On Behalf Of:

The presenter

By Request, the Author has Produced
this Self-Published, Signed, and Dated
Limited-Edition Volume
Especially for the Pleasure and Benefit of:

The presentee

Set_____ Volume_____ Edition_____

The MH Edition

In honor of the

MILLENNIUM CHRISTMAS

2000

BOOK DESIGNED & PRINTED BY:

C. JOHN COOMBES

EBOOK ISBN 9780982221358   0982221355
PRINT ISBN 9780982221389   098222138X

ALL RIGHTS RESERVED BY C. JOHN COOMBES
COPYRIGHT 2000 2008 2010 2013

CLAUS

A CHRISTMAS INCARNATION

A novel by
C. J. COOMBES

Escape to a time
When life was an adventure.

Our nation was young,
And so were her people.
A time of struggle and setback,
Of pain and perseverance.

A time also of freedom, joy,
And the birth of new traditions.
The future was fearful and uncertain,
But no more so than for the children.

For them, let us say,
Fate brought forth a man.
He was wealthy and influential,
He was good-hearted and generous.
A man of conjecture and mystery.
He was there for them, a savior,
A second chance, a hope.

Only one person may have known him.
A person who struggled to understand him
Through the eyes of a child,
Through the heart of a woman.

A disciple named Elizabeth.

ILLUSTRATIONS BY:

C. JOHN COOMBES

THE M HART EDITION
THIS EDITION REPRESENTS THE FIRST EDIT
OF VOLUME THREE UNDERTAKEN SPECIFICALLY FOR A
6X9 PAPERBACK PRINTING

It would be preposterous
To assert that
Fact is born of myth.

Conversely...
It has been proven
Myth is a child of truth.

BOOK THREE

The disciple

PART ONE

THE M HART EDITION

Is it possible?
Souls in life so fused
So entwined by roots
Seemingly inseparable by design
Would diverge with consequence
No less dramatic
Than their former union
And yet

Is it possible?
Such dramatic divergence
Draws suddenly insignificant
Suddenly irrelevant
Suddenly invisible by
A flashing glance
A passing breath
A single syllable

If distance brings no burden
If time bears no cost
Are kindred spirits
Eternal
It is Possible?

ONE

She returned unexpected.

The Mistress of Winter let loose her final breath and drove temperatures down to kill. From atop the peaks, she suffocated earth with an impenetrable layer of misery. Memories of a season past were resurrected one frozen tear flake at a time, each piling and pressing upon the land until the last remnant of living warmth had been squeezed out of existence. In fields of waist-high whiteness, life had been abandoned.

I had spent my day circling the cabin. Not outside, but inside, wall to wall, corner to corner, around and around, returning impatiently every few moments to release the latch on a door that held firm against the onslaught of a winter returned. More than my need for heat was my need to stare out into the blinding brightness where no color remained to meet my eyes, where no warmth remained to caress my face. There was no sign of movement to attract me; not outside, not inside—nothing save for a buffeting wind that ferried its biting cold disposition south from the frigid arctic regions, drawn down by the great Stony Mountains sluice.

This anomaly of June was in stark contrast to May, which had been a month of warm spring weather—days of undisturbed life-renewing sunshine. Those were mornings when one held arms outward and face tilted upward for the sole purpose of succumbing to the glorious sensation of an early springtime sun as it penetrated deep into the flesh.

May had been accommodating in every way, enough so that Christopher had given Helena time off to visit her people in the south. Her young cheery temperament was now noticeably absent. She was gone, and on a day like this, it made the cabin unbearably quiet and lonely.

Gone, too, was Christopher. He had insisted on escorting Helena partway on her journey, for he had business in that direction. He was obligated to meet with the rail crews on the North-South Poles run. They had departed together, but unlike Helena, Christopher had promised me his return in a fortnight. That would have been three days ago.

It was for this reason, knowing he was out in the blizzard that I paced. It was simple—surprise storms meant sudden death. Folks, especially travelers, caught unprepared for such events paid a steep price, usually with their lives.

This date, late in spring or early summer, meant the gear of winter was stowed in favor of lighter dress. I looked over at the wall and noted Christopher's furs hanging heavy on the hook, a silent warning that, despite my convictions, he wasn't wholly invulnerable.

In the stillness of my surroundings, I stood motionless while absorbed by the large tinted maps on Christopher's desk. I was fascinated by the trails that snaked through the blushes of color highlighting mountains and valleys, their distances calculated by the precisely spaced puncture points of Claus's needle dividers.

The focus of my concentration passed through the maps and into mental images of danger not evident within the orderly artistic swirls that graced the parchment. These thoughts of danger were hardly subdued when my gaze shifted back to the icy crack of light that edged the barely opened door.

I peered through the vertical slit into the blinding snowstorm, again studying the trail with intent as far as I might for a sign, but nothing was revealed—*absolutely nothing*. Fear had gripped me sufficient enough. I found myself wiping my eyes and blathering aloud.

"This is nonsense. Crying like a baby, you dolt. If Christopher could see you now, he would laugh until you crawled with embarrassment. He will be fine. He will be fine, Elizabeth."

I repeated the same frail assurances a thousand times, each time followed by a long, deep breath. I worked to settle myself, but my mind resisted.

As I looked across the porch I recalled how, months ago, at the onset of winter, I stood nervously upon those weathered planks. They were placed years before my appearance, and remained butted tight and secure, a testament to the skill of the builder. The center of this wooden structure showed its owner's inescapable connection to the world. It was well worn, buffed smooth by sand embedded in the boot heels of many a weary and hopeful traveler. I imagined smiles cracking open their dried-out faces as the sound of latch and hinge was quieted by a hearty welcome and invitation to sanctuary and promise.

I recalled my hesitation to cross both the physical and mental thresholds on that cold starry night, and also the joyful relief after having done so. As if only a day ago, I remembered Christopher closing the door firmly against the frosty autumn air. Sanctuary was too frivolous a term for the warm side of the rustic portico where we sat in our seclusion and whiled away strings of nights that led us in and out of winter's threats. Cozy in conversation, we discussed life and bridged our worlds. Night after night after night, I saw him satiate himself with my presence. I saw myself turn away from him...*tortured*.

I gazed across the room to where stood a bed of no small proportion. Simple in design, well-constructed of polished knotty pine logs many times the girth of my arm. Ready to withstand an avalanche of snow or emotion, the bed triggered vivid memories. The bed represented the first delicate difficulty to confront us. I recalled how the girls at the office had warned me about finding Christopher married to another. I remember how shaken I was by the thought, a thought I refused to dwell upon. The girls had warned me about a number of things, but how could anyone imagine a bed would become an issue?

My first night's stay, Christopher insisted I take his bed, saying he would sleep alongside Helena on the floor. Of course, Helena didn't exactly sleep on the floor. She slept on a cot that was inserted into the wall in the typical fashion, and also enjoyed a comfortable mattress cut to fit. Christopher did his best to find comfort *very much* on the floor with whatever rugs and blankets could be collected.

I was most disturbed by the unfairness of it all, and each passing night served only to further escalate my embarrassment. Claus was insistent that we continue this arrangement, whereby I suffered to watch him night after night sleeping upon the rough-hewn planks. As certain as every night was followed by day, so too were his assurances that a new mattress was in the making and soon to arrive. In spite of a mound of quilts, after the better part of a month, I could no longer stand to imagine his discomfort upon the floor, and so my state of mind surfaced to be heard. Helena had already fallen to sleep, leaving Christopher and I standing alone to confront each other clad only in our nightclothes.

"Claus."

"Yes."

"I absolutely refuse to spend another night in the comfort of your bed, which I might add is big enough for three of me, while you suffer on that wretched floor, amidst a collection of quilts, rugs, and bugs."

"It's nothing. Honestly, my child, I have slept on the slopes of the Stony Mountains many a time. This isn't nearly so bad. Allow me to say, I'll sleep far more peacefully knowing you are tucked in tight—knowing you are warm and comfortable. Now get in and go to sleep." He grinned.

"I *am not* getting in and going to sleep." I laughed. "I would graciously accept a patch of grass in place of a pile of rocks on the Stony Mountain slopes, but that is the point. We are not out on the slopes of the Stony Mountains. We are in a cabin—in *your* cabin to be more specific. And we are discussing *your* bed."

"How could I stand to have you sleeping on the floor?" he replied. "You would freeze to death and I would feel terrible. I would never forgive myself."

"Oh. And you don't get cold and stiff laying down there?"

"No."

"No? That is nonsense, Claus. All night, I listen to you turn to and fro—first this way and then that. I can hear you creak when you get up. Every morning you serenade us with a chorus of groans as you awake. I hardly believe you get a good night's sleep on that floor. It's cold and it's hard and—."

"Elizabeth—."

"No."

"Elizabeth—."

"No."

"Then what do *you* propose?"

"I'll sleep on the floor, or better yet, we'll take turns. That only seems fair. You have been more than hospitable, gracious to a fault as usual, and I would be ill-mannered and uncivil to allow such an inequity to continue."

"That will not happen. I will sleep outside before I have you sleeping on a floor in my presence. And that's the end of that. I'll be outside or I'll be inside. You may choose."

I was exasperated. I knew I could never persuade Christopher to be less than a perfect gentleman. And so we stood there staring at each other, I being unsure of what next to say or do. It was plain to me that I would not win in a confrontational test of wills, but I was bound and determined to resolve the issue that afflicted me with such awkwardness.

As we stared each other down—no sign in either of our faces giving hint of retreat—the candle began to sputter. Spent of its wick, it promptly died and so took with it the only available light in which to read the other's obstinacy. Now we stood in the void of night with only voices left to take up this battle. Our demeanors were markedly changed. For one thing, a second of silence without a facial expression of stubbornness was like an hour-long intermission. Many seconds went by. Finally, I pitched a proposal into the darkness.

"Allow me to suggest, we might both sleep in the bed until the arrival of the mattress."

"I wouldn't risk the shame that might be brought upon your character," he stated flatly from some place before me.

"I have known you since childhood, Claus. You are nothing if not a perfect gentleman, and I trust you implicitly. Besides, there is common sense in keeping each other warm in the cold of night. Or let me clarify my point by saying I would welcome your warmth, for I have scant little heat to offer in return. This is not about defiling my character, Claus. It is about common sense in the dead of winter. Besides, Helena is right there, and presently on account of your pig-headedness, I am freezing."

"Pig-headedness! I rather think not, and suggest that Helena sleep with you. I will sleep on her cot."

"Ha! That would be a sight to see. You wouldn't manage that cot if I hacked off your legs and then some. Not to mention, half your weight would snap it off the wall."

There was a year of silence.

"Please, Claus. I am about to catch my death of cold. I no longer feel my feet."

I had little doubt but my proposal would have failed miserably in the light of day. It was a sudden thrust into the isolation of darkness, the discomforting situation one instinctively strives to avoid that made the difference. From that same overwhelming blackness, came a woeful breath of painful resignation.

"Ohhhh, myyyy word. *As you wish*, child. Now, *pleeease…* get in bed before I change my mind amidst such nonsense. We'll discuss it further in the morning."

It had been a most remorseful resignation to be sure.

TWO

I started to sob.

…A gush of tears, heaves, and pitiful squeals.

"What is the matter with you?" I yelled.

I demanded an answer from the emptiness of the cabin.

"God Almighty, the man is a father to you, not a son…*not a lover!*"

The last quip flew right out of my mouth.

"Oooooooh. Where did that come from?"

It was a most unsettling slip of the tongue. Even worse, spoken aloud the words stirred something deep within that frightened me, the implication too close for comfort, too close to revealing something unspeakable.

25

My frown of puzzlement faded with the release of another deep breath. I had hoped to exhale away my tension, but to no avail. I remained worried. In fact, I was worried sick about all of it. I worried for Christopher; I worried for myself, should he not return. I worried for the children. They also set out for the summer, having given up the security of their winter quarters here at the cabin. My worry disallowed me to settle or sit, and so I paced the room, only to return again and again to the door to stare, to wait, to pray, to wait, to wait—*to wait.*

Very unlike the East Coast with its mollifying ocean air, a wholly unpredictable weather was a fact of life in these parts. The terrain was troubled, the winds that crossed it—turbulent, and contrary to the blizzard at hand, we were not only past spring but well into early summer. The days were, in fact, growing longer. Of course, one might not realize it, but for the way in which late afternoon light tended to dam up behind the granite cliffs. It then dribbled feebly into the valley, where it was further diluted by a mixing with the shadows of the wood.

The light was blended murky at this hour, and the trail had grown obscure in the dusky twilight. The long shadows of the desert floor were unseen on the slopes of the mountains. Here, it was as if God turned back a lamp wick to soften the light of day and remind all of His creatures it was time to go home— apparently all creatures except Christopher.

The relentless pacing pained my knees and hips. Finally, I stopped my rambling, tormented thoughts long enough to return to reality and look around the cabin. The openly spacious interior had filled with shadows as it succumbed to the pressure of dark that welled up in the canyon. Utterly spent from worry, I was relieved to leave my dismal routine long enough to freshen the fire, sample my stew, and slip back into the comfort of my nightclothes.

The cabin had returned to its chilly winter feel, and I was compelled to gather my wraps and sit before the invigorating heat of the embers. Everything seemed colder when Christopher was gone.

The sound of the blowing wind did little to warm me. I shivered to shake out a chill and drew my robe and blankets up tight. Except for the wind with its endless variety of wails and whistles, the snow effectively quieted all. And so, when I heard boots being stomped upon the porch, I was given quite a fright for I had never heard a horse approach.

"Claus?"

Spinning about, I called out nervously as the door swung inward.

"Were you expecting someone other?"

He joked aloud while still mostly out of view. Stepping fully inside, his searching eyes found me. Straight off, he broke into a broad grin. He closed the door, fit the latch, and rubbed his hands together hard. He shook himself and stomped his boots one last time.

"Ho! It is cold out there, my dear!"

"I have been worried sick for you, Claus, worried sick. Who would believe such weather? It's insanity." I let out an air of complaint. "It does my heart good to see you home. I feared little sleep tonight but for all my worry. Can you believe this storm, this snow? My word, does June mean nothing in these parts?"

Christopher laughed. And with that, I could relax. I was so happy to have him home. I wondered if he could see how he washed me free of this day of worry. I wondered if he could know how long my heart raced with anxiety, only now to slow in his presence. Could he hear how it fluttered as I took in the sight of him, as I soaked up the serenity in his voice?

I hoped not!

I quickly stepped behind him but—was it to take his coat, or was it to avoid eyes that might uncover my secrets. I set about dismissing these thoughts. Yet make no mistake, I was grateful Christopher was home. I was indeed grateful. As always when nervous, my tongue set off to flap.

"I fear for the children, Claus. If only they had stayed on a couple of more weeks, they would be safe. I don't know…I don't what—."

Christopher placed his hands on my shoulders.

"They will be fine, Elizabeth. I passed a good many of them on the trail today. They were headed back this way. In fact, I would swear there are thrice as many headed up here toward the cabin as what struck out to begin, maybe fourfold. Word of warm food and lodging gets out fast. I dare say some thirty or forty camp at the bottom clearing as we speak. I have already seen to it that those in need have food and blankets. In fact, I asked Ezekiel to open the barns for their benefit and a good number appeared inclined to take up lodging. You needn't worry further about the children, Elizabeth. Besides, this weather will pass quickly, a day or two at most. They will be fine, I promise."

"Oh! Thank you, Claus. Thank you for tending to their comfort."

Christopher's generosity brought me both comfort and a smile.

"It's a disgrace. Those children have no idea how you put yourself out in their behalf. Must it always be me, will it only be me who thanks you? Honestly, it isn't fair." I shook my head in dismay. "Who takes care of you? Sit down now. The weather is unfit and foul. I was worried sick for your well-being."

He rocked his head back and forth and crouched to look into my eyes. A smile moved lightly across his face.

"These hard blows are new for you, Elizabeth, but I have lived them many a time. Nothing a good glass of brandy won't tame."

I could feel the day's tension flow from my frame. I enjoyed the relief. I laid my head over to rest my cheek upon his hand. I then took hold of it.

"Come. Come sit down, Claus. Rest yourself. I have plenty of stew and it will chase the chill out of your bones. Please me and sit down."

I led him to the couch.

"Hot stew! Oh, ho, ho. Yes, that sounds wonderful." He inhaled deeply. "Mmmmm. What splendid aromas. Have we enough wood for the night?"

He looked over toward the fireplace. I moved to block his view of further concerns.

"Yes. Yes, there is plenty of wood. Sit. Just sit. Please—."

My eyes suddenly welled up with tears.

"Elizabeth?"

A look of shock crossed his face.

"What is this?"

"Nothing. It's nothing."

My chest suddenly heaved. It made a liar out of me and I was embarrassed to the core. I turned away, but Christopher caught my cheek with an enormous hand and gently persuaded me to face him. I was unbearably self-conscious and avoided his eyes. I fought to hold back any further show of emotion.

"You tremble? My word, Elizabeth, what have I done? Is this my doing? If so, you must believe, everything is fine."

He stared deep into my eyes to fill me with confidence, to assure me, to fill me with peace.

"I know well how to deal with these storms. You either learn quickly or die quickly in these parts. You needn't worry about me. In fact, you have every right to scold me for being the cause of such concern. Had I known how much this upset you, I would have afforded every effort to see my way back sooner."

Christopher slid his thumb across my cheek to catch a tear.

"I apologize, Elizabeth, I apologize. Now, hear me out. Look at me. Look at me."

I raised my eyes to meet his.

"Fill your head with good thoughts, and let us enjoy that wonderful stew and whatever remains of the day. I am happy to be home; I am happy to see you."

I nodded with a smile. "You owe me no apology, Claus. You did nothing wrong. Being alone is a bad recipe—reason enough to work one's self into a lather. Pointless lather no doubt, but so it goes—it's done. Now, just sit. That's all I ask. Sit."

Christopher's massive frame fell away from my fingertips and collapsed upon the couch. I followed him down, falling to my knees so I might untie the laces of his boots. I wanted to untie the laces. I wanted to remove his boots. I wanted to assure myself he would stay put. I worked the cold stiffened leather free of his feet and removed his damp stockings. I went for his glass of brandy and a basin of heated water, and upon my return, submerged his chilled feet into the warmth.

"Your feet feel half frozen!" I protested.

Little more than a mumbled acknowledgment moved past his lips. His head was laid back, his eyes closed. He was visibly raddled. I toweled his feet dry and fitted him with a fresh pair of socks. Unconsciously, I rubbed his feet before placing them upon the footstool to face the fire in hopes of forcing out what chill still circulated about him. I fitted his slippers. I laid a throw across his lap, set his brandy aside, and went for the stew.

"It is a freak storm, Elizabeth," Christopher let out in a low voice. "Rest assured a thaw is fast on its heels." His words came slow and calm. "In a week's time we will be sweltering and fighting the bugs for a good night's sleep. You just settle yourself and make the best of it, child. Besides which, right now it's nice and cozy. The fire is warm—the stew is hot.... We have each other's company. What else might one ask?"

Christopher let out a long, deep breath. He never opened his eyes. He was most certainly worn out. For a second—hours long, I stood at the hearth filling my soul with the sight of him. Then came the gentle rumble of sleep. The sound flushed my eyes with tears and my heart with peace. My thoughts dissipated. My mind cleansed itself of every ill concern. I was at last settled, emptied of anxiety.

Or so I thought.

* * *

Claus was safe at home. I might have believed no worry could possibly remain had I not felt myself stumble. Something tripped me. Something unwelcome, unnerving, a feeling I wished to avoid. I wanted to edge away, but the sensation only gripped me tighter, forcing its recognition. To my alarm, I was being driven to acknowledge my one darkest fear.

Caged cats came to mind. Those skittish creatures I espied upon the main deck of the WAVERLY back in St. Louis—that howling tangle of frightened animals that so amused me with their comical antics. To them I now felt unwillingly connected.

31

I now sensed what they must have experienced, maybe even suffered, as they paced endlessly back and forth, back and forth in those cages, frantic and fussing.

I had been doing just that and more. For the last several days, I had been pacing the cabin, fidgeting, jabbering to myself, asking questions aloud, and rationalizing my less than honorable designs and sordid desires. I did so for hours on end, as might an imbecile seeking some form of spiritual forgiveness.

I wondered if a supreme power was looking into my cage, watching over my soul with grave concern...or great amusement—laughing over these inane antics of mine as well. These thoughts only served to raise new anxieties for a weary mind. I was unconsciously kneading my knuckles to the point of pain.

My cage was invisible. It wasn't as simple as bending the bars to escape years in prison. My cage was one of inhibitions—emotional, irrational inhibitions—the kind that would allow me to stand up straight and kill a man, but faint before I could ever kiss one.

"Oh, please!" I spoke aloud to my ghosts.

I took a deep breath, held it...and then let it blow hot like scorching steam through a teakettle valve. With the faintest wail, I let loose the hot run-away pressure of my nervous energy. I tried hard to disavow my attraction for Christopher. I tried hard to avoid admitting that feelings had grown recklessly out of control in spite of my efforts at restraint.

Each day that I had wintered over in his cabin—in his presence, *in his bed*, was a day that further dismantled the forbiddances of my upbringing. I struggled to believe, to convince myself, that I was a daughter. It was unthinkable, immoral—*incestuous*—that I should see Christopher in any light other than that of a true father. Sadly, the harder I fought to subdue my feelings the further I suffered to acknowledge the insanity of the truth.

No, my mind was not empty. But it was being silenced forcibly by something deep inside that rebuked all my rationalizations, all my fruitless deceptions. Now coming unraveled was a life-long work of illusion, a pattern of falsities and misguided beliefs long knitted by a lonely heart. My time for decision was past. My sense of direction disproved. My stay at the wheel relieved. I would no longer be allowed the reins of my destiny. By whatever power, I had been judged a failure in the orchestration of my purpose. I sensed something other was about to make decisions in my behalf, and it was this realization that thoroughly terrified me.

Christopher opened his eyes and they met mine straight on. I was certain he looked into my soul. I retreated at once. I dashed for the stew. I turned to the fire and sought to bury a moment of awkwardness.

"You napped."

There was a crushing silence.

"Elizabeth…. Are you well, my child?"

"I…I…I'm fine, Claus. Thank you." I busied myself scooping his stew into a bowl. I handed it to him. I fetched a spoon. I handed it to him. I fetched a napkin. I handed it to him. I searched for something else to fetch.

"I don't know…," he said. "I sense something…I'm not sure. Maybe I should have kept Helena here a while longer to keep you company. I know it can get lonely up here. You were certainly distressed upon my arrival. I thought for sure the children—."

"No! No! You did good. You did the right thing. Helena longed to see her family. She was very excited. It was very kind of you to allow her the time. I'm just, you know, moving about to ward off the chill. I just keep moving around…. It's been chilly all day. I…I…I don't have to tell you. I mean….Eat! Please, eat."

33

I wished him to stuff his mouth, to block any further word from escaping to undo me. I returned to stir the stew. I over-stirred. I wished I could have stood over the pot and stirred for an hour. It was terrible knowing that I was visibly nervous. I could see my hands trembling. I imagined my face to be flush red.

I was fearful of an impending impossibility for me to further contain a lifetime of longing. These forbidden feelings buried deep within my being were now rising to the surface of an awakened heart. Something about this night was very different. It felt out of my control. I sensed an emotional explosion in the making that would rip my insides apart before it relented. I felt as though I were being pushed, being forced to accept this reality, to stay the course this one night or finish out my life deservedly dissatisfied and remorseful.

I traded the soup ladle for the coffee pot and walked it over to the dish counter. I needed to move beyond Christopher's attention. Supported by quivering arms, I hung my head over the basin. I braced myself against an urge to vomit. I was queasy. I raised my head to look out the window into the darkness of night. I asked myself again if all that I dreamed was what I truly desired. Was I certain? Beneath all the lies, the answer remained the same. Yes. Of this, there was no longer any doubt.

My focus changed from beyond the window to the glass itself. I looked at my image in the reflection of the black mirror, into the distortion of that obsidian-like pane that thankfully revealed nothing of blemishes and signs of age. I was not one to fall for its lies. I had long since accepted the loss of my youth, but desperately wished there might be some leftover scrap of the feast I once displayed for a young man's eyes.

If only once a young man had dined at my table. How many times had I wondered why one hadn't—*was it my character*? Could it be flawed in a fashion so visible to others, yet invisible to my mirror? Was it some small disgusting detail, a thing that hung from my nose for all to see, all of whom would deny knowledge of its presence—all of whom would study it intently from behind masks that sported smiles, and words of encouragement and kindness, but masks that covered cowardice and the lack of stomach or courage to save me with a discreet whisper?

I simply didn't know. But all would allow my inadequacy to evolve into a drama, discussed privately at first within my inner circle of friends, and later as talk of the town by everyone, save me.

I reached for two clean mugs. I rubbed their innards with a towel.

If it was indeed my character, why then did I have such wonderful friends, both female and male—longtime friends who never shunned me? Maybe it was only the men who understood something of my nature as a woman, something I had yet to discover. Maybe I actually was—how did Mary put it—*too Miss Claussen*. Did they assume I could not be sensual? I had always imagined I could, always believed it so, but who could say for certain? After all, no man had made a proper woman out of me, and that was the truth of it.

If only I had risked my reputation whilst a child by kissing the boys. It might have earned me the paddle, but then one suitor might also have revealed to another that I was a good kisser. Someone might have then said I was passionate. It might have been thought aloud that I would make some lucky man an affectionate wife. It might have proved a good thing remembered— a rumor to flourish and serve me well in later years.

Of course, this was now but speculation, for the boys were all grown and I was no longer the young girl. Sadly, they had become men, husbands, fathers, whereas, I was left behind, forgotten and deprived of my chance to grow into the woman I had always envisioned. I was left in a garden of despair, to be viewed like a beautiful flower, brilliant in the light of day, but empty of purpose at night, the uneaten apple. I had played the same games, shared the same dreams, but for some unknown reason, I was to be different. I was to become—*the spinster.*

I tipped the pot and poured hot water into the mugs.

Just the sound of the word crushed me. It was vile. It made me feel diseased and naked. Everybody could see it. They looked at me at first with those questioning eyes. *'How could someone as pretty and proper, admirably successful in society, and so well connected go unnoticed? It was such a pity, a shame. It was disgraceful.'* Then, with expressions steeped in sorrow, they would look at me and shake their heads in sympathy.

I imagined myself seen by many as a pitiful creature that faced each day alone. I, bereft of nature's way, would live a life unfulfilled and ignorant of the most blessed and pleasurable act. Indeed, the act that was ultimately intended to be the most powerful, purposeful, and rewarding reason for a woman's existence.

I spooned coffee into the mugs and stirred both the coffee and my thoughts. I rested the spoon on the counter, but my mind raced on.

I looked back at the window glaze. I had no wardrobe of silk or satin, no clothes whatsoever to entice a man. I therefore decided to make myself the only thing I could hope for with reasonable success—*inviting.* Possessing an open heart was the one quality I believed true about myself. It was a virtue that either was or was not an element of one's nature.

With my hands shaking clumsily, I removed a simple necklace from my pocket. It was conservative, typical of my life, and slow to draw attention. It went well with my plain robe. I struggled to fasten it with fingers I could barely control. I felt them moistened by the perspiration at the nape of my neck.

I brought my hands around to cover my face, and I closed my eyes. I would never make it through the night without a miracle. I raised my head and again questioned my reflection. *Who are you? Do you realize what you are doing? Do you realize the risk you are about to take?* I glanced back at Christopher, who was finishing his stew. I returned to view the midnight mirror. I placed my hands under my breasts. I lifted them. They were still firm—breasts of a virgin—*breasts of a spinster*, I reminded myself.

Yes, I was afraid beyond all measure, but I knew exactly what I was doing. I straightened my robe and pulled at my hair. I reached for my jar of lavender cream and opened it. I held it up to my nose and inhaled its alluring fragrance. Immediately, it reminded me of Lady Rebecca and I felt cheap and dirty.

"Don't judge me!" I rebuked her under my breath. "You've had your love and your passion. You can't possibly know."

My throat tightened and my eyes misted with emotion. I was not about to be condemned by Rebecca's ghost, no matter how right she might be, no matter how deep my guilt. I ignored her. I rubbed the cool cream into my skin…such a splendid perfume. If only it might replenish the softness of skin and heart that time had taken away.

I summoned up all my courage as I reached for the mugs of hot coffee. I stopped one last time before the window to look at myself. I hoped he might see me as something of the young girl I once displayed. My heart pounded in my chest. It was useless trying to will it to slow. It had raced too far ahead for me to catch. I left the sink, the mirror, and Lady Rebecca's memory. I was now a perfect emotional hurricane as I headed toward Christopher.

THREE

"You're fussing too much."

Christopher was studying me.

"Come here. Come here and sit by me. Come here and sit by the fire, Elizabeth. Let me put my arm around you, and I promise you will warm quickly. I'm never cold."

He was insistent.

"Come on, now. Sit by me. Come. Come."

He patted the cushion.

"You need to relax and let me take care of that chill."

My state of panic soared. Why on this very night, when I felt such as I did, would he ask me to sit by his side? He had never done so before. *Put his arm around me?* Was he reading my thoughts? He was! He was reading my thoughts! Was it so obvious, so visible, that I was not myself? Could I hide nothing? I turned away. I couldn't look at Christopher under any circumstance in my present condition. I was in such a state. I had no control. I placed the mugs clumsily on the side table. The coffee sloshed and spilled.

I reached for the back of the couch to steady myself with one hand while I unconsciously stroked my hair with my other. Oh, my. I was perspiring. I told Christopher I was chilled and I was now perspiring. What next! My temples were wet with perspiration, my forehead, my…. Oh, mother of god! It was more than just my temples and forehead. It was embarrassingly more, unspeakably more. I looked down horrified. Oh, lord! Oh, lord! I strained to take a breath but my chest wouldn't allow it. I pained to take a breath.

"Ohhhh."

Christopher was now fully turned about on the couch and staring at me. "Elizabeth. Something *is indeed* the matter. What is it, child? Are you not well?"

"I...I...I'm faint, Claus."

I attempted another breath. If ever I spoke the truth, it was now, for I felt ready to drop. My knees had abandoned me. Christopher leapt to his feet and bolted around the couch.

"Steady," he commanded.

I released my grip on the back of the couch, and without intention, found myself held tightly within his embrace. He walked me around the couch and as he seated himself, he brought me down gently to be cradled by his form. I rested my head upon his chest.

"I am fine...fine...suffering a spell, nothing more."

What should I tell him? What should I say; that I was suffering airs, that I was a nervous wreck, that I was worried sick for him the whole of the day? That maybe, just maybe, I was scared to death to admit I might be in love with the only man ever to mean anything to me in the whole of my life?

Christopher's lips brushed my hair. He kissed me on the top of my head. This barely perceptible gesture of affection marked the closing chapter of twenty some years of adulthood as I had known it. How one simple kiss could rupture me so deeply, could turn me inside out to a degree whereby wave after wave of emotion should flow unrestrained from within, would never be explained.

The bands about my chest snapped and I heaved. I clenched his shirt, frantically trying to lose myself, or hide, or disappear. There was no place to go and so I drenched him with a torrent of tears. Behind my tightly closed eyes, I saw a single kernel of corn resting amidst rows. It was brought to the flame, whereupon it burst open to reveal its heart, to disappear behind an unstained

39

flower of purity, white perfection made visible for all to see. It opened for the sole purpose of being devoured. It was a form of explanation. Why the vision should bring me peace, I couldn't imagine, but that it did.

I stopped crying.

"Elizabeth."

"Yes."

"I so deeply regret what I have put you through. I had no idea you might worry yourself into such a state. I have made you sick by it." Christopher was sincere. "Let us call it a night. I think it best we retire. A sound night's sleep is the only remedy for a weary mind. Come. Let us find the comfort and warmth of the bed. A good night's rest and I promise tomorrow you will view the world in an entirely better light. ...A new day to start afresh. In fact, tomorrow, I shall make you breakfast, a grand one indeed."

Christopher lifted me to my feet. He walked me over to the bed and after turning down the covers, he urged me to climb in.

In the soft glow of candlelight, I watched him undress. In spite of the cold, Christopher still preferred to sleep in long breeches and shirtless. I prayed he could not read my mind, for if not, he possessed no knowledge of how the sight of him prepared my body to accept him. He climbed into bed and doused the candle. The blackness engulfed us, but as always I found the comfort and warmth of his presence.

The room was silent. I noticed that, as promised by Christopher, the storm must have spent itself, for its ferocity was much diminished. If only my mind could be so stilled, so calmed, but it was wildly awake, thrashing as might freshly netted trout from the stream below. I lay there listening to Christopher's every breath. I lay there listening to the pounding of my heart, which I was certain Christopher heard as well. What I didn't hear was

Helena. Her absence singularly made all impossibilities possible this night, should I have the courage to sate my urges, to satisfy my carnal cravings. Vile, sordid, despicable harlot I might become, in this respect, how much worse could my life be?

"Elizabeth."

"Yes."

"Why are you still crying?"

"I don't know."

"I also don't know. I thought this was about my being in the weather. Have I misread your anxiety? Is there something worse, something you must share with me?"

"Yes. I believe so."

The pause was profound.

"Go on, then. I am prepared to face the worst of what troubles you so deeply. Just know in your heart, whatever you need, be it advice, or finance, or something more, I will do anything in my power to support you. Certainly, I can help in some fashion."

Every moral fiber of my soul, of my existence, screamed for me to retreat—to keep buried for eternity my darkest of secrets, but how could I listen? For the first time, my heart determined to overrule all other aspects of my life, my upbringing, my morality, my misgivings, my insecurities, my inhibitions, and worst of all, my life-long denial of my need for Christopher.

My heart was bleeding. Its essence began to flow thick and heavy from my breast. I could feel it spread across my awareness and knew there would be no ebb to this tide. Time had come.

"Would you put your arm around me?"

Christopher reached out from under the covers and took me into his embrace. I was close enough to whisper my love.

"Will you be patient with me?"

"Haven't I always?"

"Yes, you have, always."

Christopher waited in the silence of night, waited for me to take whatever time needed to spill my confession. And so I started down the road of ruin or rejoice, but most certainly not one of return.

"Tell me, Claus, what do you want from me?"

"Pardon?"

"You heard me. I am asking you. In this darkness where there is only your voice, where I can't see your eyes reprimand me, in this isolation, in this place where there is no witness, I am asking...what is it you want of me?"

"What is it I want of you?" Christopher repeated my question in a tone of confusion. "What...what...I don't know how to answer that question. I'm not sure I understand."

"Try."

I waited but Christopher said nothing, so I continued.

"I believe now, I understand how I saved everything, sacrificed everything I had to offer so I might in some fashion be a part of your life. Soon, I will have nothing left to lose. I will have no pride of any measure to call my own, no decency to enlist. I will be spiritually, and to say the least, morally bankrupt. And for these reasons, I only ask one thing of you, Claus. What is it you want of me?"

There was silence. But this time Christopher did answer.

"That is such an odd question, Elizabeth. I'm still not sure what you mean. What is it I want of you? I guess I would say...I want you to tell me you are happy. That is the only thing I ever wanted from you—to know, to hear, to believe you're happy. I want you to be happy. I want you to succeed. Whatever it takes, whatever is in my power to grant. I would support you without reservation. Your happiness is what brings me pleasure. And for that...anything...anything in the world, Elizabeth—you only have to ask."

"Make love to me."

"WHAT!"

FOUR

Christopher was on his feet before the blankets had a chance to settle.

"What! What did you say?"

"I said make love to me, Claus."

The tone of my request came out in a level and direct command.

"It's time."

I heard a scratching sound. Abruptly there appeared a tiny explosion of fire. Christopher looked at me in the light of the lucifer and then touched it to the candle. The room took on boundaries. He stood motionless in his britches, bent over the candle, face turned toward me, eyes wide with wonder or shock. Which, I didn't know.

"I have *no idea* what to say to that."

He shook his head and then turned from the candlelight and walked away. He grabbed a blanket from the couch and wrapped himself. He turned back momentarily to stare at me, or maybe glare at me. Again, which, I did not know.

"What am I to say to that? I don't know what to say to that," he repeated.

He sat down, drew his legs up beneath him, and turned away as if afraid to face me. The gesture was almost childlike.

I may have been mistaken, but instead of repulsion or disgust, my instincts told me that Christopher was genuinely shaken. He was in shock. This was something in the whole of my life I had never seen. My words rocked him to his core. If ever I worried about him reading my mind, at this moment the reverse was true. I was reading *his* face, *his* eyes, the script of *his* soul. He was stunned. Did he tremble, or did I only wish it so?

No matter how inappropriate my reckless behavior, one thing I knew for certain—Christopher was, above all else, a gentleman. He would respond to me as he would have to Lady Rebecca, with respect and sensitivity.

Christopher rose to stoke the fire. He reached for the poker and stabbed at the logs, shoving and pulling at the burning wood. I thought of my earlier need to stir the stew. He then stepped back and sank to the couch. He was deep in thought, lost in the dance of the agitated flames. I watched flickering firelight pattern his features as he turned to glance my way and then back to study the quieting blaze. I spoke.

"Do you remember the day you rescued me from that brute in the tavern?" I hesitated. "I wonder what you would think of me if you knew how enthralled I was by his attack."

"You are tired, Elizabeth. You are in genuine need of sleep. Clearly, you have had a long and trying day, and I am certain you are weary beyond any state of sensibility."

"You are wrong, Claus. In fact, it feels as if I have slept the whole of my life, and it was but a moment ago I woke up."

The stillness of the room was beyond measure. It felt as if each word spoken hung permanently in the air.

"Who are you, Claus?"

I waited.

"Who are you, Christopher Claussen? What are you? Are you a man? Are you a god or a saint? I thought so as a child. I thought you controlled the heavens. I thought you controlled the seas. I thought you controlled my life. In fact, on that point even unto this day, I am not entirely certain you don't."

I watched him from the bed. He sat silent. I did not.

"I have lived my life as though I am the shell. Am I supposed to be forever empty? No pearl?"

I fought back a sudden urge to cry.

"What is it that will satiate me, Claus? Is it you? Are you here to fill me with life? Are you here to give me a heart and soul?"

Again, I waited. Christopher sat motionless.

"Can you see that I am not a child, Claus? *I am not a child*, Claus—I am not *your* child! I don't know what I am to you, but I know I am not your child. You are not my father, Claus. I am not in love with my father."

I scarcely believed I heard those last words escape my mouth. Even in my present state, I understood those words could not be retracted. I understood the impact of what I had confessed.

"I have spent my entire life chastising myself, cursing myself for my inability to drive you out of my mind…to find some fault in you, something, anything to make you less perfect in my eyes—in my heart. In spite of every warning given, I have crossed a continent to be by your side, and I can't even explain that insanity to myself. Why would I undertake such foolish and inconceivable folly? Is this your doing, Claus? Is it you?

"If ever a person could be burdened with guilt, it has to be me. I honestly don't know if you even see me, Claus, but I wonder if I haven't suffered for you every single day of my life. What is it you want from me? I ask you, Claus. What is it you want? Do you hear me?"

Christopher might well have died. He barely breathed, let alone flinch or move a muscle of that massive frame. His eyes remained locked on me, and I knew for certain that he was profoundly unnerved. Even in the subdued light of the fire, I could sense his state. It was in perfect opposition to my own, for I had come to settle down. A burden carried by my heart for years had been lifted. Emerging from beneath the weight of a lifetime, I now spoke in a softer tone. I was calm and my thoughts collected.

"I want your love, Claus. Now that I have finally come to accept what I have spent my life denying, I find it easy to say. I am not your child. I am not your adoptee. The only thing I am for certain is a spinster, and this luckless achievement attained in part or whole by a misguided attraction to you. I am no longer your ward, Mr. Claussen. I am in fact, an adult, albeit crude and without class or manner, I fear, but an adult nonetheless. I am a woman, and incomplete as that may be, I am still a woman who exists for a purpose. I am a mature, single-minded soul who has never been afraid to speak her mind freely about any subject save one. And tonight that has changed. I want your love, Claus. Time has come."

Christopher thought long. I was prepared to wait until hell froze as cold as the Mistress of Winter. I would wait until one of us dropped dead.

"I would like to wash."

"Thank you."

FIVE

I lifted up the covers as if to encourage this man to find me. Instead, he sat upon the side of the bed keeping a blanket wrapped about his freshly washed body. He looked down at me. I sensed he wanted to say something, but he turned away, clearly a change of mind. Slowly, almost ritual-like, he leaned over and reached out to snuff the candle. His fingers glowed pink briefly before the pinch, leaving us to suffocate in the closing darkness. Again, I raised the blankets.

I felt the bed shift and at once my stomach began to tighten. I felt my anxiety awaken. My heart picked up its pace. Over and over, I willed myself to relax, but to no avail. Having no idea what I should expect, nor what was expected of me, each passing second placed me closer to a worrisome panic.

Christopher moved up tight against my body. He was lying on his left side and facing me. I could feel his breath wash over me. He placed his hand upon my stomach; it was still damp. He slid it gently up toward but just shy of my breasts. I hardly noticed, for I was too preoccupied with thoughts about his manhood. Was it going to touch me? My heart resonated within my chest, and I was certain Christopher could feel its panicked pounding beneath his hand. I was nervous. Maybe "nervous" was too mild a word for how I felt. One thing was for certain: I felt uncomfortable with the darkness.

"Claus?"

"Yes."

"Is it normal to do this without light?"

"Mmmm. I have heard that lovers do this in the daytime— especially early afternoons."

I laughed. My heart slowed at once. It felt good to relax.

47

"Would you prefer me to light the candle or a lamp?" he asked.

"Do you mind?"

"Not at all. I'll be the first to say...darkness does beauty no justice. Should I put more wood on the fire?"

"No, just the candle."

Christopher moved away from me. He sat up and reached for the night table. My anxiety eased back a notch.

"There's something about the darkness. I don't know. I thought it would support my modesty. I suppose it does, but I feel like I can't breathe. It's as if I'm alone. Does that make sense? It soothes me when I can see you. Do you understand what I am saying?"

There came that faint scratch and pop, and the little explosion to follow as the lucifer ignited. I watched Christopher direct it to the candle wick. The combined flames seemed brilliant in the surrounding darkness. He pulled back the splinter of wood and blew out its life. He twirled the smoky stick in his fingers.

"I dare say, it doesn't really matter if I understand or not. It matters only that you are comfortable. Are you comfortable?"

"I am now, thank you. I realized that in my million make-believes, I could always see your eyes."

Ouch. I impaled myself with mortification.

"I don't mean...I mean, I meant not *your* eyes, I meant...you know...my lover's eyes. I never...um...ah...pictured this moment occurring in pitch blackness."

I wanted to crawl under the bed. I should have left the room dark. Leave it to me to complain. My slip of the tongue, truthful as it was, caused me to blush profusely. Hopefully, the light was too dim for him to see it, but my face glowed like a bed of embers.

Christopher was back to where he started, sitting upon the edge of the bed. We both stared at the flame, mesmerized by the way in which it flickered and swayed. It danced about to shift objects in the room. Oftentimes, it would remain perfectly still as if by command, and I would be compelled to blow at it for reason none other than to upset its tranquility. But I couldn't because the peaceableness of the flame quieted my blundering tongue and the restlessness of my heart. And so, I was momentarily at ease, a fact most evident to me, after a 'long trying' day.

The flame that barely flickered seemed not only unnatural in behavior, but burned unmoving as a testament to the stillness in the cabin. Even the boisterous winds had abated, leaving not so much as a draft to cross the floor. When I chose to break the stillness, the silence, my voice sounded unwelcome.

"Do you ever get lonely?" I asked.

"Lonely?"

Christopher didn't answer right away. I imagined him to be looking back over the years of his life. I imagined him thinking most of Lady Rebecca's death.

"I suppose in a fashion I am always lonely. I just never think of it in those terms. I find myself restless, always restless. If I think about it, I reckon soon enough I realize my determination not to wait about. I have no desire to sit around here in the cabin or anywhere for that matter. I feel better when I'm moving, meeting folks, the fresher the face, the better. It has always been the hovering crowd that makes me lonely. I much prefer to ride out, to remain apart, to stay ahead of the loneliness, if that's what you wish to call it."

"I'm amazed, Claus. It's as if you drew the very words across my lips. I understand precisely what you say. I might have said it myself exactly that way. I swear all I have done with my life is move from project to project, event to event. Run, run, run, so as not to look behind. Anything to disallow the emptiness that trails me, anything to assure it never catches me. To look back is to see this horrible void.

"I so envy Mary and Allen. They complain how they can't slow their busy lives enough. They want the world to stop so they can savor life, so they can enjoy each other and especially the boys. They look back always, and do so with great joy. Their past is filled with memories to be cherished. You could sit around and listen to them all evening. They make you laugh. I am happy for Mary. She glows. Whenever I see her, she always glows."

"Mary was, and I am certain as you say, remains a fine woman. I always was most fond of her. It pleased me to see her marry well."

We continued to stare at the candle. I enjoyed looking at Christopher in the dusky light. Even to this day, he remained one of the most handsome of men in my eyes. He reached for his glass of brandy and emptied it. He looked at me.

"Would you care for some brandy, Elizabeth? It's strong but it will settle you."

"Ohhh. It sounds like a needed blessing. Please."

Christopher and his blanket arose and walked across the room in search of the brandy bottle. He picked it out of the shadows and returned to the bed with bottle, blanket, and a second cup. He sat back down and as he prepared to pour brandy afresh, I let my thoughts loose.

"My life truly is incomplete, Claus. That's how I feel, and I can't escape it. Incomplete or cursed, it's the same thing. Whatever you want to call it, I ended up childless, unmarried, unfulfilled, lonely—I can't even remember if there is pleasure to be taken from a kiss.

"I beg you to appreciate the irony in my disclosure. You see, after enduring a lifetime of men who failed to see me without effort, when finally does come a man who makes it embarrassingly clear that he is attracted to me, and more than willing to satiate my appetite, a man who actually earned my respect—he ends up dead within days—in my arms, no less. I ask what would you make of that, Claus? Would it be fickle fate, bad luck, a curse? Is that your doing? If it's heaven's idea of a prank, I find it cruel…." My voice trailed off.

Christopher handed me a generous portion of brandy.

"Drink up."

"Thank you." I sat up and accepted the cup. I swallowed a healthy swig of the fiery liquid. "Whew, that is potent brandy."

"Yes, ma'am, but smooth—an ingredient of wealth." He continued. "If you must know, I don't believe we ever truly escape loneliness. We surround ourselves with family and friends beloved. We go to the taverns. We keep pets and memorabilia for companionship. But we choose not to see reality. All that we love can be taken from us in the blink of an eye, ripped from our hearts in an instant. We come into this world alone, and ultimately we die alone, as alone as heavenly possible."

I filled the silence that followed his words.

"I suppose. For my part, I would much rather die alone as a widow than die alone as an unmarried spinster. And if I am never to be married, better to die a whore—."

Christopher coughed.

"My lord, Elizabeth, you have a way with words this night."

"Yes, yes, I do. It was you who encouraged my speaking fearlessly, as I recall. It might as well be your ears that suffer to hear it. I refuse to end my life a virgin, Claus. Ending it as a spinster is bad enough. But to end my life as a virgin is to die believing there wasn't a single man born in God's infinite creation who could make a woman out of me. That is the most depressing death bed reflection I could ever bear to face.

"I believe all of my best years have gone by me. My beauty fades as do my dreams. I am determined to know what it means to be a woman. I pray it be you who shows me. Consider it your last and most fitting lesson. I am far away from those who know me and this affair would be nothing if not discreet. I have already tossed aside my self-respect. I no longer have that to lose. So, what *do* I have to lose? *Your* respect?

"I have bared my soul before you, and it's too late now to worry about your opinion of me—not that I don't. But I trust you, Claus. You are predictable. You are kind and good in your heart, always have been, always will be. I believe you will do this for me in spite of all your reservations, simply because it's my need. For that reason, I won't have anyone other, even if I enjoyed hope for a choice.

"I have felt for you the respect and wonder that a daughter feels for a father. I have felt for you the bonds a sister holds for a brother, the respect of a student for her teacher. I have felt a closeness no one can imagine, this from the years of encouragement and consolation you have bestowed upon me. But now I need to feel for you the way a woman feels for a man."

"And the feel of a man is enough to satisfy you…nothing more?" Christopher asked with a hint of reprimand.

I slid back down upon the pillow and closed my eyes.

"I wish no obligation on your part. You needn't worry. My interest is purely selfish—a sin of the flesh. This sexual union seems to be very special and my intention is to experience it. I have heard and seen the resulting happiness. I have seen the bonds born of those unspoken delights, the secrets that all those about me share with common knowledge. I only know for certain, as the truth of all truths, if I fail this night, I shan't ever be a party to their kind. It's all I ask, Claus, just once to know, just once to experience the bliss so I might walk with them and laugh *knowingly* about lovemaking."

Christopher listened intently to all I said. His eyes never left the pinpoint of light that seemed to guide us through the darkness of night and possibly the darkness of heart. I had nothing left to say and remained as he, transfixed by the flame. As if by cue, our eyes turned away from the light to meet. It was then he spoke.

"Allow me to say this, Elizabeth." He seemed to structure his thoughts. "I have listened and understood all that you have confided. I am filled with a profound sadness that your fate has been so unsighted, so unkind in this matter. There can be no rational explanation for such unfairness, for even a blind man would sense not only your exquisite beauty, but also with certainty, your genteel character.

"It is true one can never entirely describe the pleasure of sexual fulfillment. It must be experienced. It does form a particular and long-lasting bond between lovers, friends or strangers alike—for better or worse, but a bond rarely disregarded.

"In this way, our union will not go forward unforgotten. It will not be dismissed. It will never be a venial act, but for excessive drink or the like. It will be a union chiseled as deeply into our memory as a record set in stone. I am afraid I share anxieties at this moment, much as you. I have never thought of you as a friend, nor are you a stranger. I have always thought of you as my child, and so your request strikes deep into my conscience. I need a

53

moment to adjust my perception of you. You are still a little girl in my mind, and even in view of what I saw in the saloon, even in view of what I see now. In spite of all you have said, those little girl memories still linger to haunt me."

In the thickness of shadows, I could feel Christopher's eyes boring into my soul.

"I would expect nothing less from your conscience, Claus. But you must understand now, this night, I am so far removed from that little girl you remember; it is but a hallucination. I often wish it weren't so, for those were years when everything seemed possible. If I knew then, what I know now, I would have changed my life in many ways. I would have reconsidered my ambitions. Unfortunately, time travels quickly in but one direction." I smiled sadly.

"Everything you say is true…all of it. We are not of the same blood, Elizabeth. Yet, we have always been closest to heart—this is truth. I am filled with pride by how you stand on your feet, by how you have grown into a woman who has the courage to demand what she desires. It's plain that this problem is entirely my own, and caused not in part by anything you have said or done. I wrestle with the question of whether incest is a matter of the physical relationship or the spiritual." Christopher took a breath. "I am plagued by these thoughts, Elizabeth. This troubles me deeply."

"Again, I understand what you say, Claus. Truly, I do. But is this not the very same guilt that has suffered me for a lifetime? If I were a child, you would be wise to be troubled. But I am all of a grown woman, by every measure. I am of a single mind, and not one to be held sway by your advances if unwanted. I am not your child, Claus, and to be treated as such now insults me. Let us do this willingly and free of conscience. I have waited far too long a time."

Christopher took a gulp of his brandy and immediately followed it with another.

"As you wish, Elizabeth."

Christopher gathered his thoughts.

"Notwithstanding, have patience, for I am compelled to say one last thing. I hope this for your benefit." He paused. "I cannot deny my perception of love for you is confused. It is obvious. But know in your heart, by whatever measure, my love for you goes without saying. It knows no boundaries. It remains as much a reason for my will to live now as in times past.

"In spite of these many years of separation, I do still cherish you, Elizabeth. I do with all my being. You want so badly to experience this act that I fear you may confuse the feeling of sexual fulfillment with the feeling of making love. They are not the same, and for me, what we do tonight could never be simply an act of sexual fulfillment. It would devastate my self-respect. It would empty my character of all merit. I could never hold you for the sole purpose of self-gratification. It is important for me that you know that."

An enormous wave of joy moved through me, as did an unconscious smile cross my face. I raised the blankets—again.

"Come to me, now," I whispered.

SIX

Christopher shed his blanket and slid beneath the covers. Now again, he moved toward me. But this time, as if to crush a mental barrier, he immediately framed my face with his hands and kissed me passionately. His body enforced his kiss. His will dominated me. I felt my own body begin to change. My senses awakened. Christopher covered over me and lowered himself. He kissed my neck and shoulders.

He raised himself and gently moved his knee across mine. He was pressing me, prompting me to spread my legs for him. As I did so, he shifted his body squarely above me and then settled down not upon me but somewhat below. He protected me by supporting the weight of his broad shoulders upon his elbows. His head hung from above to kiss first my neck then moving down to kiss my breasts, softly, respectfully. He caressed my nipples with his lips. My eyes filled with tears. I knew at last, at last, I was engaged in an act of sexual intimacy. To my benefit, not as a slut, not a whore, but as a person loved.

I was aroused. I was hungry, craving something more. My wants seemed not only to be reflected but strengthened within Christopher. I could sense his growing determination. I could hear his breathing deepen—full breaths. He raised his head from my breast and looked at me. He moved up to kiss me on the lips and as his lips met mine, so too did we meet sexually.

I braced myself for whatever might happen. From one second to the next, each seeming hours long, I took in every sensation, every nuance. I was stimulated by his drive to find me. I burned with the pleasure of his pressure, his nudging, his gyrations. His hands then brushed lightly across my breasts and went on to caress them. My nipples responded at once to his touch and rose to meet the warmth of his lips that drove sensations of heightened pleasure through me in waves. I succumbed to this pleasance with no account for time. In fact, it was so enjoyable, I believed we were making love, and it was everything for which I had hoped.

Joyously, I moved ahead emotionally, going, flowing, losing myself in this newfound bliss until I was confronted by another sensation that instantly clipped my heavenly flight. A change in Christopher's behavior led me to question whether he was becoming distracted or unbelievably...*losing interest!* The fear grounded me at once. Was it possible we had concluded this union? I certainly hoped not, for everything within me was demanding more, much, much, more.

Was I supposed to be left wanting? Was there a residual yearning after making love that kept couples together until the next time? I felt troubled and uncertain. Was it, or was it not, my imagination? If not over, then what, Christopher's focus was now clearly removed from the kisses and caressing I had so enjoyed.

I might have been saddened by such conclusion, but any thought of our intimacy being over was promptly put to rest as Christopher's hand suddenly slipped between my legs with purpose. I was taken aback by this unexpected and morally unsettling advance. I forced myself not to overreact and determined to give him the benefit of my trust as I worked to quell my inhibitions.

He massaged me at length, sometimes tenderly, sometimes aggressively. During those moments that I could turn away from my self-consciousness, I found his caresses nothing less than thrilling—more so for the mental thrill that I should allow such a blatantly carnal act to occur for the sake of my pure pleasure.

Regardless of where was my mind, Christopher was refocused, and his kisses were again passionate, and his thrusts even more ambitious than before. I let him have his way with me and discovered the more I relaxed, the greater my pleasure. The kisses, the caresses, the intensifying desires.... To my relief there seemed no end in sight, but that was unfortunately another mistaken assumption.

Christopher stopped his motion and let out a breath that seemed every bit to be one of resignation. I was sure of it. It was certain, I never knew what next to expect. I simply had no idea. Up to now, I had been gently escorted from one pleasant surprise to another, but even so, I sensed a certain resignation in Christopher's manner.

"Claus?"

"Yes."

"I am so grateful, that you are patient with me. I…I don't know…. I just don't know what I am supposed to do. I am utterly embarrassed even to speak of it. Is there anything—?"

"Elizabeth, you have done everything that could be asked, for you have made yourself warm, inviting, and beautiful before my eyes. No man could ask for more, but I suspect in your make believe, you failed to consider that sex is pretty much a clumsy affair especially the first time around. All too often, it is an exercise in humility. The more lovers learn about each other, the less obvious the indelicacies.

"I can't imagine any honor greater than to be the man with whom a woman has chosen to relinquish her virginity. What greater compliment can there be? Still, with that honor, with that being said, an experienced lover knows nature isn't always as willing as the participants for such a joyous union to take place. For that reason God gave us bear grease."

I didn't respond. I kept running the words 'bear grease' through my head over and over. *Bear grease.* How odd. Mary never mentioned anything to me about bear grease. Not even in her secretive and cryptic manner. I never heard any innuendos or whispers about it. I wondered if bear grease was possibly a French term for some exotic act. Christopher interrupted my thoughts.

"Actually, I hope Helena has some lard in the cabinet. That doesn't smell so bad."

I was stupefied. Dumbstruck!

"You mean bear grease as in *bear grease?*" I asked. "…As in mosquito repellant?"

"Same bear grease. Dreadful stuff. Wait here. I'll be back."

Christopher got out of bed for the third time. He left the blanket behind.

"I am certain Helena has lard around here someplace."

"Second shelf on the right side of the sink," I responded with disbelief.

I had waited an entire lifetime for this moment. I attempted to fathom the amount of sacrifice and suffering of the soul I endured over an act I assumed to be everything except associated with bear grease or lard. I placed my hand on my forehead. I rocked my head back and forth in mild dismay. It became apparent that the number of false starts may have tempered my expectations and lofty illusions, but it also brought a sense of reality and normalcy to the night, and offered me a tremendous reprieve from the stress I had suffered earlier.

"I noticed that bear grease is exceptionally proficient at reducing stress," I uttered in a barely audible voice. I heard Christopher chuckle.

"Yes. I can see how you might think that. Not the most romantic facet of lovemaking. Disgusting actually, but I found the lard."

Christopher returned to the bed. This time instead of raising the covers to invite him in, I almost felt as though I were raising the covers in order to *let* him in. The thought was unfair in every way, for Christopher was making every attempt to see that my comfort came before all else. The lessons were to be mine. I was beginning to understand that the act of making love was not angelic and surreal, but earthly and almost inexcusable.

SEVEN

My eyes opened wide. It was quite a surprise.

I was a prolific dreamer, and I always spent the better part of an hour waking up. It wasn't that I was one to oversleep or labor to leave my bed; I always enjoyed spending my final hour of rest thinking about whatever issues required my attention or brought me pleasure. It was my morning state of equilibrium, that time of perfect balance between dreams and reality.

This morning, my eyes simply opened up. I just popped into reality. I was hardly prepared, for it happened without warning. Any other morning, to awaken in this manner would have left me unsettled. I would have assumed the onset of an illness. I would have been especially attentive to my body's signs, its state of well-being. On this morning, none of those concerns entered my mind. I realized without question that I was particularly well rested—unusually well rested. I must have enjoyed a fabulous night's—.

"Claus?"

I whispered his name in a combined state of joy and mild panic. Instinctively, I slid my hand across the bed. It was an uncontrolled reaction for I sensed beforehand that Christopher was not with me. I raised my head and looked around the cabin. I was alone.

"Oh, thank you, thank you," I whispered with relief.

I was pleased—grateful in fact. There was nothing about to cause fear or regret, no guilt to be had by—*him*. What a perfect way to start out the day. I wasted no time exploiting this privacy and the opportunities it offered by falling back onto my pillow without a care in the world.

Within moments, I was plowing through memories of the night past. It was by far the most memorable night of my life. It was a remarkable night. It was a perfect night. It was a night to stay with me forever, and I was still floating high within its rapture. Just thinking about it….

I settled deeper into the coziness of the covers, and with eyes closed, I formed a fresh vision of Christopher that hovered just inches above me. Slowly, I let the vision of him settle upon me. I let it embrace me. I could feel his breath rush past my ear, I could smell him. I could feel the rough texture of his beard upon my cheek. My head turned as his lips brushed my neck; it rocked slowly side to side upon the pillow as I responded to his memory.

I raised my hands as if to embrace his body. I drew them back beneath the warmth of the covers. My hands slid slowly across my ribs to meet his, and then back and forth purposely across my breasts, lightly at first, and then more deliberate, departing only after being summoned by a more pressing need between my legs. I was certain that it was a night of lovemaking that left this wonderful glow, this residual body of heat beneath my hands. It was now being drawn back to the surface, now spreading outward.

I allowed myself to pursue and even encourage the overwhelming urges that began to flow through my body. Knowing at last, exactly what it meant to make love, my imagination tuned itself to perfection by way of reflections and comparisons to the night before. My imagination was more than enough to fuel this rising pleasure, this heady sinfulness.

My thoughts of Christopher were intensely arousing, incendiary. I was spilling grease upon the fire. I relived his advances, his thrusts, the exhilaration of his strength. I focused on each second as he brought me to a state of such penetrative physical pleasure that my fears forced me to stop him, to still him, to push him away. Yet, he persisted. Gently, he returned with renewed ambition and so too returned the rushes, and so too did I again reject him as before.

61

I felt the perspiration upon my forehead. My eyes remained closed tightly, disallowing the smallest ray of light to fade or dilute the memory of Christopher's final determination. I was now acutely aware of every detail of this man before me. It was more than the look of him, more than his fragrance or the beating of his heart. It was more than his eyes. I was aware of *him*, his presence, his ambience. It moved through me like breezes of spring gusting through unfastened hair.

"Will you be patient with me?"

I asked aloud, for now I was unsure. My thoughts were fracturing, my emotions were swirling, spiraling out of comprehension.

"Yes."

His assurance receded into a distant awareness. This time the fear, the runaway exhilaration, the unknown destination, and my struggle to keep a sense of sanity, to control my world—my body, were to no avail. Christopher forced me to stay the course, to stay with him until came that most unexpected explosion of euphoria. The wildness of my surrender drove him crazy with passion. He closed in upon me, encasing me in a cage of steely flesh. I was held immobile in the crushing jaws of his release. He had total command of my body, and his unbridled passion ripped though me in a wave of fear and awe serving to further fuel this maiden's voyage until I was entirely beaten into submission by exhaustion.

The insanity passed like rogue thunder in the night. What remained was a profound sense of stillness. A peace gained from the knowledge that two souls had merged. Two souls that had worked tirelessly to chip and chisel away, to strike, to hammer, to smash into smithereens hardened shells in order to drink, to be drunk, to drown in the sweet nectar of gratification that pooled within. I pulled back ever so slowly, savoring the sensation. It flowed through me, warming my insides—*Christopher's smooth brandy.*

The act of making love was exquisite. Like bubbling butter and cinnamon in a baking apple pie, no amount of words, no perfect description, no emphatic promise, can prepare you for the exquisite aroma. Until you've experienced it, you just can't know. Bless Mary for trying.

I withdrew my hands.

I licked my lips as if finishing a feast. I sat up on the edge of the bed and shook out my hair. I started to laugh.

"Claus, you were an absolute prince." I laughed *knowingly.*

EIGHT

Looking back, Christopher and I had conversed at length before he felt comfortable showing his affection for me in a physical way. I am certain it wasn't the physical love of a husband and wife, but in view of all I didn't know, I believed the tenderness and warmth were genuine. He made me feel beautiful—special. He made me feel *wanted.* He was patient with me, and if it was true that he hadn't enjoyed the company of a woman in many years as he had confessed, his experience in this matter was profound and entirely to my benefit.

I should have thought of nothing but our union, except it was so much more for me. I could now sit at Mary and Allen's table, and blush about discreet matters out of experience, rather than from ignorance and embarrassment. I could now speak to Mary as one woman to another. Now, after so many years of life deficient, I felt complete. I could go forward and snicker in all honesty with my *'knowing smile.'*

63

I thought about the bear grease and broke into self-conscious laughter. The lard was still on my hands. It was time to wash. I stood up from the bed and walked over to the door. The sunlight streamed in through the tiny windows with a burning intensity. I swung open the door and was nearly blinded by the light as it reflected off the snow. The air was so much warmer outside than in the cabin. I pulled the door open as far as it would go in order to hasten raising the temperature of the room as well as to invite in the joy of summer sunshine returned. I noted the number of children now camped in the clearing. They greeted me with waves and smiles, and it did me good to see they appeared safe and spirited.

As I contemplated Claus's whereabouts and my lack of plans for the day, I turned to look about the room and immediately noticed a note centered upon the table. As if a treasure to behold, it beckoned, and I darted toward it. It spurred memories of the first letter Claus sent me when I was a child.

Good Morning, Elizabeth,

You were sleeping soundly.

I couldn't bring myself to awaken you.

I shan't forget my promise of a grand breakfast.

I shall return within the week.

Take care.

Claus

A week!

"Shhh. Lie down and sleep, child. Be still now."

Memory of the gentle command returned to me. It had come during the night. I read his note ten or eleven times for sure. I read it as if every word were an embrace and each letter a kiss. Because Christopher had penned it, it made me feel good. I rubbed the remnant of his presence lightly across my lips. I brushed it with a kiss and instinctively pressed the parchment to my chest before returning his words to the table.

It was a brief missive. I wanted more. I craved more. I wished a word or two might have at least hinted of our time together, of our hearts opening to one another. A word of affection would have been welcome.

That thought hung suspended in the stillness of a morning air. Christopher was so much a part of my life; he was a part of me. He was the second beat of my heart...the rhythm beneath my song. A piece so important, that when it was missing, I felt empty, moody, and restless.

Yet, the thought of being his wife seemed to be utterly absurd. I don't know why, but it didn't fit. Maybe it was because Lady Rebecca still held a place of adoration in my heart and, in my mind, Christopher belonged to her. It was never my desire to diminish that relationship. I might love him above all others; I might wish for the feel of him next to me, but I would never dream to be his wife. This limited prospect didn't bother me. I accepted without question that it was the natural state of our relationship.

Christopher granted my wish that he make a woman out of me, but my association with him would always be something more than physical. It would always be spiritual. It was for that reason I wished dearly there had been something from the heart in his written words.

The note brought to light a reminder that I have always possessed a mind that seems to take joy in torturing me. All too often, I am served up double doses of reality, and it looked as though now was to be one of those times. This fact that Christopher made no mention in his note about the previous night rolled through my head over and over. Not a single word. He didn't even bother to pen *'Love, Claus'* at the bottom of the page as was often his custom. I couldn't deny how this oversight, intentional or not, lessened my blissful state of mind. In fact, I preferred not to think about it at all, but for my fear of facing truths that would be much worse.

Based on what my friends said about their husbands, I might believe no man would have enough sensitivity to make mention of such a wonderful night. But Christopher was nothing if not a man of sensitivity, especially in regard to my feelings. He was a master at reading my mind. He was supreme in knowing my needs.

I fought to avoid these thoughts. I preferred not to acknowledge that I knew Christopher as well as anybody could. He was not a man of oversights. If I chose to reject the omission as being an oversight, then I opened myself up to the possibility he held deep regrets after all, and for me that meant collapsing into a world of unimaginable pain and embarrassment. I turned away from the table and whatever distressing realities might exist between the written lines. I chose to think about how beautiful was the day. How glorious was the sunshine.

NINE

Christopher's absence neared a week's time, during which the sun literally steamed away the snow. In fact, the heat of day was too oppressing for a body still purging winter's thick blood.

I was moved to sit on the porch and seek relief in the cool mountain air that I knew would be breezing down through the valley.

I lifted my hair up over the back of Christopher's rocker and let it fall. I let the breeze brush past the nape of my neck as it swept away the annoying winged creatures of early summer.

As I swatted the air, I paid half-hearted attention to a nearby group of chatty children carrying on. It was mindless entertainment and I found myself chuckling over their antics for some time before forming the thought of a proposition. No doubt, it was the rag-tag sight of them that prompted the idea.

"You!"

I pointed at a thin brown-haired lass.

"What's your name?"

"Belle."

"It's a pleasure to meet you, Belle. My name is Elizabeth. Who's that older boy over there?"

She turned about to see where I pointed and replied.

"Daniel."

"Fetch Daniel here for me, would you, Belle. Please?"

"Yes, ma'am."

Belle trotted off and broke into Daniel's horseplay. She towed him back toward the porch.

"Madam."

"How are you today, Daniel?"

"Doin' well, ma'am."

"Daniel, I wanted to offer you and the others a proposition. I am of a mind to make up some soap. And...if you, Belle, and your friends fancy a first-rate meal, I would be willing to seat the lot of you to a fine spread, fresh rhubarb pie an' all, in return for setting up the ash box and working it."

"Yes, ma'am!"

The two youths answered in eager unison as if to inform me that should one have doubts the other had none. I expected nothing less, for there was little if any understanding of commitments, schedules, or demands in this land of no restraint. This was a place where one lived for the day, for time had no meaning, and in all matters the quality of life was measured by the amount of energy expended or exported to another. Along the way, I adopted something of the attitude and was intent on avoiding the unsavory work and awful mess of the ash box.

In my defense, it must be said that the children couldn't be more of a mess and would hardly appear worse for such work. I determined when finished they should be first to enjoy the benefits of their toil—*a hot soapy bath*. And so, I sent the stronger boys off to the stream with the heavier wooden buckets for fetching water to leech out the lye, the lightweights to setting up the leeching box and filling it with ash, and the girls to gathering fairy slippers near a wooded stream in the north meadow for scenting the bars with some fragrance.

A few of the girls returned early with some fresh blueberries for my benefit. It seemed the children would have done my bidding gladly just to please me, but the offer of a sumptuous meal in trade kept my heart happy, my hands busy, and my mind distracted from Christopher's absence.

Albeit chaotic, soap-making was eventually underway by the children's own device, leaving me to return myself to the kitchen and heat of hearth. I had busied myself there for some time working up bread rolls, rolling out dough for pies, and making up a large bowl of rhubarb filling. I doubted sugar would be found for a thousand miles of this place and yet, here in the pantry, Claus had a stockpile large enough to sweeten a wagonload of rhubarb without notable loss. To the impoverished, it would have been nothing less than miraculous.

A large bed of glowing embers was not to be outdone by the light of day and so served to bake not only my rhubarb pies, but also a sizeable quantity of buried potatoes, corn, and me as well. And so, I stood up to wipe my brow, ease my back, and call quits to the heat. The cabin door was wide open, but that wasn't enough to cool me. I again made for Christopher's rocker on the porch. This time, I sat down as much for the benefit of my back and feet. I raised my sleeves to chill the perspiration on my half-cooked forearms.

I sat and watched with further amusement as the children mixed lye-leeching with horseplay. At some point, I gazed beyond their unruliness, outward to where my focus was drawn toward the numbers of children milling about in the clearing below. My smile slowly disappeared.

Over the last few days, the children commenced to appear out of nowhere. It took some time before I fully realized their numbers. At first, I was pleased to see them. It brought a sense of relief to know they were in good shape and safe from the elements. Then as the numbers grew it became more a sense of wonderment. Now, however, the day's sudden increase seemed entirely unnatural and reason for concern. They appeared to be waiting, to be watching for something. They instilled within me a feeling of dread.

I had no rational explanation for my uneasiness, but I soon realized that it began even before I fully appreciated how many now gathered in the clearing. The children were in every way friendly and sociable, all smiling and agreeable. Yet, my uneasiness was increased by the peculiarity of their behavior in one single regard. They were seemingly concerned for my well-being.

In fact, when I stood up from my rocker, I was positive that all activity halted as faces, to the farthest extent of the clearing, turned to observe me, asking with riveted eyes of what were my intentions. I supposed any movement on the cabin porch would attract the attention of some, but each and every one? It sent a numbing chill up my spine.

I scolded myself for assuming this could be anything more than my outrageous imagination. I knew I was merely overreacting to what would be normal behavior for anybody returning to a place that cared for them. Out of courtesy, they all asked how I fared, what of my needs, what of Christopher—all inquiries to be expected. In fact, not to ask such things would most certainly have been rude and unconscionable. Yet, the whole of my life I felt I possessed a sixth sense. Oftentimes, being the *'chosen one'*, as the old fortune teller claimed, set me back to question if indeed I did possess a little something out of the ordinary.

What wasn't imagination was the fact that even the children readily admitted to the oddity of so many showing up at the same time. Speaking with any one child would garner only that they were driven back by the recent snowstorm or simply passing by and happy to be back for a stay, if only for a chance to eat freely until fully stuffed.

Back to my earliest years, I understood that when Christopher showed up so did all manner of children, orphans, urchins—the mudlarks of the world. After all, children of the world loved gifts, and his generosity toward them was legendary. I witnessed how the poorest of the lot would endure the kicks and curses of teamsters, stevedores, and dock hands in order to gain the briefest glimpse of the man. Oftentimes, their number brought business to a halt, mobbing the docks at first sight of REBECCA's brilliant vermillion hull cresting the horizon.

Now, fully unsettled, I found myself contemplating at length the memories of those children waiting at the docks, waiting at all places he frequented. How could they have known his itinerary in those days? How could they know it now?

"It is impossible," I said aloud.

Yet, the question nagged. Who arrived first? I wondered if, in fact, the children *always arrived first* in order to herald the coming of Claus. No matter how outrageous, at this moment that indeed was the question, for at the farthest point of the trail a lone figure moved our way.

TEN

I could never misread Christopher's silhouette. Even at distances that required an eyeglass, his form was unmistakable. He had returned. His presence sent a stirring through the children that moved in a wave-like wind across wheat. They twisted their spindly stalks until all appeared focused in my direction. No part of my dreadful feeling was due to imagination. An unnatural panic raced through my body and soul.

I was acutely aware of my anxiety, my rapid breathing, the tightness of my chest, the trembling of my hands. As he neared, I stood up on legs that felt ready to break at the knees. I stepped off the porch and began walking across the clearing to greet him. I worked to bury concerns behind a smile that was genuine.

Christopher halted his horse before me. He stared down at me.

"Hello, Elizabeth."

"Claus."

My heart lodged in my throat. My worst nightmare was realized. There was no warmth in his countenance. The glint of pleasure at seeing me was absent from his eyes. He appeared, as I feared, to be filled with regret. He dismounted.

With the utmost reservation and caution, I raised my arms to embrace him. Christopher held his arm up to block my intention.

"No, Elizabeth."

I understood. I dropped my arms as I dropped my head and looked away. I stood there unsure of what next was expected of me. I could never again look into Christopher's eyes so I listened in the agony of humiliation. His voice reverberated through me like thunder, like the bowels of earth opening before the gates of hell. My face burned from the heat of his presence.

"This mistake was only mine, Elizabeth. A mistake of magnitude only I could make. A betrayal. I wish before God and all His saints that I might undo what I have done. I have destroyed every ounce of self-respect I possess or shall ever hope to earn. I will carry this disgrace with me all my days. Unlike my pathetic mortal carcass, this cannot be buried. Forgive me, Elizabeth, but you must know I cannot stay in your company. Not now. Not for a while to come. I need time to repair the damage I have inflicted upon both of us.

"I thought myself above the temptations of flesh, but now we both know how badly I was mistaken. My arrogance has been my downfall, Elizabeth. I stand before you to plead your forgiveness as I confess my sinful lack of character. To rape you of virtue behind words of comfort and love, no matter how true, is unacceptable by any man, let alone one who devoted his life to the role of father and mentor.

"You will come to understand the truth of what I say. You will see. I beg you believe when I say that that you have done nothing wrong. You have done nothing wrong, Elizabeth. There is no crime in being curious, in searching out answers. The blame for this misfortune is not yours to carry. You are as pure in heart as any creature God blessed me to encounter. The remorse should be but mine alone to bear.

"I have nothing further to say. I will ensure you are provided the best of care. You shall want for nothing. I have made the necessary arrangements to have you escorted back to civilization in comfort and safety."

As he had done on the night we made love, Christopher reached for my chin and drew my face upward to meet his.

"Look at me, Elizabeth."

I did as he said, but could see little more than a kaleidoscope of color behind a veil of tear, a distorted apparition of the man I loved, a ghost of the present.

"I have always adored you, Elizabeth. I adore you now. Just as with Rebecca, your needs, your wants, have always been my crusades. I thrilled to love you the whole of my life, Elizabeth, but never in this manner. Never once did I envision this. I betrayed you when you were weak and most in need of my support. I beg, Elizabeth. I beg you forgive me."

His apology, albeit sincere, cut me to ribbons. The crush of my embarrassment was all about me, inside and out, the blow staggering. I wanted to shrink away, to disappear. I wanted to shut out the world. I wanted to hide from myself, but there was no place, no space, where I might retreat to be distracted by some other catastrophe. The heat of humiliation radiated from face to chest, from heart to soul. My conscious mind was paralyzed by his words, and so I was unable to respond. Instinct alone turned me away from Christopher to walk a footpath upward into the northern meadow.

"Good bye for now, Elizabeth—."

Without turning about, I raised my hand to silence him. I never looked back. I walked away from all that I loved, and in

73

short time I heard the hoof beats of Christopher's horse sound across the clearing as it trotted back into the wilderness from whence it came. I found breezes fresh enough to cool my face and skin, but hopelessly inadequate to cool the scald of my shame.

Only after I no longer heard the echo of his departure did I allow myself to break down. I held a hand firmly over my mouth in an attempt to muffle sobs that struggled to be released. Tears cascaded across my knuckles and fell away into thickets of wild geraniums flush with lavender petals as if to remind me I had given rise to Lady Rebecca's wrath.

Wishing to avoid her vaporous reprimand, I turned back down along the path. At once, I noted the congregation of children spread out before me across the sloped meadow below. They had been watching our every move, our every gesture. A sizeable number of boys were disappearing into the wood. Many of the young girls lingered and appeared to have been crying. For what reason? Could they have overheard our conversation? Did they understand the significance of my walking away from Christopher? I sensed they knew too much, but worse, I sensed they knew all of this long beforehand.

The children's eyes remained fixed on me as I returned to the cabin. They halted their activities, but made no attempt to confront or console me. They simply observed in silence from near and afar. I entered the cabin, a space that no longer felt like home, yet I was much relieved when I closed the door that severed their haunting stares.

I stepped over to the window and peered outside. The children were in a state of flux, moving restlessly, disconnected, drifting away. They appeared agitated, always looking back in my direction. This behavior, all of it, upset me to my core. Goosebumps crept across my flesh. I wished this was nothing more than the childish prank whereby one would point up at the sky and stare, and before long, there would be two, then three, and then a dozen fools staring up at the empty heavens. I wanted to hope that one child had pointed and stared my way, causing all to follow suit. Every hair standing up on my neck knew better.

Within the dim light of the cabin, I cried. I cried hard. I cried until the stress in my heart seemed less than my exhaustion. I accepted the fact that whatever was left of my life as I knew it was over. I had no idea what I was supposed to do next except maybe serve dinner to the children.

I opened the door and shuddered with shock. Not a child in sight. Not one. Even my helpers, whom I promised dinner, were nowhere to be seen. It was nothing less than horrifying. It was cruel. I closed the door that invited summer breezes, and walked to the bed where I would continue to suffer.

I lay down with little choice but to surrender my memories of a night I desperately wanted to remain perfect. Dismantling these dreams would be devastating. There was little point in putting it off, and so I succumbed to my sorrow. I wept. I wept. Lord, how I wept.

I remained in bed the remainder of the day and in my peripheral awareness took note of the dimming light and approach of night. I was deeply depressed and made no move to undress or light a candle. Rather, I pulled up the blankets for security, and allowed myself to be smothered by the encroaching darkness wherein only my thoughts and visions provided light.

I was exhausted, but bound to a restless mind, a mind that would not sleep. I was drowsy and so moved in and out of reality. I dreamed of flat thin islands of glass that cracked ominously all about me. I knew this place. It was a place that haunted me. It was a place where tortured souls gathered. I found myself swimming desperately in an attempt to surface from the unknown abyss below. I was held under by the sheets of transparency. I struggled for air. I pressed my lips into the fractures, stealing one breath at a time. My hands pushed up against the glass-like barrier and as the cracks slowly closed, I could see the glittering lights above, beckoning me to play. My lungs were bursting.

Abruptly, I sat up in the bed. I gulped for a breath of air. My eyes burned from being opened too fast. I looked around the room in a state of panic. I had been dreaming. The glittering lights that had beckoned me to play were nothing more than the light of a new day.

"Oh, my word," I gasped.

Even after waking, I remained exhausted. I collapsed back upon the bed. My night terror had been draining. I wondered what strength, or salvation, or answer could my mind possibly extract from such a traumatic fabrication. I was tired. I was cried out, dried up. I began to think about my position. A feeling swept over me that was too uncomfortably close to suffocating under the invisible barriers in my dream. It was the pressure upon my chest, the stress of my memories. It was the suffocation of my embarrassment.

My regrets might dissipate over time, but my humiliation would never pass. I loved Mary and Allen with all my heart, but Christopher was the omnipotent figure in my existence. He had always been the light to guide me, the answers to my questions, the approvals I sought, and the comfort I required for peace. Ours was a relationship that was measured in lifetimes, and now it was dramatically changed for the worse by my selfishness, worse but for my base carnal curiosity. Yes, Christopher would hardly suffer alone. Humiliation of this degree would stay with me to the grave as well.

For two more days, I suffered depression and despair that only worsened by the hour, by the minute. Guilt and remorse fed upon themselves until they grew beyond any sense of reason. I had thoroughly convinced myself that I would never again be able to face Christopher under any circumstance. I wouldn't face Mary, nor any friend close or distant that was within his reach.

I had to find a means of escaping all that was familiar. I had to lose myself. But most of all, I had to get out of his bed. One thing was for certain. I couldn't bear to wait around like a sack of potatoes that needed moving by another's hand—*Christopher's* hand to be precise. The push I needed to get on my feet finally came in thanks to the alarming realization that I had been staring at a knife on the counter and wondering half-heartedly what it would be like to slit one's wrists and witness the outflow of blood and life.

Whereas one crime of curiosity proved my undoing, this dreadful curiosity proved my salvation by returning me to sanity. I was not just shocked, but terrified by the depth of my curiosity, my contemplation to commit suicide. I had to leave this cabin. I had to leave it now before it was too late. It was the waiting combined with an unknown future that left me at the mercy of rampant depression.

The knife severed my bonds of depression. My spirit was suddenly lifted and I felt free and filled with purpose—I would leave at once. I attempted not to think myself into reckless abandon, but I was certain leaving would be necessary in order to regain my self-will and relieve Christopher of his obligation to ensure my safety at a cost of reliving his self-damnation.

I worked determinedly, stuffing my trunk and gathering whatever extra belongings I could manage a pack horse to carry. I had arrived with little, and was about to leave with less. I dragged my belongings and a chest onto the porch. I pulled closed the cabin door and at once felt its security drain from within. To snap the wave of panic, I called out to the stable hands and had them fetch and ready a couple of horses. While I waited, I stepped off the porch and walked out a few paces. I looked out across the lower valley and then turned to face the cabin.

"Well, lady. You traveled a couple of thousand miles, nearly killed yourself—did in fact kill a couple of others, all to finally understand you loved a man who was a myth. You nearly destroyed him in the process, but in the end—you came out of it a woman. You got laid. Yes, ma'am, you got laid. Mary...don't tell me anything more about watching farm animals. I figured it out—*the hard way.*"

ELEVEN

I mounted my horse, and with the pack horse in tow, I started down the trail toward the South Pass junction. It was all of a morning making the trip to South Pass, and I was both hungry and tired by the time of my arrival. For these reasons my first objective was to ease the stiffness out of my back. The morning ride served to remind me that I was out of condition for a jaunt let alone a journey. I had spent too many months being pampered, and that reminded me that I only wished to find a meal and relax a spell. My second objective was to find a wainwright, which I did in short order. A flyer directed me to his establishment.

"Mr. Jaerbyn?"

The man turned to look my way. He had been studying something in a pile of parts that were weaved together by the tall grasses.

"Yieh."

He walked toward me. I held up the flyer.

"I'm looking to purchase a small, sturdy wagon that can make a trip down to the North Platte and eastward from there. I'm headed for St. Louis and I'd like to be on my way by nightfall or first light at latest."

Kayle Jaerbyn

WAINWRIGHT
CARPENTER

GIVER & TAKER

cooper • coffins
funery box maker

Large Selection of Wagons
New & Used Wheels, Hoops and Underparts

East of Town on

Red Sand Road
Between
Lacy's Eatery and Dawg's Dry Goods & Stores

"Yi got yerself a teim?"

"No. These horses belong to Claussen and they stay."

"Well, now, I do hiv' some fine inimals."

"I'm not of a mind to drive horses. ...Much prefer mules. Mexicans at that...."

"Oh, then agin' mebbe I don't hiv' such fine inimals ifter all. Whit yi got agin' horses?"

"I don't have anything against horses. But I have worked with mules in the past, and I find they take the heat better, they drink only what they need, they won't overeat and get colicky, they are far more surefooted, they seldom get sick, they are smart as the devil...should I continue?"

"No, mi'am. I see jus' where yer comin' from, but yi did fergit 'stubborn'."

"I'll give you that."

"I kin find yi a team, an' I kin build yi inythin' yi like—."

"I'm of a mind to leave today, soon as I arrange for supplies."

"Oooh. Till order in short tam'. Whit kind o' money yi lookin' t' piy out?"

"I can do one, one-fifty. I suppose in my situation, I will pay whatever it takes within reason. Understand I have yet to buy supplies."

"Hmmm. Mmmm. Humph."

The man looked back over his shoulder. Side to side, he scanned his collection of heaps. It was a broad assortment of debris drowning slowly, disappearing into the depths of prairie grass. He appeared hopelessly lost in thought.

81

"Certainly, you must have something affordable in your yard," I said.

"Thit'd be axle breakin' country, mi'am. How smill yi lookin' t' git?"

"A bed long enough for me to lie down and sleep, plus a couple of inches, and not a hair's length more. I'm traveling light and I don't want to see my team overworked."

The wainwright pushed his mustache back and forth and then stroked the bottom of his nose with his forefinger.

"Well, now. Lemme see. I'm i-thinkin' I might hiv' jus' the thing fer yi. I got me i-little rock hiuler bick there thit used t' be i smill firm wigon. Sturdy piece o' work, she is, mostly oak, mostly rebuilt from ground up—bed'll stind up t' 'bout inything. I fit it with heavy ixles in' wheels i while back fer i hiulin' job. Built them wheels myself wit' stout spokes; mid' them fellies in' rims wide to hindle the weight o' rocks without sinkin'. Should do yi good crossin' country, sind, desert in' ill." He interrupted his rambling to study me. "In' by the looks o' yi, I say the bed'll be right perfect. Com'on bick here in' I'll tik yi t' see it."

I followed the man through his maze of wagon beds, underparts, wheels, and what-nots.

"Most o' whit I got's been used fer hiulin' stone on the r'ilbed. Mostly, busted up in' in fer rep'ir."

We arrived at a large draped oilcloth that he carefully dragged off the wagon. He tossed a number of planks to the side that had spanned the bed to support the oilcloth. At first sight, it looked pretty rough.

"Not the nicest-looking wagon I have ever seen. Why would you keep this covered up with an oilcloth?"

"I wisn't. I wis mendin' the oilcloth."

"Oh."

That made a lot more sense.

"'In' real pretty, I idmit, but she'll tik' i reil beatin'. I promise yi thit."

"And the price?" I asked.

"I could do this one fer ibout fifty-sixty. I kin git yi i respect'ble teim o' mules fer 'bout one twenty. Twenty on odds n' ends. Yer lookin' t' be on the other side o' two hundred before it's over."

"Two hundred! Ohhh. None too cheap," I replied.

"No mi'am, but this 'in't New York. W'it til yi buy them supplies. Yi'll fig'er I'm givin' this iway."

"May I ask about hoops and canvas?"

"Mmm. I got me some hoops lyin' 'bout, but they're too big—need t' be cut down. Most o' the bow clips git knocked off by rocks, but I got more. I got kinvis. Bows fer three. Twenty fer kinvis." The wainwright began nodding his head in the affirmative. "Yeah, I think we kin get somethin' igreeible to yi. I need t' look it one o' the wheels." He pointed out a loose rim that I hadn't noticed. "Don't pia't no mind. I'll fit it with a new fellie plate in' shrink thit rim bick on. Be is good is new, but I'll need ill o' whit's left o' today. Give me thit in' I should be ready fer yi."

"Give me a final price."

"I won't go over two-fifty."

"That's for sure. If it does, you'll still own it by day's end. I'll promise you that."

"Ha! Yes, mi'am. I don' doubt it." He laughed.

I returned a few hours later and was thankfully pleased with the progress. The hoops had been cut to size and mounted to fresh sideboards. Canvas had been tossed over the hoops and was being sized and fitted by a couple of Indian women who looked my way and smiled. I was especially satisfied with the team of mules now in the yard for me to inspect. They were sturdy-looking animals, all of a thousand pounds apiece, and by sight looked to have lots of Mexican blood in their breeding. The choice of animals made me very happy and feeling assured of the wainwright's competence; I left all to their work.

I returned to the street where I continued to purchase stores for the trip. When I felt I was stocked up sufficient for the journey, I returned to the wainwright and saw the wagon hitched to the team of mules. If appearances were a measure of success, then the outfit met my every expectation. I walked slowly around the wagon and team of four.

"Well, whi'dyi think?" he asked.

"I think I am impressed. Expensive, but well done."

I paid the man a fair price and then some. In a show of gratitude, he insisted on accompanying me about town to pick up my stores and help load the wagon.

"Besides, I'm w'itin' t' hear 'bout them prices. By the end o' day, I'll look like i barg'in." He prodded me.

* * *

I looked at the storekeeper in near shock.

"Coffee—two dollars a pound! Flour—six dollars a sack!"

I stepped out of the store and looked at my supplies piled up on the walk. I turned to the wainwright.

"I felt like there was a gun to my head."

84

He laughed. "Yi see, my wigon wisn't near so costly is yi wis thinkin'. I kin ilways find wood in these pi'rts to mik' whit I need, but yi kin't go growin' coffee in' flour on trees or rock. They got t' be brung in. Folks're stirtin' t' show up in these pi'rts, 'specially now since there's work t' be hid buildin' the r'ilbeds. Ever'thin's in demind in' thit's driving up prices somethin' fierce. If they ever get to tr'inin' in them supplies from out East, it won' be i diay too soon fer me. No, mi'am."

We said our good byes, and with a setting sun at my back, I left the civility of South Pass to enter the unforgiving realm of nature in reasonably good spirits. For the first time in a week, I felt free of depression, free of despair, guilt, humiliation, and, most important of all, free of Christopher's influence. I left town feeling nervous but much relieved as I watched dust and desert sage dress my wheels before daylight called it quits.

I confess, any sane gal would have spent her night enjoying the comforts of an inn at South Pass, but I preferred nothing of the kind. I wished for the very solitude I knew I would soon come to curse. I put in another two hours' worth of travel between me and my wretched memories before calling it a day. By that time, I was beat, utterly spent, and it was a fool's game to travel after dark. One might travel at night to escape Indians, but the odds were probably better to face them. I unhitched the team, crawled under covers spread across the bed, and slept as if I were dead.

I awoke late the next morning. I slept hard and it took some time to get the stiffness out of my body. I had nearly forgotten the amount of time and effort needed to gather up some wood and set it ablaze before enjoying a simple cup of badly needed coffee. The wait was excruciating. Helena had spoiled me rotten. I hitched the team so I didn't have to dwell on the time it took for water to get hot. Afterward, I enjoyed what, in a few days, would be my last taste of fresh eggs.

I traveled in a southwest direction toward the mountains that rose above Hell Hole. Traveling by wagon was much slower than riding by horseback, but I needed time to sort out my intentions and final destination, and so the slower pace was not without its advantages.

I was hesitant to return by way of my arrival into this land. That way was every bit as torturous as a southern voyage, every bit as dangerous, and most certainly much longer a route. Many of those who milled about South Pass Junction had come by way of the northern fork of the Platt River. There were now a couple of trails along its banks. One, often mentioned as of late, was the Oregon Trail. From talk overheard, traveling the Platte seemed as survivable a route as any, and if for nothing more than the sake of curiosity, I elected to travel it.

Once pointed in the right direction, all that was left was to think. And in my thoughts, Christopher assumed top billing. I could see that it would take both an eternity and countless miles of risk and hardship before I might free myself from thoughts of him and all attached humiliations. I was even surprised to realize how thoughts of Lady Rebecca's death seemed to hover over me, as if I needed something else to weigh upon my spirit.

The worst part about leaving South Pass was having departed without determining where best to go in the end. Home would always be Boston, but home represented a myriad of unwelcome scenarios. There simply was no place or persons I longed to see more than Mary and Allen. But the thought of my indiscretions coming to light before either of them was excruciating to say the least. Of course they would accept my fall from grace with the utmost sympathy and undoubtedly attribute the misfortune to my impulsive nature—a minor lacking that would always be beyond my ability to control.

In spite of her unquestioning loyalty to Mr. Claussen, Mary would hold Christopher equally to blame—for my benefit—even if she thought he was completely innocent. We would both know he couldn't be blamed. Besides, I would never allow him to be blamed. From every angle, my situation appeared impossible.

At this time, facing Mary and Allen or any of my friends back East remained out of the question. My anxieties were eased in knowing that they were thousands of miles distant. I would first focus on finding Rachel and Caleb, who, hopefully still resided in St. Louis, the closest reach. I knew that my visit would be temporary at best, but for now it gave me a sense of direction, a purpose. Finding them would bring me peace and comfort, for I would consider nothing less than Rachel and Caleb yet being together, and after all this time, most certainly reunited with their son, Isaac. The whole of it seemed a good first move.

As the miles passed and I further pondered my options, I found most appealing those thoughts of returning to see Dorrie and her boys. That was the one prospect that truly warmed my heart. Whereas Rachel and I were well acquainted, Dorrie and I had formed a bond that struck deep into my heart. To think of her brought me closest to the sense of the peace I shared with Mary. Of course, given a hundred more miles and a thousand more thoughts, I would undoubtedly change my plans at every step.

TWELVE

After a few days of solitude beneath the desert sun, my brain was having no problem adjusting to the state of mindless insanity that accompanied me on my journey westward from Rapid Run to the Stony Mountains. My back, however, was a different story. The past six months spent in leisure about Christopher's cabin softened me to a degree that my back pain was the one thing capable of disrupting my intolerable conscience and all things Christopher.

The wagon was built strong and purposeful, built to haul rocks but not me. The seat springs must have been made for a pair of three hundred pound men, for they offered no give to comfort my small frame. I might as well have lost all my teeth by sitting in the bed. The constant jostling and jarring had bruised my spine until my back pain was intolerable. I first placed a thickly folded blanket between the bench and my bottom, but to no avail. I then loaded additional weight on the bench seat to get more spring, but after halting the team repeatedly in order to pick up whatever weight bounced off the seat, I gave up.

The longer I sat on the wagon bench the more my back suffered spasms caused by the constant compressions. I found myself crying out in pain at almost every turn of the wheel and finally had to accept that this trip looked as if it was not about to happen. It would have taken days for my back muscles to relax in the best of times, without adding the endless jolting of wagon travel.

I was down to my last option, which was to walk. Walking seemed to work out the knots as long as I didn't trip or stumble. And, as long as I was supremely careful about climbing up and down off the wagon bench, which guaranteed a fresh round of pain in either direction. I chose to walk during the early morning hours when the air and ground were cool and I could get out from under the awning. This morning was no different.

Unable to simply jump to the ground, I turned myself inboard toward the center of the wagon, and reached out over the driver's wheel with my left leg. I lowered myself until I was able to place my left foot upon one of the horizontal spokes and then eased my weight onto it.

I then collected my skirt, holding it up and clear of the handbrake with my left hand, while gripping the wagon seat with my right. I moved to lift my right leg off the wagon and over the same wheel to find a second footing. Suddenly, in spite of all my care, or most likely because of it, my left foot slipped cleanly off the spoke, causing me to lose my grip on the wagon seat, whereby I came crashing down onto the rim of the wheel.

My right leg had not yet cleared the top of the wheel, and so hooked there to pitch me over onto my left side. My hands shot forward and managed to grab the rim of the wheel, but not before my left knee slammed hard into the ground. The massive jolt to my inflamed spine literally crippled me with pain. I was frozen in place, unable to move in any fashion.

"Eiieeee."

I cried out, exhaling slowly through clenched teeth. My back muscles locked up instantly. Only by flinging my arms over the wheel, did I prevent myself from falling away from the wagon directly onto my back. I hovered there somewhat spread eagled with my hands clutching the wheel rim, my right leg pointed awkwardly upward toward the sky, and my left knee perfectly impaled upon a godforsaken prickly pear. There was no problem remembering the sensation of being pricked by the cactus as that horrid tingling shiver shot up through my body. Still, the sensation was short lived and paled in comparison to the unrelenting complaint of my back.

"Ahhhh. Oh, that hurt. Oh, my word, that hurts. Ouch, ouch, ouch." I spoke aloud.

I struggled to gain a breath. My ribs served only to amplify the slightest attempt and skewer my spine like twisting knives. I remained snagged by the wheel, and determined it best not to move so much as my pinkie for at least one lifetime. I most likely would have waited out eternity had it not been for a second, and much more violent, shiver that coursed through me—this one surprisingly notable in comparison to the first tingling.

I reached down to check my knee, the one that flattened the cactus. I couldn't get near it, but for revengeful needles awaiting my groping fingers. Having no choice, I gritted my teeth as I drew myself back up along the wheel, pulling my knee free of the cactus. I stood up and endured the newly arrived spasm that wished to squeeze the life out of me. To save myself further agony, I laid bent over across the wheel while plucking out the embedded needles. In that position, I quickly noticed the smear of fat or wax that coated the blameworthy spoke. I could hardly blame the wainswright for his liberal application of the lubricant that had oozed out from the wheel hub. The blame was to be mine, and so I went on to rub my knee gingerly until assured I had found every last needle. I next removed the little miseries from my skirt.

"Even walking is going to be unbearable," I commented aloud.

I commenced to take baby steps in the direction of my mules. I stopped twice in that short distance in order to arch my back. With hands placed squarely on my hips, I bent myself side to side. I bent myself down, easy, easy, easy, each time with a little more bounce to stretch the taut muscles along my spine.

Slowly, my muscles gave way and allowed my back to relax. I was free to move with some confidence. I looked up into the blue sky. It was hot. I was suddenly aware of a driving thirst. I hadn't noticed it before, but I was very thirsty, and most disheartened to know that the water barrel was inside the same wagon I had just killed myself to climb out.

I arched my back again and did my sideways dance a time or two more before proceeding back to the wagon. Water barrels were often kept strapped to the sideboards on the outside, but I yet preferred mine kept safe within. I didn't like the thought of losing my barrel to a bump while plodding through the desert only to discover it missing about three hours before certain death. I kept the barrel in a copper wash bin that collected any leakage from poorly fit staves. I would simply sop up the water with a rag and wash with it, or treat my face to a cool damp freshening. Another added benefit was the way it humidified the inside of the wagon and gave some reprieve to my sinuses and lips when I slept.

With considerably more attention paid, I scaled the spokes and worked myself back up onto the seat. I rested momentarily, for it was precisely that sitting position that my back so disliked. Unconsciously, I went to rub my knees not realizing how tender they were—bruised no doubt. I rubbed both my knees vigorously and slid my hands down my shins.

"Ouch!"

I snapped my hand back as if slapped for stealing candy. I frowned momentarily and quickly surmised I was yet a victim of the heartless prickly pear. I held my skirt out before me and searched the material but saw nothing of a needle. Obviously, it had to be lodged in my skin. I pulled my skirt atop my thighs and bent over to search my left shin for that remaining devil of a pricker.

My leg was now reddish looking and somewhat swollen, no doubt soon to be black and blue. I placed my hand upon my knee and was about to slide it down my shin to feel out the needle, when I caught sight of it in the light. I moved to pinch it with my fingernails, and the moment I touched it, the pain was instant and very irritating. It annoyed me. It was an odd-shaped scrap and I wasted no time in pulling it out of my leg. I rubbed my shin, to alleviate the burning sensation.

My attention returned to the needle between my nails and I placed it in the palm of my left hand. It was peculiar and precisely upon noting its curve, a bolt of fear knocked me almost senseless. I stared in disbelief as my mind raced to comprehend what I was looking at. I yanked my skirt up and looked at my reddened leg and the telltale marks. I let my dress fall back so I might stare with undivided attention at my palm where lay a single curved fang.

"Oh, God."

A rush of adrenaline flooded my body. Snakes. I felt them crawl all over me. I shuddered. Instantly, I recalled the snake thrown in my wagon by Luke's killers. It was horrifying. Instinctively, I raised my feet onto the dash. I looked about and beneath the bench where I sat. I turned around quickly to inspect the wagon bed. I studied every space and shadow in the wagon until I felt fully assured there was no immediate threat behind me. I then looked out across the desert floor. I saw nothing, no movement of any kind. I studied the team. They were calm.

My eyes moved upward to scan the horizon. The mountains surrounded me. The familiar peaks I left behind, those to the west of me, remained in full view, but their distance was shrouded by deception. They seemed so close, but I had traveled days in an easterly direction and I knew all too well that those peaks were way beyond offering me help. Now I stood at the north slopes of the same southern mountain range that lifted Hell Hole above the desert floor to see across the pass.

Hell Hole was my only chance of finding help if this bite should be poisonous, and I knew it was. Only poisonous snakes had fangs. All others had rows of teeth that left nasty bite marks. This snake had struck me in the shin and busted its fang off against my bone. I knew I was fortunate in that the wound couldn't be too deep, but that offered me scant consolation. I had seen some wicked snake bites.

Again, my gaze passed across the slopes of this range alongside me. How I would have loved to hear just one riotous bawdy song echo down a valley, but to show me the way, to lead me up to that incorrigible little piss pond. That was a wishful thought and, truth be told, I hadn't the faintest idea how far I must back track to even be in the vicinity of that rowdy bunch. Memories of those boys were soon interrupted by tingling sensations now evolving into a dull burning. I was in trouble. I was in serious trouble.

Instinct told me that walking was not a good idea, but my back was dead against riding in the wagon. I laughed to myself and shook my head in wonder.

"This is truly amazing. I can't walk. I can't ride. I have hours at best to find help that has no reason to be here in the first place. I'll never find Hell Hole. To think different is lunacy." I searched the slopes half-heartedly for any sign of trails.

"I am a dead woman. I'm dead." I thought of my life-long savior, Christopher, and I started laughing. I couldn't help myself. I laughed as hard as my back would allow.

"I know…. I wanted to be a woman. I wanted to be fulfilled. I wanted to be loved by a man before I died. That was all I wanted, and by God I did it with a few days to spare."

I laughed. I then yelled out across the sand and brush.

"I am fulfilled! Yes-sir-reee! I *am* fulfilled!"

It was hard not to laugh at my situation. And I did. And after settling down, I looked out ahead of me and then back from whence I had come. I knew somewhere up ahead I would find folks traveling this way, but I had even less of an idea of when or where that might happen than I did of the whereabouts of Hell Hole. Turning to look behind me, I noted the sun was in retreat as was I.

"Well, Elizabeth, chances are, should you head for Hell Hole and never make it there alive, somebody at some point is bound to find your body in this covered coffin and give you a fitting burial."

I agreed with that thought. And so I coaxed the team about and into the sun. In spite of my snake bite, my back was still the more painful issue, and it forced me to lie across the bench seat upon folded blankets to relieve the pressure. I shuffled myself from one position to another every twenty minutes until I had

93

done so enough times that I was now staring into the brilliant orange glow of a sun dying off like myself.

It had been a good three or four hours since the bite, and if I had checked my leg once, I had checked it a thousand times. Not once did it look better than before. It was now badly swollen, bruised, and throbbing. I feared facing the night alone. I knew night would soon be upon me, but to be alone for the whole of a night and not knowing what I was about to endure was frightening beyond measure.

I brought the team to a halt when the desert floor was lost in shadow. The mountains to my left were bathed in an intense wash of orange and red against a cool blue sky. I looked up to see the first stars now glinting back at me. The sight of them offered some solace, a spellbound moment that subdued the discomfort that engulfed me.

My back had eased its complaint and although it was easier for me to climb off the wagon, placing my weight on the bitten leg produced unmistakable pain that throbbed in great beats. I unhitched the mules so they might forage. At least this is what I told myself, for barely beneath this thought was a second, one of death. It was my wish that the animals be free to wander in case I didn't wake up.

I climbed into the wagon and made up my bed. I felt chilled but cared little to seal the canvas. I propped up a pillow and pulled the covers over me. I stared out the front of the wagon and into the distance where splendid layers of purple and violet ribbons of light settled upon the flat open land of the pass. Looking up at the collecting stars made me feel closer to God. My back was finally at rest, leaving a wickedly painful leg to be my sole focus. The pain overrode any other thought. I prayed for merciful sleep.

Sleep I did. And I awoke in a completely different world. I awoke terrified. I was momentarily closed in by the darkness of night, and grateful to see stars watching over me out the front of the wagon. The pain in my leg was now extreme, but it was the inability to breathe that set off the run-away fear. I expanded my chest. I arched my back upward as I attempted to take deeper breaths, but I was fully panicked by the sensation of suffocating.

My throat felt as though it was swollen, as though air would not flow freely. My dry mouth and thickened saliva served to make me gag and choke. My pulse was racing. I felt light headed. I tried to calm myself. I reached down to check the swelling of my leg and was frightened by its enormity.

I blurted out a slur of words.

"It's the darkness, Elizabeth. If you could see it in the light of day, it wouldn't be anything out of the ordinary."

...But in the darkness of night with only the ability to feel, it dominated all else—Claus, *help me please.*

A vision of Christopher burst into my head, and I was desperate to hold on to it. My need for him stampeded over all other thought. I would confess; I would crawl; I would grovel. If only he would not forget me. If only he would favor me with a miracle. I believed, I believed.

The more time passed, the less I could focus until eventually his image was overrun by stray thoughts and nonsensical dreams. I was losing my mind. I was losing my mind, and I realized it. I cried. Maybe I dreamed I cried. I felt abandoned by life. I felt left behind by all things good, all things warm and joyful. I felt alone and terrified.

Each passing hour served only to feed this morbid pain. I vomited all over myself, but I was too weak to change matters. I was now unable to move, except for the shivering. The shivering was intense and unrelenting, but I could no longer move my arms or legs. I waited for my chest to stop its rise and fall. I waited. I watched or maybe I dreamed I watched.

I was a corpse with nothing left but my thoughts and they were unsure…my thoughts were…. It was hard to stay focused. I was too confused—dizzy. It was too dark. I couldn't remember where I was. It occurred to me that Mary might know, but she was…. I couldn't call out to her. I couldn't breathe. All that mattered was to breathe, Mary, to stay perfectly still and breathe. Breathe…. Breathe….

THIRTEEN

Gracie was a phenomenon in her own right. This was a fact readily apparent to anyone who might chance to meet her. The trouble was, in her short life, the total of all people met could nearly be counted on the fingers of her delicate hands. Having entered another summer, she could now lay claim to her tenth year. She was young, bright, white through-n'-through, born to English parents; and she was as rare as a doctor in the western wilds. Most of her wilderness siblings were dark headed half-breeds of either French or Indian heritage.

Her daddy called her 'Booty' from the day that she was born. He claimed she sprouted hair as rich and gold as the nuggets he found when panning or setting traps in the streambeds. Soon after she arrived on this earth, he tucked both her and those golden locks into a large leather boot that he had fashioned into a papoose with pride. It was certainly fitting and foretelling of the life before her. He was a furrier, a trapper, a panner, and their world was and always would be one of continuous movement. Few, at any age, had traveled but half the land her young eyes had surveyed.

In view of its history, the boot-papoose was not just a prized possession, but a shrine in the eyes of Gracie and in the hearts of her family. Along with Gracie, it too had grown over the years. Its adaptations reflected her life. Once outgrown as a boot-papoose, her father refashioned the leather into a travel bag for Gracie's diapers, baby clothes, and belongings. As she grew older, he fitted it with small pockets to keep up with her collection of lucky stones, lucky bones, and curios that only a young imaginative mind could appreciate. In time, Gracie acquired a hand for leatherwork and began to fashion her own compartments. The growth of this unique piece was limited only by her strength to carry its weight.

The 'boot-papoose-diaperbag-backpack' was a conversation piece to be sure. There was much pride in pointing out the fact that not only was the original bootlace still used in snips to tie down the pocket flaps, but also one could yet make out the original boot sole on the backside. This keepsake was older than Gracie, had traveled farther, and was affixed to her young frame not only by straps and belts, but also by bonds that she felt to be sacred.

Gracie ran her slender white fingers back and forth across the twisted spirals of sinew that fastened her pocket flaps secure. Twirling the lace between her fingers, she passed it lightly across her lips, unconsciously assessing the texture while deep in thought. Now and then, she would be compelled to open a pocket for the purpose of taking inventory or organizing her 'things' familiar. She clutched the boot-backpack close to her chest, and lay carefully backward across the mound of rocks that covered her dadduh.

In the stillness of the wood, she looked up through the trees, past the leaves, and far into the purest of blue sky. She dreamed of seeing her father hovering overhead in the heavens above. The dream was shattered by the screech of a passing hawk that brushed the tree tops and drew a stream of that cool blue sky down the slope in its wake. The chilly stream stirred the pines, and even more so, it stirred the silence that surrounded her. It brought a memory of prayer that she whispered aloud.

"Ought I be a feathert dove

Aloft upon bespreaded weng

I woult scrape thy sky above

I woult hover high en' seng

Praise the Lort, praise the Lort

I woult find thy fragrant scent

Brought forth upon a breeze

Soon passed over wild flowers spent

Ta tiddivate as He please.

Praise the Lort, praise the Lort

I woult hover high en' seng

I woult scrape thy sky above

Aloft upon bespreaded weng

Ought I be a featheret dove"

The uncomfortable breeze invaded Gracie. She drew her legs together and crossed them at the ankles for warmth. She pulled her coat up tight and attempted to gather herself beneath the boot-backpack that lay pressing upon her breast. She wasn't sure what was worse: the chill of the mountain air, or the chill of loneliness.

Gracie wasn't one to cry. Her life was built upon survival by the hour. After ten years of facing cold winters, *colder*-blooded opportunists, sweltering summer heat, starvation, thirst, blistered feet, bug bites, bears, wildcats, snakes, and finally rashes beyond recount, Gracie had been toughened to a degree where she now looked at her mother with numb acceptance.

Her mother didn't feel the cold or the swarm of flies. She was still breathing, but she hadn't moved in two days. That was in stark contrast to the frenzied pace she had maintained for a week prior. Gracie barely kept up with the severity of her situation. It seemed as though every minute required her to relive details in order to make sense of what had come to completely change her life.

It began with the summer's first new moon at which time her father set off for a rendezvous at Horse Creek in Mexico. He planned to trade away his pelts and furs for fresh supplies, a special 'sump'unt' for her mother, and most important, a birthday gift for her.

'I cain't take ye weth may, Booty. Ye gawtta understant, gril, them trappers en' pannahs get ta drinkun', en' brawlun', en' chasun' wemen en' young-uns alike. I cain't kape ye safe agin' so many ovva mine t' 'ave 'eir own way. They't be a bat lawt, piggy-widden. Ye jus' promise may t' coupie down, stay low en' close ta yer momma's side en' I'll bring ye sump'unt' gurt special fer yer birthday. I give ye may word on thet, Booty. Ye jus' be gut en' pay mind ta wot yer mama says, en' by ferst full moon at summer's aind, I'll be back long dreckly t' kiss ye up down boat sides, love.'

He returned by the full moon as promised, tired but safe. Instead of pelts and furs, now the pack mules carried wares, dry goods, *and gifts*. For her mother, he had brought back a nice iron pot. She was thrilled. Her dadduh said it was cast at the Earl Foundry in Pittsburgh, Pennsylvania. It sounded like a magical place.

'*Fram the forks o' the O-high-o,*' he had boasted with a large grin.

Her mother was elated and so was she for her gift was no less wonderful—a beautiful looking-glass and matching blue-handled brush. Her mother loved the blue-handled brush, but wouldn't have anything to do with the looking glass.

'*No thank-ye, love, I ownt one jus' like et years back long, en' all et dit was make may older en' more 'arable avery time I looked en et. Now, when yer dadduh says I luk beautiful, I might call 'um a sweet talkun', lyun' sinner, but I got no way a prove 'um wrong. Ye jus' kape thaccy maggoty lookun' glass 'way fram may, ye hear?*'

But for Gracie, it was the first time she had ever seen herself. She spent hours staring at the glass to see the reflection of tiny flecks in her green eyes, the lashes that surrounded them, the texture of her skin, the white of her teeth, and the stuff in her nose.

And this was only the half of it, for there was the ability to see what lay around a corner or behind a tree. A particular thrill was to bend the sun and send it shooting across a valley. The mirror was an endless source of fascination. It demanded a pocket of its own.

Her dadduh had brought back something else. He called it Cholera. It began with his complaining of a bad stomach and ended shortly thereafter. Being sternly warned, Gracie stood alone and distraught at a distance behind her mother. From a place apart, she watched in silent horror, as her father's body emptied itself of life.

'Stay back! Damn ye, love! Stay back. It's Cholera. D'ya hear may? It's Cholera. I knaw it. Stay wi' Gracie. Stay back lessin' ye come down with it. Don' fuss wi' may. Don' get near may. Hark ta may! It'll kill ye, love. Please. Please! Go away. Gracie'll be needun' ye soon enough. I ain' got ought fer ye. I ain' got ought fer ye, love.'

Her father ranted. He begged. He pleaded with her mother to ignore him, to leave him be, but he was too weak to enforce his wishes, and too weak to take his leave. In a day's time Gracie watched her dadduh go from begging and pleading, to uttering sheer nonsense, to silence.

Gracie watched the center of her world, her invincible father, her protector, her teacher, her wilderness god, break down and cry for the first time in her life. He cried hard. They were tears of despair, tears shed because of her mother's refusal to abandon him. She watched from that distance as her mother fought valiantly to clean her dadduh, to bring him water, and to ease his fears. She cradled him in her arms, and between sobs and prayers, she spoke to soothe him. Her mother's last effort was to cover her dadduh with rocks. *'A proper burial,'* she called it.

Gracie went on to watch benumbed as her mother fell to her knees, going down with the last stone meant for her dadduh's grave. Exhausted from her labor and the days of dedicated attention, her mother commenced to suffer the same dreadful fate. She crawled weakened, out of the woods, and collapsed onto a blanket from which she never arose.

Her devoted mother demanded with the severest cruelty of love that no matter what she might say or do, Gracie was not to come near. Her mother consumed her last coherent hours telling Gracie how much she believed in her and what was needed to

101

ensure her survival. Gracie last heard her name floated upon her parent's dying breath.

The memory of her mother's and father's voices never stopped instructing her on what she needed to do in order to live. Her mother repeated many of the same instructions given to her from her father.

'Hait north en' west, en' seek out the South Junction Pay-ass. Kape eyes out fer injuns. Stay clear o' stranguhs, piggy-widden, 'spesh-lay menfalk.

'Be careful o' the water ye drink.

'Kape eyes out fer bears en' snakes, Booty.

'Find yerself a kint soul goin' east-ways 'long the north fork o' the Play-ette. Fallow thac course far uz it ud take ye. Always be a-askun' which way be it t' St. Louis. Take up livun' in St. Louis, Booty. Ask ta werk fer yer stay.

'Ray-member, wot yer dadduh praicht, kape yer eyes out fer injuns, use them 'arable haits', Booty, ye hear? Use 'em god-awful ugly haits.'

Gracie's father was familiar with Indians, and wise to many of their ways. He spent years trading with various tribes, often for profit, occasionally for his life. The Shoshone, Cheyenne, and Arapaho were friendlier than the Comanche, Sioux, or Crow.

'Them cusset Crow, I swear et times I believe they es the devil's own spawn. They'ut kill ye soon es look et ye, Booty.'

Gracie had traveled enough to know that she was camped well south of the marauding bands of Blackfeet that swarmed about the northern ranges, as well as the Sioux, who were now hunting north and east of them toward the Upper Missouri. For now, the Comanche should be far south and west of her.

'Should ye be lucky enough ta wamble 'cross some Day-laware, knaw they're trustwor-thay.'

'Hait east—stay clear o' man—stay close ta knife.'

Her father had advised. Gracie and her mother always paid strict attention to his words.

Gracie could do nothing now, but stand guard against animals of the wood and wait. It was her mother who now struggled to breathe—a mother, who had spent her life cooking, cleaning, and picking up after the three of them. Now it was she who lay amongst blankets soaked in vomit and diarrhea. She was covered with flies that were attracted by the stench of a corpse that was not yet dead. Her mother would have been appalled to see herself immersed in such filth.

Gracie spit out the leather lace held between her lips, and leaned forward. She pushed herself off the stones. She stood up. She fixed her eyes upon her mother's lifeless form. To do so was hard. The putrid smell was her mother's warning to stay clear.

'If ye disobey may child, Eh swear, God'll send ye ta the averlastun' fars o' hail!'

In spite of the longing in her heart, Gracie's eyes turned away. Her gaze moved past her dadduh's mound of stones, across to a small meadow where the movement of a rabbit caught her attention. Instinctively, her hand slid to touch the steel at her side. She moved a step or two toward the creature, but decided it was too far away to kill with a throw. She dismissed the animal and looked beyond it—down the rock-strewn slopes of the mountainside.

Her eyes followed the cutting edge of a brilliant blade of light that bounced up from the desert below. There were many such blades streaming in parallel as they knifed their way through the wood from slits between tall trunks in the tight stand of forest. She enjoyed this light, which split open the shaded morgue about

103

her. She was mesmerized by these shard-like rays, and contemplated their radiance, so welcome in the sad darkness of her day. She understood the beams filtered in from a harsh land that she would have to face—a place that held little mercy for her plight. She wondered when that confrontation would come to pass.

"Somewhen." She whispered aloud as she waited for her mother to find God and her dadduh.

'There ain' ought out there, but one gurt waterless sea unfit fer life.'

Her dadduh spoke of the desert's severity often, and of the luckless souls who died of thirst, or insanity, or crazed Indians who inhabited it. He kept his family under cover of wood upon the slopes and higher ground where the number of threats was reduced to an occasional wild Indian, wildcat, or bear—all of which remained formidable and still required at least one eye to be ever on the lookout.

Gracie's folks watched everything and everyone on the plains with an eye of distrust. One could easily spot a rider on horseback a day's travel out from these hills. Gracie wasn't a stranger to the open land by any means. She had absorbed enough experience to respect it, and to recognize the safety of seclusion on the slopes that surrounded it. On the high ground between the desert floor and the upper tree line, food was plentiful and water flowed abundantly.

Her dadduh's life had always been one of involvement with the Indians, and for the most part, he felt they had always been friendly. That was, up until the white man's greed and dishonest motives had gone about changing them for the worse.

'Twasn't always so. Twasn't thet-a-way en years back long 'fawr ya wuz born, Booty, 'fawr the great fur wars en' the Americain lies en' do'uns. Twasn't thet-a-way 'fawr the Astors en' McKenzies give 'em injuns guns en' pumpt 'em full o' whiskey en' reason t'

104

kill off the rest o' us trappers. Din't use' ta haf' ta be on the
lookout av'ry bloomun' minute. Din't use'ta haf' ta be afeerd.'

The Indians lived or ventured through the mountains much farther north, but as a rule, in the south, Indians occupied the wide open spaces of the plains to hunt buffalo and make use of the unlimited views that offered security for their villages. If buffalo dung or water was in short supply, squaws might be seen moving about the foothills visiting streams and collecting firewood. Gracie hadn't seen any for a long time.

Gracie leaned down, unfastened a pocket flap on her boot-backpack, and pulled out a spyglass that had been in her dadduh's possession for as long as she could remember. She slid the cool metal barrel back and forth across her lips as she squinted to dim the brilliance of the sun-baked landscape. She then extended the brass tube and placed it against her eye in much the same manner as her dadduh had done countless times before. She commenced to peer into the distance.

There were no longer conversations to be had, no games, no chores to shoulder with her family, and so the spyglass became a diversion that opened up her world. On the one hand, its reach fooled her into believing she could touch a soul, miles away, and this alleviated her loneliness. On the other hand, its reach presented all those barren miles of distance in painful clarity and served to amplify the very loneliness that suffered her. Gracie wondered a great deal about what uncertainties awaited her in that vast sun-scorched country. She scrutinized the eastern horizon for the minutest sign of St. Louis.

She strolled down to the first of many clearings. She sat down and leaned back against the rough bark of a tree. From there, she stared through the telescope, fascinated by shimmering waves of heat that distorted the distant views. Methodically, she sorted out the various features she happened upon, each worth study, each made all the more interesting by the fact of their great distance. It was all about *'peek-a-boo, I see you.'*

It was during one of these 'peek-a-boo' passes across the desert floor that Gracie's attention was snagged by something she might have missed a hundred times before. It was more a thought than a feature, like a mirage, or her imagination, or maybe something as simple as a smear of dirt on the lens. She fumbled to find it again. She felt she had seen something. It would be out there somewhere, bobbing about and shifting in the undulating waves of heat. She repeated her sweeps, back and forth, carefully stepping the spyglass lower each time until....

"Well, 'ark a' may. There et be," she whispered quietly to herself.

She was positive that it hadn't been there before. After all, she had spent hours studying the plains over the last couple of days viewing multiple perspectives of the same lifeless landscape. Now, she held the spyglass rock steady and studied the semi-apparition it had captured. She refused to believe this ghost of an object had escaped her watchful eyes and gone unnoticed during her methodical observations.

"Chinny reckon. Empawssible."

She spoke in wonder. She shook her head in doubt.

"No, no, no. Tidden there b'fer. I knaw et weren't. Es thaccy there a wagon, dadduh?" she asked her father's spirit aloud.

Preferring a less obstructed view through the woods, she rose to her feet and leaned securely against the giant pine. Her eyes watered under the strain of staring long and hard at the image she held centered within the brass tube's shadowy vignette. In and out of the surrounding terrain popped this silhouette, so vague, so blended into the background, so seemingly camouflaged that she remained undecided as to whether or not she was truly looking at a wagon.

The spyglass fell away as Gracie closed her burning eyes for relief. The blurriness was due more to her tortured eyes than distance. After a moment she opened them but looked upward in the direction of her mother. She raised the glass and trained it on the lifeless form. She waited patiently to see the chest heave for another breath. It rose—it fell—and so she turned to leave the tree, and walk a short distance farther down the slope to an area in the clearing that offered a more advantageous northern view.

She held up the glass and made a general sweep along the horizon from east to west. Satisfied, that nothing further remained to be found, she refocused her lens upon the object that so awakened her curiosity.

"Momma, I say now, there's a wagon comun our way. I knaw thaccy there's a maggoty wagon. I seen un b'fer, ye knaw...when we went ta the rendezvous year 'fer last weth dadduh. We saw un, 'member?"

Gracie prattled on freely for ears that could not hear. She watched this supposed wagon for the better part of an hour until her eyes were again half-blind from the light and strain of staring through the glass. If it was a wagon, it seemed in no hurry to travel. It didn't appear as though she was about to miss anything, and so she decided to appease a growling gut that strove to return her to the tent, which her dadduh had filled with fresh supplies.

Her father had returned with a sizeable quantity of stores, and so Gracie had no reservations about satiating herself on the dried buffalo meat. While gnawing on pemmican, Gracie's attention shifted back and forth between her folks and the desert.

"Why woult et jus' be settun there, momma?" D'ye thenk et's always ben there? I don't. I woult o' seen et. I woult o' seen et, dadduh."

107

In spite of her knowing it was a pointless effort, she periodically picked up the spyglass, and attempted to find the wagon from the campsite. It was next to impossible seeing the desert itself let alone any insignificant detail therein from the camp's secluded location in the wood.

"Mebbe et's jus' a clump o' sagebrush blown up agin' a rock 'r cacti, er a funny lookun pile o' chump, sump'unt akin t' thet. I wish et wern't so far away...." Gracie fell silent.

"I wish et woult move 'r sump'unt, momma. I wish et woult. I wish some' un be out here-there."

Her hunger alleviated, Gracie wandered back to the lower clearing, and in short time centered in on that blur of a distant curiosity. It certainly didn't make sense that a wagon should remain stilled for so long. One could have eaten a dozen meals in that amount of time. Maybe the wagon was broken. Maybe it had been sitting abandoned for years. No matter what the reason, in time, falling shadows gave rise to fearful thoughts and stifled further speculation. Gracie grew anxious to find the security of her campfire, tipi, and blankets, and so called it a night.

FOURTEEN

Before Gracie was fully awake the following morning, she was puzzled and sensed something amiss. It was the silence. There was a lack of movement and the familiar sounds of morning floating about to herald a new day. The drumming of her dadduh's deep voice speaking to her mother in lowered tones, the crack of firewood being snapped in to smaller pieces, the clinking and scraping of a spoon against an iron pot, the swooshing of her mother's clothes as she bustled about. The popping and snapping of a breakfast fire as it gave rise to aromas of tea and freshly killed game.

All this seeped inside the tipi and into Gracie's dreams long before her eyes were ever open to the pale gray of first light. She habitually pulled the blankets up about her face to force out the morning chill. She rubbed the fabric across her lips , for there was always comfort in the warmth of her wrap and the knowledge of her parents' presence.

Although this morning's puzzlement was there, it was less pronounced. The facts of reality came quicker with each passing day. This morning the sounds, the smells, the presence of her folks felt more like what it really was—a confusing blend of dreams and wishes. She opened her eyes and searched for her mother. The dream ended the second she spotted her lying still, uncovered in the cold. Gracie waited for the telltale heave that prolonged her mother's passing.

Immersed in a morning stupor, Gracie's gaze remained fixed upon her mother until the moment a memory of the mysterious desert object flashed through her awakening head. The remembrance stirred within her an excitement and a rush of impatience that raced through her body. She needed to jump to her feet for a 'look n' see.' Maybe now, the wagon would be nearer the mountain. Maybe now she would see someone coming her way.

Believing half-heartedly that she had seen her mother take a breath, she felt free to go and so leapt to her feet. With the spyglass held firmly in one hand, she pulled the blanket tightly about herself with the other and set off at a trot down the path to the clearing.

"'Ark a' may, Gracie...thaccy there's a horse...er a mule.... Ha! There's another un. Issn' thet comical."

The sight of the horses or mules sent her spirits soaring. It was not what she had expected to see. The animals were obviously closer to her, close enough to identify even at a distance due to their movement, but not so the object she knew was not a cart,

109

and thought to be a wagon. Gracie knew from listening to her father that wagons were pulled by teams of horses, mules, or oxen. The questionable object was now most certain to be a wagon just as she believed from the start. The thought of its actuality tumbled over and over in her mind. It was exciting to see a traveling tipi. It was a riveting notion that someone else should be in these parts besides her.

"Hmm...tell me, Gracie, why ain't thaccy there team... hitched?" she asked herself.

Gracie remembered well the first time she had seen a covered wagon. It was at a rendezvous, and it had made a sizeable impression upon her. She was astounded to discover her father had once owned just such a wagon. The few people she had seen always traveled on foot and occasionally rode a horse or mule. But then her life was lived in the mountains, and according to her father, one might be lucky enough to see a small cart on the slopes, but a wagon—never.

Her father often told her stories about wagons, about coaches and carriages, stories of kings and queens, and parades with prancing horses. Many a night she sat at the campfire and listened to him tell of cities with roads instead of foot trails, roads that were bordered with buildings, each and every one stocked with silks and candies, and all manner of wondrous things. He would talk about roads flanking seashores that stretched forever, rimming vast blue oceans of water covered with white-tipped waves as far as the eye could see. He spoke of how the waves would roar toward shore and crash in magnificent splashing sprays that created clouds of mist to catch the sun and make sensational rainbows. It all sounded so unbelievable; a magical scene larger than life, wider than the desert itself. If she hadn't heard such things from her own father's mouth, she would have dismissed it all as nonsense.

Gracie's rush to know what next took place on the plain was now tempered by her desire to eat a morning meal. She walked up the slope, still wondering why the team wasn't hitched, still believing she could tell her momma about the animals wandering on the flats. She was reasonably confident that the wagon wasn't going anywhere, although the thought of it disappearing was unsettling and remained foremost on her mind until something else, something even less pleasant, crept into her consciousness.

Her attention swung back from her mental misgivings to focus squarely on her mother's chest. Gracie stood perfectly still, her breathing halted as she waited and watched. She rubbed the blanket wrapped around her lightly across her lips. No heave, she thought to herself. She stood unmoving and concentrated all her senses simultaneously to determine one unsettling answer. She wondered if her mother's time had come to pass, and if she was at this moment truly alone in the world.

"Momma?" she whispered.

Her eyes began to well up with tears. This irritated her because the tears clouded her observations. She wiped her face with the blanket, and gazed with grief-stricken realization that her mother was indeed beyond the call of this world.

And so, Gracie Castleman began her morning burdened, hungry, and alone. She began her day searching for stones, not small ones, not lucky ones, not pretty ones, as she did when a child, but stones to be counted by the hundreds, stones that were protective, stones that were heavy. Her mother had collected all the nearby rocks for her father's burial, and so Gracie's task was made all the more difficult. One by one, she sought them out, walking farther into the wood or along the stream bed and back to gently place another upon her mother. This she did, in a fashion only just learned days before—for a 'proper burial.'

Gracie's tears moiled many a stone. She cried openly during the course of her labor. She dearly missed the conversation, the love and attention of her folks. The only relief came from her thoughts of the wagon. Each time she took a break from the strain of carrying rocks, she would walk to the clearing and pick up her dadduh's spyglass with arms that were shaking with fatigue.

Here too, she faced disillusionment. All day long, while she proceeded with the burial of her mother, she had been carefully marking the position of the wagon. The wagon never appeared to move. As best she could tell by lining up trees to sight across, the wagon was in the same place it had been all morning and the day before. The team remained scattered.

"Mebbe et wern't a brokun wheel 'r anythun o' the kind. Mebbe the driver es sick 'r dyun. Mebbe he's jus' plain dead out there...out here-there en the meddle o' nawhere."

All these thoughts and more seemed bent on burdening her. With a heavy heart and more questions than answers, Gracie returned to the task of fetching stones for the last time. She finished her mother's grave just before nightfall. In the length of her day, one that was torturously long, hauling stones from mid-morning to late evening, the wagon remained unmoved.

FIFTEEN

The following morning, there was too much mist in the woods, and it prevented Gracie from seeing out across the plains. It had rained and everything was raw. The clouds and humidity were trapped within the trees, and stood between her and the endless miles of clarity beyond the slopes. Gracie was annoyed, but also fraught with understandable concerns. She was slow to rise for her body was woefully stiff and sore, discomfort being the cost of yesterday's toil. Even if not for the morning's painful reminders, the damp mists gave one but little incentive to leave the warmth of bed and blanket.

Eventually, hunger drove Gracie to fetch some fresh water from the stream, and set it to boil over embers restored to a flame. In short time she was simmering a mash of potatoes, corn, and wild onion. She cut up some pieces of pemmican to toss into the mix. Having worked so hard and having eaten so little the day before, she found herself famished.

Even so, thoughts of the wagon, and apprehensions of heading out alone across the desert filled her with anxiety and worked against her appetite. She was restless, and that also made eating a solid breakfast more of a chore than a pleasure but she managed. Afterward, she washed herself with heated water and then retreated to the tipi and warmth of her blankets. There was little choice but to accept nothing further would become of this day until the mists burned off.

Gracie fidgeted with the pockets of her boot-backpack. She fidgeted with the spyglass, slipping it open and closed. She conversed with her dead parents, now hidden beneath mounds of stone, too cold to be warmed by a campfire. She was growing nervous and desperate. She was beginning to pour all of her hopes into the mysterious wagon that never moved.

Occasionally, she would face the chilling damp in order to walk down to the clearing and have another look through the glass. Her impatience served no purpose other than to increase her anxiety, for there was nothing to be seen and this only further raised her fears that the wagon would move on beyond the mist and disappear from her sight forever.

She struggled with the telescope and frustration for the better part of the morning. She could do little but fuss until the warmth of the sun did its work. And so, slowly, as the day warmed and brightened, the glass peered deeper into the murkiness and its scope reached farther out across the plain until it finally found the horizon. To her surprise, the mists had cooled the day and straightened out the wavy disturbed views in the spyglass. Now it produced a distinct and undeniable image of a covered wagon. To both her relief and concern, the wagon remained fixed in place.

"Appen the driver really es sick."

She said out loud, then, another consideration.

"Appen the driver *really es dead.*"

Indian killings crossed her mind, and that was soon joined by the thought of Cholera—contemplations that left her shaken. She presented these notions to her parents, whom she was certain could hear her in their own way. She was a quick-witted girl, and in no time finalized plans of procuring the wagon for her own needs in crossing the desert. If nothing else, the animals would be valuable for trade. She looked back at her parents and felt they were encouraging her to leave, giving her a sense it was time to go.

Hurriedly, she picked up the camp. She had left everything scattered about for the last week, but now felt an urgency to account for all she had come to inherit. These things were suddenly *her things.* She scoured the ground until satisfied she had missed nothing. She packed up the family stores, rolled up her bedroll, struck the tipi, and saddled the mules, which was difficult at best due to their height and the weight of the saddles and goods. This had always been her father's doing with her mother's assistance. It was now managed with the aid of time and a rocky ledge. She went about checking the straps, tightening them as she saw fit, carefully securing everything, as she had seen her father do many, many times.

The family owned five animals, one for each rider, and two that served as pack mules. She tied the mules head to tail to keep them from wandering. She then mounted her mule, 'Kelly,' a gentle animal selected for her earlier in the year when she had reached ten years of age . Satisfied that everything was in order, she turned one last time toward her folks and blew them mournful kisses and tears.

"I love ye momma, en' ye uz well, dadduh. I have ta go now."

From the foothills, she looked out across the vast plain below. She took a deep breath and set her course. Somehow, her young mind understood there was no place for fear in her journey to live. When the time for true fear was at hand, she would know. Now was a time to survive.

She rode the remainder of the day, leading her pack of mules down the mountainside, down the slopes of security, and toward the outer edge of the foothills that provided her haven. Beyond the foothills, the desert floor spread out infinitely before her. It was as incomprehensibly flat as the mountains were tall, but unlike the mountains, once you set foot on its surface, you found yourself exposed to all creation. It was a frightening consideration, and for her a compelling reason to refrain from hasty moves.

The following day she traveled with more confidence and speed. Keeping a wary eye open for strangers, she continued along the northeastern edge of the mountain and noted good places to hide. She observed and recorded every nuance of both the slopes and the desert that flanked her right side.

Producing her glass, she determined from her current position that the wagon was now within a safely reachable distance. It was a half day's ride, but not a trek, no matter how short, she wished to undertake in the broad light of day for the flat land was simply too open for her liking.

As the brilliance of the desert day was diminished by the approaching dark of night, so too was her anxiety diminished by the secrecy of the unlit world. Well shrouded within the wood, she determined it best to rest for a few hours. She would then ride out before the break of dawn and claim her find.

Gracie pressed a hard biscuit against her lips, now and then nibbling at it as she assessed her surroundings. She relieved the mules of their burdens, dragging the loads off their backs and letting them fall to the ground. She often stopped her business in order to listen. She stopped her jaw to silence the crunching that echoed between her ears so she might better hear the excited chatter of night creatures disturbed by unwanted intruders, grockles.

There was no such chatter, no rustling of the leaves, no snapping of twigs under foot. The world was silent, and so feeling reasonably safe, she laid herself down and disappeared into the shadows that blanketed the ground. The shadows moved quietly upward past the treetops where they merged and became one with the night sky. The reflection of stars vanished from her weighted eyes, and she was soon lost to her weariness.

SIXTEEN

Gracie awoke of her own accord, and did so well before the rise of the sun. She had slept without the benefit of fire in order to remain as inconspicuous as possible. It was an illogical act that left her open to an approach by wandering bears or wolves, which presented far more danger than a chance meeting with an Indian. But her fears were immature at times and not always rational.

She had been chilled by the night air, and now withdrew deeper into her blanket. Beneath the cover, she blew warm breath into her hands and filled her small space with its heat. She remained quiescent, stilled in the absence of light, listening as attentively now as before her drift into sleep. Again confident nothing lurked in the vicinity, she arose to brave the morning air.

She wasted no time in working off the chill. She packed her bedroll, saddled the mules, and headed out onto the flats. It was unsettling at first, as she emerged from behind the cover of trees and confronted the undefined plain. The ground beneath her had no discernible boundaries. It was a black splash of empty space that flowed out before her until it reached a distant veil of stars.

She was entirely blind of the wagon. Not only because it was too dark to distinguish anything at a distance, but also because once off the slopes, the lay of the land had unanticipated swells that moved subtly up and down between her and her prize. This would have been a problem had she not been a bright child.

As it was, she had given much thought, not only to the wagon, not only to what treasure or terror it might possess, but also what path of approach offered the least risk. Whether desert or wagon was most to be feared, she couldn't say. But in both cases, she concluded it most sensible to make her advance at night. And so, falling back on her father's lessons, she made a careful observation of the stars above its location. Now, she rode toward those stars.

She found herself awed by the enormity of the heavens. It had been a long time since her father had taken her to view the desert night sky in its full glory, without a pine needle or aspen leaf, without a mountain ridge or ghostly mist to obscure even the faintest twinkle. The scene above her head on this barren, unlit lay of land was hauntingly spiritual.

Between the northern and southern horizons, across this still and shadowed expanse of earth now obscured under that speckled heaven, Gracie believed she might be the only person alive. She believed in the God her parents had raised her to trust. She believed that He could hear her beating heart, that He could see the light of her soul. Being a lonely creature filled with insecurity, a lonely child left to face a fearful future, her belief in the spiritual world brought badly needed comfort.

In her desolation came sadness. She searched for solace in the memories of her mother and father until at last, the sky took on the dress of dawn. The stars and lessons had served her well; and now, in the thin film of light that emerged from far off to the east, she began to sort out the misleading shadows. She homed in on the wagon with much relief. It was near.

As she proceeded, she attracted the attention of a foraging mule on a rise off to her right. Much to her delight, the mule moved at once to intercept her. A second mule then appeared from behind a rise, and fell in behind the first animal, which continued to approach her. She knew from experience this was a natural instinct for herding animals, especially mules, which could be ornery but hated being alone. The animals walked mountain trails in line, one behind the other, and so she had no need to catch them. They came to fall in line with the mules she had in tow. With a total of seven mules, hers was not to be an unnoticed arrival.

She worked quickly within the comforting shroud of the murky morning light. She dismounted Kelly and immediately produced her collection of shrunken heads. Their appearance was accompanied by a discordance of sound as the bells were inadvertently jostled about. At first, the shattering of silence gave her reason for pause, but then her father's words filled her head and she adorned herself as he had advised.

'Don' fergit them injun's dislike they haits, Booty. I'm on may last leg, child...ye ark ta may, ye hear. Git the black bear grease... en' work et ento yer hair. Make yerself luk...god-awful en'...hang them thar skulls all over ye...en' the mules uz well. ... Talk ta the sky, go on crazy-like, child. Uz sure uz I'm dyun, Booty...I promise ye...them injuns'll...think thrice...'bout gevun ye any trouble. Sperets make 'em...a might nervous, Booty...en' don' ye...be forgettun et.'

His voice then gave way to the tempo of broken, labored, breathing and fatigue.

"Yes, dadduh."

She whispered aloud, as she strained to listen from afar, from a place and time that was now but memory.

Numerous shrunken heads now swung from Gracie's frame, they twirled about her, each staring in a different direction with dark lifeless eyes. They scraped the sand with their adornments, leaving snake-like trails as she stooped down to reach for her backpack. Its feel, its presence, which brought with it the history and substance of Gracie's life, raised her spirits and confidence.

She lifted the flap upon one of its many pockets and removed a pouch filled with bear grease that had been worked full of black campfire soot. She slipped her fingers into the pouch and dragged them through the thick paste. She worked the grease into her hair, and smeared it across her face and forearms. She then complimented the black lard with the reddish purple stain of berry paste. She produced her blue-handled birthday gift and opened her eyes wide to see a reflection in the dim light.

Believing she was a sufficiently fearful sight, and emotionally prepared for a bad encounter, she set out to travel the remaining distance on foot. Silent, but for the eerie tinkling of bells, as if a nightmarish ghost afloat, she moused toward the wagon. Each step closer increased her anxiousness.

Gracie's hand slid down to the sheathed knives at her side. They were the source of her courage. Her favorite game had always been knife-throwing with her father and at that she was wicked. They had spent countless hours competing with each other for the title of *'Supreme Thrower o' the Blade.'* The title came with exaltations, special salutations, and the highly coveted, carved and decorated trophy of a wooden tortoise. In the center of its patterned shell was a slot where the winning knife stood proud.

Gracie was too small to match her father's throw for distance and force, but what she lacked in strength, she more than made up with astonishing accuracy. Much of the time that her dadduh was out trapping or panning, she remained at camp practicing with stubborn resolve. From the day her dadduh came back to camp and found a rabbit roasting on the spit, caught fresh on the end of her blade, her challenge to his title was something to be reckoned. Now, having felt the cool steel at her side, she removed her hand and moved forward.

Gracie was highly suspect of strangers, this being bred into her by both her parents. She wasn't afraid of them; she was cautious to a fault. And so, literally on tiptoes, if that were even necessary out of doors, she crept forward furtively those final few hundred feet of sand. The closer her approach, the lower her stance until she was little more than the shadow of a sage bush rolling about between the wooden spoke wheels.

She crawled underneath the bed of the wagon between the rear wheels and listened for any movement or sign of life. She was patient. She waited through the duration of a gentle passing breeze, but there was nothing to hear. The hour was early, and surely she would have heard the snoring of someone fast asleep. But there was nothing.

Gracie expected to find no living thing and prayed to find nothing dead. Her mind conjured up all sorts of unspeakable imaginings. She fought to distract herself from visions of mutilated bodies, victims of Indian torture. At the worst of it, she suddenly realized there was no smell of rotting flesh. This raised her spirits immensely, dispelled the visions, and so without further concern, she stood up and peered into the small cave of canvas over hoops. Her eyes were still adjusted to the dark of night, and as the morning light intensified by the moment, it gave her ample luminance to discern beyond a doubt that this wagon was indeed empty.

"Yut, yut, yut," she whispered.

Her face broke into a broad grin. Her eyes opened with delight. She was elated. Serious for only a fleeting moment more, Gracie looked again far out ahead and then into the distance behind the wagon. She looked all about the surrounding area. She saw nothing to raise her suspicions, and so, eagerly climbed into her new home.

She settled upon blankets that covered the bed of the wagon. Inside, it was cozy. This wagon didn't look anything like the one she had seen at the rendezvous. It was built much smaller, and the bench seat bounced. Still, it provided ample room to be a home of sorts—much smaller than the tipi, but still acceptable.

Right off, Gracie spotted a wooden chest and the sight of it made her giddy with excitement. *What wonderful treasures it must contain*, she thought to herself. Her imagination went wild as she ran her hands over its surface, but she was unable to open it. She fumbled through various items in hopes of turning up a means to open it, but to no avail. She considered prying the chest open with her knife, but disliked the idea of ruining its beauty. Besides, she thought it better to wait, better to be undistracted, better to move the wagon to safer ground.

Aside from the chest, there was little more to be found other than an assortment of clothes, guns and ammunition, a water barrel, and a good deal of dry goods. The guns would bring a handsome profit. She couldn't help but to sift through some of the clothes. They were very well made, not at all worn out. By quickly sorting through what was there, she was surprised to discover little of man's attire. There were a couple of sets of trousers, but all in all, there was nothing about in the way of tools and whatnot that spoke of a man's presence. It would appear the wagon belonged to a woman. That was odd, she thought to herself—*couldn't be*.

Gracie fumbled through the belongings a second time, and assured herself there were no men's garments of consequence to be found. She reached for a blouse lying upon the blankets of a makeshift bed and held it up in the brightening light, and as she looked along a nicely laced sleeve, her eyes were distracted by a litter of wood shavings spread across the forward end of the bed. She noticed a knife lying amidst the debris. She looked above the knife to see letters carved into the back of the bench seat. She scratched her greasy head as she struggled to remember something of her mother's lessons. She stared hard at the letters. She ran her fingers firmly across the carvings leaving a streak of soot and berry stain to collect in the grooves.

"Eeeeeee. Ellllllaaaaah. Iyeeeeee. Zeeeeeeeedd. Aaaaaaaaa. Beeeeeeee...."

It was a long word. Gracie recognized some numbers at the end. Maybe, it was a sentence. Maybe, it was a message. It probably was important, but her memory failed her amidst all the excitement, and so it was with some minor disappointment that she let it go.

It didn't mean she wasn't thinking. Indeed, she was wondering why a woman would be traveling alone out here in the desert. It was so dangerous. Maybe, it was a runaway team that finally came to a halt at this place. No, mules weren't exactly the runaway type. Besides who freed them from the harness? The woman probably just plain got lost—ran out of water. At that thought, she looked over to the water barrel. She noticed it was damp at the base.

"I knew uz much!" she exclaimed aloud.

Now it was certain that she had seen the wagon's arrival from the camp. Had it been here for any length of time, the water would have been long gone. Besides, the team would have wandered miles away in their foraging. That thought brought to mind that

122

she had seen the wagonpole, and from what she remembered at the rendezvous, it seemed much too long for only the two mules. There must have been a team of four. If two mules fell in with her pack then there were likely two more mules wandering about. Mules were good for trade. They had worth.

Oh, yes, she thought, *they had worth.*

Gracie sat up and directed her attention outward from the front of the wagon. She scanned the country ahead, but saw nothing of life. She then crawled back past the trunk, clothes, and water barrel, to the rear of the bed until she was able to lean out and search eastward along and beyond the two lines of wagon-wheel tracks that vanished into the distance of a brightening horizon. She was hunting for the mules, but haunted by the missing driver.

For that reason, her attention fell to the ground immediately before her. The morning light had intensified enough that she was able to study the disturbances of the sand. There were harnesses and lines laying all about. There were footprints everywhere, going in all directions. They were small, like her mother's. They were tracks of a woman. Step—skid—step—skid, the left foot dragged. They wandered all about the wagon, but no one was to be seen.

Gracie's scrutiny gobbled up ground as far as the dawn light would allow. An uneasiness swept through her as thoughts of the woman being kidnapped by Indians entered her mind. Her eyes snapped back up to the horizon, looking for any hint of movement. She studied each bush, each cactus, anything that might provide a hiding place, but there was nothing.

There was also nothing of tracks by any other human, horse, or man. Gracie determined there was only one woman who must have wandered away. For what reason, she could not imagine. There were water, food, clothes; the wagon was not damaged.

It must have been precisely as her father warned—in the desert, the woman went *insane*.

The onset of morning was making Gracie feel further exposed and uncomfortable. The time for play was over. There was much to do, and so she jumped out of the wagon amidst a cloud of swinging horrors and tinkling complaint. She went for Kelly and the other pack mules, brought them to the wagon, and lashed them to the wheel. She was suddenly stymied by what to do with her two newfound animals.

She walked over to the wagon pole and looked at the lengthy beam. She observed the doubletrees and singletrees lying alongside. She turned to make sense of the harnesses and tangle of lines that lay spread out upon the sand next to the wagon. The complexity of hitching a team had never occurred to her. This was a terrible setback, and would have to be figured out in quick order if she planned on owning the wagon.

She stared down and studied the confusion of straps and chains until it became painfully clear that the mules wouldn't be hitched to the wagon anytime soon. With a great exhalation of disappointment, Gracie turned away from the mess and went about cutting her only good rope in order to tie the two wandering mules to the wagon. Once done, and now standing in the full light of morning, she removed her spyglass to survey the distance surrounding her. Almost immediately, she spotted the third and fourth mules. With dismay, she again shortened her prized rope. Working against time and the ever increasing chances of being seen, she set out at a brisk pace to retrieve the animals.

"Oh, yes," she repeated her thoughts. *"They have worth."*

The morning was warming rapidly as she strode out. Aside from hunger, and a concern for snakes, she was actually at peace in spite of her past days of horrible misfortune. Four extra mules assured her additional financial security, and ownership of the wagon with its guns and supplies most certainly added to her worth. It was just this matter of conscience that needed to be addressed.

Gracie wished dearly to appease her instincts and sidestep her conscience, for her instincts were straightforward and unclouded. They compelled her to remove the wagon and all of its amenities back into the hills with speed before the light of day betrayed her presence.

Gracie's mother would have understood these instincts, but would also have nodded knowingly of her daughter's inability to sidestep her conscience. She would search for the woman whether she liked it or not. A stranger might have said that Gracie would seek out the woman to fend off loneliness. Her mother would have said, yes, maybe—but more likely, it was due to her being a child of heart.

The remaining two mules were foraging a fair stretch from the wagon, but fortunately were to be found near one another. It would take time to reach them and return. Ever the more nervous, she stepped hurriedly while swinging her freshly cut lengths of rope in arcs as she walked.

Gracie soon discovered why the last two animals stood together. A couple of moments, a couple of hundred feet, and she would have been scratching ears and sweet talking mules to follow her back to the wagon. Instead, the idea was all but abandoned as she stared down at the lifeless driver. It was indeed a woman. Older, near her mother's age, bare skinned, and just possibly, most likely—*dead*. Well, maybe not….

Gracie moved as close as she dare, taking care to stay out of reach. The woman didn't share the same look of her mother and father—that ghostly bluish white look. No this person appeared *pure and painfully* red. She was severely sunburned and badly blistered, but maybe not really *dead* dead. In any event, Gracie wasn't about to be tricked, and so stood there impatient, guarded, but intent on watching the woman for a spell.

In time, she sat down to continue her wait. It wasn't as much a lack of patience, as it was a sample of the sun's escalating heat that prompted Gracie to take some action. She had been unconsciously sifting the sand, sorting out pebbles and debris, which she now began to toss at the woman's face. She long since discounted the possibility of Cholera. The woman was not a mess and did not smell. The flies did not seem to be swarming her, but at every glance upward the vultures grew in number, gathering to circle overhead.

Growing restless, Gracie moved in very close. She crawled on all four to within inches of the stranger's face and then lay down alongside her. Their faces were so close she could sense the slightest breath passing across the stranger's chapped lips. She thoroughly studied this lady who lay death-like before her on the ground. Beyond the burn and blisters, she found the woman attractive. It pleased her that they shared the same color hair. It also made her sad. It was also the color of her mother's hair.

Gracie's heart opened up to this suffering stranger. She felt urgency to help, but also desperation to have this person's company. Filled with need and courage to match, she reached out to gently sweep away the veil of blonde hair that hid much of the woman's face. She then stroked the woman's head with her delicate berry-stained hand.

Gracie brought with her not only two lengths of rope, but also the compassion and innocence of youth. The gesture was acknowledged by a weak response from the woman. Gracie sat up straight as the sun poured fresh pain into the stranger's face. She wondered how she might provide for this person. She wondered where was the woman's blouse?

SEVENTEEN

The pain was unbearable. It was excruciating. My head felt as though it were being crushed. Nausea twisted my stomach into unstable knots. The whole of my upper body was broiling. My poisoned leg now seemed to be but one painful issue of many, no longer the sole focus of my attention.

As my wits surfaced, scrambled and confused from the depths of near death, I began to sort out a sense of my past, my memories—amongst them a desire to end my life. In fact, I gained enough sense to realize I probably had ended my life, and most certainly had received my sentence from God. I had been condemned to Hell for committing suicide, and the heat of the inferno now scorched my skin and soul. I refused to open my eyes for fear of what I might see until I heard the sound of bells and bustle.

I felt something near me. My instinct for survival, the need to protect myself, forced my eyes open so I might face this unknown threat. I saw nothing at first, felt nothing, but searing light and heat. The intense purity of damnation and eternal fire. Then came the primal fear, for there was indeed movement, frightening flickers of shadow. Slowly, these swirling silhouettes began to take shape.

Gripped by bone-deep horror, I deciphered visions, glimpses of hideous, hellish creatures swarming and whirling about me. They flew over me, dragging wisps of hair, or worse, webs across my face. I stared at this collection of dark-eyed spidery creatures circling over me, moving in and out of my consciousness, and I accepted the fact my soul was irrevocably lost. Invisible tears streamed down my parched face.

In one final desperate attempt to ask God for mercy, I blurted out a silent breath of air. It was meant to be a remorseful request, half scream, half prayer, words from a repentant heart, but I had

127

nothing left of strength within to entreat. I had nothing left at all but a motionless body burning.

"Cham Gracie, who might ye be? Hell-loooo-oh. Cain ye h'ayr may? Are ye dyun? Cain ye h'ayr may?"

The words made me gag. My tongue was swollen, caked in sand, and stuck in my dried-out throat. I choked because these melodic words instinctively rushed me to plea for mercy, to beg forgiveness, but I was unable to speak. Who belonged to this angelic voice? I wanted to be near it. I was frightened beyond measure and its music settled me. It tugged my soul. Did God actually hear me?

"Woult ye have a drenk then? Wot be ye do'un wamblin' about here-there?"

That mellisonant sound, that sweet voice...the voice of a child. I moved to raise my head, but was riveted with paralyzing pain. Pain so acute, it instantly sapped my strength. It left me stunned. I could do little more than open my eyes. They too were invaded by sand, and after substantial effort to see, I wished dearly I had not.

Hovering close over me was some hideous form of human remnant, blackened and charred by hellfire, a drover of demons. Another soul lost in hell, another wretched creature wandering the inferno in blind search of non-existent love or sympathy, or forgiveness, or *food*. The voice of an angel in the form of a fiend; I wondered if my roasting flesh gave it appetite. I realized how its sweet voice poisoned me, how it seduced me. How I was drawn toward it, to be quieted by its melody. How many more of these things would come to feast upon my frying carcass?

In desperation, I looked for a means of escape. I looked around only to be halted by sudden puzzlement. My gruesome thoughts were momentarily suspended as I noticed the lace on a blouse that I very much enjoyed. That was odd. That lace touched another garment, and another that I also recognized to

128

be my own. This caused me to undertake a broader view of my surroundings. Was that not my chest, my guns, my water barrel? Was this not my wagon? Would these things exist in Hell? Even in my state, that seemed ridiculous, but it opened a door for other possibilities. All manner of things started coming back to me. It was as if pieces of a puzzle were whirring in rotation, then falling one by one into the framework of a pattern that my mind could comprehend.

I glanced fearfully at the demon from the corner of my eye. I didn't like it. I preferred to look at my frilly garments—they bought comfort. I recognized more of my belongings. I studied the wagon hoops that pressed up against the canvas overhead. This all made sense to me. I desperately wanted it to make sense because more than life itself, I wanted a door, a path out of this Hell.

My surroundings seemed contrary to the fiend that hovered over me. The two did not mesh in my mind. They seemed of two different worlds, and so I chose to believe in my surroundings, to put faith in things familiar, things I understood, things that brought me comfort. My belongings gave me a mental footing. I decided this creature might not be from Hell as first thought, but rather some sort of sick and demented worldly clown, most likely another of those luckless desert wanderers who went crazy. Yet, I was unsure, and so I gathered up my courage.

"What…are you?" I gasped.

"Gracie."

"What?"

"Gracie…Gracie Castleman."

"Gracie…Castleman…." I repeated her name with a voice I had never heard before. It was raspy, dry. It was weak. I was moving in and out of consciousness and so having difficulty understanding this horrible creature.

"What are you?"

"I'm a grill."

"A grill…a grill? A girl? No…I don't think so," I quipped. "A girl? A girl?" I suddenly realized what she had said, but I was thoroughly confused. "Gracie Castleman…. Do I know you?" I asked in a whisper.

"I don' reckon anybody knaws may."

It was a relief to know my mind was sufficiently revived to understand her response as being peculiar. I was elated to know that I could appreciate the oddity; I could follow something of the conversation. My life had been given back to me and I wanted to cry with joy. An enormous burden had been lifted and so I happily returned to the realm of deep drowsiness or sleep, but this time the fears were lessened.

My mind seemed to whir below my consciousness, conjuring up questions and answers that came to me in dreams until at last I was again called back to the light.

"Hayl-looo-oh. Hayl-loooooooo-oh."

My eyes opened to a brighter light and I quickly focused upon my strange companion. This time I could clearly see a young girl behind the frightful filth. I even recounted how forlorn had been her last comment.

"Gracie?" I remembered her name.

"Yut," she whispered.

"Where… are we, Gracie?"

"En yer wagon."

"Yes…I mean…where is my wagon? Where…are we?"

"En the desert."

"Yes…. Gracie…I know, I know. I mean to ask…more specifically…where…in the desert are we…*precisely?*"

"Ohhhh, I knaw wot yer askun'. Uhh…I cain't say fer certun'. I knaw we're east o' the lower range, mebbe half day's ride out on the flats."

"I see."

In truth, I didn't. I fell back into a stream of surfacing memories in order to piece together my life. I remembered being in the desert. I winced as I recalled the snakebite and the pain. I remembered the fear of not being able to breathe. I thought to myself. It's coming back…it's all coming back, then I grimaced. Oh, there was a memory I could have done without. I recalled there was other pain, worse than the physical pain that was able to heal itself. There was the pain of humiliation, the pain of Christopher.

"How long…have I been here, Gracie?" I asked, my voice slurred.

"Ye mean en yer wagon?"

"That too."

"Ye been en the wagon sence the mornun. I dent thenk I'd aver get ye back en et. 'Fer that ye's layun out there en thac sun bakun. The vultures 'er wamblin' about up 'bove knawun ye's pretty well cookt. I spied yer wagon on the h'rizon three days b'fer today…. I don' knaw how long ye been out here-there. I don' knaw how long ye been en the sun, but yer burnt sump'unt fierce."

She shrugged her shoulders.

"Would you help me…to sit up, please?"

"Yes'm."

Gracie was eager to give assistance. She reached for my bedroll and eased it carefully behind my back and shoulders. She helped me slide back against the bench seat. My head throbbed fiercely. It was all I could do to open my eyes and look at myself. I was naked down to my waist, down to my skirt. Why wasn't I wearing a blouse?

"My blouse...."

The child must have seen the confusion in my expression, for she reached behind her at once and held up my missing blouse. The sight of it instantly filled me with dread. It brought back the fear of suffocating. I knew at once why I removed my blouse. I hadn't been able to breathe and panicked.

"I dent wanna put et on ye, cuz ye lookt desperd painful bein' plimmed up en' all. So, I jus' covert ye, en' triet t' kape ye cool."

I was damp. Most of me was damp. I assumed it wasn't from sweat, but rather from water the girl had recently poured on me, or spilled in an attempt to get me to drink.

"That was kind of you. Is there any water left ?"

"Yut." She offered me her mug. "I sprinklt some on ye...t' cool ye down. There's stell a gud amount en the barrel."

I knew better than succumbing to the urge of gulping. I moistened my cracked lips to begin, and then let the liquid slide across my tongue and slosh the roof of my mouth. Slowly, I let it move down my throat, sand and all. My tongue freed itself; and now unstuck, it could be of use.

"Thank you. As I see it...you saved my life."

"Et was nawthun', nawthun' et all, apart fram tryun' ta get ye back-long the wagon."

"How old are you, Gracie?"

"I jus' turnt twelf." She thought a moment. "Well, nawt really. Cham really fifteen. I jus' turnt fifteen."

"I trust...you know your age."

I took another sip of water.

"I don' count gud. Fifteen. Cham fifteen. My birthday es en the summer."

"I see."

I opened my eyes just enough to glimpse her. Eleven made more sense to me.

"Are your folks outside?"

This question changed the girl's demeanor markedly. She said nothing at first. Behind all the face paint, she looked at me most suspiciously as if to determine whether or not I was fit to be given an answer.

"They're off a ways...nawt too far. They left may 'ere ta watch over ye...en case ye woke up 'r sump'unt."

"Or something? You mean...like died?"

"Mebbe." The girl shrugged her shoulders.

"Hmm. Answer me this, Gracie. Why are you ...why are you... you know, why do you look like that? You gave me quite a fright."

"Oh, ye mean like thiccy?" She looked at herself, then back at me, and broke into a broad and absolutely beautiful smile. Her eyes flashed like green crystal.

"Ta sceer off enjuns. Don' ye knaw?"

"Indians? I see. Well, I don't know about Indians, but you sure gave me a good scare. What on earth...are those horrible things hanging from your neck? Are they heads or—?"

"Speret haits ta protect may. My dadduh made 'em fer may."

133

This young girl was friendly, almost overly so. She was trusting. She was too trusting to be left alone. There was something about her. I couldn't put my finger on it, yet my instincts told me something was amiss. I wanted her to talk and so encouraged her to do so.

"Tell me…about your dadduh. You say he made those things? How ever did he go about…doing that?"

Gracie went on to explain how her father understood the depth of Indian connections to the spirit world, and how he used this knowledge to his benefit. She was taught that white men could also be superstitious, but not nearly like the Indians. Gracie's father worked this fact to his advantage.

"When my dadduh got holt ov a bat pelt, like when a beaver get old 'n sick, 'r en a fight en' get scagged up en' all, he woult take they skins en' stretch 'em over a stone 'r a skull. He woult burn the hair ov a spot ta make a face. When the pelt was gud en' dry, my dadduh woult cut out holes fer eyes en' off'times a nose en' mouth. Uhh…see…thic un 'ere don' 'ave a mouth." Gracie snatched one of the heads out of air as it swung beside me. "After thet he woult work the driet pelt off the stone en' stuff et full o' grass 'til et felt like a hait. Ye wanna feel et?"

I reached up and fondled the false demon, but that didn't lessen its distastefulness. In the meantime, Gracie chattered freely.

"Dadduh tuk the most time fittun teeth en the mouth. He used t' set at the fire efter we ate, en' whittle a piece o' wood ento a jawr. Then he woult steck et en the coals t' blacken. When he figer'd et done, he't let et cool en' make holes en et t' fet the teeth.

"He showt me how t' make glue by boilun down a piece o' sken en' mixun et weth pine sap. We woult dep the teeth en hot sap en' steck 'em en the jawr. We woult work t' make 'em look jagget en' fearful. See…look at thic one, tidden nawthin' perty, bissly issn et."

Gracie snatched another swinging devil from flight and turned its attention toward me. The teeth were every bit as nasty as she described.

"Thiccy one es really gud. Off'times dadduh woult jus' pull a sken over a skull..." Gracie stopped to think. She tilted her head and gave me a look of concern. "But the enjuns knaw all the teeth o' animals en' so et's harder t' fool 'em thet a-way. Et's better t' make two rows o' teeth. Ye knaw like, puttun one animal jaw enside anawther. Thac es really sceery—see...see thiccy one hayr?

"Efter all the teeth 'r glued, then my dadduh woult take some mule hair—like thiccy here—hair fram the tail es really gud... en' glue et ta the hait. See how long et es?"

She pulled on the strands and then fluffed them.

"Efter thet, we woult collect some beetles 'r bugs, en' bones, 'r lettle stones thet lukt strange en' scraggy. Dadduh always use't some sage 'cause sage es gurt powerful medicine ta enjuns. We woult tie some o' these thengs ta the hair. See how they all 'ave sump'unt? Glue don' work so gud fer thet, so we tie 'em. 'Hair's purty strong, ye knaw.

"See the bells, here?" Gracie studied the head as her fingers worked to free a bell from the hairy entanglement. "Thet's the last theng my dadduh woult do. He woult tie on a couple o' bells. He hat a lettle box o' 'em. But, these are always fastent weth senew...see. So we don' aver lose a bell. Dadduh always sait, *'They don' gev they bells away, Booty.'* "

"How many of those heads do you have?"

"I hat fifteen, but my dadduh jus' made two more en' so now I 'ave se'enteen."

"I thought you couldn't count?"

135

The natural warmth of Gracie's expression went cold. She looked at me again with obvious suspicion. I could see her sizing me up. She became defensive.

"I cain't count. My dadduh sait we hat fifteen, en' then he sait we 'ave se'enteen haits all tolt."

"I see. Maybe, if we get time, I will teach you numbers so you can count on your own."

The little lady was no fool. I was certain she could count. I was amused by her instincts. On the surface, she overflowed with a simple sweetness and charm, but in the space of a blink, her green eyes would take on a penetrating stare and frost over icy-cold with mistrust.

"So tell me, Gracie. Why would your father need so many heads? Just to scare Indians?"

The question distracted the girl, and in short time the warmth returned to her face.

"Yut."

"Are you afraid of the Indians?"

"Yut."

"Why?"

"*'Cuz, some kill ye uz soon uz luk ut ye, Booty.'* Thet's wot my dadduh always sait. *'Dent used ta be thet a-way.'*"

"Did you ever speak to an Indian while your father was doing his trading?"

"No, I was tolt t' hide en the wuds en' kape perf'cly stell less'n I wantet a wheppun. I only watcht."

"Mmm. I suppose your father knows what's best."

136

"My dadduh sait enjuns used t' be gud folk. He sait they got t' drenkun en' go'un ta war, en' white folk woult swendle 'em out o' their guds, out o' averythun, even their wives en' horses. Dadduh sait tradun fer wheskey was easy, but bad business 'cuz wheskey wore off. He sait, *'Booty, jus member...wheskey wears off, en' tempers wear en'. Then them enjuns come back long t' kill ye, grill."*

"Your father sounds like a smart man."

"My father was a gurt smart man. My dadduh was the smartest man alive. He knew averythun. En, averythun I knaw, I learnt fram 'im."

At last, Gracie referred to her father plainly in the past tense. If she had a mother, she barely made mention of it. I began to believe that Gracie was surviving on her own. It would explain why it seemed she had a need to talk, a need that seemed greater than a fear of strangers. I was certain she was lonely and so I let her continue. The more she talked, the more I was bound to discover. The more she talked, the less I had to.

"You still haven't told me what your father did with all these heads. I don't doubt they were for scaring Indians, but how did he do that?"

Gracie could be easily won over by encouraging such conversation. She enjoyed holding my attention, and eagerly offered a story to entertain me.

"See...enjuns woult come aroun' fer ta trade. En' when they dit, my momma en' dadduh woult start actun strange en' do'un crazy thengs like walkun en' talkun funny. They woult ask the enjuns t' set ta our fire en' eat. Then my dadduh woult light up 'es pipe en' offer et ta 'em. Efter thet, my dadduh woult begin ta trade fer pelts en' stuff.

"Appen dadduh got ento an arg'ament, or effn he thought the enjun was plannun t' rob 'em, then he't haul out 'es sack en' shake et. Et has bells sewn ta et on the outsite en' the enjuns pay close mind when they h'ayr they bells. Most of 'em naver seen 'r heerd o' bells.

"First, dadduh woult luk up et the stars, en' then down en the shadows 'round the trees en' he woult talk ta the sperets. Then he woult open thaccy sack en' pull out a hantful o' haits. En' he woult show the haits averythun outside o' the sack. He woult show 'em the trees en' the campfire, en' he woult let 'em get a real gud luk at the enjuns. En' he woult kiss the haits en' hang 'em here-there n' hi-low on the branches mostly behind where the enjuns be sittun.

"When h'uz do'un business, he woult call out ta the haits en' he woult get up fram the fire en' show 'em the enjun pelts en' jingle the bells. He woult pertend t' listen ta wot the sperets tolt 'em en' then he woult set back down at the fire en' make an offer fer trade. Appen dadduh hat a bat feelun 'bout an enjun, he woult point 'em out ta the haits en' tell the sperets all manner o' private thengs… secrets n' such.

"Enjuns dent like them haits one bet. Even the worst o' the lot woult get real quiet. I woult lie en the woods en' watch the enjuns kape t' lookun back o'er their shoulters at they haits swingun en the nightwend. Ye coult tell after a spell, them enjuns jus' wan'et ta leave. They woult finish up business en' go on their way. But… they woult naver come back t' kill a body.

"Dadduh sait thet honest enjuns naver saw the haits en' effn they dit, they dent care so much 'cause they be o' gud 'earts. The bat uns were afeerd ta return. My dadduh always sait there wern't no reason fer 'em comun' back long, 'lessn they meant harm, 'cuz he give 'em a fair price fer cert'n."

138

"Tell me about your mother. Where is she now? Doesn't it bother her that you are out here alone?"

"Why we be dresst like thac?"

"Like what?"

"Like thac. They be clothes fer trav'lun?"

"Yes, I believe so."

"We be fram a city?"

"Yes."

"Wot city?"

"Boston."

"How es et yer alone?"

"How is it *you're* alone?" I returned the question.

"D'ye knaw St. Louis, where's et to?"

"Yes, more or less. Mostly less, I'm afraid. I've been there."

Gracie had evaded my questions twice.

"Are ye nawt afeerd o' enjuns?"

"Some."

"How es et then, we be 'avun' the same cawlor hair?"

"I don't know. Do you?"

"Ye be Anglish?"

"No. Are you?"

"Yes. Have ye aver heart o' Anglant?"

"Yes."

"Have ye aver seen et?"

"Yes."

"Chinny reckon. Es et true, then? Really, es et true."

Her green eyes went brilliant.

"Yes, it's true. I have...when I was a child."

"Have ye aver seen a coach, 'r a castle, 'r a keng 'r a quayne? Have ye aver seen an ocean?"

"Enough, enough. My word, too many questions. My head is already splitting without your help. I would have to be a lot stronger to answer all those questions. In the meantime, may I have another cup of water, please?"

"Yes'm."

This time drinking was much easier, and after finishing off the first cup, I asked for a second. At first Gracie said nothing, but studied my every move. Then curiosity got the best of her young mind.

"Why es et then, we be here-there?

"What are you asking? How did I end up in this mess?"

"Yut, thet too."

"I was bitten by a snake." I pulled my skirt up past my knee for her to see.

"I sawr et when I put ye en the wagon."

"Oh, well then, you already know."

"I knaw why ye's sick, but nawt why we be out here-there by yer lonesome. Dit ye get left behind by a man 'r sump'unt?"

"No. Not at all."

"Mmm. I dent see no man clathers n' thengs."

"There isn't any to be found."

140

"So, ye be sayun we's jus' trav'lun' alone then?"

"Pretty much it."

"Hmmmph."

Gracie was very curious about me, and conveyed an innocence that was truly heart-warming. I could have accepted this as the natural reaction of a trapper's daughter, who had seldom encountered another human being. But I knew there was more, something else behind the eyes of this bright young lady. It had something to do with her family or, more likely, lack thereof. Her interest in my traveling alone undoubtedly had relevance to her own situation.

I looked out the back of the wagon at Gracie's mules. I took note of the amount of gear that burdened them. There were far too many possessions for a young girl to have in tow. She would be robbed or worse in a heartbeat. I tried to steer the conversation.

"When do you expect your folks back?"

Again, she gave me that suspicious look. Her answer was guarded.

"Soon. They sait effn they ain't back-long fer may en a coupl'o' days, then I'uz ta hait north fer South Pay-ass."

"A couple of days! South Pass?" My response revealed my disbelief. "They just left you here by yourself? Don't they worry for your well-being?" I asked.

"I'm fifteen. I'm olt enough t' fent fer mayself," she insisted indignantly.

"Oh, of course. Of course you are, my dear, I meant nothing to the contrary. After all, you took care to save my life, and there's much to be said for that."

"I altready sait, et wern't nawthun."

She answered with indignance, her feathers obviously ruffled.

"No, it was very much something. Something I must repay in a fitting manner when the proper time and place allow. I guess I just don't understand how they expected you to guard so much valuable property. I mean, I can see at least three pack mules from here, a bundle of pelts, kitchen utensils, a tipi, it all adds up to small fortune, a camp in itself...quite a bit of responsibility I would say. I usually think of it as more of a man's job."

Gracie bored into me with those icy green eyes.

"Ye don' b'lieve may, do ye?"

Instinctively, she put a little more distance between us.

"Oh, no. No, no, no. Gracie, of course I believe you. Why wouldn't I believe you? I don't expect you to lie, not after all you've done for me."

This child was way too quick, I thought to myself.

"Nawt...nawt...ye dent b'lieve may. I cain tell, but et's no mind, cuz I haff ta go anyways. Yer better en' all. Chinny reckon ye cain fent fer yerself. I haff ta go. Chave thengs ta do."

"Wait, Gracie. Don't go. Please, not just yet. I want you to stay. Really, I do. I would very much like to keep your company."

"Nawt, chaff ta go."

"Grace, please. I know I am holding you back, but if I've offended you, if I was rude, if I've frightened you; I apologize. I know I shouldn't pry, but oftentimes I can't help myself. I confess I am curious about you, but to be truthful, I find myself concerned for you. It was a mistake of the heart, nothing more. I can see you are young, and it must be the mother in me that tends to overly fuss. But, I meant you no harm. Please, Gracie...stay. I beg you forgive me."

In response to my explanation and earnest pleas, she settled down considerably.

"We cain't stay h'ayr," she said. "Et's too open. There's no water fer the mules. Effn they die, we coult die. I'uz o' mind ta leave thic mornun et first light, but I dent knaw ef yer gurt 'nough ta travel. We best be agon sooner n' later—when et gets dimpsy."

"Dimpsy?"

"Yut. Jus' then, when the sun gets down...ets dimpsy...ets dimmet or dimpsy, ye knaw wot cham sayun."

"I swear, Gracie Castleman, I barely understand half of what you're saying, but at least I understand what you mean."

I was physically sick, too weak to move about on my own, and quite possibly cloudy in my perceptions. I needed Gracie's assistance for a few days more if at all possible. For this reason, I chose not to bring up the issue of her family again anytime soon. It was plain to me that this subject struck a tender chord within. She was very sensitive about it. Still, behind those sparkling green eyes lurked something very secretive. I felt certain she was battling life alone. I spent too much time with children to know different. Gracie was too young to be out on the desert.

My wretched condition denied me any measure of comfort or rest. Between snakebite, sun poisoning, blisters front to back, run-of-the-mill misery, and whatever else I may have forgot, I knew nothing of appetite and, quite the opposite, suffered an unending urge to vomit anything that might hope to cross my lips.

Being so sensitive to heat, I offered no objections to Gracie's wish for traveling at night. Just the thought of cooler air brought me much needed relief. Night travel would also be easier on my mules, which were plenty thirsty and would appreciate Gracie's assurances that we were only a half of day from the slopes and fresh water.

"Appen knaw where's et ta the North fork o' the Play-ette River?"

"Not in the sense of having ever been there, but I have conversed with a number of those who have traveled that route. I know it's a ways off—maybe south of us, I don't know. ...East a fair stretch for certain. We would never reach it without a full burden of water and supplies if that's what you're asking. I believe the Cheyenne River is closer, but farther north and eastward."

"D'ye thenk ye coult find et?"

"The Platte?"

"The Play-ette 'r St. Louis."

"I'm a born fool, Gracie. I think I can do just about anything if I set my mind to it. But *I am learning.* You have yet to appreciate the indelicacies a woman enjoys without bathing for weeks on end. No, maybe you wouldn't. Maybe you are still too young. Honestly, I haven't the strength to even contemplate it. At this moment, I think only of rest. I need a few days of rest. Was your last camp nearby?"

"A day's rite 'r so."

"Was it a safe place to stay? Did it have water?"

"Yut."

"That's not too far. If it's safe, I say we return there for a couple days stay. Give me a chance to get back on my feet. After that, if you're bent on going to St. Louis, maybe, just maybe, I'll go with you. That is, if you wish me to."

Gracie pondered my proposal.

"I don' knaw. My folks sait go dreklay ta South Pay-ass Junction en' then make way fer the North Play-ette en' St. Louis. 'Sides, effn we go back ta camp, ye'll haff ta leave the wagon.

144

'*Ye might see a cart on the slopes, Booty, but a wagon...naver.*' Thet's wot my dadduh always sait. We neet ta hait fer South Pay-ass 'r St. Louis."

"Well…. Obviously, I am in no position to stop you from heading out for South Pass or the North Platte for that matter. However, I'm not sure what benefit you would gain by visiting South Pass by yourself—unless of course, as you said, your parents are there waiting for you. I know the place reasonably well, and fear it would present more danger than advantage, but if that is what you believe you must do, then go. Above all, don't worry about me, Gracie. If I can find fresh water, I can take care of myself, in spite of how it looks."

Gracie grew pensive. She offered no protest, but then, no agreement was forthcoming either. Her mind was digesting the hard facts before her. Any fool would know that loving parents would never send a child across the wild lands to seek out South Pass, let alone make way for the North Platte and St. Louis. But, I said nothing. I simply laid back and watched as she fidgeted over concerns and indecision. Gracie was disheartened by the logic of my persuasion.

"I'm nawt so sure 'bout go'un back ta camp."

"Why?"

"I don' knaw. Cham afeerd et's jus' a day's ride the wrong way. Et seems ta may, we jus' be wamblin' 'bout here-there fer nuthun, thet's all."

"Gracie, in this place, a day's ride is meaningless. I've spent that much time going in circles. But I will leave it up to you."

And with that our conversation ended. No further plans were discussed. I spent the remainder of the day keeping to myself, trying not to move, drinking as much as possible, and attempting to eat. It was remarkable how fast water improved my condition on the inside. On the outside, my snakebite looked hideous.

My entire leg appeared black, but the swelling seemed to have subsided and the pain somewhat diminished. Unfortunately, the malady seemed perfectly replaced by my simmering skin, which swelled further with each downed cup of water. I could not be touched. There was no position that would afford me comfort, and so I had little choice but to lie still, suffer...and watch Gracie.

As dusk took hold in the low places, Gracie began fetching her animals, fitting their pack saddles, and securing loads. For a while, I watched her going about her business working the straps and ropes. She wouldn't look my way and although it was obvious she was upset, my health prevented me from doing anything about it. I wasn't going back to South Pass under any condition. I was running from South Pass, and thoughts of St Louis were sheer nonsense.

I had no idea where I would be headed, with or without Gracie, but I elected to get on my feet. That was no small measure, and not without a great deal of pain. Determination prevailed and I began laying out my own harnesses so to untangle the traces and lines. I worked alongside Gracie in a silence that was awkward if not comical.

In the end, Gracie decided to take my advice, but never said as much. She agreed by actions—she brought a mule to the end of the wagon pole where I stood aligning a doubletree.

"Does this mean you are you going to stay with me for a while?"

She looked to the side with lowered eyes.

"Will you lead me back to your camp?"

Gracie didn't answer.

"Thank you."

I offered my appreciation. Gracie shrugged a shoulder and took a deep breath.

"How d'ye hitch they mules?"

"Well, it takes a bit. We have to fit the halters, and then the harnesses and traces, and the bridles. The main thing is to keep everything from getting tangled. That's why I sorted all this out on the ground. To be honest, I haven't the strength."

"Chinny reckon'd a wagon woult be a maggoty theng, but et luks ta be fer more work 'n I figer't."

"Well, if you've never done it, it probably looks to be impossible. It's not all that bad, but I agree it is nothing like mounting Kelly and just riding off. Come on, I'll show you how to get the lead team harnessed first."

Following my direction, Grace helped me harness the leaders, and hitch them to the wagon pole. She watched my every move and essentially harnessed the wheelers on her own. We stepped the wheelers in place and hooked their traces to the trees. Finally, I showed her how to connect the cross-checks and run the team lines back.

"Now, if you pull the lines and your lead mules split apart, your cross-checks are set too far ahead on the lines. There's too much slack. And if they turn into each other, then the cross-checks are set too far back on the lines. They are too tight. When they're set correctly, the leaders will back up straight as an arrow and you're set to go."

Harnessing my animals made obvious how much worse they were for wear. They were thinner for lack of water, and it dismayed me to put the burden of the wagon upon them, but Gracie's mules had never been harnessed, let alone teamed four up, and we didn't have the luxury of training them.

147

Gracie topped off her water flask, which was sufficient to meet our needs, and just before nightfall, we divided up what water was in the barrel between my team to freshen them. She tied her mules in tow behind Kelly, which she planned to ride. I suspected her decision not to ride with me in the wagon was a last attempt to assert her independence.

We headed out toward the slopes as soon as the sun gave up its heat. Gracie stated as a matter of fact that she would have us in the foothills before the break of day, and I accepted her assessment without question. It was a simple matter to stay pointed to a familiar peak in the distance.

EIGHTEEN

There was little left to do but strike up conversation as we faced the hours of travel before us. I made a number of attempts to converse, but it was difficult because Gracie was either harboring resentment or hiding much. I didn't push her, but instead chose to sit back in silence and study the way she moved through the harsh black and orange portraits of a low-slung sun being smothered by the blackness of night.

I came to accept that Gracie was not only a gorgeous child, but also a child to be respected. She was intelligent, she was agile, she was remarkably confident for her age—more so than any child I could recall. She was a creature of the wilds. She was also exhausted, entirely spent. The growing body of a child, remarkable or not, could fight sleep for just so long. This was one of the very few advantages I held over this girl, and so after watching her nearly fall off Kelly for a third time, I called out to her.

"Gracie. Gracie!"

"Wot?"

"You're sleeping, honey."

"Naw, I ain't."

"Yes you are. I have watched you nearly fall off that mule three times now. The next time, you're going to fall and crack your head. Tie Kelly and your mules to the wagon and come sit here on the bench."

"Naw—."

"Don't argue with me child."

I was direct, adamant. I halted the team. Gracie began mumbling a refusal, but was cut short when her head rolled backward one last time. The falling sensation jolted her awake and her eyes opened. She said nothing, but slid off the animal and stumbled blindly toward me. With closed eyes, Gracie lashed the mules to the wagon as I insisted. She climbed up onto the bench and sat next to me. The air was now uncomfortably cool.

"Why don't you get in back and lie down? Climb under the blankets where it's warm."

"Naw."

"Suit yourself, but then favor me and grab a blanket to cover us."

Gracie obliged without complaint.

"Come now, wrap up. Put your head on my shoulder and close your eyes."

Gracie then did a most unexpected thing. She lifted my arm up over her head and moved into me. The gesture caught me off guard and I understood at once, she was so tired, she was reverting to the child she truly was. I placed my arm around her and drew her in close. She laid purposely into my embrace and succumbed to her weariness. I was deeply moved.

For a moment, I sat motionless and gazed upon her. In the light of the moon, I looked affectionately at her discolored face, framed in its thick mop of greasy, scraggly hair. Glints of reflected moonlight danced off the long white lashes and brows, garnishing that adorned those spectacular green eyes, now closed and searching for something in a dream. A coyote barked far off in the distance. She stirred. Apart from the single interruption, her breathing went deep and undisturbed.

Having this child in my arms effectively masked my pain. This was one of those rare moments where I might understand something of the emotion and protective instinct that filled a mother's heart. For the first time, Gracie's vulnerability was apparent and my heart burst forth to welcome her. She brought not only a wonderful sense of peace and fulfillment, but also a tear of affection to my dry and weary eyes. I pressed my face to her smelly head and kissed her good night.

"Uggg."

I wiped the grease off my lips.

"There is no family is there, Gracie. Where did you come from, sweetheart? Why are you out here so young and so alone?"

I started the team moving slowly toward my guide stars above a distant peak. Gracie never awoke from her sleep, but after hours of conscious effort to comfort her within my embrace, I invited an unbearable stiffness to invade my frame, a discomfort that finally forced me to stop the wagon and release her. I coaxed the child into lying down in the bed. She was drunk with fatigue, and even so, barely allowed me to fuss over her.

By candlelight, I removed what remained of those deplorable shrunken heads, fearing that instead of safeguarding, her spiritual protectors would most likely twist around her neck, and strangle the poor waif to death. Having removed the threat, I pulled up the blanket and tucked her in. I remained in the wagon awhile, watching over her in the dim light and listening to the sound of her slumber. Her gentle breath soothed my misery. I was immersed in feelings for her that distracted me from my own sufferings. I wished to take her in my arms and crush her with affection. In lieu of such bother, I held back and tried only to imagine what was her life? What stories would she tell? What wish might she make? I wondered what secrets she harbored behind those slumbering eyes.

I knew, as with all children, in time she would seek guidance through the knowledge and experience of others in order to sort out her fears and concerns. Curiosity was a powerful force, and children had an insatiable appetite for answers to the questions in their lives. I had nothing other than my instincts, to conclude Gracie would come to me for answers. Answers were always free for the taking.

I blew out the candle and crawled forward to climb back onto the bench. The cool night air soothed my skin. I looked up at the sky, rich with stars and milky streams. I enjoyed the brilliance of the moon. For one undisturbed moment, I felt an inner bliss. I snapped the reins, and found myself suddenly reciting parts of David Dusterwinkle's lullaby 'Mr. Moon.'

...Momma singing quietly, whispering in your ear

Time to sleep my little one, Mister Moon is here....

The night progressed, and I felt increasingly alone on the bench as I considered my own doubts about life. I needed to get my affairs into a manageable order. I laughed to think how my

151

plight might not be as distant from this child as I might hope. Same questions, maybe the same heartache, just more years on my part spent searching for those free answers.

Maybe Gracie had folks, maybe she didn't. Maybe I was sent here to watch over her. Or maybe God sent her to watch over me and save me from myself, save me from my remorse by instilling within me one of the most powerful of instincts to survive. Protection of the young—a mother's instinct that overshadowed all pain and hardship. The two of us were together waging battles yet to be won or lost. Friend or foe, only time would tell.

I reached the trees of the foothills before dawn, and set the mules free to forage. In spite of the heat that radiated from my flesh, I found myself badly chilled by the end of our night's journey. I wondered if I was running a fever. I climbed into the back of the wagon and laid down alongside Gracie for warmth. She remained in a deep sleep. I would have thought her dead had she not managed a breath for my sake. She made me think of Luke's last moments.

In what remained of night, troublesome thoughts drifted in and out of my consciousness. I lie questioning how run down this child must be. Why so tired, I wondered. Had she not slept in days? Was she on the run? Why did she possess a full camp? Why did she not speak freely of her folks? She was dressed so frightful with all those skulls hanging about her. The visions still haunted me and I tossed and I turned in my state of discomfort until my eyes greeted the first rays of morning light.

When I awoke for good, it was not a gentle gradual awakening, but rather an awakening on the fly as I bolted for the rear gate. I threw my head out the back of the wagon, where it released a torrent of vomit. I could hardly believe there was anything in me to lose. My head hung lifelessly as I waited for the head-splitting pain behind my closed eyes to subside. In spite of my pitiful vomit, I knew I was suffering from dehydration.

I willed my stomach to settle itself. I opened my eyes momentarily to confirm what I sensed, which was the ooze of broken blisters creeping across my flesh. The morning air chilled those places soaked in the watery discharge. I endured the waves of shakes and shivers that passed through me. From some distant place in my past, I could hear Allen warning me of the dangers of infection.

My sudden movements had no effect upon Gracie, who continued to sleep peacefully. I settled back onto the bedding, and pulled my skirt up high across my thigh. I studied my leg in the available light. It appeared entirely black and blue in the shadows, looking even worse than Gracie's face. I slid my hands up and down the wound, and noted to my relief that the swelling had gone down markedly. In fact, there was now so little pain, I was more concerned about my blisters and the looming infection. I lay back down and closed my eyes. I felt drained.

Now my wandering mind caused me to worry about the scarring my face might carry for life. I passed my hands slowly across my cheeks, taking in the alien feel of their texture. I tried to imagine what I must look like. This time it was young Caroline and the visions of her mutilated back that wedged their way into my head. After a string of such thoughts, further sleep was futile.

I opened my eyes and stared blindly up at the hoops and canvas. I felt half dead and miserable, but sleep was out of the question. These visions behind closed eyes were intolerable. It was best that I stop my tossing and turning, and leave Gracie to her sleep and the peace she might enjoy. Quietly, I exited the wagon.

I set about building a fire to boil the last of our water. This helped take my mind off my discomfort, providing I stayed upwind of the heat, which seemed to sear any skin exposed. I looked to the eastern horizon through soft pastels of color where a brightening sky heralded a dreaded sun that would soon appear.

Even the touch of its first rays would feel like branding irons upon me unless I sought shelter in the shade of the woods beyond.

I craved a cup of coffee, but that was out of the question, for there was just enough water to boil up a pot of stew. Had there been extra water, it wouldn't have made a difference, for any coffee warmer than a chunk of ice would have never made it past my cracked lips. They had been baked through and through, and were swollen to the point where it was all I could do just to pronounce words.

I would have to be content plunking dried vegetables one by one into the heated water as I waited at some distance for it to boil. I cut up some jerky and biscuits and added them to the mix, stirring all with reason, thickening the water into gravy. The simple soup should have looked delicious, but I had no hunger to satisfy. For me, the smell of food was enough to make me retch so I stirred but sat at arm's length upwind.

Between the scraping sounds of a stirring spoon and the aromas drifting through the wagon, I succeeded in bringing Gracie back to life. I heard her jostle about the wagon. I looked up from the stew to see her kneeling inside, but leaning outward and looking my way over the back gate with much anticipation. I hoped there was nothing of my vomit to be encountered. There were no devilish heads swinging about to protect her, but she remained a formidable sight with that black and reddish-blue face topped off with that mess of greasy spiked hair. What a sight she was to behold first thing in the morning. I tried not to laugh, for it stretched my cracked lips, but she surely was an eyeful.

From the back of the wagon, Gracie continued to stare at the breakfast pot with all the hopefulness of a half-starved child. I knew this look because I had fed many of those children, and their eyes all shared the same intensity of fixation. Indeed, I was happy to see her, and I smiled the best I was able, knowing I probably looked as bad as she.

"Well, then. I would say good morning, but you're well on your way to passing meridian."

It was a joke, the hour being very early. She said nothing. I knew my speech was slurred, but if she didn't understand me, she could have at least acknowledged me. Instead, she remained silent and expressionless. Apparently, she was still groggy from a badly needed rest. Maybe, she was still sleeping for that matter. I had often seen children sit at a breakfast table, staring at me, even answering my questions, while fully asleep.

"I trust you slept well. I would have passed you for dead, if I hadn't known the better."

Gracie shifted her stare, and looked straight at me in the oddest manner. I saw the green of her eyes disappear as her face began to break up. She removed herself from my view, dropping back into the wagon. Her expression took me quite by surprise. I stood momentarily confused, asking myself if I had just seen her start to cry. I cocked my head to listen with intent, and sure enough, I could hear her muffled sobs.

Clearly, I had misread this child. Yet, I knew children. I knew the look of a child who craved something, but if Gracie didn't want breakfast, why then a look of such expectation? Feeling most awkward, I raced to remember what all I had said. But there was little for me to recall and even less to have uttered callously. I simply had said nothing to warrant such a sorrowful reaction.

I was taken by a thought, and I turned about to look behind me, but there was nothing and nobody to be seen. I was standing alone. Clearly, it was something I had said or done, and yet…. Then it came to me. Not something I had said, of course not, but something I had done. I must have done something that reminded her of something. Something…or someone…someone like…*her mother—her mother making breakfast at the fire.*

155

This was all about the other side of Gracie that I could not see. It would make sense based on my earlier suspicions. I wondered if I had just glimpsed sight of a wound that she suffered. If so, she concealed it well. If not for the fact she was only half awake, only half in control, it might not have been exposed for many days or weeks to come. It was every bit the same as her placing my arm about her shoulders during the night past.

I knew this revelation had to be addressed, but I was unsure how to go about it. I didn't wish to press her. And this was certain to be sensitive. I was uncertain whether she would accept or reject my attempt to console her. Yet, my instincts about children were honed from way back and well proven. I learned from experience that children often needed to be coaxed into letting loose of the things that troubled them. Much the way Mary eased me away from the death of Lady Rebecca.

There was no time like the present to approach the issue, and so I walked over to the wagon and peeked over the rear gate. There, before me, was Gracie lying face down on the blankets. She was a greasy mess, but a greasy mess filled with a heart full of hurt. I, on the other hand, being well armed with assumptions, did my best to be tactful, to be gentle, and to ease directly into the conversation.

"I promised you I wouldn't pry, Gracie, but isn't there anything you might tell me so I could better understand? It would help me from feeling so useless. I am embarrassed to think I may have said something to upset you so."

Of course, I knew it wasn't anything I said, but I needed to give her a reason to save me, a reason to explain.

"Et's nawthun' ye sait." She sobbed.

Then without raising her head, "I'uz dreamun, en when I awoke, chinny reckon'd ye be 'un other."

156

With that, she broke down again and hid her face behind her hand. I reached into the wagon cautiously to caress her. This time she allowed it, and I could feel the moisture of emotion upon her face. I went with my instincts.

"Gracie, you thought I was your mother, didn't you? This is all about your mother, isn't it?"

She was immediately overtaken by my words. She gave way to a hard cry, now uncontrollable. The sight moved me at once. My eyes misted over, and I worked to keep my own emotions at bay. It was hard for me to speak without choking.

"What happened to your mother, Gracie? I think you should tell me. It helps to let it out."

It took a moment for her to rein in the sobs that racked her small frame. I could see she was a very strong girl emotionally and this was something she was working hard at to keep on top. She calmed down. The heaving stopped and she lay quiet for a few moments. Then in a regulated voice with heavily guarded emotion, she explained.

"My mother diet...." She halted. "My mother diet back-long a day or so...en' when I woke, I smelt fud en' 'eard the spoon en the pot en' I figer'd et was her breakfastun. I uz confus't wakin' up ensite the wagon." Again, she paused. "I wanted her t' knaw 'bout the bat dream I'uz havun, 'bout how I be afeerd...en how I lov't her...."

She started to cry afresh. She buried her face in the blanket.

I shook my head with empathy.

"Oh, Gracie...."

I bit my swollen lip. My vision blurred. I squeezed my eyes shut to push out the tears.

"I am so sorry. You must believe I know what you feel. Honestly, I do. I myself lost two mothers of sorts, and I didn't think I could ever go on living. I too was young when it happened, about your age. It was painful. It was so very painful. I haven't forgotten. Even to this day when I think of it, I end up melancholy. It is only because I've grown older that I have come to understand and accept those losses. It will take time, Gracie."

"How cain et be thet ye lose two mothers?" she asked.

"Well, to be honest, I guess you can't, but it felt that way to me. My real mother became sick and died when I was nine. My second mother was a remarkable woman, who took me in and cherished me as though I were her only child. She died in a fire at Christmas when I was about twelve. I saw her die in the flames and I was devastated. Even now, I say it with difficulty. It took a long, long time for me to accept her death. You won't ever forget, Gracie. You will just think of it less often."

"Mess Elezabeth."

"Yes."

"Cham only ten."

"I would have never known."

"En, I cain count uz well. I liet. I dit. I em sorry."

"To be honest, I figured as much. But I understand. A young girl has to be careful. She has to protect herself, especially when she doesn't have a mother to watch over her."

"I mess my folks." She sobbed.

"Of course you do. You loved them a great deal, as they did you."

Her comment almost slipped past me.

"Gracie...? What do you mean, you miss your folks ?"

158

"They diet o' the Cholera."   She began to cry again.

"Oh, my precious child, tell me this isn't true. When did all this happen?"

It took a moment for her to answer me, my eyes refilling with tears but for seeing her in such wretched despair.

"My dadduh diet back-long a week...jus' 'fer my momma."

I couldn't have been further stunned had I been kicked in the head by Kelly or any one of the mules. I was lost for words. I felt woefully ashamed to know this child before me was carrying a fresh burden of such enormity. I was embarrassed at having been concerned mostly about my bites and burns and my unholy affair with Christopher. I was embarrassed by my self-pity and inconsequential suffering when compared to what Gracie's young heart was struggling to overcome. This child had been ripped to shreds emotionally, and yet had the backbone to stand up and face her tribulations, whereas I had chosen to run. It was no longer the sun that made my face red and hot.

"I don't know what to say. There is nothing I can say, Gracie. I can only offer to keep you company if you wish. We can talk about your mother and father whenever you choose. I know they were loving people, and I would beg to hear about them—every detail."

I stood outside the wagon patiently silent. Gracie soon rose to her elbows. She lifted her head, glanced at me, and immediately looked away. Her bloodshot eyes were now added to the mask. I could see how hard it was for her to be weak. This was pride I fully understood.

"Why don't you take a moment to settle down. Come out when you feel up to it, and have some breakfast. It's ready to be eaten, and it will do you good. I promise you will feel much better afterward."

159

Gracie wiped away her tears but still avoided my eyes. She wiped her nose and the surrounding grease off onto her sleeve. She nodded her approval.

"Yut."

In time, Gracie climbed out of the wagon. She sat down, and I could see the weight of her sorrow. I said nothing, but handed her a cup of soup. At first, she kept her eyes fixed upon her cup, not caring to face me.

I held my tongue, and in due course, as I had hoped, she began to talk. Conversations about our likes and our dislikes, our joys and our fears, the good and the bad in our lives started to flow. Words flowed slowly at first, like maple sap on a cold morning, then increasing in speed as they absorbed the warmth of our friendship. We reached a comfortable and trustworthy place, whereupon she informed me that her campsite was also the gravesite of her parents.

"Appen thes change yer mind en' all? Knaw'un thaccy there be deat folk et the camp?"

"No, Gracie. I know they are kin. I know they are your parents, and that they loved you. Would it bother you to stand at my side if I were paying respects to my folks at their graves?"

"Naw, I figer et woun't"

"Good, then you believe me."

While Gracie was sitting at the fire finishing her soup, I busied myself by making an effort to conceal the wagon from view. I looked over to see her staring at me with a questionable look.

"What? Am I doing something wrong?"

"Why be ye coverun thaccy wagun?"

"I thought it might be prudent to conceal it from view, you disagree?" She turned around and looked across the desert. She turned back to me.

"Ye put down tracks fer twenty miles thet lead drecklay ta h'ayr, t' thaccy there wagun." She pointed at the wagon. "Any'un who might chance ta cross 'em woult follow 'em right ta where ye stant." She again pointed at the wagon. "Wot diff'rence does et make ef ye cover et? Why don' ye jus' hide the chest?"

She looked at me in a fashion that made me feel like an idiot. I turned away from her condescending stare and observed well-embedded wheel tracks leading to the horizon. I dropped my handful of branches and kicked the sagebrush aside.

"Yes, I see. You do have a valid point there. I'll...ah...get the chest."

Within the hour we had mounted the mules and were off working our way south under the cover of the trees. I was unwilling to leave my chest of belongings, so everything was packed on the mules. Altogether we were nine mules strong and traveling light. This was good because it would enable us to port additional water. It was bad because nine mules were easy to spot at a distance. At least, nobody could tell if we were women or men unless they rode within gunshot.

I followed Gracie obediently as we worked our way along the tree line, slowly climbing to higher altitudes and thicker forests. I was impressed by her intuition. The way I figured it, she never knew where we were at any time. Yet, by instinct, she always knew where she was going. She exhibited no fear of being lost whatsoever. This, for such a young child, amazed me. I was careful not to mention it, lest I jinx the one person I was counting on to get me back. Back to what...I didn't know.

Gracie also failed to share my fear of running out of water. She paid little mind to the issue, and made no further mention of it once we arrived at the foothills. She was way ahead of me, for it wasn't long after that, before we came to the first mountain brook. It was a joy to watch the cold, clear water gurgle its way down from the peaks above. Both of us dismounted and dropped to our knees at the stream's edge. We plunged our hands into the cold clear fluid. I brought it up to my mouth. It was some of the best-tasting water I had ever enjoyed. It did wonders for my stomach and overall vigor, which seemed unable to snap back from the sun or snake poisoning or whatever. If the mules could have smiled we all would have been wearing grins. The only difference being, the mules and I were grinning more out of relief, whereas Gracie grinned out of pleasure.

We crossed over the brook and continued on to cross many more small creeks until at a much higher elevation, we came to a sizeable stream. It was a very fast-moving body of water and when we came upon it we were well within the thick of a heavily forested vale. On approach, I heard the rush of water long before I saw sign of it.

It was at this stream, Gracie turned to head up alongside a ravine that often times cut deep into the valley floor as it constrained the reckless tumble of melting spring snow. All the while climbing, sometimes in the ravine, sometimes out, we remained in view of the rushing blue-white current. We stopped often to take our fill of it, for the water was delicious. Gracie wiped her mouth and turned to me.

"We be gettun' close now. The waters flow ento a pool o' sorts up thet-a-ways."

We rode on and my mind began to think of this poor soul struggling to bury her mother. I imagined the effort undertaken, the strenuous work, as I looked at ground that appeared mostly rock in every direction. Whether it was due to my imagination or my nose, an unpleasant thought struck me as we rode closer to her camp.

"Gracie, did you bury your folks in the ground?" I asked as tactfully as possible.

"Yut. There's nawbody else."

"No. I mean did you bury them in the ground, in the earth?"

"Naw, the grount's too hart. I watcht momma place stones atop my dadduh en' I dit the same fer her.'"

That was not something I wanted to hear.

"Hold up a minute, honey. We need to talk." She stopped and I dismounted. I walked over to her.

"Did you cover them with earth before you placed the stones on them?

She looked at me with a questioning face as though she had done something wrong.

"Naw."

She waited for whatever I was about to say.

"Gracie, I will try to be as delicate about this as I can. Generally it is a good idea to cover the loved one with dirt before placing the stones. It helps keep down the odors and other things that are part of a normal process in God's plan to return us to dust." She thought for a moment.

"Ye be sayun', ye thenk they stenk?"

I gauged her condition.

"I can't say for sure, but if they do it will be worse than anything you can imagine. I noticed the wind is blowing down through this valley as it should. I would suggest we ride out and around, and then approach the camp from upwind. Better to pay our regards with a fresh wind to our nose. It is only my suggestion, having dealt with this type of thing much in the past.

163

Don't misunderstand me; I will be at your side no matter how you wish to go about it."

There was no argument or second guessing and so we climbed out of the ravine and circled about in order to enter the camp from upwind. We were close, as Gracie said, and the grave mounds were easy to spot. We dismounted and stretched our legs and backs by collecting wildflowers from a nearby clearing.

"Now, let's not concern ourselves with unpleasant thoughts of smell, but instead hold our breath so as to cheat Cholera out of hurting us as well, alright?"

"Yut."

In a crude and comical manner, we took deep breaths then ran up to the graves and tossed wildflowers upon the stones. We wasted no time retreating. No disrespect intended, but I for one needed very little encouragement to empty my stomach. One whiff of that smell, whether potent or otherwise, would be enough to clean me out.

Keeping a stiff upper lip, I disallowed my stomach anything more than a gag and worked to adorn the graves. I did this with heart, for I believed it crucial that Gracie had someone with whom she could share the knowledge of these graves. I held this would be far more consoling in her future than memories of collecting rocks or tossing flowers. I remembered how badly I needed Mary to give me back a connection to my past. I made certain I was Gracie's connection.

We set up camp with plans to stay for the night. We did so at a safe distance upwind from the graves, for aside from the obvious malodor and concerns about drinking clean water, we also noticed a number of animals had been attracted to the area. It was the wolf tracks in particular that were most unsettling. Gracie recognized the prints at first sight and passed on her father's warning.

"Don' be doat'n 'tween scent en' scavenger."

"Not to worry."

But I did. The idea of fresh wolf tracks beneath my boots, and animals creeping around at night while I hoped to sleep was enough to give me the jitters. I longed for the company of Shadow Hunter.

We settled in safely upwind of the drifting scent, and after unpacking the mules, I agreed to collect firewood so Gracie might go off hunting. I offered her a gun, balls, and powder, but she shunned them because the noise and smell scared off the game '*fer eternity.*' She preferred her bow and arrow and our agreement was she would hunt first and if she returned empty handed, we would go out with the gun. She returned within twenty minutes with a plea to help her drag back two deer. *Twenty minutes.* I was genuinely impressed and frankly—once again embarrassed before this wondrous child.

Gracie was exceptionally adept at gutting the animals and cutting up the meat with a superb swiftness. She was no stranger to the art of making jerky. I expected to be camped here for a while, so doing the best I was able, I helped her arrange the firewood and set up sapling rails. We sharpened stakes and skewered the butchered meat. We laid the cuts out carefully in tidy rows over the heat of a low fire. The meat slowly dried out and the smoke served not only to keep the biting flies at bay, but it also prevented Mr. and Mrs. Castleman from meandering upwind in the still evening air. The smell of the drying meat was wonderful, but it came at a price. We stood ever watchful for wolves and bear. The vultures circled overhead in number—they also drawn by the scent of meat.

It had been a long day preparing the jerky, and well into dark before all was packed in bags and made ready for the mules. We hung the bags high in the trees for the night so the wolves wouldn't be able to reach them. We then stoked the fire and were fast to sleep. We were left unmolested by man or beast the whole of the night, but try as I might, a sound sleep still escaped me. Much of my night was spent watching over Gracie and keeping the fire well fed.

NINETEEN

I managed my best rest in the early hours when the first sign of light filtered down through the trees. Maybe the wolf tracks played too heavy on my mind; maybe it was one of a hundred other things. Whatever it was, I awoke same as always, tired and dismayed at the necessity of facing another day feeling half dead. I arose from my bed, smiled down at Gracie as she stirred, and moved to freshen the fire.

Gracie sat up, and that signaled a new day. There was much to be said about being counted amongst the living. As was my way, I had little appetite for breakfast and so laid back to watch Gracie feed herself. She was full of spunk this morning and doing a respectable job of distracting me from my discomfort. We chatted freely.

"I may feel haggard, while you feel refreshed, but I am here to tell you, between the travel, the mule sweat, the sweat and grease collected from standing all night over the smoke pit—*you stink.* The apple didn't fall far from the tree."

I alluded to her parents. She took the insult in jovial stride.

"Oh! En' yer sweet? I don' thenk so. *You* stenk!

"You stink."

"Ah! En ye thenk yer a bowerly sort? Ye billid diddlecome, yer a festerun' bag o' blesters. Ye stenk, stenk, stenk! At least I don' luk like I stenk."

"Oh, ho! I beg to differ. Fine, I stink. Not as bad as you, but I concede. Point is we need to wash. Do you mind fetching a pot and filling it with some water? We'll make good use of these embers."

"Wot fer? We cain scrub en the flow."

"In the stream? You can't be serious."

"Cham serious. Et'll wake ye right up proper, ye doattie. Make ye jus' biver n' scream."

"No, no, no, no. I don't think anything about biverin' and screaming sounds good."

"Oh, quit yer crewntun', Mess Elezabeth, ye ol' grammer. Don' be so afeerd. Et'll clean yer twily sken o' thet mess right nice. Make ye feel en' luk like a new piggy widden."

"Make me freeze is more like it."

"C'mon, Mess Elezabeth. We'll take our bath en the stream. Ye'll feel better, I promise. Ye'll feel perfec'lay clean en' fresh. Come on now, don' be doat'n."

"I feel better just lying here, right now. That water has to be freezing. I think best to boil some water and save my heart."

"No, no, ye always feel better efter gettun up en' movun 'round 'cause then ye don' thenk 'bout bein' all plimmed up like ye be."

"I'm getting too old for all this malarkey, jumping in and out of streams, and traipsing about the country. I'm not ten, Gracie. I'd much rather go home and see my dear friend Mary. I would sit in her lawn chair, sip my summer tea, smell the delicious fragrance of her flower garden, watch the ships sail, and waste away the afternoon."

For a moment, I may have been positively radiant. I looked over at Gracie. There was a pause in her flow. Her face was empty of emotion. She looked at me with distant eyes.

"Cham sorry," she said suddenly.

"Sorry for what?"

I sensed her change and was puzzled.

"Appen shoun't o' brought ye back long weth me. Chinny reckon ye have other thengs t' do."

Her comment was out of character, and at once I understood I must have hurt her feelings by my mentioning Mary. Gracie didn't have friends, and for me to be her first wasn't unthinkable. I had just snubbed her without even giving it a thought. It was to be a delicate relationship.

"No, Gracie, it was the best thing you could have done for me. It isn't me that is helping you, sweetheart. You are helping me. I have only ever had one other friend who did that for me. It was when I was your age. Her name was Mary and to this day when I feel ill or depressed, I often dream of her caring for me. It's a daydream, of course, because we are all grown up now and lead different lives. She has her family and all, but I still think of her. She was always a good friend to me, Gracie."

"Chell care fer ye, Mess Elezabeth."

I couldn't help but to smile broadly, in spite of hurtful lips.

"Come here."

"Why?" She smiled.

"Just come, here. Lay down here, next to me."

She studied me for a moment, and then rose to her feet and sat down next to me.

"Come, on. Lay down here by my side."

I pulled on her and she leaned over, falling next to me as I asked. I put my arm around her then pulled her in close.

"This is how Mary used to hold me when I was sad or unhappy, or lonely, or just in need of a good hug. We would lie like this for hours. She was only a few years older than me, but when you are young, a few years is a world of time."

I laid there for some time with Gracie in my arms. Lord, but the child brought me comfort. I closed my eyes and let my mind flow with the gentle breezes. Countless memories I would have thought long forgotten came back to me. Unfortunately, they all swirled about one man, pointed in one direction, brought me to one place, the present. I believe Gracie might have laid in my arms the whole of the day, had it not been for my breaking the silence.

"You kept asking me why I was out here all alone. Do you still want to know?"

"Yut."

"Well...I started out west from a place called Boston. That's where I lived with my friend, Mary. It's a wonderful place, Gracie, and I left it to find a man who meant the world to me. I think I may have been in love with him, you know, I wanted to be with him like your mother and father wanted to be with each other. Do you understand?"

"Yut."

"I am sorry to say that it seemed he preferred not to be loved, and that made me feel very sad. I felt I had to leave him, and so I rode out into the desert. I guess God didn't think that was such a good idea and He sent you out to find me. I think He wanted you to bring me back. I don't know why He wanted you to do that, but here we are…just you and me."

I wanted to kiss her on the head, but having done that once before, I knew better.

"Were we fixin' t' hait back-long Boston way?"

"More or less."

"Were we go'un ta travel the desert alone? My dadduh sait et was dan'grous. He tolt may, et makes folks go ensane."

"I suspect all too often that's the truth of it. But now that I have met you, I don't think I can do that."

"Do wot?"

"Travel alone."

"Why?"

"I'm not sure. Would you like to know what I have done most of my life?"

"Wot?"

"I have taken care of children much like you. It seems like I'm led to people in need, especially children. Do you see how strange this is to me, Gracie? You have just lost your parents, and here I am. I was convinced I had left every vestige of my life in another world…in that place called Boston. Can you understand what I am saying? I was the only person alive out here in the middle of nowhere, and all I wanted to do was leave my life behind. Instead, I end up being rescued by a child, who has just been orphaned. Do you think that is some kind of miracle, Gracie? Or is it just the most preposterous coincidence you've ever heard?"

"I don' knaw, Mess Elezabeth. I don' even knaw wot words yer sayun, but I cain tell ye thes. I uz sittun en the wuds en' dadduh was buried under they rocks; momma was only breathun a bet now en' then. I 'member the wend blowun through the trees en' I button't my coat agen the chell. I thought I'uz the only person alive en the worlt. I jus' set there by myself en' wondert wot I'uz suppost ta do. I wern't really sceered, but I'uz...alone. I'uz so alone, Mess Elizabeth. Then I saw thaccy there maggoty wagon. Now, *thet* was a mir'cle effin aver was one."

She said nothing more and that time I did give her a kiss, grease and all.

"Ohhhh. You are a mess, girl."

She exploded from my arms, jumping to her feet.

"Come, on now. Let's wash up. Weeeeee!"

"Oh, no, no, no, Gracie."

"Yes, yes, yes. C'mon, jump en the stream weth may. Et'll be fun, en' ye'll ferget 'bout all the bat stuff. C'mon, Mess Elizabeth."

"Oooooh, my word, Gracie. All right, all right!"

I relented in spite of much better judgment. Gracie tugged gently on my arm, pulling me to my feet. Maybe because of her youth or her innocence, she stripped down before me, harboring nothing of shame or hesitation. She then danced toward the stream as if she were a pure child of nature.

I stood in her wake laughing under my breath. I shook my head as I felt the pressures of my ingrained inhibitions flare up at once. I refused to be stifled by my old world ways and so let my clothes drop to my feet. I looked at my exposed body, and besides the blisters, the burns, the black and blue ravages of the snakebite, the dirt under my nails, a various assortment of nicks and scrapes, and finally the smears of grease from Gracie, there remained some scarce vestige of youth to be found. Or so it seemed at least on the thigh of my right leg and possibly my virgin-like breasts. I could never again be a Gracie, but I wasn't yet a decrepit old hag, and I most certainly was not a virgin—a fact that quite unexpectedly sprang upon me.

"Hmmm. That was an odd thought," I noted under my breath. I did, however, thank Christopher for that reality.

Revealing every inch of my flesh to the world gave me a feeling of overwhelming freedom. I hadn't moved an inch, but felt as though I had run miles with the wind blowing through my hair. I imagined this sensation to be reserved for the joys of childhood until I recalled doing this once before when alone and wandering the desert in search of Christopher.

One thing was for certain, I couldn't even begin to imagine any one of my friends back home stripping down before me, or I before them, to jump into a river. You would never find yourself reading of such things in Boston. Such exhilarations were unimagined.

I had no sooner spewed out this thought about reading, when suddenly I was engulfed by a sensation that I had written some-thing of consequence. Was it a note? Maybe a letter, something that had to be read. I couldn't see the images of this memory, but I could feel it. The sensation haunted me enough so that I momentarily retraced all my activities clear back to South Pass. But I sensed South Pass to be too far back. The sensation lasted only seconds, it being shattered by a barrage of energetic screams.

"Come on! Come on, Mess Elezabeth! Be queck 'bout et. Like thes."

Gracie thrashed about splashing water in every direction. She rubbed herself down with the soap. She then fell to her knees and dropped forward, face down, and disappeared beneath the current. A second later she sprang upward like a waterfall in reverse and ran for shore.

"Do et queckly, en' et'll rense ye perfclay clean. Ye'll feel wonderful."

She squealed. She toweled herself off briskly as she stomped and ran around in circles trying to outrun the obvious freeze following close behind. "Wot ye be waitun fer?"

She badgered me. She prodded me to hurry with her eyes and a nod of her head.

"I'm going, I'm going."

I walked cautiously to the stream bank. I knew the water was going to be cold; mountain streams were always cold. It looked cold. It looked freezing. It reflected the air in these mountains that might seem warm, but in reality was always 'winter cold' barely hidden until a breeze blew away the summer fakery.

I didn't want to appear feeble. I didn't want to be outdone by a child. And I most certainly didn't want to draw any unnecessary attention as I stood before Gracie's waiting stare naked as a newborn. I was already freezing, and all I had done was look. I couldn't afford to think about this so I took a breath and plunged in.

I didn't squeal like Gracie. I couldn't squeal like Gracie. I couldn't get my jaws to separate.

"Huh, huh, huh, huh, huh. Oh…my…God-d-d!"

I managed one constricted gasp as I stumbled for a foothold and daylight. To save my soul, I could not take a breath. No air went in and no air came out. I don't believe my toes ever touched the streambed. It was more like a wishful wash. In my two-second dunking, I endured a cold so excruciating, my breasts, my chest, my arms all tautened, my skin looked like a plucked chicken, but blue as death. All of me went blue as the snakebite on my leg. My teeth trapped my tongue in a clench so tight, I feared they would crush themselves.

173

"Oh, G-G-God! Is that c-c-c-cold!"

I looked over at Gracie, who was falling all over herself in an uncontrollable convulsion of laughter. She was doubled over and spit was running out of her mouth.

"W-w-w-w-where is t-t-t-he s-s-s-s-s-oap?" I demanded of sorts.

Gracie nearly crawled to the water's edge to hand me the bar as the tears streamed down her face.

"You t-t-t-think t-t-t-that's f-f-f-funny?"

I reached down with both my hands and slapped the water to spray her good. She jumped backward with a squeal as I lurched up the bank to chase her across the clearing with two fists full of riverbank sand.

I couldn't yet breathe, but Gracie was screaming for all she was worth. Injury or no injury, the cold made me run the fastest, and I pitched both handfuls of dirt squarely at her back and into her freshly washed hair. She came to an abrupt halt and turned to face me with the look of a killer.

"Ye best nawt let may ketcha 'r...."

Gracie lowered her head and glared at me. As she reached down for her own muddy projectiles, I spun around and ran for my life. I could hear her fast on my heels and so headed for my only safe harbor—the gurgling glacier. In I went, my only protection being adrenaline and stupidity.

There we were naked as God made us, running, screaming, laughing, as we plunged in and out, criss-crossing back and forth across that liquid ice from one bank to the other until at last my condition got the best of me and I was forced to a complete halt and a number of revengeful muddy attacks.

"You w-win…y-y you w-win. I c-c-can't…go…anymore. I'm d-d-done."

"Ye best nawt be messun weth Gracie Castleman."

"I agree. You…w-w-win…you w-w-win."

Gracie relished her superiority for barely a minute before having a change of heart.

"Ye be all right, Mess Elezabeth?"

"Yes. Fine. J-Just out of b-b-breath…just out of b-b-breath… and f-f-freezing."

She moved in close to my side and placed one hand on my back and the other on my stomach. She watched me intently, waiting for my breathing to slow. I smiled at her and then I dropped back beneath the surface of the fast-moving currents to wash away the sand.

When I surfaced, Gracie emerged from the current at my side. She then insisted on soaping my back, and in spite of the frigid water, I held my place against the current, for I couldn't remember being treated with such tenderness since Mary's care. I returned the favor and together we rinsed off. By that time we were both shaking so severely that Gracie took my hand firmly and walked me toward the clearing so we might dry off.

I was toweling off and whining through chattering teeth about the mercilessly cold water, the obvious insanity of anyone who should willingly cleanse themselves in such a grueling manner, and the cruelty of a certain young person well versed in this little water ritual, when something blue caught my eye. Gracie began brushing out her hair the best she could, it still being coated with the remnants of bear grease. In her hand was a certain blue brush that I positively recognized at once. In one hand she held the brush, in the other a mirror.

"Gracie! What have you there?"

I came across dead serious. The sudden change in my demeanor stopped her laughing at once, she thinking something went wholly amiss.

"Where?"

She spun around to look behind her.

"That brush and mirror?"

She looked at me queerly, and then at the brush and mirror, rotating them slowly as if expecting to discover some hidden jewels heretofore unnoticed.

"Where did you get those?" I asked.

"My dadduh. He gave 'em ta may jus' 'fer he diet. I tolt ye thet. Don' ye 'member?"

"Oh, yes. Yes, you did. I do remember, but I don't recall where you said he got them."

I approached her.

"Et was et a rendezvous up near Beghorn. Es there sump'unt special 'bout 'em?"

I reached out for the brush. Gracie handed it to me willingly.

"Incredible. Unbelievable."

The idea in my head was too outrageous to even contemplate.

"I am certain I purchased a brush and mirror identical to this for a young Indian girl who was badly injured by a runaway coach. That was in Albany, New York, early last summer. Her family was forced to move out west by the army, the last I heard. It was a sad affair to say the very least."

I crossed my breasts with my arms and commenced to shiver vigorously.

176

"Where't they be et now?"

"I don't know. I never found out, I'm sorry to say." I was momentarily pensive. "Shall we get dressed?"

I wasn't about to wait for Gracie's answer. I was cold and sped away in search of warm clothes.

All truth be told, I was invigorated by the chilly waters, and for the moment felt alive and healthy, but I knew this would be short lived. I could feel myself failing rapidly as my body returned to the business of repairing itself. Still, I wished a few more minutes before being bowled over by mounting wave of weakness or worse, nausea. I looked over at Gracie and admired her youthful splendor.

"How would you like to smell as wonderful as lavender?"

"Wot's thet, lavender?"

"Oh, my, my, my. Lavender is my favorite fragrance. Come. Let's open my chest of treasures."

I was again nudged by that ghostly memory that I could not decipher. I struggled to hold on to the fleeting impressions that again vanished at first sound of Gracie's voice.

"Es sump'unt the matter?"

"No, why do you ask?"

"I don' knaw, ye lukt so thoughtful."

"I was trying to…I don't know trying to remember…something. I just can't put my finger on it. It'll come sooner or later."

Gracie moved to my side as I pulled the chest free of the tangled collection of camp gear. I inserted the key, gave it a turn, and lifted the lid.

"I'uz go'un ta open thet weth my knife, but I den't wanna mark et up."

"Well, I certainly appreciate your consideration."

I reached into the chest and removed my jar of lavender cream. I released the leather strap that held the top in place.

"Here…smell this."

I held the jar under her nose.

"Ohhhhhhh."

"Yes, exactly. It's my favorite. Hold still."

I slid my finger across the cream and rubbed it on each side of her neck below the jaw. I did the same for myself.

"There."

"Thank-yeeeeeeeee!"

"You're welcome."

I turned to replace the jar and moved to arrange the items in the chest, now strewn about by the forces of travel. In doing so, I spotted a folded paper in the pocket of the fabric lining. I knew at once—this was the memory calling for my attention. I pulled out the paper and unfolded a letter.

"Wot's thet?"

"Shush."

'No matter how devas------ my situation no matter how far youve watered across the globe when I find you I know I come -----t That's how I feel. I feel is Mary You make me feel --e m--- important. Over the years ---- - feeling that has influ------ me in every way and that's all that matters is the water water is the water. As for back as I can remember it is always been that way.

178

'I've reasoned that life would be an illu---- little more than a ------ if there were no one with whom to share it. Its only wate can I drink Its only It's only by the memories of another that I might exist at all. Its only because I have stored in you memories of me that I am able to go --. I can go back to you say this is who I am and this is where I come from I have done these things good bad and some day I will go from you --- when I return you w--- know me still. The more I look back the more I realize how true ---- is If I didn't have you and Mary if I Mary is I would have anything at all. I love you very much, Claus, plea-- ----- -------------now'

"I love you very much, Claus, please don't leave me now," I whispered aloud.

I remembered only the last line.

"Wot?"

Gracie was burning with curiosity.

It was odd how I was unable to remember writing anything, let alone this fragmented work of a letter. I was amused at how the words seemed to be from the hand of a stranger, but written for my heart alone. Even as clarity abandoned me, even when I was in the worst of condition, my desperation was for Claus. Remembering the last line brought with it all the emotion of my childhood when I believed Christopher could control the seas. Emotions ran deep and sorrowful. I folded the letter and returned it to the pocket.

As expected, my brief explosion of vitality came crashing down, and I found myself barely able to keep open my eyes. I napped much of the afternoon. Later, I joined Gracie in preparing a dinner that held no temptation for me. I picked lightly at a piece

179

of meat then returned to my bed. I spied the blue brush and mirror now lying on Gracie's blanket. I could hardly escape the thought they might very well be the same set I had purchased in Albany.

The brush I had bought wasn't the run-of-the-mill sort, and neither was Gracie's. The chance was astronomical that it should be the same. It was beyond comprehension. How it might have ended up here in the middle of nowhere, out here where only trappers and traders could be found would certainly be a tale to be told. Most unsettling was the idea that such a feat held an uncomfortable possibility that hard times had befallen the child whom I had given the present. I contemplated these impossibilities until my questions slowly merged with my dreams. I recalled nothing of Gracie cuddling up next to me.

* * *

It was the day after next before I awoke truly refreshed and so witnessed Gracie tip-toeing about the camp early of a morning in an attempt to saddle the mules as best she could. She was considerate by nature. She called out to me, only after I began to stir, so I might help her with the tent and my chest. These were the two most cumbersome items in our possession. She was now driven to move on in spite of, or maybe because of, her vague sense of destination.

Either way, I agreed to leave camp on this morning in thanks for the days of rest she had afforded me. The hellish pain of my sunburn was now much subdued. After a winter in the sunless cabin, my color now changed notably darker. My leg was also improved. The swelling was also markedly reduced, the color now changing to match my burned skin. The skin around my bite was starting to crust and shed, and I suspected soon the rest of me would follow suit.

180

We mounted up, and after paying our last respects from the saddle, we started down the mountainside. My attention was riveted to the trail. At times, I was both amused and terrified by its treachery. Although obvious, it must be said that travel on the desert had its vistas, but also at times indescribable boredom, whereas the mountains could equal the views, but on the way up the ground was in your face, and on the way down you felt ready to fall a thousand feet. It was never boring. I couldn't afford to be distracted by anything other than my will to survive the many obstacles intent on spilling man and beast alike. I already possessed enough injury for show.

Gracie continued to make her way north along an unseen path, and as always, unconcerned about her exact whereabouts. Her lack of worry often rattled me. I had to accept this country was second nature to her mind. She didn't question it; she didn't fear it. She simply flowed with its valleys and streams, surefooted and stable. Young Gracie was in her element and genuinely serene.

I was the opposite. I found myself to be nervous, ever queasy, and even disoriented at times. It might have been general fatigue, or the heights and the thin air, but I think I was just plain tired of the situation as a whole. I wanted to go home, but there was no home, and I sensed melancholy creeping close behind to usurp my positive outlook. I imagined the joy of being lazy, to be waking up from a nap at Mary's home in Boston, in my old bed, instead of stammering forward in a relentless drive to survive. I was being mentally attacked by the sheer impossibility of returning to civilization. I reminded myself sarcastically that it was I who wanted something in my life called adventure. I gave up every-thing to have it, and now I would give up everything to lose it.

TWENTY

We had returned to the wagon. It remained unmoved and undisturbed, found exactly as we had left it days before. Unsurprisingly, nobody spotted its miles of tracks, or followed them to steal it away. Gracie now stood alongside it, and stared out across the vast expanse of land she so deeply distrusted. I began to remove my belongings from the pack mules and place them back into the wagon amidst a cloud of uncomfortable silence. A tense and difficult conversation was underway.

"Ye kape sayun' yer my friend, but ye'd leave may, ye'd part ways ta rite out here-there?"

"I have no choice, Gracie. I am too run down to keep up with you. I have no desire whatsoever to return to South Pass, whereas you do, and I can't stay here. My only option is to seek out the Tsistsistas. I believe they are my friends, and if so, they will care for me until I can fully regain my wellness.

"These past few days of rest have helped me immensely, but I'm not yet myself, Gracie, not by a long shot. I do feel better, but I'll need much more than a few days' rest before I take off clear across country. That, my dear child, will require a perfect mix of health, fortitude, and stupidity. I have plenty of stupidity, possibly the fortitude, but lack the good health. A few weeks of honest rest, time enough for these wounds to heal for good, and then after that, then maybe the North Platt and St Louis.

"This much I know for fact. I won't be of any use to you if I am eight hundred miles out and dead. Now, you may come with me if you like—and I wish you would. In fact, I want you to. Or you may set your own course. Should you choose to come with me, I promise you will be safe."

"Safe? Oh, I don' thenk so, Mess Elezabeth. I don' thenk so."

182

Needless to say, my idea of comfort and security was not shared or well received. The look upon Gracie's face might have been described as a driblet of dismay and a bucket of disbelief. She was shaking her head negatively in quick shiver-like movements as she searched for a convincing argument against my designs.

This idea, so unthinkable to Gracie, came to me in a state of despair after I dismounted to stretch beneath the last of the trees. It was then that I observed a column of smoke far to the north and east across the seemingly lifeless plain.

My imagination erupted with visions of Tsistsistas on horseback riding hard to drive buffalo, funneling them into a trap by setting the plains on fire. The Indians would be farther north, having followed the buffalo into the cool green valleys, where the herds grazed the grasses and roamed more agreeable climates for the summer.

A wonderful sense of security and safe haven washed over me. I felt as though every minute I delayed in finding Chief Ho'neheveho and Talk-a-Lot only served to amplify my illness. I wanted to be smothered by the closeness of community. I wanted to nap peacefully during lazy afternoons in tipis teased by the aromas of roasting food. I wanted to lower my guard and recuperate in the care of those I trusted. I wanted to lose myself in a place that suffered no ties to any world of mine.

One thing was painfully obvious—my talk about seeking out the Tsistsistas devastated Gracie. As I finished transferring the last of my stores, she grew visibly anxious, visibly distraught. Thoughts of Indians clearly mortified her. It would take a concerted effort on my part to stay ahead of such deep-rooted anxieties. Who, better than I, understood the difficulty of overcoming these childhood fears? I had suffered many a nightmare after listening to horrific stories of Indian barbarity from the Americans.

I could only imagine the stories her father had conjured up in order to assure himself she would stay quiet and hidden when he deemed it necessary. There were many occasions when I overheard Mary tell the most preposterous stories in order to frighten her boys away from swamps or strangers or anything else that caused her concern.

To me now, those outrageous tales were laughable, even hysterical, but remembering those occasions kept me from blaming Mr. Castleman. I understood. Yet, it would be up to me to protect his daughter emotionally, and at the same time bring a new and balanced point of view into her life about these colorful and inspiring nomadic people.

"How many friends do you have Gracie? How many friends have you ever had?"

"Frients?"

"Yes, friends. You know, children your own age. Children with whom you play hide and seek, and skip rope, and make believe, and all the things children do. Friends, Gracie, just friends, nothing more, nothing less."

"I..."

Gracie's mind stalled. Her eyes were blank. She couldn't answer my question. She couldn't even shroud the confusion I infused behind those dazzling green eyes. The thought of *friends* seemed to make her almost as nervous as the thought of Indians. I could see that the idea of encountering others was not an easy prospect for this girl. She knew nothing of relationships. She knew nothing of friendships. She knew only survival.

"My word, Gracie, you are countless years too old for your age. You think of me as your friend—and I am your friend—but there are other types of friendship, important friendships that stay with you for life. My friend Mary has stood at my side, has supported me, has given me her shoulder to cry upon since we were children, the same age as you. I would give up my life for her, Gracie. That is what friendship means.

"Out there, where the Tsistsistas live, there are hundreds of children your age. They play together, they hunt together, they sit around campfires and sing together, they dance together; they grow up together and remain friends as did Mary and I. You could have many friends for life, Gracie. But you first have to meet them. And that won't happen wandering alone out here in the woods because friends aren't found hanging upside down from trees you hike beneath."

Gracie stood quiet and studied me. She digested every word I said in silence. She was struggling to comprehend my words, struggling to envision what I pictured. Still, fear remained the overriding factor.

"Cain't I fin' frients en South Pay-ass 'r St. Louis?"

"In St. Louis you could find a million friends. In South Pass there are very few children, and it would be difficult. But for you to get to St. Louis, you are undertaking one very long and difficult journey. If you made it there with only scars, let alone your life, it would be a miracle of no small significance. I made that journey, Gracie, and have no doubt when I say I saw the many faces of death.

"On the other hand, if we spend time with the Tsistsistas, we would be better prepared. Should we stay a while, you would learn a great deal about life on the plains and how to survive the trip to St. Louis. You would learn to ride horses and fly through the wind. You know the woods and high country, Gracie. Now it's time to learn the vast spaces of the flat lands. They would teach you well."

It was not at all easy. Gracie took her daddy's words to heart and believed with the strongest conviction that she should be heading northwest to South Pass. It didn't help that I appeared exactly what I was—*weak*. She could see that plain enough, and was certain to have entertained fears of me dropping dead on her, as did her folks, and leaving her miles out on the plain amongst what she considered to be a bunch of wild, heartless, butchering heathens.

It wasn't Gracie's fault she suffered such fears, but she would have to face them if she planned on staying with me, for I had no doubts about the direction I was heading. I felt bad for her because I could see she was caught between terrible apprehensions of being separated from me, should she strike out alone across an unknown land, or remaining at my side to feel temporarily secure, but later be trapped in the fearful clutches of Indians and all her childhood nightmares.

I was in no need to hurry my departure, and most certainly preferred to take whatever time necessary to address Gracie's long list of dreads. I wanted very much for her to accompany me. I knowingly feared for her safety traveling anywhere by herself in this world. She was too young and too pretty. Her youth, beauty, and naiveté would be her demise in a man's world.

I stayed with her for a final night's rest before leaving the woods and striking out eastward across the flats. During our evening, we filled our bellies with fresh meat and berries. We filled our heads full with engaging conversation about the Tsistsistas in general, and about how I met Chief Ho'neheveho and Talk-a-Lot.

The discussions continued over breakfast the following morning. She was both curious and captivated by my stories of these two Indian friends, and that was a good thing. She was beginning to identify them as caring people with hearts and ideals.

"Do you trust me, Gracie?"

"Yut."

Her answer came truthfully, but not without reservation.

"I know I appear weak and sickly in body, but here in my head, I am only focused on caring for you. If you trust me, I will see you to safety, and I promise to show you a world that is all of the stores, and streets, and ribbons and bows, and dresses, and carriages, and every other imaginable wonder your eyes might ever dream to behold. This I can do, and this I promise."

After hours of exhausting conversation, I prevailed. I succeeded in, if not dispelling, at least diminishing the heretofore undisputed teachings of her parents—this being no small feat.

"Very well, time has come. How about we try and harness the mules once again?"

"Esset better ta take thiccy wagun 'r leave et?"

"To take it. For now, it is best to keep the mules ladened and the wagon light. But when we first spot an Indian, if at all possible, we should place your stores into the wagon and hide them from view. There's no point in us first having to face hearts blackened by the temptation of all that glitters."

Gracie said nothing further. She was wary, but after all was said and done, I managed to coax her down the slopes of her mountain home and towering fears, and out onto the desert plains with me. Of course, only I could have known who rode at my side because Gracie wasn't about to forward one foot into desert sand searching for Indians without following to the letter her daddy's instructions. In spite of the fact she had managed to wash out most of the mess in her hair, she showed no hesitation in greasing up and sporting all the shrunken skulls.

I agreed she should do whatever made her feel most at ease, but I could only shake my head with wonder. She did herself up, and studied her work in that blue-handled looking glass. When she concluded her final touches, I was forced to admit she once again looked like one of Hell's own, plucked straight out of Satan's lair.

187

TWENTY-ONE

I believe Gracie spotted the first Indian we were to see, hours before he ever arrived. Her dread of this inevitable encounter became an obsession, an all-consuming fear that was certain to drive her crazy. She hardly spoke a word as the tree line and mountain slopes fell away behind us lest her attention, now entirely riveted to the endless miles of nothing, be drawn aside, leaving her prone to unwanted attack.

She scoured every passing foot of the surrounding plains, and never failed to suspect an Indian or some other unknown danger lurking in each one of those nearly imperceptible shadows. Shadows, I could only hope to discern in the penetrating light of a midday sun. Shadows, her fragile-looking finger pointed to somewhere far off in the haze of distance. We were bound to run into Indians at some point in time, but not nearly as many as we were apt to find within the realm of an overactive imagination. Given half a chance, Gracie could have stared through solid stone and spotted Indians.

All the effort Gracie expended searching hills, scrutinizing shadows, and anticipating ambushes proved to be a monumental waste of energy. Her efforts were entirely unnecessary. For when the Indian appeared, he sat proudly upon his horse before God, all creation, and the two of us. The outline of the man was clearly defined on the horizon. He was not stooping behind sagebrush, cowering, or crawling about on all four. He was not lying in wait half buried in the sand.

Quite the opposite, in fact, he sat forward and erect, and it was clear he had no reason to hide. We were in his land and we could feel it. All the while we watched him, he watched us as the wagon and our mules plodded along carrying Gracie and I closer to his command. It remained thus for some time, a visual engagement, the three of us staring at each other before the lone

188

Indian was apparently satisfied sufficient enough to leave. He turned about and disappeared over a distant rise. Gracie was numb with fear.

"Where's et to, he went?"

"I'd say he's going to tell the others that we're approaching camp. It won't be too long before a scouting party comes to meet us."

"We gawtta go back! We cain't go on. We gawtta go back now!"

Gracie was adamant, having been struck by pure panic at the thought of a party of Indians heading our way. All my prior coaxing went out the window.

"What are you saying?"

"We gawtta go back! We gawtta go now 'fer they come back long ta get us."

"Go back where, Gracie?"

"Back long ta they mount'uns where et's safe, wot d'ye thenk! I don' like thes one bet, Mess Elezabeth. Injuns, they be terr'ble, terr'ble. Ye don' knaw wot they're gonna do. They coult ait us, er tie us ta a stake en' shoot us full o' arrows...er...er roast us 'live. Ye don' knaw. Now, let's jus' get outta here, Mess Elezabeth. Please, let's git! Let's jus' git."

I halted my team as I watched Gracie prod Kelly to turn about. She wasn't even looking back to see if I was following. She was urging her mule to step up the pace, but the animal wasn't having any of it. I hollered out to her backside.

"What are you thinking, Gracie? You can't go back. You're riding a mule for heaven's sake. They are riding horses, and very fast horses at that. You wouldn't put a mile behind you, before they caught up with you."

189

"Appen ef we git now en' hurry!"

"Gracie, listen to me. Look! Look before you." I raised my hand to point westward. "Look at where those mountains lie. It's too late to go back. First of all, it's too far. Secondly, go back to what? Do you wish to live up in those hills, and wander on your own until who knows when, until you stumble into another wandering soul who hopefully is still sane or crazy as you? I would hope not. Accept it, Gracie, you are surrounded by Indians; Indians here; Indians there; Indians everywhere! This is their land, and that's the long and short of it.

"I hear you say to me that you are headed for St. Louis. Well, the only thing between you and St. Louis, Missouri, is a thousand miles of wide open space, all of it inhabited by Indians. Now you can run and they will be upon you within the hour, or you can shake in your boots and mess your pants, or you can stand up and face what comes your way at my side—your choice."

I quieted momentarily so to gather my thoughts.

"I don't want you to think I ever said you should be a fool or throw caution to the wind, I didn't. I only said, I have lived with these Indians, they are hospitable, and they are survivors. They know this land and they know how to deal with it. I spent time with them, and they aren't as savage as you might think. They may be your only hope out here, especially on this ground."

I pointed down with emphasis, but her eyes were fixed away from me, steadfast upon the mountains in the distance.

"And, Gracie, sweetheart… If you can't see it with your own eyes, then let me spell it out. I—don't—feel—good. As a matter of fact, if you want to know the truth of it, I feel downright miserable. I need to rest ,girl, and these people can give me a chance to get my strength back. They can give us shelter and food for whatever time we need."

If I hadn't raised the smallest doubt within Gracie that the Indians would have reached her before she could have made it back to the foothills, she would have left me without so much as a glance to the rear, not even taking her belongings. But she did look back. She halted Kelly. She looked back over her shoulder to study me.

"Don't forget what I told you. I am Chieftess Vehona'e. I am Chief Woman—."

"I don' thenk so," she said from the safety of distance. "I thenk yer Chief Crazy, ef anytheng. Chinny reckon yer Chieftess Too Long en the Sun."

I didn't have to see her emerald eyes. I could feel them.

"Really!"

I looked at her disdainfully.

"You think I just made all that up? You think I lie? Fine! I'm a liar. Why not? Liar, spinster, whore, killer, I'm everything else these days."

"My dadduh always sait, *"Booty, thet desert drives people ensane."* I'd like ta believe all them thengs ye say but—."

"I'm not crazy, Gracie. I know I told you some stories that seem unbelievable, but how could I make up so much? I told you before: the Tsistsistas made me a chieftess because they believed I proved myself to be brave and generous. I brought them many gifts—."

"Yut, ye also sait thet those gifts came fram a wagon thet hat ghosts livun en et weth ya," Gracie interrupted.

Unfortunately, I had said as much. There was no way out of that. It occurred to me that this time around I wasn't going to win through persuasion.

191

"I can't argue that. Oh, well...I will tell you this, Gracie. Crazy or not, I am headed for the camp. You can continue heading back to the mountains if you like, but it won't make much difference. The Indians will catch you, and I will be seeing you in camp one way or the other—a guest or a prisoner. So, till then."

I nudged my team forward. It was my turn not to look back.

"Better unhitch your mules from the wagon; you're going to need all that gear."

Having left her with that thought, it wasn't long before I could hear the bells that adorned her collection of heads as she closed in on me from behind. I stopped the wagon when she came abreast.

"Get your belongings off the mules and into the wagon, and be quick about it."

I had nothing else to add, and my patience wouldn't have allowed much additional. We were both irritated and shared nary a word as we prodded the mules and scanned the horizon for what we knew was about to come.

It was late afternoon when, as I suspected, a party of braves, numbering about twenty or so, streaked diagonally across the horizon, returning in force from the northeast. They had come to investigate what their lone sentry had seen. They were riding swiftly and disappeared into a distant hollow for a brief moment, their position divulged only by a thick cloud of yellow dust rising out of the lowland before they broke once again into view over the crest of a closer rise.

Gracie was riddled with fear. She began to fumble about nervously through the pockets of her backpack. The passing hours of silence had settled me and I honestly felt bad for her cause. I knew all about her fear, having experienced it many times. I couldn't help myself but to try and console her.

"Now what are you doing?"

"Nawthun."

She was curt.

"Oh my word, not more of that stuff. Oh, Gracie, I don't believe you."

She said nothing in reply to my disbelief, but went about at frantic pace, adding grease to her hair and stain to her face. She opened the bell-covered bag that hung off her saddle, and yanked out the remaining shrunken skulls to display about her mule. Poor girl, I thought with ruefulness.

The sun was barreling across the desert from the west, it being at our backs. It glared from the lowered angle of late afternoon working to scrape along the ground and wedge light between the earth and darkened storm clouds lying heavy in the northeast.

A hard amber light washed over gentle waves of sparsely covered land that rolled ahead to lead us. The infinite sunshine swept through the Indians like a golden wind to slow their advance. They took a stance before us, upon a rise that crossed to our left. As they sat abreast upon spotted horses in their vivid dress and face paint, they countered the intense hues of a waning sun. Garnished in such prominent displays, they rose up spectacularly from the ageless sands of insignificance that threatened to swallow us.

My heart went out to Gracie, she being in the worst way. She was unable to speak and so sat squirming in her saddle, whereas, I on the other hand, found myself lost for words to describe how thrilling it was to see these warriors again. To be sure, I wasn't without concern, but my apprehensions were tempered by what small understanding I had gained of these people through my former acquaintance. I could never say in truth that I knew the Cheyenne, or that I was perfectly comfortable with them, but in my brief stay with Talk-a-Lot and Chief Ho'neheveho, I discovered many things, some things obvious to the average eye, others learned only by close association.

Based on my learning, I believed these men to be Dog Soldiers. They were a fair distance from us, but the crisp notes of their whistles moved easily past us in spite of the wind in our ears. I could make out the necklets pulled about their necks, which I knew, fastened the collections of eagle bones. It was these bones used for making whistles that the younger warriors blew so fervently. I also perceived the diagonal shards of black raven feathers jutting out from their hair. It made for a silhouette I had seen in the distance many times before.

"They are Dog Soldiers, Gracie, the most ferocious of all the Tsistsistas' soldier bands. Their bravery is above question, for their role is to sacrifice themselves in battle to defend their tribe and families. When a Dog Soldier stakes the earth, he commits himself to death before dishonor and vows to stand his ground. Only if and when a comrade in battle should remove the stake shall he be set free to retreat from battle. Can you imagine such character?"

I looked at Gracie and realized anything I should say would serve only to further her fears. So this pleasure was to be unshared. To see them was exhilarating—a mixture of excitement and danger. We were wholly at their mercy. It was like cuddling with a catamount.

Contrary to what Gracie believed, I knew that I was considered a good spirit amongst many of the Tsistsistas, as well as an honorary chieftess, and my appearance would be cause for celebration in the right circles. Of course, what I didn't mention to Gracie was how much I pinned hopes on one of these Indians also being aware of these same facts.

Five or six of the Indians broke rank and bolted forward at once, moving down the slope in our direction. Another five or six followed on their heels. Fast into a gallop, the horses kicked up dirt and dust that sailed upward in their wake, falling back to earth behind a show of fluttering feathers and flapping leggings. The youngest of the Indian braves came at us first with many of the older boys following in close pursuit. They were hollering, blowing their whistles, and whelping out their war cries.

"Mess Elezabeth…. Mess Elezabeth!"

Gracie's voice rose in both pitch and desperation.

I looked across at her. Her face displayed the severity of strain she endured as she struggled to keep her courage. Her eyes clearly revealed her terror. I dismounted the wagon in our last moment and stepped over to console her. I held out my hand to take hers.

"Come with me, Gracie. Things will work out. I know you think I must be insane, but I promise you I'm not. Come with me now."

By the look of her, she had resigned herself to a horrible death. She wavered between instinct and reason, but in the end as the braves drew near, as the thunder of their horses' hooves met our ears, she gave me her hand and all her faith, for there was little else she could do.

I helped her and the tangle of shrunken heads slide off the mule. My hands gripped her waist firmly and because of it, I could feel her body quaking. Her breathing was shallow and rapid. Her knees were failing as I assisted her to the ground. She gripped my dress and clung to me so fearfully, I was unable to move at will.

"It'll be fine, Gracie. I promise. Relax a little. That's better. Now let's walk out and meet them."

She seemed so young to me at this moment. Had it not been for all the grease, I would have taken her into a tight embrace and reassured her. I would have kissed her affectionately upon the head as a mother would her child. Instead, I unclamped her fists and pulled her by the arms, firmly guiding her around to my side, so we might walk forward together from where the wagon rested. I mostly dragged her to greet the braves.

I was correct in assuming these Indians to be Dog Soldiers. I found myself relieved beyond measure to know positively that I had located the Tsistsistas instead of the dreaded Blackfeet or Comanche. I knew no other tribes and so feared those Indians as much as did Gracie.

The youngest boys, those of about eight to twelve years of age, came riding in first full of warrior dreams and fighting spirit. But once they were close enough to appreciate Gracie in all her glory, they turned about abruptly and began high-tailing it back across the field. Their actions immediately raised concern in the minds of the older boys who were following them in a second wave. The older boys, now themselves wary, slowed their approach and likewise turned back at the sight of Gracie. The odd behavior of these young warriors was well viewed and witnessed by the older experienced men, who remained on their horses, side by side, along the crest of the rise.

A sense of relief forced a smile to creep secretly across my face. I couldn't help but be amused by the reaction of these warriors, whose bravery was legendary. They stumbled the instant they got an eyeful of Gracie. Not unlike the older men atop the ridge, I also knew what was supposed to have taken place. I understood that the older warriors realized something was amiss long before they received word from the returning boys. I knew about the taking and counting of coup. I learned it firsthand in Chief Ho'neheveho's lodge.

"Well, Gracie, you most certainly made an impression. There's no denying it."

"I tolt ye injuns dent like speret haits," she whispered.

"Yes, you did say that."

Gracie easily read the troubled and suspicious looks upon the warrior's faces. Their response filled her with a small measure of reassurance. I had learned enough over time to know that although clashes between warring braves was a blood-letting ordeal, if given the opportunity, braves always preferred to first approach the enemy without the benefit of a weapon. It was for the purpose of touching their foe.

"They only wanted ta touch may?"

Gracie was bewildered.

"They wanted to count coup. But that didn't happen."

"Count coup?"

It was a good thing that Gracie's curiosity always overshadowed everything, including her fears. I was more than happy to have a conversation that might help me regain something of the trust she had lost.

"Well, oftentimes, in spite of what you might think, these Indians have no intention of harm whatsoever. Their only ambition is to prove their bravery by simply touching you. But don't misunderstand me, that is no small feat, and except for what just happened here, their intent generally scares the daylights out of the person being touched, not the person doing the touching.

"Unfortunately, when these Indians come riding up like murdering maniacs with faces all painted up and yelping and carrying-on, most people assume they are about to be hatcheted to death or worse. I have little doubt it has cost more than one brave his life, getting himself gunned down but for a complete misunderstanding of his intentions."

"Any fool who does sump'unt thet stupit des—."

"Not stupid, Gracie. Not stupid, and not a fool. Just something you don't understand. I mean, look at you, standing here shaking in your boots. You can barely speak…your voice quivers so. I'd like to see you walk up there and touch one of those warriors."

"I sait *injuns* were stupit, nawt may."

"Well, keep that thought in mind because here comes another one, and he isn't a boy, and I'll just bet he isn't stupid either."

Gracie's emerald eyes went wide open. We watched as an older, more experienced brave bolted out from the line and headed directly for us at a full gallop.

"I promise you, this warrior won't be of a mind to retreat. If you're smart, you will show him of what you are made. You just stand up straight, stay put, and hold your ground."

Gracie had yet to learn that in a society where courage was the backbone of survival, to charge weaponless into the ranks of the enemy and touch him on his own ground was one of the highest forms of bravery that could be exhibited. It earned a man enormous respect amongst his peers and the accounts of his feat would be told over and over again. Not just in his honor before the younger warriors, but more important, to reinforce the importance and degree of courage required of every warrior. He would be called upon by the chiefs to give an account of all his courageous acts at social and religious events for all the years of his life.

"The warriors will want to touch *you*, Gracie, because you are the more fearful of us. By a long shot, I might add."

"He won' hurt may?"

"I don't think so. Of course, he might have heard you call him stupid—sound certainly carries on the wind. I know I wouldn't care much for that."

I didn't take my eyes off the approaching warrior, but I imagined Gracie went faint. The comment was utterly cruel on my part, but I didn't like the way she so quickly degraded something she didn't understand. Still, I had to relent for I knew she was but a child.

"I'm just kidding, Gracie. I am certain he wants only his coup. He is going to prove himself, prove his bravery to the others."

We watched as a second, third, and fourth brave, all appearing older and experienced, left ranks to charge us. Three men were allowed to accept credit for such bravery. I spoke out the corner of my mouth, for my eyes never left the advancing riders.

"Don't move, Gracie. They won't hurt you."

Gracie didn't answer. She had lost her tongue.

"Between all of them, they can only touch you three times, after that it brings no merit. Only three men can claim the feat of bravery."

A few of the younger braves, now feeling more secure, turned back toward us and fell in behind their mentors. The remainder, not wishing to look cowardly, took up the rear of the charge.

We stood our ground and we stood tall. We were very nearly overrun by the stampeding horses as they brushed by us. Having a full-grown horse gallop past you at arm's length is frightful enough, let alone seeing it mounted by a painted Indian brandishing sticks and lances.

As I had predicted, we were struck repeatedly, sometimes lightly, sometimes painfully, but we were not intentionally harmed. In the end, I had been touched many times, mostly by the youngest, but Gracie said she had only been touched thrice. Not once by a boy. I wasn't surprised.

"Thet made 'em feel brave? Hettun two wemen?"

"One woman and a thing. Not hitting—*touching*. And I am certain that touching women does not make them feel brave.

But facing a spirit does. It was you who kept telling me how afraid the Indians were of your spirit heads. In fact, it looked to me like you were banking your life upon it. So, either it is you, who is incredibly stupid for caking yourself in bear grease and berries, or you are especially clever for being so frightful. I trust it's the latter, and you are indeed frightful, and only a truly brave warrior would dare face your spirits head on."

I felt as though Gracie got the point. Either way, after having proved their bravery, the Indians stood off at a distance for some time conversing amongst themselves. I had little doubt that everything about us was perplexing to them.

"We need to welcome them."

"Why?"

"To let them know that in spite of your greasy spiritual beauty, we mean them no harm."

"Oh."

At no time during their conversation did the warriors drop their guard. If not one, then another would hold us fixed firmly in his stare, and so it was no effort to get their attention. I pointed to myself with the thumb of my right hand and then raised my hand to make a circle in the air like a halo to signify this was about Gracie and me. I then held my index and middle finger pointed upward alongside my head to signify friend. I made a motion as if tipping a cup toward my mouth. Lastly, holding my hand to my mouth, I snapped my index finger off my thumb as if to flick something away. These gestures meant I wanted to speak, one might say, to throw out words. I repeated these gestures a number of times. By the third time, I had the attention of all.

It was just then, as if to appease an audience, that Gracie suddenly stepped forward and copied part of my signing. Only she went on to place her hands at her mid-section, and spread her hands outward. She then raised her right hand, palm outward, and pointed her index and middle fingers upward, after which she spiraled them toward the heaven.

I was completely dumbstruck.

"You know how to sign? Are you kidding me? You, the morbidly frightened, run-for-the-hills-child, know how to sign—."

I was stunned, lost for words. She had told the warriors that she was a friend of the Great Spirit. What next! I thought to myself.

"I don't believe it. I spend hours trying to coax you into going with me to meet the Indians and you just toddle forward and start signing as if you're having a tea *party social*. You told them you are a friend of the Great Spirit? Unnnnn-beeee-lievable."

I stood there, jaw ajar, staring at her. I wanted to be angry in the worst way. The girl had a way of making me feel like the stupidest of fools.

"How do you know signing?"

"I always known et. I tolt ye, my dadduh made may hite en the wuds while he en' momma went 'bout their bus'ness. Offen times, I'd haff ta lay quiet-like fer hours. Weren't much ta do but watch my folks en' the injuns do tradun. My dadduh dit aver'thun by signun cuz them injuns were fram all parts en' all talkt diff'ernt. I got ta wheres I coult knaw wot they's signun real gud fram afar—long uz there's enough light ta make et out."

I needed a moment to digest the information, trample my impulse to be angry, and overcome my disbelief.

"I see. Well…. Sweetheart, you won't be having any problems with Indians. You already know far more than I did the first time I met the Cheyenne."

"How'd ye talk ta 'em?"

"It wasn't easy. I was picking thistles out of my ass for a month."

I went back to signing, expressing my friendship, and encouraging the Indians to advance. Gracie's father knew his business almost too well. The knowledge he passed on to his daughter was as much my hindrance as my salvation. The look of her was enough to stand off the worst that a wild uncivilized West had to offer.

"I think it might be a good idea for you to put away those heads. They have served their purpose."

"I'll put away...thaccy on *Kelly*."

"Fine. Not what I had in mind, but it's a start—put away Kelly's."

Eventually, the warriors' apprehensions gave way to the inescapable draw of curiosity. And so, after a great deal of gesturing on both of our parts, trying to convince the Indians that Gracie was a good spirit, it became obvious they wished to approach. I played on their curiosity as best I could.

"Turn around, Gracie."

"Why?"

"I want them to see your blond hair. I want to spread it out. Now turn around."

I turned Gracie around and displayed the backside of her ungreased blonde hair, as I did my own. The color mesmerized the men who knew only a world of black hair, black eyes, and ruddy complexions. If it hadn't been for hair color, something I pointed out repeatedly, the Indians might not have come within ten miles of us without first going back for their medicine man.

I knew the warriors had not been initially threatened by our approach because when they returned from their camp they had brought many young boys. This was a good sign. The older would not wish harm to come to the younger, and so I imagined they would not be apt to make sudden or irrational moves when they confronted us.

But it seemed the warriors were in no hurry to meet us, and most of an hour passed before the party as a whole finally moved our way and cautiously surrounded us. The men halted their horses before us and stared thoroughly mystified. Their faces said as much. They studied us from every angle, nudging their horses first to our left and then our right, in front of us and then behind. I raised my hand in greeting in order to end the trance. I then pointed to myself.

"Vehona'e." This caused an immediate stir. The men spoke excitedly amongst themselves. I turned to Gracie.

"It means Chief Woman. See, I wasn't lying."

I tried to reassure her. I turned back to them. I pointed my hands toward Gracie.

"Gracie. Náhevése'enôtse (She is my friend)."

The men studied her the way a cat studies a snake—intently. They were wholly perplexed, unable to take their eyes off of her, and unwilling to approach too close. Because of our hair color, they undoubtedly assumed Gracie was a spirit child of mine... and visibly astonished by the horrific spirit I had fostered.

As their concerns appeared to settle, mine increased, for I was most unnerved to discover that there had been a medicine man amongst their number. I had vivid memories of how persuasive these men could be. He would have the first and last word on whatever next would take place. And so, it was now I who became apprehensive. I studied their faces, wondering what decision might be made when suddenly a seemingly small mishap occurred.

Mounted on a horse, a leading brave sat quietly watching us. He was wearing a necklet fashioned of the usual eagle claws, bird heads, feathers, and other significant artifacts. To his surprise and dismay, the necklet had come undone. Before he could catch the falling piece, it dropped to the ground directly in front of where we stood.

I knew at once the outcome of our arrival could be influenced by this turn of events. I had been told by Talk-a-Lot, after witnessing some strange behavior following a similar incident that it was absolutely forbidden for a Dog Soldier, once he was seated upon his horse, to retrieve any item dropped to the ground. Having learned of this, I acted at once to address Gracie as though pushed by divine intervention.

"Gracie, walk forward slowly with absolute confidence, and pick up the fallen necklet. Do it now, girl, show no fear and much good may come of it. Pay close attention to what I say."

To my surprise, she stepped forward without question or hesitation. Startled by her advance, the men nudged their horses back from her in unison. They were still plenty wary of her, and for good reason. From a spiritual point of view, visually, it was hard to believe she could be anything good. In fact, the medicine man was the first to retreat.

"Hold the necklet up to the sky and offer God a prayer of thanks. You might as well make it for real. We can use all the help we can get."

Gracie held up the necklet as I said, and thanked the Lord profusely for every second she stood on her feet still breathing the sweet air of life.

"Well done, that's plenty good. He's heard you. Now, lower it to the ground, and say another prayer to Mother Earth. Make this one shorter, I don't want anybody getting impatient…. That's good enough. Now, hold it up and offer a quick word of thanks to the four directions, face the East. Do it.... Now, the South. Yes.... Now, the West and then the North.... Perfect. Now, offer it back to him. Look him straight in the face; meet his stare with those incredible green eyes of yours. They think you are a powerful spirit, and I see no reason to change their minds."

She did exactly as I instructed to the word. She raised the necklet for him to accept. She looked at him with an icy green boldness, and it was he who averted his eyes. He glanced at her with much reservation, at first unsure of what to do, until the medicine man, moved forward and encouraged the brave to retrieve his possession. He did as the medicine man instructed, but it was done with a snatch. He chose not to put the necklet back on, but instead tied it to the mane of his horse. I knew he worried it may have been desecrated by evil spirits that he feared Gracie might harbor.

The medicine man slipped off his horse and walked over toward us. He was adorned with a good number of stones, herbs, bird heads, animal claws, dead lizards, baby turtles, and other animal remnants that possessed their particular spiritual powers. The influence of the man made me very uneasy, and I hoped he was blind to the insecurity I attempted to conceal. I remembered all too clearly my first encounter with Ma'heo'ôhme'ehnêstse (Medicine Comes In Sight), the medicine man who visited us in Chief Ho'neheveho's lodge. He carried much weight and scared me half to death before I earned his friendship. That friendship did not come easy.

This medicine man opened up a pouch and removed what looked to be a piece of bitterroot, which he put into his mouth and chewed. He then held out his palms and spit upon them rubbing the saliva about. He raised his palms to the sky and then turned them over and held them over the earth. He held them up to the four directions and then passed his hands over his arms, his shoulders, after which he did the same to both Gracie and I. He

205

raised his rattle and shook it all about us, front and back, side to side, and began to chant. When he was finished purifying us, he looked me in the eyes.

"Nétónêševéhe? (What's your name?)"

"Vehona'e. Nétónêševéhe? (Chief Woman. What is your name?)," I asked.

"Hotoama'heo'o."

I did not understand the meaning of his name, but immediately followed my question with an assertive suggestion.

"Nóheto ov tipi Ho'neheveho (Let us go to tipi of Chief Wolf)."

Hotoama'heo'o was much surprised by my request and turned to speak to the mounted braves. After a lively discussion, in which many of the others offered some advice, he turned back to me and motioned with his arms.

"Nóheto! (Let us go!)"

Once the boys overcame their wariness and abandoned their wide-eyed stares, there commenced a great melee. The youngest braves made most of the noise as they fine tuned their war cry skills, blew their eagle bone whistles, and worked their way through the older braves in order to touch us. They were counting coup amongst themselves as a game. They were very aware of Gracie's young age and flocked to be near her.

The oldest of the braves must have determined all of this to be a good sign, and so appearing filled with new confidence, he barked out an order. Two of the men nearest him dismounted at once and offered us their horses. This was in keeping with their values of honor and generosity, both mandatory virtues if a brave should aspire to become a chief later in life.

I motioned with signs that Gracie and I needed to drive the wagon. I was certain to include Gracie, who had reattached herself to my dress. She showed no desire to leave my side, and so I asked if she wished to ride with me. There was no second thought on the matter. I climbed onto the wagon. And after quickly lashing Kelly to the gate, Gracie climbed up alongside me. In fact, she mostly sat on top of me. Her insecurity brought me a perverse sense of pleasure, for it made me feel needed as the mother I might have been. The feel of her nearness was inexplicably soothing, and I was contented to have her.

"We be really a chieftess then?"

"Yes, and if you don't do as I say, it'll be me who ties you to a stake, shoots you full of arrows, and eats your roasted remains."

Gracie laughed, but it was an uneasy laughter.

TWENTY-TWO

By best guess, we rode some three hours, most of the evening in a northeasterly direction toward a towering rock formation. The sun had fallen away, and the rock remained the only feature tall enough to snag the last reddish rays of light along hard edges of its uppermost reaches.

By contrast, the trees crowding its base disappeared into the shadows of the plains as darkness washed through the wood to rise higher and higher, clinging to the striated surfaces of the vertical walls of stone. Within the murkiness that blanketed the escarpment below, we entered a large sweeping canyon that fed and followed a wide shallow stream. In the silence of nightfall, the stream funneled us upward toward an immense shimmer of activity.

We had arrived.

Off in the distance, in what little light remained, one could make out various sized groups of Indians heading quietly up the valley, returning to their lodges after a day's work. I knew this life. With eyes closed, I would know men were returning from the hunt. Women who joined them were bringing back bloody slabs of bison draped over their horses. Other women were bringing back bundles of firewood for the morning fires. Braves, standing watch over women gathering firewood or digging for roots, would now be escorting them home in the twilight of day's finality. Young boys charged with guarding the horses that grazed on the slopes would be driving their small herds back toward camp to be staked at their owners' lodges for the night. I knew the sight of our wagon making its approach would escape none of those vigilant eyes. Word of our approach would reach camp long before our arrival.

The settlement was spread out evenly across the gently rising slope. To the farthest extent of the camp, fire pits were lit that formed stark triangular silhouettes in the foreground. The bases of many other tipis glowed softly from within, each lodge expressing the comfort to be found hovering about their warming fires and embers. Occasional sparks could be seen escaping through smoke holes, spiraling briefly upward along plumes of hot air that rose faintly in straight columns as if to support the blue-black expanse of a stilled night sky. The infinite uncaring universe above our heads only added to the allure of humanity below with its beckoning images made all the more cozy and inviting.

The sensation was strange. I was at once both unsettled and serene as if floating undisturbed upon the surface of a deep mysterious pond. I suffered no pain but to know what fear lurked beneath. Viewing the camp did make me realize how tired I was, and how much I wished only to lie down undisturbed upon the thickest buffalo hide to be found so I might sleep forever.

Contrary to that wish, any desire to sleep was unshared in this place before us. The later the hour, the darker the earth, the more evident was the activity. We were in earshot of the tribe, and the strange and exotic sounds of nightlife emanated from there within. The campfires were casting their flickering lights, and the rhythmic songs of prayer and feast chants carried across the expanse. The children could be heard, their voices joining in a continuous din of yells and laughter as they stampeded amidst the tipis, playing hide and seek, hunt and kill, or any one of a number of games that taught boys to become formidable braves, and girls…squaws who would one day command respect. To the outermost tipi, silence was ruffled by the random eruptions of drum beats, whistles and yelps, the chorus of betting gangs—the winners and the losers. Even the softest whispers beneath blankets draped over the heads of courting couples added to the mix. All of these sounds merged into one voice that was ready to eat, ready to play and relax.

We eased the wagon carefully across the stony, rock-strewn bed of the stream. Beyond the banks, there was a covering of grasses and wildflowers sporting subtle glows of white and yellow flowers barely perceptible in the dim light of a crescent moon. A moon that began to bounce rays of cold light off standing pools of water. A woman could be nothing, if not immediately sedated and intoxicated by unseen blossoms blending fragrances of vanilla, almonds, honey, and the intense currents of spice.

A mist softly padded the riverbed. There resounded a chorus of frogs and toads, some rapidly clacking, some grunting and chirping, others sounding their *um-rum-um-rum* in the reeds like seasoned cellos. Now, the howl of the wolf and the bark of the coyote summoned life at our feet to awaken and stir. Life, hiding from the heat of a suffering sun, now sprung forth to enjoy the security and coolness of night. The drone of crickets and unseen creatures carried through the air, being fractured only by the clomping of horse hooves or the sound of the prayer drum—the beating of which played upon my ears and Gracie's fears.

For me, these were all reassuring signs testifying to the tenacity of life, the way in which it held on in this harsh, desolate land. This was the music of God's creation where, in order to overcome the odds, man merged with nature in perfect harmony. The collection of sounds and sights served to instill within me a sudden rush of euphoria, a rush of memories that spoke of a better time. I was grateful to be returned.

"Isn't that the most wonderfully peaceful sight you have ever seen—the glow of the tipis, the fires, the children playing, the richness of life in this brutally unforgiving land?"

"Fer ye, mebbe."

Gracie had a way of dampening my perfect mood in the split of a second. It felt like a wasp sting. This time I stung back.

"The word is *you*, Gracie, not *ye*; it's *maybe* not *mebbe*. The word is *for*, and not *fer*. *Fur* grows on animals. *For* means many things, but nothing to do with animal hides. If I manage one thing only, in my acquaintance with you, it will be to teach you to speak some form of English that the rest of us can understand."

"I do speak proper Ainglish. My par'nts were fram Ainglant."

"Debatable. You grew up conversing with trees. How would you know?"

My sudden fall from tranquility left me irritable.

"If it's of any consolation, had they planned to eat you, Gracie, you probably would have already been skinned, scalped, and gutted by now."

She didn't reply and the silence brought me regret.

"Oh, Gracie, please! It's just a joke. We'll be fine. As I have said, I am a chieftess."

"I'm hopun fer et."

Gracie made her snide little remark in a stern, dead flat growl with no inflection whatsoever. It was more of a whisper than anything—intentionally concealed from the party of braves who drew into a tighter formation as the night closed in. It may have been fatigue, but I found her far too young for a quip delivered in such stoical manner. I thought it excruciatingly funny and burst into laughter.

"Stop et." She whispered harshly into my ear. "They be lukun et us."

I laughed the louder.

Fully unnerved, she lashed out with a pinch in earnest. I couldn't escape her, and I believe she thought she had the power to subdue me with her finger and thumb. It was as bad as being tickled. The harder she pinched, the harder I laughed.

She was right about one thing, all the braves were now looking at the two of us. I turned to them and, to Gracie's utter horror, I pointed at her indicating that she was the cause of my outburst.

"Gracie," I said aloud.

The Indians looked at me oddly and spoke amongst themselves. Then seeming to size up Gracie, they turned to me, played with their hair, and called out a name repeatedly until I finally understood the meaning. I absolutely convulsed with laughter. The men joined in the laughter as well.

"Wot's so maggoty funny?"

Gracie sported a frown that forcibly distorted her face. She demanded an answer using her dry, most impassive, and hysterically funny voice. Her manner drove me into a fit of insane laughter. I couldn't speak. I was fully choked up, half crying, blinded with tears. I managed to sputter a few words.

"They call you, Amêške'hehe. You know, they had me stumped, trying to figure out what the blazes that meant. Then all at once, I got it. Grease woman!" I howled.

"Yer lyun."

She hit me on the back.

"I swear! I swear it's true. Why not, Gracie...Greasy, sounds about the same to me. Lord knows, you look like a Greasy." I roared.

Gracie was appalled. Filled with spite, she drove her head into my side, and rubbed her greasy hair all over my clothes.

"Oh! You nasty little tart! I ought to wring your neck. You wait till we get off this wagon. I'll have these braves strip you down and give you a sound washing in the creek with sand for soap. That'll be something you won't soon forget."

"I'll die first."

"And you might."

She never so much as cracked a smile, the poor girl. I, on the other hand, needed a day and an hour to regain my composure. After the way everything had been going in my life, and how miserable I felt as of late, it was a relief to know I hadn't forgotten how to have a good, gut-splitting laugh.

We were inside the perimeter of the camp now, and many of the younger braves had ridden ahead to confirm the news of our arrival. In the light of the open campfires, my attention was diverted by a group of young boys who were splashing about one of many reed dams used to trap fish. I looked past them farther up the stream, and noted the way the water's flow snaked along peacefully back and forth through the tipis and up the length of the rise like a dark ribbon. It wasn't far before its banks disappeared from view in the translucent mist of campfire smoke and shadow.

I saw three riders emerge from between the tipis and head in our direction. Noting the riders appeared to be women, my spirits began to rise with anticipation. Sure enough, I recognized my dear friend Talk-a-Lot riding at a full gallop to welcome me. Above the sound of pounding hooves, she was hooping, warbling at the top of her lungs, calling out to me from afar. I knew the sound of her voice at once and was thrilled.

"Elizabeth! Elizabeth!"

"Talk-a-Lot! Ného'héve'hoomâtse (I have come to see you)."

"Héehe'e (yes), Héehe'e (yes), Elizabeth, I come!!"

She was pushing her pony hard and fast, but she was no more overjoyed to see me, than was I to see her.

"Ne-toneto-mohta-he? Tosa-a ne-hesta-he? (How are you? Where did you come from?)" She brought her panting horse to a halt alongside the wagon. "Elizabeth, né-háeana-he? (Elizabeth, are you hungry?) Are you thirsty? You must come. Hotoama'heo'o waits to see you."

As Gracie listened to Talk-a-Lot jabber in her excited mix of Cheyenne, French, and English—words accompanied by frantic gestures of the hand while signing; as Gracie observed the Indian's infectious smile, and fondness for me, exhibited by the fussing, the reaching out and touching; I could see the much needed assurances finally soften the edges of Gracie's life-long fears.

On the other hand, it was anything but assurances for Talk-a-Lot ,who kept an uneasy distance from my young companion. Talk-a-Lot made certain not to touch Gracie or meet her hypnotic eyes. In the light of the moon, each time Talk-a-Lot dared look into those colorless glass-like spheres, she was filled with trepidation and continually glanced away. At last, unable to further contain her concerns, Talk-a-Lot abruptly went serious and questioned me directly.

"Nevaahe ta-tohe? (Who is that?)"

She wouldn't look at her, and only nodded her head in Gracie's direction. I couldn't help myself, and started to laugh a second time.

"Naa hë'e, náhevése'ènôtse (She is my friend)," I blurted out.

The braves were clearly waiting to see the expressions of the women when they took in the full measure of Gracie. They too now laughed with me.

I could barely spit out the words.

"This...this is...this...is...Gracie."

TWENTY-THREE

I was thoroughly overjoyed to see these people again, and I soaked up the profound sense of security and solace that came at once with their greetings. Their lives were hard but simple, and the simplicity eased my mind of all the burdens of memory. We rode into camp, and there was a great gathering as word spread that *Vehona'e* had returned. Having once presented an entire wagon of supplies, now to be seen entering camp with another one was cause for great expectations.

This time, when asked by Talk-a-Lot if I was menstruating, I understood at once the importance of the question. There would be those who wished to see me. There would be lodges to welcome me. And for these reasons, I must be free of blood

214

that signaled questionable spirits. I was clean, but heretofore, I had no reason to consider Gracie.

"Gracie, are you menstruating?"

"Wot?"

"Are you menstruating?"

"Am I wot?"

"Is it your time of month?"

"Wot?"

"Never mind."

Gracie studied me with a look of utter bafflement.

"We are clean," I assured Talk-a-Lot.

After some effort to convince Gracie that she was with friends, I left her in the care of the other women. Talk-a-Lot escorted me directly into the lodge of Ho'neheveho. The chief was very happy to see me.

"Welcome, Elizabet! Ne-toneto-mohta-he? (How are you?)"

"I am tired, but I am well. Ne-toneto-mohta-he? How are you? How is your leg? It looks good."

"Leg good. Medicine good." He slapped his thigh hard with his hand.

Talk-a-Lot explained to Ho'neheveho that I had come to them in the company of another person. A person who was fearful to gaze upon, but whom a medicine man believed was a good spirit. She told Ho'neheveho we had no place to sleep. The chief insisted we be given robes and blankets and that we be fed and given a bed in his lodge. This was the way of a chief. His generosity would have no limit. I told him, I came with few gifts. This pleased him even more, for he was now able to offer me everything I needed for nothing in return, which brought him honor.

Ho'neheveho asked to meet Gracie, and she was escorted inside. She was brought in no farther than the opening and stood there, fully illuminated by the fire. Her blonde hair stood up perfectly to the four directions, molded in its sooty grease, and radiated away in streaks of vivid reddish purple from her berry-stained face and icy-cold eyes. The shrunken heads dangled from her neck. It was not a heart-warming vision, and the chief sat up straight at first sight of her. He was taken aback. I didn't doubt he was questioning the conclusion of the medicine man and his own decision to have her spirits enter his lodge. I placed my hand upon his arm, and gave him a look of understanding. I arose to my feet and walked around the fire to Gracie, who was apprehensive.

"It is time to put away the heads, Gracie. They make everyone nervous and it isn't polite to do such a thing when these people are offering us shelter and food."

I began to remove the heads one by one, lifting them by their cords of sinew and letting them fall to the ground at her feet. She said nothing. Neither did anybody else in the lodge. They watched in silence, in amazement, clearly placing their trust in my judgment to bring such spirits into the lodge. I remained momentarily focused on Gracie.

"I can't have you sleeping on their furs with all that grease in your hair, so tonight you will have to sleep on the ground with your blanket as usual. Tomorrow we will get you cleaned up and turn you back into the beautiful girl I know you to be. Now place these heads into your parfleche and keep them out of sight. Do you understand?"

"Yut."

"Yut? Is that the same as yes?"

216

"Yut."

As a sponsor, I positioned myself behind Gracie, and placed my hands upon her shoulders. I looked up to Ho'neheveho, and presented her.

"Naa hë'e, náhevése'ènôtse, Gracie (She is my friend, Gracie)."

"Héehe'e, héne'enáotse (Yes, I understand)."

The chief nodded in acceptance. He was visibly relieved to see her without the heads. His eyes kept darting downward, toward the pile of shrunken brown faces, their gnarly teeth sticking out as they jerked about in the flickering firelight, but he nodded his approval of Gracie. He passed his fingers back and forth before his eyes in an attempt to acknowledge the splendor of Gracie's eyes. I responded in kind, indicating I understood. With that, he asked that we might sit with him, to his right, at the back of the lodge.

Hotoomee'e (Shelter Woman), Ho'neheveho's wife, and Talk-a-Lot saw to it that we were fed. Gracie was famished, but I, not so much. I spoke with Ho'neheveho and Talk-a-Lot about things in general, catching up on things over the past seasons. Ho'neheveho was very concerned to know I had returned after becoming ill. He was visibly upset at the sight of my leg wound and immediately instructed his wife to act on his bidding. Snakebites were not uncommon here and there were rituals plenty to be performed by the Medicine Men to assist in the healing. Hotoomee'e left the tipi at once.

By this time, the hour was late and Ho'neheveho insisted I lie down and sleep. I thanked him from my heart and took my place upon the bedding that had been set out for me. I was too tired to worry any further about Gracie, and feeling so pampered by the softness of the furs, I fell asleep at once.

TWENTY-FOUR

When I awoke the next morning, I was covered with a heavy robe. Everyone else in the tipi was still sleeping soundly. Gracie was asleep on the ground between me and the warmth of the coals. I had warned her the night before not to sleep on the bedding until she washed out all the grease in her hair. Under normal circumstances to block the warmth of the fire would have been considered very impolite. I was certain that while I slept, my hosts noted the disrespect. I also believed they would have overlooked the indiscretion after witnessing the child's anxiety and my affections for her. I had little doubt about Gracie's determination to lie as close to me as possible.

I wished to be as the others, still traveling the world of dreams, for the bed was soft and the robe that covered me was thick and warm. It kept out the night air. Regrettably, my whole system seemed to be running afoul, and what little food I had eaten before retiring didn't sit well with me now. I was suffering from nausea. My stomach was burning and churning, and it felt like it had taken on a life of its own. I attempted to lie still, and willed my insides to settle down, for I didn't relish the idea of getting out of my bed to face the morning air, nor had I any desire to disturb my sleeping hosts.

Unfortunately, desire made little difference in the matter, and I found myself moving quickly to untie the flap and distance myself from those sleeping inside. Breaking into a run, I had barely enough time to reach an out-of-the-way place to vomit. Once I emptied my stomach, I discovered that not only did I not feel better, I actually felt worse than ever. It was as if I had left my soul and spirit in the bed of buffalo hides, and only an empty shell of me now stood outside quivering in the field. I was shaking as much from weakness as chill. I stood there writhing in discomfort, bent over with eyes closed, hands upon my knees to keep my frame from falling forward.

"Mess Elezabeth?"

"Oh, Gracie! You startled me half to death."

I leaned over to vomit again.

"Wot's the matter, Mess Elezabeth? Why we be so seck?"

"I'm flushing out poison, honey. Flushing out poison…." My voice was shaky. "Poison from that blessed snake, poison from the sun. Maybe even poison from bad water or bad food. Whatever it's from, it has been dogging me for so long, I can only say, I don't have to fear it being Cholera, or I would have been dead, right at the outset."

No sooner had the words passed my lips that I winced with regret. *Good night*, I thought to myself. *What have I said?*

"Oh Lord, Gracie. Forgive me." I gasped. "My mind has surely abandoned me. That was a horrible and insensitive thing for me to say. Please forgive me, I…I just wasn't thinking."

Gracie said nothing. No reprimand, she merely raised her shoulders and shrugged it off, but I knew it must have been a painful reminder. It made me realize how strong this child had to be, how she had to stand up and face the loss of her parents, and yet cope with all of the new obstacles that now confronted her. Seeing me sick, being in a strange place with people she feared, living day to day without being loved, her world made mine seem serene. I felt woefully embarrassed.

I had blurted out one of those unintentional, irritating blunders that would haunt me. It would remain embedded in my memory like a splinter. There was no calling back the words, and so I went on talking, hoping to cover my shame before her young eyes.

"I guess I am just plain wore out, Gracie. I have no desire to do anything but sleep. I think it may be I have been on the move for so long that I have simply burned myself up. I'm not the young

219

girl you are, Gracie. I am not strong like you, and I seem bent on discovering the hard way, where lie my limits. I reckon I have reached them all."

I stood up straight and placed my hand upon her shoulder.

"Don't fret any, Gracie. I'm not one to go down without a fight. I should think, given a good month's rest, I'll be up and kicking, healthy as a horse. Bear with me now, and you'll see it soon enough."

Abruptly, I turned away from her and retched.

"Yer scarun may, Mess Elezabeth. Promise may ye'll be gittin' better 'cause yer makun may fayrful. I don' wanna be left hayr alone."

"Not *yer*, honey, *you're*. And I promise…I pro—."

At that point the lights went out.

Next I knew, I was looking up at a clear sky bordered with the faces of Talk-a-Lot and Hotoomee'e, who were standing alongside Gracie, and looking down at me with much concern. They joined forces in lifting me to my feet and escorting me back into the tipi to lie down. Ho'neheveho had arisen. He glanced repeatedly in my direction, and after much quiet discussion with Hotoomee'e, he stepped out to take his bath.

I lay prostrate and uncomfortably chilled. I pulled the heavy buffalo robe up about my ears. Hotoomee'e prepared a hot cup of tea that she boiled out of ground up stems and leaves from a plant that possessed a pleasant mint odor. Talk-a-Lot called the tea 'He heyuts-tsihiss ots,' and said it would stop my vomiting and put some warmth back into me. She fed the fire. As she worked the embers, she sang songs that chased away demons and beckoned good spirits. The tea seemed to work, and soon the nausea passed. Within the hour, I was sitting up and conversing. Gracie was all teary eyed and uttering sighs of relief, one after another, after another. Her unspoken show of anxiety and fear for my well-being endeared her to the others who could see the child's unintentional display of devotion.

Gracie was eventually calmed down. But, to the dismay of everyone, none more so than me, the tea's magic was to be temporary. I grew progressively weaker by the day. I was no longer able to keep down food of any kind. I was losing weight at a frightful rate and becoming anemic. I looked ghastly, both drawn and pale. My appearance and condition started to wear heavily on everyone in the lodge. Concern for my health and that of everyone else had now come into question. It was feared that I brought a very troublesome spirit within their midst.

According to Talk-a-Lot, Ho'neheveho had asked his tribe to construct a lodge for my privacy, and for the protection of others from whatever bad spirit afflicted me. The response was over-whelming. Most all of the people were recipients of my original gifts and they readily offered something in return. This was an opportunity to show gratitude.

My lodge was not to be the typical tipi for a sick person or a widow. It was larger than a menstrual lodge. It was outfitted with beds for me and Gracie, and guests as well. It was furnished for my comfort. We were given food and gifts, and the women came, offered prayers, and lit the fire pit. I was happier now that I had been moved, and no longer felt myself a burden to the others.

I pleaded with Ho'neheveho to accept my team of mules in gratitude. He did so, but with great reluctance, and immediately summoned an old man to be brought before us. In my name, he gave the old man one of the animals to take home to his family. The old man was instructed to offer praise and announce to all the generosity of Vehona'e.

It was determined by Ho'neheveho that his medicine man, Ma'heo'ôhme'ehnêstse (Medicine Comes In Sight), should be

221

summoned at once. The call was put out. In truth, I was surprised I hadn't seen him earlier, if not for his medicine, at least in greeting, for we had formerly become friends during my first stay with the tribe. The man was a trusted advisor who usually stayed very close to Ho'neheveho. I was told that Ma'heo'ôhme'ehnêstse had been riding with a hunting party on the plain since before I had arrived. He had returned only this morning, and upon hearing the news of my return and of my affliction, asked to be summoned to my side as soon as possible to drive away whatever demon possessed me.

It was a most bizarre irony to have this man whom I once feared greatly, come now to assist me in my time of need. Seeing him enter through the opening raised my spirits. Even though his methods and actions were wholly pagan to me, knowing that he came to pray for me, to fight for me, offering me the best of his ability to drive out my demons and encourage the good spirits to favor me with strength and well-being was music to my ears. To see only the determination on his face made me feel honored and in the best of hands.

He arrived with his wife and insisted that everyone leave. Gracie protested, but he would have none of it. He growled at her. His eyes flashed with a hint of his temper, and she nearly fainted on the spot. Ma'heo'ôhme'ehnêstse had not had the benefit of seeing Gracie all dolled up in her spirit heads. Talk-a-Lot rescued her, and led her out the tipi. Gracie had grown comfortable with Talk-a-Lot and I was free of any concern.

Ma'heo'ôhme'ehnêstse had come fully prepared to perform his purification ceremonies. It began with the sweeping of the floor, followed by the laying of sweet grass. I watched him remove a pulverized mixture of sweet grass, sweet pine needles, and sage from his parfleche. He sprinkled the mixture over the hot coals of the fire pit, filling the air at once with incense both sweet and heavy with fragrance. This would strengthen the effect of the medicine.

He next lit a bundle of sage, and waved it about the tipi with one hand, while he produced a rattle and shook it vigorously in his other. As he circled around the fire pit, stepping in a dance-like manner, he swept the walls of the tipi with the smoking sage bundle. He then gathered up the air and whatever bad spirits within, and forced them out the tipi opening.

He then concentrated his sweeping motions and attention to my area and, holding out his arms, he collected any evil spirits hovering about me, and forced them out the opening in like fashion. At that point he bid the outside world farewell and sealed the flap. With the help of his wife, he hung a number of colorful feathered amulets and leather shield-like plaques. Each of these was covered with painted symbols, and sprouted streams of leather tassels adorned with down and dyed quills, which dangled to the ground.

Once these artifacts had been placed to his satisfaction, he sat down to his medicine pipe. The bowl had been placed in the center of a circle that was drawn by his wife in the dirt. The stem was pointed eastward toward the opening of the tipi, the direction of the rising sun. After lighting the pipe, he raised it to the sky, lowered it to the circle earth, and then presented it to Nivstanivoo, the Four Directions.

He sat and smoked his pipe in privacy even requesting his wife to leave. It was now only the two of us. I lay at the back of the lodge, close to the ground, curled up under my robe. He sat cross-legged at my side with his arms outstretched, wrists resting upon his knees. Ma'heo'ôhme'ehnêstse faced the fire pit and raised his head upward, his eyes closed in meditation.

The smoke from the pipe filled the lodge. The sun bore down through the fire vent at the top of the tipi in a brilliant shaft of light. It illuminated the thick haze within and transformed my cozy space into a wild borderless dreamlike place. The sun's rays singled the medicine man out and intensified the radiance of paint purposely scrawled across his face. The glow of color that emanated from his features enhanced the hues of amulets and shields that tinted the fog, and heightened the overall surrealism of the setting.

When Ma'heo'ôhme'ehnêstse finished his pipe, and carefully emptied out the bowl, he began to chant. It was a sign for his wife to reenter. She stepped to my side and removed the robe that covered me. She stripped me of my clothing, leaving only a swath of material across my waist. For the first time in my life I found myself to be honestly indifferent about my nudity before others.

The woman began to wash me. This was followed by attention to my hair, which was adorned with bundles of herbs and artifacts possessing strong spiritual powers. After having done this, she again removed herself from the tipi. Ma'heo'ôhme'ehnêstse returned to sit down before me. He lit his medicine pipe a second time.

After Ma'heo'ôhme'ehnêstse completed a second round of ritual smoking and meditation, his wife returned with a large dead rattlesnake and busied herself with preparations. In time she produced a bowl that contained the pulverized innards of the reptile. Alongside the bowl was a pallet of paint.

Ma'heo'ôhme'ehnêstse continued to chant while he swirled his fingers in the paint and dipped them into the bowl of snake paste. He began to apply this unguent to my face and then my chest, all along my torso and down my legs. He covered me from head to toe with patterns. Even my hair was streaked with paint. He explained to me that he wished to make me look terrible so that when the demon spirits were driven out, they would be afraid to hover near me or re-enter my body. The pulverized snake's spirit would call the poison back from my body. After this, in privacy, he sat down for a third time to light the pipe and smoke while meditating.

During the last segment of the ceremony his wife did not reenter the tipi. Ma'heo'ôhme'ehnêstse finished his pipe and set it aside. He sprinkled more 'vih o ots', *sweet grass*, upon the embers, and another plume of fragrant smoke billowed upward. He began to dance and chant with great deliberation. He shook his rattle and worked himself up into a dripping sweat. He was praying in earnest, giving everything he had to drive out demons that he believed possessed me. He entered into a state of trance, and in some inexplicable manner he brought me with him.

Nothing could have prepared Mary, Allen, or my friends back home to accept what I was experiencing at this moment. They would have been horrified. Maybe only Allen would have understood what I felt. He was an open minded and intelligent man. For the truth of the matter was, I felt wonderful. I felt so much better than I had in the last few weeks that it was nothing if not miraculous.

My upbringing would never allow me to believe that demons had been driven from my body. It also never would have exposed me to the power of persuasion that such ceremony could foster. I was grateful that Ma'heo'ôhme'ehnêstse demanded privacy. I think I now understood the need for it. I was embarrassed at my condition and the fuss I was causing. I was embarrassed at the attention I was drawing from others even when I knew it was out of genuine concern for my well-being.

It was only after some time alone with the man, only after I could see how serious he was about his medicine and his prayer that I understood he was talking to his God, the Great Spirit, for my well-being alone. It was an intimate affair. It was personal. I respected him. I accepted what he was doing as appropriate. Instead of embarrassment I now bathed in the glow of his attention. Each time he placed his hand upon me or even touched me in the

225

lightest manner, waves of euphoria moved through me. I felt spiritual, elevated. He concluded the ceremony some six or seven hours later. He departed only after seeing to it that I drank from a bowl of hot tea made up from the top and stems of a plant that he called 'Mis ka tsi.' It quickly put me into a deep dreamless sleep—a state of perfect peace.

TWENTY-FIVE

While I was under the care of Ma'heo'ôhme'ehnêstse, the medicine man, and subject to the purification ceremony, Ho'neheveho issued a call to gather wood for a great fire. It would be a night of feasting and dancing—a night to offer prayers and thanks for the gifts of the earth and my return.

The tea that had been administered to me was a potent sedative, and I slept virtually comatose until the setting of the sun. I awoke to the pulsing rhythm of the prayer drum. Its vibration passed through my body. I sensed it was late, but I felt wholly rejuvenated. I had regained considerable energy and appetite. The sounds of pandemonium played upon my ears, tugging at my senses until I was obliged to open my eyes and satisfy my curiosity. The fire pit was giving off warmth and light, enough for me to see Gracie sitting alone in our tipi. She was sitting quietly on her bedding, working a pair of moccasins that Talk-a-Lot had been teaching her to make.

"Hi, Gracie."

I greeted her with little more than a broken whisper.

"Oh!" she gasped. "Mess Elezabeth, how d'ye feel? Ye ben sleepun so sount. I triet nawt ta wake ye."

She moved at once to my side.

226

"You didn't, and I feel quite rested. I see you washed your hair."

"Yut, et's clean."

"*Yes, it's* clean"

"Yes, it's clean"

"It looks wonderful. I like it. Why is there so much commotion outside? I've been lying here listening to the drums and everybody running back and forth past the tipi."

"They be havun a feast ta give thenks fer...*for*...a good hunt en' for yer...your...comun back long."

"Oh, Ho'neheveho...I told him not to do that."

"Talk-a-Lot sait they were too slow t' give thenks fer yer...*for your* return."

"I know, I know, Gracie. It isn't true, but I'm no match for the spirits."

Talk-a-Lot entered the tipi as we spoke of her. She broke into a wide smile upon seeing me sitting upright.

"Népévomóhtâhehe? (Are you feeling good?)"

"Yes, thank you. Náháéána (I'm hungry)."

"Hémêseestse (Come eat). You come. Come, come."

She motioned for Gracie and me to follow her outside. Gracie helped me to my feet, and although I was yet shaky, for the most part I felt revived. We left the tipi as a group and walked to the center of the camp where there was a large fire blazing away. The Indians were painted up and costumed, and I fit right in, being painted with spiritual patterns that covered me head to foot. I watched as more and more Indians came into view, dancing, praying, and singing out their songs. They were moving clockwise around the leaping flames of fire in the center of the camp.

227

Talk-a-Lot asked us to remain put, while she moved through the crowd and made her way up to where her brother, Ho'neheveho, was seated. She spoke to him briefly and then returned. There was an appropriate seating arrangement adhered to in these festivities and social gatherings. The innermost circle, closest to the fire…front row seats if I were in a Boston theatre, was occupied by the chiefs. Seated in the next concentric circle outside of them were the highest ranking warriors and men of bravery and honor, medicine men, and the like. In the following circles were the braves and young men. Lastly, seated in no special order behind the braves were the women and children.

This was not meant to be demeaning to women, but was more a practical matter. In order for the men to hear and witness the business of the day, they had to sit in close proximity, which formed the focal point. Their advisors sat behind them, and news emanated from the center outward. The families were kept at a distance so the young would not disturb nor distract the proceedings of the chiefs. Any child that was unruly or bothersome was not reprimanded, but whisked away to the perimeter, farther from the vicinity of business. On this night the order of business was primarily entertainment so the children were allowed to make as much noise as they wished.

Holding firmly on to Gracie's hand, I towed her behind me as Talk-a-Lot tugged on my hand, leading me through the ranks of the women, the braves, and the warriors. She brought me to the side of Ho'neheveho. He was pleased to see me and asked that I sit to his right. I took my place; Talk-a-Lot and Gracie sat down behind me. Because this was not a business function, many seated in the inner circles often faced outward or to the rear and conversed with those occupying the outer circles. This was routine posturing to be social.

There was a bounty of victuals to be had at the fire pits inside of the tipis, or at numerous small fires burning in close proximity.

The aroma of roasted meat permeated the air, and I found my mouth salivating for food. There were all varieties of stew, rabbit, skunk, deer, antelope, bison, all boiling with additions of sweet potatoes, and assortments of tubers, roots, stems, leaves, and berries—most of which had once been foreign to me. I turned to Talk-a-Lot.

"Námésêhétáno (I want to eat)."

"Nôhtseno'é, nôhtseno'é (Wait, wait)."

Talk-a-Lot jumped to her feet and raced away. Gracie and I were left to face each other. She looked around in amazement, not quite accepting that she was sitting with the chiefs in the center of this large gathering of Indians.

"Now do you believe I am a chieftess?"

"Yut." She hesitated. "How does a woman get ta be a chieftess?"

"I can't truly answer that, Gracie, but I can tell you that the Tsistsistas hold their women in high regard, and also that they value generosity. Remember, I told you that I gave them my wagon full of wares. I will also give them this wagon and whatever else I am able."

"Wot will we use?"

"Mules. I have learned much from you, Gracie. I have watched you move an entire camp across mountain and plain, and I see the wisdom in what you do. It is efficient, no harnesses to fuss with, no washouts to worry about, no broken or dried out wheels. I have learned much from watching you."

I only smiled, but Gracie beamed with delight.

Talk-a-Lot brought food for everybody. She placed a large gourd filled with stew in front of us, then handed each of us a wooden spoon. Neither Gracie nor I wasted time in helping ourselves to the aromatic meal.

"E'tóne'éno'e? (How does it taste?)"

"Nápêhévé'áhta, e'pêhéveéno'e. Éháoho'ta (I like its taste, it tastes good. It's hot)."

"Do you like it, Gracie?" Talk-a-Lot asked.

"Yut."

"Yut means exactly nothing to Talk-a-Lot," I injected.

"*Yes.* Héehe'e."

We took our time eating and enjoying the food as we watched the dances and enactments. The food, the commotion, and the festivity all helped to remove me from my own sickly condition.

"Épéveéno'e? It tastes good, yes?"

Talk–a-Lot motioned for us to empty the gourd so she might refill it.

"Épéva'e (It's good). No, no more. Thank you. Náéšená'so'enohe (I am now full)."

Our appetites satiated, Gracie and I relaxed and watched as the braves were called upon to count coup, and tribute was paid to others for their admirable deeds. Ho'neheveho had given away a horse to a poor woman in gratitude for my safe passage. He also gave away two more of my mules to old warriors in remembrance of their lives of bravery.

Periodically during the evening, I observed a spontaneous outburst of excitement sweep through the crowd, whereby a number of people would look to the heavens and then applaud with approval. This happened four or five times as the hours passed into the deep of night. Finally, my curiosity winning the

230

best of me, I was driven to ask Talk-a-Lot for what reason these repeated outbursts were taking place.

She giggled and passed my inquiry on to Ho'neheveho, who in turn laughed heartily and rolled his eyes with delight. He responded by saying that I had brought with me the falling stars, and that this was a good omen that warmed the hearts of all Tsistsistas.

However, the full explanation of this omen didn't come from Ho'neheveho or Talk-a-Lot, but instead was translated by her, as being given to Gracie and me by a respected brave who was all too healthy looking. The man had done well in the hunt, and was seated next to Gracie in the company of Ho'neheveho to be acknowledged and paid honor.

The brave began to explain through Talk-a-Lot that the Tsistsistas were told a story by their ancestors of an event that occurred many, many, seasons past, in the time before people, in a time when only the sacred bison roamed the earth. In those seasons the earth was still a young woman. One night in particular, in the bright light of a full moon, the Great Spirit saw the young woman earth weeping with much sadness and despair. The Great Spirit asked why she was so sad.

She replied that she had been left alone in the darkness of the universe. She cried of her loneliness. Her wailing was the wind. Her tears flowed as rivers across her face, and splashed down mountainsides to form large lakes and pools of water. She asked the Great Spirit why, when all the stars played and lived together in the sky, had she been forgotten? Why was she unable to reach them, to go to them and enjoy their friendship?

She wished only to have company. She wished only to have another with whom to pass time as she grew old. Her beauty was hidden behind her tears, her sadness, and the emptiness of her heart. The Great Spirit was deeply moved. He was so filled with

231

pity that he came down to her from his place in the heavens, crossing the night sky as a great streak of light. He mated with the young woman earth and, having touched her with his spirit, she was blessed with a child and great joy.

The child grew into a man and gave his mother earth all the love and care for which she had hoped. For the Great Spirit commanded that he take care of his mother all his days. Mother Earth watched over him and provided his needs, his food and his shelter. He appreciated her blessings and generosity, and showed his respect for her and his gratitude by always offering a portion of his good fortune in prayer and sacrifice.

Now, all women know that the moon illuminates Mother Earth, and a woman who wishes a child might mate in its light so to be seen by the Great Spirit. He will know she is lonely and longs for the love of another. He will be filled with pity and will descend in spirit to touch her. If one watches quietly in the darkness of night, one might see a sign of the Great Spirit coming as a star, falling from the heavens to touch a young woman. The stars are noted—each believed to be a child en route. The children to come are counted and marked with notches on a blessing stick, and the foretelling becomes cause for much rejoicing.

"Oh, yut. I remember!"

Gracie blurted out a remembrance of one of the enactments that she had watched earlier in the night. I too remembered how the women danced before us with exuberance. As they moved past us, I noted how beautiful they looked. Each woman was dressed in her finest attire and adorned with bright articles of jewelry easily noticed. The sides of their faces, their arms, and their ankles were painted up with spots of white that blended into their dress and hair.

About them was an Indian brave painted with a large white circle on his chest and his back. White streaks of paint radiated out from the circle along his arms and legs. He was the moon and he carried flaming torches that shed light on all the women who surrounded him so the Great Spirit might see them.

The women wailed and screamed. They rolled their heads about and buried them in their hands. They reached up to the sky and pretended to cry in despair in order to fool the Great Spirit. Sadly, I feared more often than not, they were desperate in their hopes, for Ho'neheveho had once confided that their numbers were dwindling.

Of course, I must add that the beauty of the legend, which I found so enchanting, was squarely offset by the vulgarity of the storyteller. He stood up, to tower over us, and in a manner entirely void of modesty, he displayed all his enthusiasm and hopes for the night with wild pelvic contortions and gyrations that left nothing to imagination. His moves were obscene enough to damn the entire East Coast Protestant population to the eternal fires, should they glance his way. I only succeeded in encouraging this behavior, for the more appalled I appeared by his gestures—my first thought being the issue of Gracie's exposure to such lust—the more he and the warriors seated behind him roared with delight. Even Ho'neheveho and Talk-a-Lot were laughing at me.

I knew that the hunter meant no harm, and that he wasn't trying to be rude, for the Indians didn't have the profound divisions of right and wrong or *rudeness* as we Europeans understood it. They viewed life as honorable or dishonorable. To steal or kill… acts considered wrong by any measure in my culture, more than likely would be considered very honorable in this tribe.

No matter how outrageous children behaved, they were never thought of as doing anything wrong. They were raised by example, learning what brought honor to their family. The Indians were every bit as disciplined in their rules of behavior as were we, but their rules were incomprehensible to all but a few Europeans. In any event, I was unable to walk away from the morals of my culture and upbringing, and I found myself floundering in an attempt to protect Gracie from this open show of sexual wantonness.

Even a quick change of the subject wasn't nearly as simple as I hoped. Gracie had a vague impression of union because there had been times she awoke to find her parents together. It was clear that they hadn't satisfied her curiosity about such matters because she was forthright in questioning me directly. And although, for the first time in my life, I fully understood the meaning of congress from experience, I was in no position to explain it to her satisfaction. I had just received my first taste of what Mary endured when I had been searching for these same answers at about the same age. I had to remember that this was one of the very few times Gracie had seen people, let alone men, let alone *naked* men but for breech cloths that did little to hide manhood.

This explicit theatre of sexual desire would have filled the churches back east, but to these people it was a natural part of their lives, something to sing about, to act out in dance. And honestly, I wondered who was I to be judge or jury? I could have told Gracie to simply watch the dogs and horses, as Mary told me. But I remembered how badly that lesson turned out. Maybe the better lesson would be for Gracie to sit and watch, so sit and learn with all the other young girls of her age. It was a distinct clash of cultures before us, but possibly a better balanced school of learning that might save her from many of the frustrations that I often believed had ruined my life.

Brimming with benevolence and hopeful prospect, the hunter offered to mate with me in the light of the moon before the Great Spirit, but I declined with all politeness, feeling it a bit much for my limited experience. After all, I was still relatively new to this. The man remained determined and it made me very nervous. As for Gracie, I just pulled her in tight to my side and told her in no uncertain terms, I was positive he was a good man, but to ignore him or I'd peel the skin off her ass.

My anxiety baffled her, and she was hardly inclined to drop the issue. I, on the other hand, was in no mood to continue the conversation. Beneath the waiting hunter whose eyes alone were raping us, I reminded Gracie that it was she who didn't believe I was a chieftess, and she would be well advised to shut her mouth and accept my advice now, before the warrior elected to carry her off, have his way with her, and leave her someplace never to be seen again. Truth or not, Gracie got the point, shut her mouth, and saved me one unwanted box of worms.

TWENTY-SIX

The festivities lasted far into the night, nearly to the break of dawn, and I had fully anticipated sleeping late into the following day. Yet, for all the night's celebration, for all the weariness I felt when I finally reached my bed, I awoke early the next morning as sick as ever, followed by the usual mad dash and bout of retching.

Another week passed with further deterioration in my condition. There was nothing left of me now but skin and bones. I spent most of my days confined to the bed, for I was too weak to remain on my feet for any extended period of time. Gracie and Talk-a-Lot were kind enough to offer me company and care for me by encouraging me to eat and keeping the fire.

Being bedridden as I was for the most part, and having little more than time on my hands, I whiled away the hours investigating the hidden side of my tipi mate—time I spent peering into her world, and discovering who was Gracie Castleman. The answer was quick in coming and as obvious as looking at her. She was an angel of a child; self-sufficient, capable, strong willed, yet as

235

innocent of worldly ways as any person I had ever met. She knew nothing of people or the most common facets of civilized living.

She may have been raised to know good manners and be respectful, she may have been taught cleanliness, but I could hold her attention for hours by just describing an ordinary street in Boston or a horse-drawn buggy. A ship was almost beyond her comprehension, as was a lace tablecloth, a hutch, or a piece of polished silverware. Her world was one of complete isolation, a world of woods, water, and the art of survival. Her newly acquired proficiency in the use of a bow was just one of her many skills. She could throw a knife in a fashion as wicked as anything I ever witnessed, and she raised many an eyebrow amongst her Indian male counterparts with those knives, for they believed white people only used guns.

Some days later, I was awakened to my usual state of nausea, it occurring at about the same time that Talk-a-Lot, Hotoomee'e, and Gracie entered the tipi. They had returned from the stream with fresh water. They studied me somewhat quizzically, and after looking in on me and saying a brief good morning, they removed themselves from the tipi. I felt the sickness welling up inside, and dressed quickly to hurry out, so as not to mess the furs. It was such a routine part of my day that now I simply took it in stride.

I stepped outside and was astonished to see the ground all about our tipi sprinkled lightly with wildflowers and sage grasses. I looked about and noticed immediately that no other tipi was decorated in such a manner. I saw women flashing smiles at me, and their men careening about to have a better look in my direction. It was all very odd, and although I was curious about this unwarranted attention, I was forced to move on for the sake of my stomach.

As I stood, crouched over, looking out across the valley, Talk-a-Lot, Hotoomee'e, Gracie, and a few of the other women came up behind me, and began to pamper me with smiles and affectionate touches. This was a far cry from the apprehension some of the women had exhibited earlier having believed evil spirits resided within me. I was baffled and somewhat amused as I studied them, noting their knowing glances and outward displays of approval.

I was trying to decipher this change of attitude, when Hotoomee'e, who was very caring and kind to me, and whom I liked very much, began looking into my eyes and making great sweeping arcs with her hand and nodding with an understanding. She made gestures, indicative of my vomit spewing outward. This was clear enough to me. She would then make a similar sweeping arc at her stomach. First, at her mouth, then at her stomach.

"Mé'êševôtse?"

"What? What is it, Hotoomee'e? I don't understand."

I noticed Gracie stood aback, oddly silent, but watching everything with fixed intensity.

"Mé'êševôtse?" she repeated.

There were three other Indian women with Hotoomee'e besides Talk-a-Lot, who were also giggling at my expense. I was as naive as Gracie about some things, and I stood there trying to make sense of what she was saying. No doubt my condition had diminished my wits, leaving me slow to render into English what it was she was trying to tell me. Then she cradled her arms and everything changed.

"Wahhhhhh!"

She mimicked the unmistakable cry of a baby. Back and forth, she rocked her arms.

"Mé'êševôtse?" she asked again, and patted her tummy.

"Baby...yes, I understand.... Huh? Oh my word! They think... they think I'm pregnant," I stammered aloud, utterly astonished.

I looked at Gracie, who said nothing but continued to study me.

It was the most preposterous assumption they could have ever entertained.

"Ha!" I laughed. "What could these people possibly know about me being pregnant? For the love of god, I practically grew up in an infirmary. I was more virgin than a nun. I would surely know if I were pregnant of all things." I looked at Gracie. "At my age, Gracie, nothing works. I mean I've never even—."

Been with a man; the thought dealt me such a horrific blow, my knees nearly buckled beneath me.

I sank to the ground. I felt like a bomb had gone off inside me.

"Pregnant? No! That can't be."

I shook my head in disbelief, trembling at the mere thought. *It wasn't possible!* How long had it been since my last flow? Five weeks, six…seven…how long had I been sick? I had no calendar. Who paid any attention to days or weeks? They just moved from one into another. Time was meaningless out here in the desert unless it was a season. If it was hot it was summer, if not, winter. Besides, my flows were as erratic as…. This was not about to happen. I rose to my feet.

"I *am not* pregnant!" I insisted. "My lord, I nearly died from snakebite. I mean, forget the snake, I nearly died from sun poisoning after laying unconscious in the desert for who knows how many days. My back was already killing me because of that stupid wagon. Of course, I'm in a state. I know I'm in a state, but who wouldn't be after enduring such things. Nobody has appetite after such ordeals. That's not uncommon. My body chooses to purge itself of these poisons, and I may not know what all poisons suffer me, but I do know this. I am not pregnant!

238

Absolutely—not!" I looked directly at Gracie. "I am not pregnant, young lady!"

Gracie stood silent, unsure, while the others approached and began caressing me with gentle touches and tender gestures. I looked around at them. They were a collection of smiles, so secure in their diagnosis that it scared me out of my wits.

"No, no, no—."

I raised my hands to reject their advances, but to no avail. I then placed my trembling hands over my face, shaking my head in defiance, unwilling to accept this one horrifying possibility that had never occurred to me.

If fate could be truly cruel in my life, this would be the ultimate blow. The truth was, I never cared to acknowledge my ignorance in this matter, and any open discussion of sex or pregnancy simply was not tolerated while growing up.

I didn't have a clue, as to what I might experience if I were pregnant, but women did get sick. I remember on many occasions, Allen having to look in on the expectant. I just never would have given it a thought. Hit me over the head, if you will, and I still wouldn't have seen it. I saw Mary almost daily, while pregnant twice for her boys, but she never ailed. I was never actually present when Allen attended a birth, or when Mary mid-wifed. These were very private matters, the details kept secret and the issue rarely discussed in good taste. What then would I know?

There was no escaping the fact I had slept with Christopher. The knowledge was ripping me to shreds, suffocating me. I had practically forced him to sleep with me. I thought to myself, could this be my punishment? Was this the price I was to pay for my indiscretion?

This was to be my sin of sins. I was worse than a whore; a whore had little choice but to take a man in order to survive. I chose to take a man for no purpose other than to satisfy my carnal curiosity. I had sinned indeed. Sinned before the eyes of God, and now I might give birth to a bastard child who would suffer the aftermath of this unholy union. We would both go through life, the child being living proof, the inescapable proof of my immorality. If I was with child then my fate was sealed. The shame would prevent me from ever returning home. I broke down and sobbed. I cried out of desperation, I cried in humiliation. If I should be with child, there would be no honor left to my name, only inescapable disgrace.

"Don' cry, Mess Elezabeth. Ye'll be fine."

Gracie had come to kneel at my side. She caressed me with her hands.

"Oh, Gracie, you can't possibly understand. You don't know about people and what they think, the way they judge. You don't know what things I have done. You don't know. I have lusted. I have fornicated; I have murdered. God has seen it all and He knows I have done these terrible things."

"Nawt all terr'ble, I knaw wot ye done fer may."

"If I am pregnant, Gracie, I have cursed a child for life. What if I have a son? I would have to make up a story, live a lie until the day I die lest he live in shame before friends and family. I would have little choice in this matter but to lie. Lie through my teeth.

"How would I raise this child? I have no husband. A child needs a father. Who can raise a child proper without a father? Oh God, let us pray this isn't true, let us pray this isn't true." I writhed in agony. "I would rather die of snakebite than be pregnant. Let me be sick, please, please Lord, just let me be sick—sick as a dog. Let it be the snake, that devil of a snake. Oh, Gracie, I need to be sick." I sobbed.

Gracie pulled me up toward her small frame and wrapped her arms tightly around my neck. Her eyes began to mist over as she felt my pain. She spoke to me in that peculiarly impassive voice.

"I want a mother, Mess Elezabeth. Don' cry. I want a mother. Ye'll be a gurt good mother, I knaw et."

TWENTY-SEVEN

The Indians enjoyed such uncluttered relationships. They not only embraced, but also embodied the very sanctity of life and death. The spiritual aspect of their lives was so closely aligned to their daily activities that at times their mortal bodies seemed mere personifications of their spiritual selves. The events of birth and death served to reinforce the simplicity of passage between those parallel worlds.

They held dear my pregnancy and reveled in delight knowing a newborn was eminent. It was the purest of pleasure in their world, and made me all the more special in their eyes. I was so different from them in both looks and manner that my situation drew unending attention. I was always to be a focal point, the talk of the tribe. People, whom I did not know, were relieved to discover my sickness was a spiritual purging of evil and filth in order to become clean and prepared to accept a child. They seemed to feel the severity of my sickness was equal to the depth in which I had cleansed myself. I had earned much respect for my suffering.

Strangers now passed my tipi daily leaving sprinkles of wildflowers, sage, or medicine bundles. They presented the gifts to help me in whatever way they might by attracting good spirits and repelling those unwanted. It was common knowledge that I had come with the falling stars, and now it was evident one of

241

the notches on the blessing stick was mine. The Great Spirit had assuredly sent me to them to be cared for while I was cleansed for his blessing.

Sadly, I suffered from a considerably more complicated view of life. My understanding of the Great Spirit, *who touched me*, was much more down to earth. I saw him as a big, strapping, blue-eyed, blonde-headed Swede, and in return for this new life given me, I was stripped of my old life, which I now coveted. He had left me quite burdened, fully two thousand miles from reality.

I now existed for the sole purpose of serving the needs of a child I didn't know, a child I didn't want. I resented this unborn stranger. Everything and anything that had been relevant to me as an individual now seemed to have evaporated. Whoever I was, whatever I did, however grand my accomplishments, the handholds of my existence were removed. A person who could no longer gain support from the foundations of her past had replaced me—a person who was to be a mother—a person given no choice but to start life over at this random place and stumble ahead in circles. I was embarking upon a future that I could not envision nor escape.

I sobbed until my eyes were raw, until my ribs hurt. I knew I was not a young woman of childbearing age. I also knew another fact of pregnancy, a secret that was closely guarded. The grave-yards were littered with remains and reminders of loving wives and caring mothers who died at the end of their terms. I had spent years placing countless orphaned children into the homes of those fortunate mothers who had managed to survive the ordeal where others had not. It was in great part due to this reality that sex and pregnancy were issues discussed in whispers or not at all. Pregnancy was a time for prayer—a time to plead for the safe delivery of healthy children. It was a time so fraught with fear for the mother's ordeal, one dared not ask anything more.

Gracie coaxed me to my feet and walked me back to the tipi.

TWENTY-EIGHT

It was the last of June when I left Christopher in South Pass Junction. Now, aspen were cloaked in dazzling gold, the vistas had streaks of flame-red that ran like unspooled ribbon across hill and dale. The air was thick with the seeds of Showy Milkweed. Bison sported rich dark coats. The night skies were hosted by *Se ma omeve-ese he*, the *starting-to-freeze-moon*. I knew from these signs and more that it was near middle October, and that would make me a little more than three months into term.

Gracie and I spent a lot of time with Hotoomee'e and Talk-a-Lot in the lodge of Ho'neheveho. I was often embarrassed in their presence, for my appetite was now wholly insatiable. I was starved from sun-up to sundown, eating everything given to me. Gracie would go slack jawed every time I made mention of being hungry. She was embarrassed for both of us, for food was not nearly as plentiful during the winter months. Thankfully, morning sickness now out of my system, my pregnancy gave me the renewed vigor needed to remain with the Tsistsistas as they migrated south. Even so, the snow was often too deep, or the ground frozen too hard, for us to dig for roots or plants to enjoy, but the women understood my needs, and did their best to see I ate as much as possible.

We always managed enough food to get by. We dove into our stores of pemmican and dried fruit, but still there was to be had bison fresh from the hunt. As long as the men were dressed warm, oftentimes it was easier to catch bison in the winter because the animals could be driven into the snowdrifts and killed. The meat was either roasted or stewed, often with red currants and other dried fruit cakes. We also were able to enjoy fresh fish that could still be caught in streams flowing fast enough to be yet unfrozen or by breaking ice on the surface of pools.

I had maddening cravings for fruit, and I would bundle up and spend hours outside in the cold gathering up haws, which clung to the hawthorn bushes all winter long. The Indians called them 'nah ko tasi mins'; I called them good. To me they tasted much like dried apples. I also ate a substantial amount of boiled gooseberries that also had been compressed into dried cakes during the summer months. They could be really tart at times, and we would mix them with a sugary syrup boiled out of the sap of Box Elder trees.

I took great comfort from the support I was given by the tribe. A healthy appetite returned one of the great social pleasures in life, and at each gathering to eat, the fuss and attention paid me forced the initial shock of pregnancy and the mental anguish that followed to wane.

I resigned myself to my situation, for I was determined to put the child's welfare above all else. After doing so, I discovered myself filled with inner peace. I was learning to cope and no longer viewed my pregnancy as my undoing. Those feelings of remorse and despair were replaced by a mother's natural concern for her baby's well-being. I would talk to the child for hours, and it would bring me profound feelings of purpose and fulfillment. I would walk out into the fields of snow on bright sunny days and talk aloud, assuring the baby that although I had made plenty of my own mistakes, I would never falter in my responsibilities as a mother.

The stillness of the winter months about the camp and our frequent confinement to the tipis gave me endless hours to focus on the many changes taking place. The first of which, after my bout with morning sickness, altered my sleeping habits. I now had to lie on my sides or back, for my bed, although softened by the furs, was still too firm for my breasts. They had become swollen and exceptionally tender to the touch.

The morning sickness and accompanying terror had now long since been replaced by a state of well-being that surpassed anything I had ever experienced. I felt almost euphoric. I felt as though I were perfect in every way. I felt beautiful. My hair seemed thicker and grew faster, as did my nails, which now seemed stronger than ever. I was brimming with energy. The smell of roasting meat was intoxicating, the taste was indescribably delicious. I watched for other changes to take place, but they came later, in the dead of winter.

The Indians called this the time of the Big Hard Faced Moon. It was often brutally cold outside with winds blowing down upon us from the north. Nothing separated these people, Gracie and I included, from death other than the hides of the tipi draped over their lodge poles, the fire pits within, and the warmth of the robes that we laid beneath. I enjoyed a particular benefit that nearly made me immune to frigid weather…fat. It seemed to be collecting everywhere on my body. It didn't make me happy, but it did make me warm.

I assumed it to be about late December or early January, and about my sixth or seventh month when Gracie and I determined, as I stood before the fire pit, that my belly was most notably distended.

"There's no denying my situation."

I held my robe open.

"Sure as cain be. You're all plimmed up."

"Plimmed up?"

"Mess Elezbeth, averthun on you es skinnier than a blade a grass, averthun cept thet there."

She pointed at my belly. I looked down and took a deep breath.

245

"Isn't that the truth of it."

I was no longer tormented, and sight of this big belly brought a smile to my face. The old me was gone along with all the worries and humiliations. No longer was I plagued with doubt; no longer did I reprimand myself for past deeds. My new life was only about here and now and to hell with the morrow.

And now, I was content to be alone with Gracie. We had finished eating a fresh kill of buffalo, and were in our beds being lazy and staying warm under the robes when I sensed a spasm. Little alarms went off, as is usual when a muscle gets a cramp or takes on a life of its own. I thought it queer, and I rubbed my side, but it continued. I raised myself upon my elbows, and began to pay closer attention. The spasms continued but felt nothing like the spasms I was accustomed to. And so the child let me know.

"Gracie."

"Yut."

"Yes."

"Yes."

"Come, here. Be quiet."

"Wot?"

"Come, here. Give me your hand."

She did as I asked, and I placed her hand upon my belly.

"Wot?"

"Shhhh." I waited. "There! Did you feel that?" I whispered.

"Feel wot?"

"That movement…the baby."

Gracie's eyes grew wide with anticipation. It went on for nearly half an hour as the baby made little movements that I could sense, but were too weak for Gracie to feel. Wearing a frown, having given up, she sat back disappointed, but I was elated. I was thrilled. I was grateful. I rubbed my hands across my belly around and around. It was a gesture that I found myself doing continuously from that day forth. It was a caress, a reassurance, a protective act, a possessive act, an affirmation that this baby was alive, healthy, and all mine.

TWENTY-NINE

The hours of winter stillness turned into weeks, and eventually the dead of winter gave way to the first warm southwestern winds of spring. The comforting breezes seemed to be fanned our way by the millions of geese and returning birds winging overhead on their migration north. With these changes came my own, now more notable than ever, and I found myself utterly fascinated by my metamorphosis.

Never in my life had I questioned my control over my own body. It was mine to will, and yet here before my eyes I was quickly being transformed into something different. A butterfly I hoped, but I might become a horse or a buffalo in view of how I appeared. It was out of my hands. All I could do was watch the change take place. I was to have no say in this chain of events until the Great Spirit was finished with me.

The Tsistsistas called springtime *matse omeva* and those warm winds from the south now worked hard to chase the Mistress of Winter from our minds. Spring was flooding the land with new life. My child would be in good company when it entered this world. I knew the child was soon to be, for I had reached a point where the fascinations of the last eight months had worn off. We had moved camp, and traveled many days to the north before setting up camp for rest. I was most uncomfortable and becoming ever the more irritable. My feet hurt, my back hurt, my stomach was always on fire. My only escape was my dreams.

They were exceptionally vivid, sometimes consoling, sometimes very disturbing. Unlike anything I ever experienced before, the dreams left me so filled with emotion, at times I would find myself sobbing and unsure of when I was awake or asleep. I questioned whether I lived in this world or some other. I often laid still in the silence of night staring through the darkness into the soft reddish glow of the fire pit or upward into the heavens through the smoke vent. I would lie there and consider how the Indians put great stock in their dreams, how they were so close to their spiritual world, and how all of it made me wonder who really knew God, the Europeans or the savages.

"Mess Elezabeth?

"Mmm-mm"

"Ye sleepy?"

"Mmm."

"Wot are ye go'un ta name the baby?"

I opened my eyes at once.

"Now that's a question." I thought aloud. "If it's a girl I was thinking of Dawn, Rebecca, Mary, Gracie, Dennison-Claussen. If it's a boy, well...oh...maybe...I think...Luke."

Gracie remained silent for a moment thinking the names over.

"Thet's the worst name I aver hert."

"You don't like Luke?"

"Naw, I don' care fer no Dawn, Gracie, Jenn'fer, Erbecca, Willie Nillie wotnot. Who'ud name a baby grill thet? Et sounds like a supply list."

"Girl, not grill."

"Girl."

"Well, don't worry. It's going to be a boy."

"Oh!" Gracie's eyes opened wide. *"Ye cain tell?"*

"Well, no. But I know it's going to be a boy. I know it."

"How d'ye knaw? How cain ye tell?"

Gracie was brimming with curiosity.

"Feels like a boy. It just feels…like a boy. I don't know."

"I like Luke. Luke…Luke. Et sounds gurt strong."

"Say it again."

"Luke. Luke. Luke Dennison."

"You're right. It does sound strong. I like that."

I smiled with his name on my lips, and drifted off to sleep.

THIRTY

"Wot be ye starin' et?"

I turned away from the tipi opening to look down at Gracie.

"I was watching the children. They seem to be everywhere."

"Wotever they be do'un?" Gracie asked as she stood up from her bed to come to my side and look into the bright outside.

"The most normal thing on earth. Playing. Isn't that what all children do?"

"Does the noise bother ye?"

249

"The noise doesn't."

"But somethun does? Is thet et?"

"You can count. How many children do you think are out there right now?"

Gracie stepped in front of me and surveyed the area.

"Mebbe fifty."

"I would say every bit of fifty and then some."

"Thet troubles ye?"

"*That* troubles *yooooou.*"

"That troubles yooooou." Gracie mimicked.

"What troubles me is some crazy old hag once telling me I was the chosen one. To any soul alive, those would be the five most useless words ever uttered. But not me, you see, I am the one exception who is stupid enough to even question that prophecy."

"I don' git et."

"I don't either. But I'm beginning to believe that when I see lots of children, I should be nervous."

As with times before, it was easy to explain this collection of children for any number of reasons. For example, Gracie was a child. She was unique. Her blonde hair and green eyes were spellbinding. She drew a crowd of children wherever she went. They always wanted to see her, to be near her. They often played around the tipi in hopes she might appear or come out to play. A group of children, whether standing about or making a playful ruckus, is guaranteed to attract more children. They are simply curious about everything. They find interests, excitement, or simply security in numbers. There were at least seventy or eighty before me now to prove it. It was a simple explanation. And, yet…something inside….

THIRTY-ONE

There was no set pattern for the delivery of a child amongst these Indians as far as I knew. In general, first-time mothers stayed in their tipis, or close to camp where their fears could be allayed by the experienced. Those mothers who had given birth prior often left camp to find an isolated place that was peaceful to them, and saved having to clean up a mess in the tipi. I had heard on one occasion, of an Indian scouting party searching for a mother, who was believed to have died in some isolated place giving birth.

Back East, I had read accounts of women found murdered while in labor, presumably by Indian haters back before the forced migrations began. Rival Indian tribes would have been more inclined to kidnap the mother as a slave, and not harm her. The child would have increased their numbers. The white man was more inclined to kill a female Indian and her child.

I was safe from that worry because I was both white and deep in Indian country. It was the only fear I didn't have. My greatest concern was always my age. I was not as young as the average first-time mother. I was constantly attended to by Talk-a-Lot and Hotoomee'e. They went out of their way to be affectionate and nurturing, to be supportive.

Gracie was as afraid of my delivery as was I. That was my own fault. I had acted stupid in confessing my fears of death during childbirth. Although she made no mention of it, she suffered for fear of her prospects should I die. It was a needless worry for the tribe had taken well to her.

As I passed farther into my term, Gracie became more and more obsessed about my well-being. During the past month, my pending delivery becoming obvious, she spent virtually every moment awake caring for me. She was suffocating me, but I exercised patience the best I could. I felt badly for her, for I knew in her worried mind I was the only connection between her and the world she once knew.

"Gracie. Gracie!"

"Wot?"

Gracie stirred, but could not open her eyes.

"Gracie, wake up something's happened," I whispered.

"Wot? Wot is et, Mess Elezabeth?"

Gracie fought her way out of the sleepy grip.

"I'm all wet. I think my water broke."

I had remained still amidst the moisture for quite some time while thinking back on what Mary had said about her water breaking first and soon thereafter going into labor. I had been having mild contractions for more than a month. Now, I was very nervous knowing something different was headed my way. Gracie lay in her bed for a moment before speaking.

"Wot's the meanun o' thet?"

"I think the baby is coming."

"Oh may wort!" she gasped. "Wot t' do now?"

"I'm not sure. I guess we'll just have to wait until...."

I hadn't finished my thought when I was suddenly clobbered by a contraction as painful as anything I had experienced when falling off the riverboat and breaking all my ribs.

"Oh, God! Oh, God! What was that? Oh, *my God!*" I was racked with fear.

"Wot is et, Mess Elezabeth? Wot's the matter? Wot is et, Mess Elezabeth? Wot woult ye have may do?"

Gracie was frightened half to death, as was I.

"Something's wrong! Something's wrong. Get Hotoomee'e, Gracie. Get Hotoomee'e now. Hurry! Something's wrong!"

Gracie flew out the tipi screaming for help.

When Hotoomee'e, Talk-a-Lot, and Gracie rushed back in, I was sitting up straight in bed, knees up in the air, legs spread, and leaning back on my hands. I had experienced another of the contractions and was now as scared as a hare in a hound's pen. Hotoomee'e looked at me and spoke soothingly.

"Háo'omó'e. Háo'omó'e (Calm down. Calm down)."

Hotoomee'e looked at Talk-a-Lot and spoke.

"É-anétanó. É-anéotse (She is in labor. She is giving birth)."

"Ée'tóhtahe (She is afraid)," answered Talk-a-Lot.

Talk-a-Lot turned to me.

"Hotoomee'e say to be calm. Sssshhh. She say everything good. You have baby now."

In other words this incredible terrifying pain was perfectly normal. That realization scared me more than the contractions. This was to be my lot for however long it took.

My delivery was pure hell to be specific. I will forever be a one-child mother. It was inconceivable to me that I could have lived through the ordeal, and I decided the only explanation was the devil didn't want me. There is absolutely nothing romantic about giving birth. I saw many people arrive at Allen's infirmary, and many with serious injury. I never saw any of them suffer anything the likes of this. It was merciless and incredulous that any woman should have to be subjected to such torture to further the species.

I swore at Christopher for his part in this disaster. I was positive that he impregnated me with a child in his image, a child

253

the size of a horse. I knew I was suffering through the same labor that women of all walks of life endure. I didn't care. In my defense, I wished to add not only were most younger, but also great numbers of them were now dead. It was no wonder no one discussed birth. If they had, we would not be a species.

Maybe it was my age, maybe just my luck, but the delivery didn't go well. During the first couple of hours, there seemed to be little concern by anybody but me. Hotoomee'e had removed my clothes and kept an eye on me. She sat next to me patiently and talked to me in her native tongue. I discovered that once I had become tired, it was impossible for me to translate her words. Even my powers of reason were shutting down, giving way to an infinitely more primal instinct.

The day had passed and by nightfall, I was an exhausted, sweaty, overheated, ball of convulsing flesh. The contractions continued through the night, and left me delirious. By some venue of awareness, I understood the women were now concerned about my life. They toweled me and kept fresh water at hand for me to drink. It was inconceivable to me that any muscle in my body could continue to react this violently, for I no longer had the strength to keep my eyes open. I hadn't opened them in what might have been hours. I couldn't support myself any longer so I just lay in my bed coiling and uncoiling, fighting like a dying dog trying to get back onto its feet. I heard the women screaming; I sensed movement, and everything went black.

The medicine man was hovering over me. I could feel his breath. He ran his hands through my hair. No...it was Mary's hand that caressed me. No....

"How do you feel, Elizabeth?"

He asked. I listened to his voice.

"How do you feel, Elizabeth?"

254

He asked me a second time. The sound of his voice resonated through me, but I couldn't answer because I didn't know this feeling. I was separated from my pain. I was aware of myself, but I was lost. It was a man's hand that moved though my hair. It went with the voice. I knew this hand. I knew this touch.

"Where am I?

"Shhhhh. You are safe."

He was attending to my needs, watching over me, but not with words. He stroked my head with his hand. His breath swept over me again.

"He's strong."

"Is that you, Christopher?"

"He's strong."

"Where's my baby, Christopher?"

"Look, Elizabeth, Look! He's healthy and handsome!"

I tried to see. I looked through the darkness. I was desperate to find my child. I could see a point of light far, far away. I moved toward it. I looked into it. I struggled to open my eyes. The light broadened and spread out before me in a golden band. It was the radiance of a morning sun rising to greet me. It was still very low in the sky and it entered the opening of the tipi, which always faced the rising sun. Gracie was sitting cross-legged on the ground at the foot of my bed. She was alone and the sunlight was baptizing the head of a baby cradled in her arms.

"Gracie?"

She spun around, eyes wide with excitement.

"Yer awake! Luk, Mess Elezabeth. Luk, he's gurt strong en hantsome."

"My child."

255

"Et's a boy jus' like ye sait—jus' like ye sait. He's gurt strong—kecks like a mule. Look, look! Ain't he a sight? Et's a boy, Mess Elezabeth, just like ye always sait. Cain ye believe et?"

She placed the little bundle into my arms.

"Here's yer lettle piggy-widen."

He was sleeping, breathing so lightly. Long blonde lashes adorned his tiny eyes. They remained closed before the sun, which glowed upon his face with the warmth of God's love. From the moment Gracie laid the boy into my arms, I was aware of nothing other than my son. He was an emotional eraser that wiped clean my slate of worrisome thought, my heartbreak, my humiliation, my fears, and every torturous hour of pain. Everything bad in the world vanished in that instant.

There was nothing in my life at this moment to disappoint me, to depress me, or to sadden me in any way. I simply bathed in an overwhelming sense of wonder, knowing I had brought forth a soul into the world. In my consciousness, there was now only the joy surrounding this one tiny issue of new life. I was terrified of this fragile flicker of light. With all my heart, I wished him the strength to live as I promised he would be all for which I lived.

THIRTY-TWO

I was left alone and undisturbed during the following weeks. This was not common practice amongst the women, who were known at times to go about their business within hours of a delivery. The tribe was pampering me. They were concerned for the well-being of both me and my baby. I sensed them having an air of reverence or spiritual interest regarding this child born with the sun in his hair and the sky in his eyes. As was Gracie, as was

I, he also was a sight to behold, and their attention was riveted to him. The tribe assumed that the blonde-headed woman, Vehona'e, a person of great medicine, naturally gave birth to a son, who by all appearances was equally as spiritual. In this matter, even Gracie with her blonde mop and swinging dead-heads earned much respect and consideration. We three were a mystifying troupe that spurred their curiosity as much as their concerns.

I imagined the Indians viewed all our strangeness and existence as peculiarities of the spirits, and what appeared wondrous might turn catastrophic if ill fortune befell any of us. A turn of events Ho'neheveho assuredly had no desire to face. He encouraged Hotoomee'e to spend as much of her free time as possible looking in on me. She slept in my tipi the first three nights, leaving Ho'neheveho to his own devices by choice.

Hotoomee'e brought to me her experience in nursing babies and oversaw my son's care as well as my own. Amongst other things, she spent the first days sitting alongside me cutting up the roots and stems of a certain plant, which she then steeped in boiling water. A small amount of fat had been added to the tea. She called this tea 'motse iun,' and explained it would stimulate my flow of milk and make it more agreeable to the baby as well.

My breasts were indeed filling. I took my first wary step in learning the "how to's" of motherhood—*breastfeeding*. It was the *most* sensuous experience imaginable…for about two days. I was then *most* unhappy to discover that the blissfully serene image of a wholesome mother breastfeeding a babe cradled in her arms was dreadfully misrepresented.

I decided this lie was perpetuated through the ages with oil paintings brushed by men who probably never stayed at home to support mother and child long enough to learn the truth of it.

The truth, which I discovered after little more than those two or three days, was that breastfeeding proved to be impossibly painful. Almost at once, my nipples became raw and chapped. I was torn between the guilt of holding back from a perpetually starved newborn and facing the utter agony of satiating the angelic creature staring up at me.

It may have been due to the dryness of the desert air, but I was too embarrassed to ask my Creator, let alone ask or admit my discomfort before these people who were as hardened as steel to these small and laughable distractions. I gritted my teeth and suffered as Luke cooed with content while filling his belly.

Thankfully, all the guilt haunting me about breastfeeding, about whether or not I knew how to mother properly was put still by Hotoomee'e. She knew. She understood my discomfort at once and prepared an herbal salve to coat my nipples. She brought me a wet nurse who appeared honored if not thrilled to breast feed the blonde-headed babe with great medicine. My breasts readily agreed to the temporary reprieve before I was able to utter a word contrary.

Gracie always stayed close. She was fully taken by the child, and learning on the go as was I. The two of us would stare at him for hours, watching the way he reacted to the simplest things, like turning his head to look our way as we spoke, or wrapping his fingers around one of ours. He was irresistible. He was remarkable in every way.

Ho'neheveho waited until Hotoomee'e and Talk-a-Lot assured him the time was appropriate to pay me a visit. I was pleased to see the chief, and felt honored by his presence and his attention. I took him by the arm and seated him before my fire pit. I placed the baby in his arms.

"Nee'ha (Your son)," he stated with pride.

"Héehe'e, nae'ha (Yes, my son)."

"Épévoéstomo'he (He has a nice personality). Éována'xaetano (He is content)."

"Épêhévetano, héehe'e (He is happy, yes)."

"Épévahe (He is good looking)".

I beamed with pride.

"Néá'eše (Thank you). Hámestoeotsé'tov, Ho'neheveho (Sit down, Ho'neheveho)."

Talk-a-Lot had told me before hand that Ho'neheveho wished to call on me, and so Gracie and I had prepared tea and fruit for his enjoyment. He sat down as I had asked, and held the baby with great care taking time to know the child. The smile never left his face. He looked up at me many times and expressed his approval. In time, I exchanged the child for tea.

"Népévomóhtâhehe? (Are you feeling good?)" he asked.

"Nápévomóhtahe, héehe'e (I'm feeling good, yes)."

"E-tahpeta (He is strong). What name this boy?" He asked me in English.

"Luke."

He gave me an odd look. He leaned back frowning.

"Étšêškéʼo (It is small). What mean, Luke?"

"I don't know." I shrugged my shoulders. "Short, but strong name amongst my people. Name is in the story of Great Spirit."

"Hmmph."

Ho'neheveho thought this was a very strange name. He pinched his fingers together, expressing the notion it was too short, insignificant. It had only one syllable. This amazed him as much as me having bestowed a name with no meaning. He couldn't comprehend a name so short and not rich with significance.

He called for Talk-a-Lot to enter the Tipi and sit with us. He spoke to her expressing his concerns. She gave him a questioning look and then she spoke to me.

"Ho'neheveho wishes to give your son a Tsistsista name. He wishes a name that feels good to our people. He wishes to call him Hotohketana'ôtse, or Ota' Exanehe."

She explained to me that Hotohketana'ôtse meant Falling Star, and this name would bring to mind how I brought the stars to earth, and with them the Great Spirit with babies for his people. On the other hand, Ota' Exanehe meant Blue Eyes. Luke's eyes were becoming as blue as the midday sky; they embodied a perfect reflection of his father. Blue eyes remained endlessly mystifying to most of the Indians, and so were the talk of the tribe. All the Indians, including Ho'neheveho, were forever gazing into them, finding them indescribably fascinating.

"Ota' Exanehe."

I nodded my head, approving his choice of this name.

"Ota' Exanehe!"

He bellowed aloud, swinging a fist into his chest with pride.

"Ota' Exanehe! Épéva'e, héehe'e? (Blue eyes! It is good, yes?)."

"Héehe'e, épéva'e (Yes, it is good)." I laughed.

THIRTY-THREE

From day one, Luke proved to us all, he was here to stay. He was a feisty little thing, well…maybe not so small, but he was feisty. He ate like a horse, kicked like a mule, and, best of all, possessed the disposition of a saint. Luke was good natured, playful, and a pleasure to cuddle.

After his first month, *he* slept peacefully through the night, which meant *I* slept peacefully through the night. There could be no denying, he was *'easy on his momma,'* and his cheery temperament proved essential in uplifting my own. Thanks to his gentle demeanor, I was able to move forward in my new life as a mother with few, if any, concerns. Hours turned into days, which in turn became weeks, and I found myself growing naturally into the ways of motherhood.

Luke was bouncing merrily upon my lap when suddenly he was startled by the unexpected yell of a nearby crier. We all turned in the man's direction. I noted how his message was instantly picked up and spread by others. It was repeated, and resounded through the camp like a war cry.

The message was delivered with such exuberance that I missed what had been said. I could see that Talk-a-Lot was listening with intent as the man ran off sounding his announcement repeatedly. Immediately thereafter, everybody was roused, running about from tipi to tipi, and talking excitedly with frenzied jabber and gesturing. If I wasn't already in a great mood, Talk-a-Lot improved it by translating the news at hand.

Apparently, a great ceremony was about to take place. The proclamation stirred up quite a commotion. Talk-a-Lot conveyed to Gracie and me that the crier had announced a decision agreed upon by the chiefs to construct a large pavilion in the center of camp. The work was to commence at once. The structure was being built to accommodate a number of upcoming events, including dinners and dances, prayers and purifications, announcements, various rituals, and numerous social obligations that needed to be addressed. She explained that the time had come for the tribe to demonstrate their appreciation for the gift of new life, the bounty of roots and berries, the herds, and blessings of all manners given by Mother Earth.

There was also to be recognition and appreciation by the tribe for individual health and personal gain. Braves and soldiers would give their thanks for past protection given by the Great Spirit—some may have escaped injury during a successful hunt, others may have returned unharmed or victorious in a battle that brought them honor within the tribe. It was customary for members of the tribe to show their gratefulness publicly. Many Indians had made vows of personal sacrifice in return for favors from the spirits or good fortunes bestowed.

And then there was always this matter of my presence in their lives. It wasn't about my bearing gifts, but more a perception of my adding the strongest of medicine to the tribal spirit. The tribal spirit was of supreme importance and believed to be strengthened by the contributions of each individual.

The Tsistsistas still spoke of how the falling stars had followed me into their midst and brought blessings of children to the hopeful. The spray of new faces bouncing on loving mothers' knees only served to perpetuate the recollection. They recounted with thankfulness how my spirit came to assist Ho'neheveho in regaining the use of his leg. This summer, the herd was near and food was plentiful. The tribe was healthy and at peace.

So much good fortune was attributed to the woman favored by the Great Spirit, the woman with the sun in her hair; I was forever steeped in mystical relevance. Despite my desire to diminish my role in such fortunes, I was held to accept my contributions to the festive air and consensus that the spirits had been generous. It was for these reasons and others similar that the voices of the tribe came forward to ask for the ceremony.

There were four large events held each year. This one, ofttimes called the Sun Dance ceremony, sometimes New Life

262

or the Medicine Lodge, was considered the second largest, but occasionally ended up being the largest of the annual events. It was the only one that focused primarily on the men of the tribe. The women assisted in the preparation, offering food, drink, prayer, and encouragement, but the rituals by design were for men. Within two days, the preparations were underway in earnest.

Around a week into preparations for the ceremonies, Talk-a-Lot approached me with Hotoomee'e at her side.

"Hotoomee'e' ask me to ask for a gift from you."

"Anything."

"Hotoomee'e' want to know if you would honor Ho'neheveho with prayers to give him strength and courage."

Apparently, Ho'neheveho was to offer a personal sacrifice in the upcoming ceremonies. Talk-a-Lot went on to explain the events that spurred Ho'neheveho to make a vow that he planned on honoring at the lodge. He paid me honor by stating that my return to the camp was one of the factors in taking his vow. But there was also another factor of great significance.

We three sat down and over tea. I was asked to recall my last visit when the tribe struck their tipis to head south for the winter. Talk-a-Lot told me it was then that the tribes split into two groups of thought. One group preferred to stay forever in the south. The other group chose only to migrate south for the winter and return. She told me that the tribes wishing to remain in the south hoped to do much trade with the white men now constructing a new outpost near the southern hunting grounds.

Through the translation of Hotoomee'e''s words, Talk-a-Lot stated that Ho'neheveho was party to the group of chiefs that preferred to remain in the north, and hold claim to that ground, which he considered to be their ancestral home. Also, past conflicts with whites along the Santé Fe Trail may have also been a factor in his preference.

The chiefs who stood by Ho'neheveho threw their weight upon the words of past elders who cautioned against contact with the white man and his ways. At recognition of the inevitable split, there was held a great council of all the chiefs. It was during this council that Ho'neheveho made a public vow to the Great Spirit promising a personal sacrifice should the whole of his own tribe return with him to the north and remain one people.

I understood without explanation from Talk-a-Lot that a separation of the people meant devastation to the spiritual strength of the tribe. The realization brought great disheartenment and anxiety to many, but none more so than Ho'neheveho. The thought of accepting anything that would diminish the spiritual strength that protected his people was inconceivable to him as well as most other chiefs.

Hotoomee'e' smiled broadly when conveying her story to Talk-a-Lot for translation. She gushed with pride as she relived the return north for the summer. Numerous Tsistsistas remained with a few chiefs in the south, but all members of Ho'neheveho's tribe along with the majority of other chiefs and their tribes determined it best to summer in the north. And so, at least for this year, the split was minor, and the spiritual force of his tribe remained intact. Ho'neheveho's prayers had been answered. Now time had come to fulfill his vow, for to postpone a promise to the Great Spirit would certainly bring ill fortune to him and most likely those under his care.

I was flattered by the request to pray alongside Hotoomee'e. I felt honored to be held in such high esteem. I agreed at once to do whatever was needed of me. It was my wish to bring her husband honor. My acceptance of Hotoomee'e's request brought her enormous relief. She was ecstatic. Both she and Talk-a-Lot believed when Ho'neheveho most needed my prayers I would hold great sway over the spirits and bring him physical strength and fortitude.

In all honesty, in spite of my acceptance, I rarely gave thought to the spiritual significance attached to the three of us in the minds of these people. It was true neither Gracie, Luke, nor I looked anything akin to Indians, yet we managed to live a simple and unassuming lifestyle within their midst. We followed them through the same day-to-day routines, partaking in all the often exhausting activity needed to survive—we were something similar to three thistles sprouted within a thorn bush—prickly as the rest, but different.

The news of my acceptance raced through the tribe and was received with much praise and appreciation, for Ho'neheveho was loved by his people, and I had brought him honor. Within a matter of hours, I was approached by Ma'heo'ôhme'ehnêstse the medicine man and asked to accompany him and a select group of scouts in their search for a suitable forked tree to be killed with reverence and used in the ceremony. The selecting process was an honor reserved for a person of high standing, and although I was the honorary choice, a warrior who had been very successful in his hunts during the past year, and unlike me, a person who knew what he was doing, offered me much needed advice. I honored him publicly by expressing my gratitude for such selfless assistance in my behalf. The tree was brought down and taken back to camp along with a freshly slain bison.

Early the next morning, shortly after awakening and feeding Luke, I walked for the first time alongside Hotoomee'e to the hills for solitude. At a place deemed pleasant, she spread out a hide and we sat down upon it and commenced to pray. The prayers were said over a collection of herbs and feathers, and other items taken from things of nature that were valued for their strengths and considered to be powerful medicine. It was believed they

265

would absorb all of our prayers and this medicine would be tapped into later as needed.

The collections of artifacts were contained in two amulets, one for her and one for me, both lying upon a small leather skin. When prayer was over, she wrapped the amulets in the leather for safekeeping, and we returned to camp. We then went about our business for the day, she to her chores and I to mine.

We repeated these prayer sessions each day that the ceremonial lodge was being built. It was a large structure, supported at its center by the sacred forked tree we had killed. The sacred tree was now stripped smooth of its branches and decorated. Affixed to the top of this tree was an outcropping of brush that formed a nest of invitation for the Spirit Bird.

Around the pole were two concentric circles of smaller poles. The first circle was about thirty feet in diameter, the second about sixty. The circles were made up of about thirty or forty additional poles, each standing on end to form roof supports around the perimeter of the pavilion. The tops of the poles were then bridged together to carry the weight of hides that would cover the structure and offer protection from the sun and wind. The sides were draped in hides, so that the entire edifice was enclosed.

There were a number of smaller lodges built around the main lodge for the business of preparations. These included the sweat lodges, which were occupied most of the day for cleansing the spirit. Many of the women were kept busy heating rocks and bringing water for their men who were purifying themselves.

On the day the festivities began, the tribe went through an internal cleansing ritual. Those of us in the company of Hotoomee'e started out by drinking an herbal tea together that promoted vomiting. The tea was most effective, as I soon found out, but I was bound to follow suit, vomiting as they, but not accepting it nearly as graciously.

I had little choice in these matters, for I was following Hotoomee'e's lead. And as a chieftess, I couldn't afford to look weak, knowing the extent to which she was counting on me for support. At least the 'inner cleansing' ordeal was short lived, and thereafter all members and guests of the tribe began to feast.

The dancing, the singing, the games, and an outpouring of merriment by all, young and old, were quick to follow. Other than my morning prayers with Hotoomee'e, I spent most of my time with Gracie and Luke, watching the dances and related activities taking place outside the lodge.

One dance Gracie particularly enjoyed was performed to thank the Great Spirit for the plentiful bison. In this dance, the men draped buffalo hides over their backs, and leaned over until their hands nearly scraped the ground. With a little imagination, I saw them as an impressive looking herd of bison shifting one way and the other. Next came the hunters, masculine in their costumes of feathers, beads, and quillwork. Painted up, they walked in file with their spears in hand, entering the circle and moving round and round, stalking the herd. Suddenly, they would make a mad dash across the center of the circle and touch the chosen animal with their spears...in effect, killing it.

The favored bison would collapse, and the rest of the herd would scatter, disappearing from the ring and our view. The hunters then surrounded the fallen animal. They stooped down and picked up the creature, raising it above their heads, and parading it around the circle in front of all so they might see. It was then placed carefully upon the ground with great respect, and praised and worshiped.

The dances continued, and there were many more that portrayed similar worship for roots and water and health. Through such outpouring, such communal celebration, I fully appreciated the closeness of these people. I understood the importance they placed on both their social bonds and their marriage to the environment. I continued to learn how every aspect of our survival depended on the existence of the bison herd, plants, roots, and each other.

The ceremonies went on for days. Along with the adulation came the injured and the sick, brought into the circle where the medicine men would dance about them in order to drive out the evil spirits. After the sick were provided for, the wealthy men of the tribe came forward with their possessions and distributed them freely to the unfortunate. And I mean freely, for generosity was such a highly respected virtue that all stepped forward eagerly to offer something to the less fortunate. A lack of enthusiasm would surely prevent a man from attaining greater prestige within the community. All the chiefs had proved themselves many times over to be benevolent and charitable beyond question or measure.

This shared attitude, and specifically this one event, made a profound impression upon me. I had spent my life working hard to draw wealth from the rich in behalf of the poor, and I never experienced anything near the communal outpouring of good will that I witnessed here. Whereas in Boston I had to arrange for events, coax and coddle, plead and promise, in this place to share or give was of the first order. It was their way of life.

It was this communal virtue, so prevalent, which caused me much contemplation. I had always believed that to share was to love, and to love was to share. Their way of life showed me for certain that my beliefs and the goals I had hoped to see in my life could indeed be realized. I thought of Christopher and how freely he gave. I thought of how little he said, but how loudly his actions spoke for him. He should have been born a Tsistsista. Maybe we all should have.

Tribal friends and family now shared announcements of weddings and births, good news and bad, spiritual blessings and much more. There were many distant friends and relatives who arrived during the event, and it was impossible for this time not to be one of the social high points of the year. So went the start of the event until came the seventh day, when the ceremonies took on added fervor, and by evening of that day, the pace of activity resembled a stampede confined to camp.

On the seventh day, Hotoomee'e's attitude changed markedly. She had become very meditative and our prayer sessions had lengthened considerably. I understood the time for Ho'neheveho to give thanks was near. I was committed to stand by both him and Hotoomee'e and provide my support. In a storm of drumming, dancing, and song, we two had been given our privacy. Left to ourselves, we focused on prayer undisturbed.

Talk-a-Lot and Hotoomee'e had explained to me that Ho'neheveho and a small group of other men had been performing performing a ritual dance to the beating of the prayer drum since the morning of the day before. They had first danced themselves into a frenzy, but were now beyond exhaustion and moving in and out of the spirit world. As evening approached, the prayer drum stopped. It left an eerie silence, an overwhelming impression that a secret was about to be revealed, one that was now forcing the attention of all toward the inner sanctum of the pavilion.

At last, Hotoomee'e turned to me and took my arm. She rose to her feet and led me toward the outer fringe of bystanders who watched or served, played or just stood about talking. We disappeared into the mob of people, first moving through the crowds of women and children, next through rings of visitors and faces unknown, next past the rings of advisors and warriors of high esteem, and finally into the innermost circles of the chiefs who ringed the center of the great lodge. I felt naked. I knew all eyes were upon me. I stood out. I was different, I, the only woman, the chieftess, the woman born with sun in her hair.

Hotoomee'e was proud to have me. I could see it in her face; she was showing me off. She really did believe I brought her

269

husband great honor and strength by my presence. She bid me to sit down before her, immersed in the glow of the fires and the resonance of prayer voices that filled the night air. There before us at the center of the lodge stood Ho'neheveho, wearing only his breech clout. He was awash in sweat that dripped off his face and streamed down his body, glistening in the light of the flames. To me, he appeared to be semi-conscious.

Hotoomee'e laid down her leather parcel. She unfolded it and handed me my amulet. This time the leather wrap contained something new. Alongside her amulet, there were now two stout sticks well smoothed. I sat nervously awaiting her call for support. The chanting started back up and took on a new sense of urgency. The feet of the medicine men began to pound the ground with renewed vigor—pounding that echoed the heartbeat of a tribe now driven to a rarefied level of hysteria.

Ho'neheveho and the others had halted their hypnotic movements. Still sweating profusely, he stood motionless alongside the rest; he stood silent facing the nest of the Spirit Bird atop the sacred pole at the center of the lodge.

At this point, hides fitted around the perimeter of the lodge were being raised so that all people could see inside and be witness to the final ceremony. There was much movement and commotion as the Indians crowded tightly inside, searching for an advantageous place within the confined space. The air crackled with tension. The atmosphere was spiritual, frightening, and my hair stood on end, for I sensed the ceremony had reached the pinnacle, the advent of its purpose.

I was unsettled by the spiritual storm that swirled about me. It was singular, powerful. The world was eerily unnatural and out of control. I didn't feel part of it. I felt like a bystander. I was concerned for Luke. I was concerned for Gracie. I wanted to be near Talk-a-Lot so I might be reassured.

The tribe moved as one soul under the starry night sky, merged in prayer and thought. The prayer drum started again, this time in a slower, more deliberate rhythm, which motivated the tribe into a unified chant. Their attention was now beyond distraction. Their eyes were now riveted upon the few souls moving rhythmically around the sacred tree at the center of the lodge.

I thought I should be grateful at this moment to be nothing more than an onlooker, to be sitting a safe distance from the urgency at the hub of the crowd. Ho'neheveho, the dancers, Ma'heo'ôhme'ehnêstse, and the medicine men along with their assistants were now all congregated at the center. The smoke of sweet grass and sage rolled out from under the roof of hides and wafted through the air. The medicine men whirled and wailed, and incantation and song washed over the dancers and participants. They called out loudly above the din of the crowd; they cried out to the spirits of the earth and sky.

Seated solemnly around the perimeter of the inner poles were the tribal chiefs, nearly twenty in number and dressed in their full regalia of feather and bead and impeccable leather garments. Behind them in the appropriate order were their seconds, sons of the chiefs, warriors of valor and fame, scouts, the older men and the unknown faces, which numbered in the hundreds, all chanting in unison.

I was now extremely anxious, for I felt distinctly foreign. This was all much too strange and fearful. It felt demonic. I didn't belong here. Would I be allowed to leave after being witness to whatever this all meant? I must have been visibly nervous for Hotoomee'e took hold of my arm and squeezed it hard. She gave me a look of assurance, released her grip, and by a cue that escaped me, she moved to stand up with a select number of others. In doing so, she reached for my hand and pulled me up to my feet. I stood at her side weak-kneed and waiting nervously for whatever was expected of me.

We were being beckoned by the medicine men to approach the center of the lodge. Hotoomee'e had picked up our amulets and the two smooth sticks. Following her lead, I entered the inner sanctum and stood facing Ho'neheveho, who appeared to stare through us as if unable to see the world before him. Hotoomee'e handed me one of the two sticks. She looked at me very determined, nodding assurances that I would be up to the task before me.

I was only just beginning to question why we needed the sticks, when Ma'heo'ôhme'ehnêstse, the chief's medicine man and a friend of mine, stepped between Hotoomee'e and myself and grabbed the flesh of Ho'neheveho's chest. I watched out of curiosity and was then mortified as he produced a knife and plunged it through the pinched flesh that he had pulled away from Ho'neheveho's ribs. He then forced the knife away from the ribs so as to stretch open a gaping hole. Instantly, Hotoomee'e drove her stick through the opening and let loose of it. It happened so fast that I hadn't the time to turn away.

I was stunned, still watching, as Ma'heo'ôhme'ehnêstse again pinched the flesh of Ho'neheveho's breast and drove his knife through a second time. The blood showed brightly upon the blade, but Ho'neheveho never flinched. My first order of the day became ghastly clear. I was to drive the other stick. A task that was impossible for me to even consider. My only thought was to keep my knees from giving way.

I am certain it was desperation that filled my eyes as I looked at Hotoomee'e. I saw her immediate concern. She flashed an expression of understanding my way and stepped over to assist me. She reached for my hand and closed my grip about the stick. I saw my arm rise with the wooden piece in its hand, and I felt her grip tighten as it drove the ceremonial stake through the bloodied opening, resisting the toughness of Ho'neheveho's stretched skin. I gasped as a wave of chills raced through me. Ma'heo'ôhme'ehnêstse had already moved on to the next man, while I remained standing in shock, stunned by what I had just been made party.

Hotoomee'e smiled at me, trying to ease my distress. There was little blood and Ho'neheveho never uttered as much as a moan. As for myself, my stomach was in my throat, I was woozy. It was the grizzliest act I had ever witnessed. Hotoomee'e stepped away, leaving me but seconds to stand staring into the face of Ho'neheveho, afraid to glance down at his chest lest I disgrace him with vomit.

I suddenly felt clumsy. I felt as if I were now an obstacle being jostled about by Hotoomee'e as she reached around me either to fiddle with the sticks, or to keep me from toppling over. I tried to clear my head, to regain a footing in reality. I focused on the attention now being paid my stick and then hers. I tried to grasp what next might take place as I saw long dangling leather straps being secured to the sticks.

Lifting my eyes, I followed the leather straps upward to an arch high overhead. It was a timber laid across the poles and bound in position about twenty or more feet above the ground. As I observed how the cords were secured overhead, I saw the straps suddenly snap tight at which point my eyes raced back down the cords just in time to witness the horror of Ho'neheveho being yanked upward off his feet. My senses now battered into oblivion, I watched as his skin stretched. I watched as it was pulled forcefully off his ribs. I gagged and had to turn away.

What happened to these beautiful people? Were they truly heathens at heart; were they barbarians after all? Were they going insane from all the emotion, the commotion, the dancing and chanting? Had the ceremony gotten totally out of hand? I looked at Hotoomee'e who was staring upward as if touched by the hand of God. I forced myself to follow her stare and once more take in the sight of Ho'neheveho. He was hanging by his skin slowly swinging back and forth. I was beaten emotionally numb. I stood appalled as I witnessed the Indians crowded around me, drowning in the excitement of this barbarity.

All my beliefs seemed a misconception. All my childhood fears where upon me with a vengeance. I was overrun by fear for the life of my son. I feared for Gracie; I feared for Luke. I feared what might happen to anybody not of this tribe, but I was frozen in place, too frightened to blink. Everywhere I looked, a thousand eyes looked back. I was the blonde chieftess who stood out from all others. There was no escaping this, there was no escaping their scrutiny, I was insignificant, my life meaningless in this mayhem. I felt completely at the mercy of their mood.

My focus locked onto the Bird Spirit's nest above the Sacred Tree. I couldn't bring myself to look at anything below the nest. For those about me, it cradled the Bird Spirit, but for me, it was as empty as my soul. I couldn't bear to see Ho'neheveho, to see the skin of his breast stretched hideously, to see how it hoped to rip free of the leather bound sticks that held him steadfast against the merciless pull of gravity. I was too nerve-racked to look down and into the faces of these people, knowing they studied my face for the slightest sign of weakness.

What would happen next? Was there something as horrid in store for me? I had agreed to partake in this ceremony, but had I agreed to more than the support of prayer? I would have never knowingly agreed to this. What was next? What in God's name was next? My heart was racing. My head was swimming; the world was spinning. I felt faint, my head and thoughts clouded. I was struggling to hold on to my sanity when I barely sensed Hotoomee'e raise my hand to her mouth. She bit down hard upon my finger. The pain was instant and excruciating.

Instinctively, I withdrew my hand, but it was held firm by her grip and her teeth. Forthwith, I faced her and met the intensity of her black eyes as they bore through me. Her stare never wavered. I realized she was drawing my attention away from the event and bringing me back to my senses with the only remedy powerful enough to overcome my affliction—*pain.* I swallowed hard, tears of stress welling up in my eyes. I lowered my eyes. I was torn between fear and shame. Hotoomee'e released my bruised finger and moved tightly up against me. She pulled me down and encouraged me to sit.

And I did. And I did so for the next eight or nine hours, praying for Ho'neheveho as his feet swung slowly above us. I knew he was there, feet dangling back and forth above me, but it was a long time passed before I was finally able to raise my head. Even then, I was unable to look at him, to look at any of them. It took all of my courage to accept that this was real, and that I was here seated in the center of it—a part of it. What sane person could accept this? Would this change me in some way? Was I becoming something else?

I struggled to seek relief and concentrated on prayers—prayers to a Christian God. I didn't care if I prayed for snow or applesauce pie, so long as it forced me to focus on something other than what surrounded me—a heathen madhouse of ritual beyond all reason.

Even prayer failed to suffice. It fell to the only two things in my life that might counter this event: thoughts of Lady Rebecca's gruesome death and memories of my humiliation by Christopher's rejection. Lady Rebecca's fiery death proved to be too distant for this traumatic affair, but the thoughts of Christopher's rejection still shredded my heart and self-esteem. However pathetic this diversion, it had a measure of success.

Slowly, I regained something of a grip on my composure, and in controlled doses, worked up enough daring to witness others proceed toward fulfilling their vows and earning honor for their bravery and sacrifice. They were likewise tethered to the sacred pole by their flesh. These men were not suspended as

Ho'neheveho, but remained upon their feet, leaning backward with all their weight trying to rip themselves free of their bonds.

And there were those men who walked in endless circles around the sacred tree. They had similar stakes plunged through the skin of their backs and shoulders. They were tethered to leather straps or hair ropes that were affixed to the massive skulls of bison. The heavy, sun-bleached craniums scraped and dragged at the earth, horns digging in and holding the men back, fighting their every step and horribly distending their skin, pulling it like taffy. Time and time again they went around the circle passing before my eyes, hoping for the wooden pegs to rip free and put an end to their ungodly suffering.

Forgive me that I should ever overcome the initial horror of the scene, but truth be known, my nightmare was eased more and more by a sense of astonishment. I tried to imagine how anyone could stand up to such torture. How could anyone tolerate the thought or the anticipation of such pain? I had all I could do to simply muster enough courage to raise my head and face the spectacle before me. Having one last fear to face, I finally looked up at Ho'neheveho with the same feeling of incredulity. A feeling of overwhelming amazement, a feeling of awe I could not put into words. And maybe that was the point. Maybe the whole of this night added up to one profound emotion experienced in the most extreme manner by all in the tribe—an emotion that could not be justifiably described, only understood. Respect.

As my anxieties subsided, I began to enjoy some peace. Physically, I stopped trembling. My breathing deepened and slowed. Mentally, my thoughts fell back into streams of order. My thoughts became pensive. It took me hours to settle down. It took me hours to see past the grizzly images on the surface and consider the strengths of these men. I no longer believed the men or the sacrifice to be barbaric.

I looked up at Ho'neheveho. His eyes met mine and our stare was momentarily locked. I saw him as the incarnation of courage, of valor and honor. I saw him, as he truly was, the invincible warrior, a mortal who stepped free of mortality, a man who could face insurmountable fear, the fear of his own chilling self-inflicted pain.

My stomach moved up into my throat as I was distracted by a stake that ripped free of one of the men. The second stake now being subject to all of the man's weight pulled horribly at his skin until it too was released to snap up and away. It happened faster than those who supported him could come to his aid, and the warrior dropped to the earth with a thud. The man's bloodied body lay on the ground chest up with two ghastly wounds.

Overhead, the leather straps, free of their burden, swung gently in the sacred cloud of burning sage. A number of others were relieved of their suffering, having endured as much as they possibly could. There was no disgrace in removing oneself from the torture. The vows had been fulfilled and the respect far surpassed any thought of failure or shortcoming.

I had no doubt about Ho'neheveho. He would withstand. He would suffer as we sat in silence and supported him. I sat in awe. I sat and prayed most of the night alongside Hotoomee'e, who chanted aloud without break. I realized how little thought I gave to the limits of her devotion. She would take no water or food for the duration of her man's sacrifice.

Fortunately, she wouldn't know I was often busy praying for myself. I should have prayed to God, but instead, I remembered a time in my youth when a fearful storm approached while on board the REBECCA and how I believed that Christopher had the power to thwart its progress and save us. As a child, I never doubted it. As an adult, I could only dream.

Toward dawn, Ho'neheveho fell back to earth. We set out at once tending his needs and caring for his wounds. He was a man of unimaginable stature—the kind of man that legend was built upon.

The sights, sounds, and experiences of the New Life Lodge never left me, but the days themselves did. They passed on from that night and brought me around, and around, to pass the midsummer Medicine Lodge and the glory of honor and sacrifice, many more times.

As the seasons came and went, I found myself howling and stomping, summoning the spirits to bear witness to the bravery of men putting themselves to the test, pitting their will and endurance against the unthinkable. Not just in the lodge, but in the everyday struggle to survive.

People back east would have been appalled by my actions, by all of this. All things considered by them to be un-Christian, heathen, and base. Yet, I found myself filled with pride knowing that a man didn't prove himself worthy in battle by *playing with toy soldiers.*

THIRTY-FOUR

Luke survived his entry into this world in spite of my raw breasts. No doubt, his blissful ignorance of that potential starvation saved him from a dubious personality. He survived in spite of Sun Dance ceremonies and other oftentimes outrageous celebrations that swirled about his being. And through it all, the babe became an infant, the infant a toddler, the toddler a child. Luke learned the complexities of life from his mother and the perspectives of two cultures.

I knew this marriage of diversity would offer him a wonderful insight into the future of this frontier. I allowed him to freely absorb the Indian customs that nurtured him, but I also disciplined myself to converse with him only in English. All others, aside from Gracie and Talk-a-Lot, spoke to him in the tongue of the Tsistsistas. He grew fluent in both languages.

My strict adherence to this policy didn't go without notice, and one day Ho'neheveho questioned me on the matter. With the passing of time and many conversations, his English improved.

"I hear you speak to Ota' Exanehe. Why you speak only white man words, no Tsistsista? You know many words Tsistsistas. I think this a sign soon you go east with Ota' Exanehe and Haahke'eveho. Yes?"

Ho'neheveho now called Gracie, Haahke'eveho. It meant Little Chief. The new name better complied with the Tsistsista's convention of naming one after a relative. In this case, Gracie was named after me, Vehona'e, Chief Woman. Gracie had been most elated to have shed her former name, Amêške'hehe, Grease Woman. Sadly, when it was dropped, so too were many good laughs.

"Hová'âháne (No). No. No. I stay here…with you. One day, maeto (in the future), Ota' Exanehe will walk the directions. Not now. Tséstsêhe'xove (at this time) I stay here."

I assured Ho'neheveho that as long as I was welcome amongst his people, I had no immediate plans to leave. This pleased him a great deal. I also warned him that Ota' Exanehe must leave to see the world at some time, and much of that world belonged to the white man. This the chief understood.

As one season fell to the next, Ho'neheveho and I spent countless hours seated at the fire, seated beneath the stars, before the herds, beside the streams and almost always discussing the differences between our peoples. We tried to help each other understand the difficulties those differences presented.

For example, Ho'neheveho believed the earth to be a spirit, and could not understand how the white man could be fooled into thinking he could buy a spirit or own it. He couldn't fathom why anyone would want to claim just one field of grass without bison or one river when the earth was so vast and open to all.

I pointed out that even Indian tribes fought one another to command a certain area—a certain piece of the earth. I explained if all the tribes had a piece of land that could be called their own, there might be less fighting. I explained that it made for an orderly arrangement and peaceful neighbors.

Ho'neheveho laughed at the impossibility of such an arrangement. He explained that people mostly fought and competed for sustenance and so had but little choice other than traveling great distances to find sufficient food for the tribe. I countered with the raising of crops.

I pointed out my inability to understand how Indian warriors could go about killing each other on what often seemed more of a whim than any need for sustenance. I thought this was barbaric. Ho'neheveho stated that taking the life of your enemy made you more powerful, for you absorbed your adversary's spirit and strength. He argued it was sensible. A warrior always paid tribute to a foe fallen in battle. To give your life in war was heroic and brought your family much honor. He assured me that no one killed on a whim.

As in former conversations, we remained respectful yet far apart on some issues, but we tried in earnest to understand each other's points of view. The chief and his people had equally confused and sometimes fearful opinions of us. Feelings of distrust, disdain, or hostility toward whites were not yet as profound as what might be found in those bands of Indians living farther east or engaged heavily in the business of furring.

The Tsistsistas never occupied beaver country to the same extent as many of the eastern or mountain tribes. They were mostly oblivious to the bickering and rivalries that consumed those tribes employed by British and American furring companies. They were spared the trinkets and devastating flood of whiskey given freely for first murdering competitors that the Americans or English determined had moved too close to their respective hunting grounds, and later murdering themselves in a state of drunken suicidal insanity.

The chief recalled a few confrontations with whites traveling across their winter hunting grounds in the south as they followed the Santé Fe Trail, but this was many seasons past. He said soon thereafter a great council was held, including many Indian tribes and the white warriors, and it was there that the Tsistsistas made peace with the white man.

In fact, I recalled reading a flurry of newspaper articles back in the mid-twenties about a peace treaty made on the upper Missouri between a large deployment of some five hundred soldiers and a notable number of western tribes. I suspected the chief was speaking of that event.

I also gathered that as of late, a large number of Tsistsistas from one of the sister tribes had been trading with the Americans, and soon after died from bad medicine. I pressed for more details about these deaths, and determined the tribe had been exposed to Cholera. I wasn't sure how severe was the affliction, but it terrified many, and further convinced the Tsistsistas to be wary of contact with the European invaders. This avoidance by the majority of Tsistsistas meant they had less than needed knowledge of Europeans or their culture. I yet suffered the same ignorance, my less than needed knowledge of Indian customs.

My second stay with the Tsistsistas only furthered my ability to see with clarity and disheartenment how I had grown up believing that in the wilderness these people were savages to be feared. The more time I spent in their presence, the more I came to see how respectful was their manner and how orderly was their society. Women were treated with the highest regard and not only lived free of fear and dominance, but also contributed significantly to the affairs of the tribe and decisions undertaken by the elders.

Easterners portrayed the Indians as simple barbaric minds leading simple barbaric lives on the land. The portrayal couldn't have been further from the truth. It belied the often brutal and unforgiving demands that nature made upon these people. It required them to possess the utmost in intelligence, tenacity, and perseverance to survive.

To realize the truth was to witness a culture based on acts of bravery whether in play, on the hunt, or in war. It was to appreciate a culture based on acts of honor and generosity at home. It was to respect a culture steeped in acts of gratitude toward others, the spirits, and the earth for its bounty and sustenance.

I found the Tsistsistas to be every bit as engaged in religion, culture, and family as any community back east. I didn't condone acts of Indian savagery, but I grew cynical when realizing that if a Puritan burned a woman at the stake, drowned her in a bag filled with rocks, disjointed her on a rack, or poked every inch of her naked body in search of the devil, well…that was God's work. When the men of my world went to war, burning out Indians and bringing back their heads in a bag, they were heroes. They were admired.

Everything was a matter of perspective, but one thing was for certain, the Indians had never started the brutalities by overrunning and stealing away the lands and livelihood of the white man.

I enjoyed everything about these people. However, with heartfelt regret, I couldn't lose sight of the fact that they were of a culture most likely to be pushed to the brink of extinction. Even as vast as this land proved, with horizons seemingly unreachable, signs of the white man's encroachment would eventually appear. Maybe not this year or next, maybe not for another ten or twenty, but I knew for a fact that my kind were coming. The white man set out across a world he thought was flat and made it round. He would come, and the Tsistsistas would be forever changed.

To the benefit of his tribe, Ho'neheveho seemed to sense this foreboding fact. He was both intelligent and farsighted. He was a great leader because he listened. He listened to his advisors. He listened to me. He listened to the ever more frequent news of events overheard during dealings with traders and other tribes.

His ears enlightened him sufficiently to understand that change was sweeping the land east of the Tsistsistas, east of the Great River. He rationalized that these changes would make knowing the language of the English as important, if not more so, than speaking the language of the French.

Ho'neheveho had never feared the French trappers and traders, for they lived in harmony with his people and those of other tribes, often living amongst them, often helping them, often taking Indian brides. But the English were different. The stories he told me were unsettling for him. The English chose not to share their food. They chose not to share the earth. Their words could not be trusted.

When the Tsistsistas lived east of the Great River, in the times before they hunted bison, the English gave weapons to the enemies of Ho'neheveho's ancestors, leaving them to be slaughtered and driven out into the desert. He had heard stories of other tribes stumbling about mindless from the drink given them in the camps of the white man. He had heard that much ruin had come of it.

The Tsistsistas continued to adhere to the warnings of their forefathers, to avoid strangers with the pale faces, not to trade with them, not to trap for them, and not to accept their gifts or medicine. This avoidance may have been the saving grace for his people. It kept them unspoiled. It kept them healthy and harmonious.

Nevertheless, Ho'neheveho believed a storm was blowing from the east and thunderous warnings rolled across the land beforehand to meet his ear. His people spoke ever more of trading with the whites for coveted utensils and goods. He was driven to help them prepare, to give them shelter from the threat en route. He sensed the sooner they understood the white man, the better they would fare in the war of cultures bound to overtake them. One must know his enemy.

THIRTY-FIVE

In order to protect his people from the pale faces, Ho'neheveho wished for me to teach his tribe the white man's ways, more specifically, the language. From first word of my arrival, he wanted nothing more.

For nearly two years, he never made mention of such hopes. First, he waited patiently for me to overcome my period of illness. Next, he waited patiently for the passing of my pregnancy. His honor prevented him from asking anything of me until he believed that both Luke and I were strong and healthy. Only then did he make his wish known. Only then did he consult with Talk-a-Lot, and determine to approach me.

Ho'neheveho came to ask if I would *"give good medicine"* to his tribe, teach the *"Medicine Book"* as he called the reader that he remembered from my first stay. I promised him I would do as he wished and he was profoundly grateful. He insisted we feast at his lodge that night, and during our meal, he gave away horses and many gifts to the needy in my name.

Talk-a-Lot had told me that one of the reasons Ho'neheveho ordered such a large feast and celebration upon my return was to thank the Great Spirit for bringing back a person who could add strong medicine to the tribe. It was his intention keep my *"good spirit"* in the camp as long as possible, and so Gracie, Luke, and I remained as well-treated guests of honor.

Gracie eventually offered up her shrunken heads, which never failed to impress everyone. On numerous occasions, she had been called on to produce them for the purpose of warding off evil spirits that afflicted the unfortunate. She had long since grown accustomed to her new family, but along with her knives, the heads represented her father. Talk-a-Lot made known to all this close connection when Gracie delivered the treasure of spiritual terror to Ma'heo'ôhme'ehnêstse, the medicine man.

GRACIE EVENTUALLY OFFERED UP HER SHRUNKEN HEADS

The medicine man was indebted to me for the many gifts I had passed his way during my first stay with the Tsistsistas. He repaid the favor by coming quickly to my assistance upon our arrival, purifying me when I was sick at the onset of my pregnancy. He went on to calm the tribe, who were most unsettled by the presence of Gracie and her collection of dreadful swinging heads.

The medicine man made every attempt to repay me for honoring him with my gifts, but he was hopelessly lost for a way to thank Gracie. My gifts were numerous but paled in comparison. Gracie overwhelmed him with her horrifying heads, for not only did the heads overshadow most all of his sacred possessions, but he fully understood both the spiritual significance and the sacrifice. Ma'heo'ôhme'ehnêstse understood that the spirit of Gracie's father accompanied the gift. To be trusted with such a bequest was to pay him the highest possible honor. From that day on, he considered himself deeply indebted for a gift he would never be able to return in kind. He was visibly moved, and looked upon Gracie thence forward with considerable affection.

THIRTY-SIX

I worked with purpose to fulfill my promise to Ho'neheveho. I recommenced teaching his people the white man's tongue. I was happy to do this in return for all that he and the tribe did in my behalf, accepting the three of us as their own. Teaching English was the one skill I possessed that could benefit the tribe. I held classes daily in the chief's name, and in doing so brought Ho'neheveho much honor.

At the onset, I told Ho'neheveho that much to my dismay I no longer possessed my books and would have to do my best to teach without them. Maybe later, I would attempt to acquire some readers. He praised my determination and made public news of my gift immediately. Because the opportunity to acquire this strong medicine came at no cost to the Indians, they were excited and so news traveled fast. The very next day people started to show up at my tipi, asking me when I would begin to give them this medicine that they were impatient to accept.

I asked Ho'neheveho to attend the opening of our first day of class. He did as I asked. I asked Gracie and Talk-a-Lot to have him stand before the class and call out five words. Because of his status all ears in attendance were open and all mouths shut. The girls promptly wrote the words on the sheet of shale and showed them to the class. Long before he picked his words, I had departed to walk across a field far out of earshot. Once the words were written upon the shale, I was signaled to return.

I walked up to Gracie and reached for the shale. I looked at what had been written and in a bold clear voice spoke aloud the words to a profoundly astonished lot of Indians. A few were so badly shaken by such powerful medicine that they rose from their seats and retreated some distance from where I stood. Even in a society where bravery was second to nothing, it took a good amount of laughter before the frightened were again settled.

The example of word power spread like wildfire and my class was overwhelmed by the curious, making it too large to handle for the first couple of weeks. After that, the number of dedicated students dwindled to about twenty-five, and held firm at that number. Seven or eight of my students were in my original class, and already understood some English. This made the entire prospect much easier because they were able to act as interpreters and assist in the basics. Talk-a-Lot was always at my side and her mastery of English was no longer in question. I was also held in her debt for reteaching me words such as 'Ótahe'.

The word meant 'pay attention', and I used it more than any other. There was an element of truth in the old adage about acting like a bunch of Indians. I say this because my students were not particularly adept at sitting still long enough to digest the intricacies of a new language. Who could blame them, for it was one thing to sit and listen to an elder whom you respected and admired, a person you wished to emulate as he told his stories of battles on the plains and bringing down bison by the horns. It was another, to hope one might sit still for the rules of grammar. That was wishful thinking at best.

To overcome this obstacle, I invented ways to teach by incorporating lessons into games that required physical activity. For example, if they played a quick game of stick, they would be required to yell out 'I win!' or 'You lose!' I fashioned a pair of dice and made up games where they would have to yell out the number of marks on the dies. This taught them to count with great speed, for Indians loved to gamble. Trying to remember the correct number in English added an element of hilarity to the excitement. I used these games to teach them how to trade and barter for prizes with English names.

These lessons were all accomplished with a lot of noise and laughter. Everyone stayed awake, and I was left only with the task of reining them in. So *'Ótahe!'* became a tool used mostly for explaining the rules to the games. I did make a concerted effort to include other words and began with the easiest and most helpful:

I, ná-

yes, héehe'e

no, hová'âháne

who, névááhe

where, tósa'e

what, hénová'e

when, tone'še

one, no'ka

two, nèxa

three, na'ha...and so on.

Every day thereafter, I spent my afternoons teaching class and in return I was given food, shelter, and provisions without word of complaint. I was comfortable. No—more than that—I was happy. Out here in the middle of the purist virgin land, in this wildly free country, I was teaching, and for the first time in many years, I was enjoying the satisfaction of immediate rewards for my efforts. The very same rewards that had escaped me back in Boston.

I hung a sign outside my tipi that said "SCHOOL." It was highly decorative, fashioned with beads, bones, feathers, and paints. All the students, young and old, took part in its making, and when displayed during school hours, it garnered grand admiration. For those who did not attend my classes, the letters on the sign were designs of great mystery that lacked the usual symbolic animals and plants that all understood. Oftentimes, the letters held their attention as much as a game. My previous students recognized the sign, understood it, and returned to learn. And with them came friends and children from other tribes and families.

Yes, I could say in all honesty, I was at peace with myself. I was happy living out my life with little more than the skins on my back, so long as I had the pleasure of dear friends, Gracie, and my beloved son, Luke. I had buried my past and delighted in the gratification of being relevant once again. The feelings of worth, of accomplishment—feelings I scarcely dared remember, returned to me with more than just renewed vigor. I relished providing a service that made me feel I was an integral part of society.

I gained a special sense of worth in my teaching Gracie. She had learned some basic reading and writing from her parents at a very young age, but she must have found it pointless to continue with lessons, having no practical reason to use the knowledge. Eventually, what had been learned faded into the background.

At first, Gracie might have seemed to start at the bottom with the rest in her class, but once seeing the speed in which she absorbed my instruction, I knew there were remnants of her childhood lessons surfacing from deep within. She quickly became instrumental in helping me to teach, and by being a part of my program, she was forced to focus on her own pronunciation. The resulting change in her speech was dramatic.

She taught, and she learned English with the others, but her ambitions and curiosity drove her to split her time between learning to speak acceptable English and learning something of the tribal language, something more than signing. It may have been brought on by a fascination of the people she feared her entire life. In any event, her interest earned her the tribe's admiration. She paid them respect by attempting to learn their language and ways.

In turn, Talk-a-Lot paid a lot of attention to Gracie. She took her under wing and they would converse for hours, moving through two languages and forming bonds that would last a lifetime. As one would suspect, Talk-a-Lot fully made the camp a home and the tribe a family for Gracie.

As for Luke, he needed nothing in the way of support. He had no issues whatsoever. For him life held few fences. He was unharnessed and free to run, free to explore. For Luke, life was simply meant to be lived.

As time went on, my class grew too large and rowdy. I was forced to divide the students into two groups. Each group attended class every other day. Gracie and Talk-a-Lot stayed close by my side, and together we watched over Luke and the other children in class. All the while, I tutored the two of them, and soon enough they were grasping the method and routine of my instruction. At that point, they began to teach the classes in my place, leaving me some freedom for diversion and other considerations.

One of those was my regrets at leaving Christopher's cabin in haste with little more than clothes for the road and a small chest of personal items. I regretted departing with even less thought to what I might come to need. And so, I found myself sorely missing my books and a small trove of teaching tools, including pencils and paper.

We did most of our writing with sticks in the dirt, sometimes with chalky stones on thin fragile sheets of shale. Passing messages on stone was spiritual or magical to many of the first-time students. The mystery lessened as they came to understand the technique of writing. But to really impress them, I needed to find some books and show them what a sensational window to the world the written word could be. I needed to show them how all answers could be found within books, truly great medicine. The desire to obtain readers gnawed at me. It became an obsession, a personal crusade.

To find such books meant reconnecting with my past, an undertaking for which I had little stomach. Just the thought of doing so gave me anxiety, something I hadn't experienced in years. I chastised myself for my cowardice, my ease at falling prey to past embarrassments. I lashed out at myself and then determined to remain focused on my ambition. I went on to contemplate what risks were in the offing. After much thought and discussion with Gracie and Talk-a-Lot, for the sake of our students I decided the risks would be worth the results.

I requested an audience with Ho'neheveho so I might express the importance of obtaining the books and the undesirable need to make contact with whites. We sat at the fire in his lodge. He remained silent as he listened carefully to all that I said. This was his way. When he did speak, it was obvious that he considered the affair a matter of importance because in his eyes my activities were beneficial to all. He reminded me that any prospect of my being separated from the tribe was reason for his concern. I was held in high regard and the departure of my spirit from the whole was worrisome. Prayers and sacrifice would be in order to ensure my safety and speedy return. Acknowledging the wisdom of my words, and having taken every risk into account, Ho'neheveho agreed to support me in my ambition to return with stronger medicine for his people. He sent me away to await his call.

THIRTY-SEVEN

The call came as promised. My mission was to begin by searching out a white man the Indians called 'Wilpen.' He was not considered friendly. He was an enigma, a person who could not be explained, a person who lived as a hermit. Yet, for whatever reason, he was tolerated within their midst. Aside from the rare occasion when the Indians felt desperate to trade for something they needed, they preferred to remain distant from the man. Aside from the usual belief it was best to avoid contact with pale faces, the tribe also believed he was possessed by troubled spirits. White man or not, a hermit was generally full of troubled spirits and best left alone.

On one count, the Indians were clearly interested in the increasing numbers of settlers that were visiting Wilpen's place. These white strangers were already moving through the southern regions of their sacred hunting grounds. As with many tribes, the Tsistsistas understood what it meant to be forced out of their lands by strangers. The white man looked very different, came from an unknown tribe, and raised the concerns of all Tsistsistas. It was a topic much discussed around the fire pit. It was the main reason for supporting me in my quest for stronger medicine.

Ho'neheveho instructed five of his warriors to escort me to Wilpen's outpost. I left camp in the company of five, but only three rode alongside me. The other two were always a ways off to one side or the other. My three escorts explained that the other two rode apart to ease fears that they might tread upon the tracks of our horses or cross our paths. If this should happen it was believed we surely would be struck lame or worse. This was because Ho'neheveho considered Wilpen troubled, so much so, that he sent along two contraries to travel with us.

Contraries were unique unto themselves. From my very first encounter with their kind, I was captivated, mesmerized by their ways like nothing other—contraries lived their lives backwards. The Indians called them *hohnuhk'e*, and there were never more than a handful, maybe two or three within the tribe at one time.

Contraries were often highly respected warriors. They were also individuals of substantial peculiarity, and oddly enough often entrusted to do the most serious duties, which made no sense at all when one watched their antics. And one couldn't help but watch their antics, for only the daft could pass them by and not take notice. Consider just one of their peculiarities—aside from their odd behavior, they painted themselves red, and for the most part, everything they owned was painted red.

Contraries wore caps of owl feathers, kept whistles made of wood strung about their necks, and attached buffalo beards to the heels of their moccasins. Their hair was braided and wrapped with strips of buffalo hide that was split at the ends where two small tails of buffalo beard were likewise attached. It wasn't difficult to spot them in a crowd, and for this reason, I began early on to ask and observe their strange ways.

If you told a contrary to sit, he would stand. If you told him to walk he would ride. He might walk in and out of a lodge backward. If you told him to go away and leave you alone, he would come closer and bother you. Contraries said 'Yes' for 'No.' They did everything in reverse or opposite of what was accepted as the norm. If you needed water to be fetched, you told the contrary that your tipi was flooded and needed the water to be bailed out. He would then go to the river and bring back more water.

One never chose to be a contrary, for it was an extremely difficult life of hardship and solitude. They never joked or joined in the fun and activities. Instead, like Wilpen, they were hermits, living reclusive lives in the hills or apart from the tribes. Persons ended up in this position by bowing to warnings from the spirit world after having developed an irrational fear of thunder or lightning. It was often an affliction of older men or women.

The distressed person would begin by paying an enormous price to obtain a sacred lance of exceptional spiritual power. This he would obtain from another contrary at a cost of many horses, gifts, and favors. The lance was about five feet long, and had a bird with red plumage fastened near to one end. The shaft was covered with mysterious symbols. At each end, fastened to fine strips of bear intestine, were feathers of hawks, owls, and eagles.

It was called a thunder bow, and it was imperative that the lance be treated with the greatest of respect lest the owner be struck dead by lightning. No one was allowed to touch the Thunder Bow, and it was not allowed to touch the ground. If either of these misdeeds took place, then a purification ceremony was performed at once. The bow was stored in a special parfleche made from the hide of a bison.

At the back of the contrary's lodge, instead of finding the owner seated in the place of honor, one would find the Thunder Bow. No person was allowed to pass between the bow and the fire. Only the pipe was allowed this transgression. A contrary was not allowed to sleep on a bed, and was obliged to sit on the bare earth. When he rose from his place of rest, he sprinkled the ground with sage to purify it. He had to eat from a special bowl made from the horn of a mountain sheep. No one was allowed to eat from it or even touch it. After eating, he was obliged to cleanse it by purification with sage.

A contrary was something to behold for certain, and yet, he was held in the highest of esteem. Those who entered his lodge moved slowly and with great reverence in his presence. They only spoke in hushed tones. It was a difficult life indeed, and it only came to an end when the bearer of the lance could no longer manage the weight of its responsibilities. If fortune smiled upon him, another stricken individual might come and plead to purchase his lance at a handsome price or at worse he might hang his Thunder Bow in a tree never to return for it.

THIRTY-EIGHT

And so we rode south. Four days our horses lumbered along, methodically stepping their way across the desert floor as I drifted in and out of daydreams, or mused over my two reclusive, red-painted, companions. I wouldn't eat with them, sleep with them, or converse with them in any fashion, yet they were to see to it that I traveled in safety. It was frightening to know they would give up their lives at the drop of a hat in my behalf. It placed a burden of responsibility upon me that I preferred not.

To escape the colder climate of the Black Hills and northern prairies, the tribe annually passed through Wilpen's vicinity during the autumn months. The Indians told me that Wilpen's place was a way station of sorts that sat along a path well known by the Tsistsistas and settlers alike. The path wandered through the bottom of an expansive ravine that at some point in prehistoric times fed water into the Platte's north fork. I suspect it still did when a driving rain sent a gully washer roaring down between its walls.

Of course, it rarely rained, and everything about the place was as dry as the sand and unfastened tumbleweed that shifted and bounced across the hardened riverbed. The Indians tolerated the outpost for various reasons. For one, the place was remote. For another, the Indians could easily emerge from and retreat back into the cliffs, appearing and disappearing like mirages. But the main attraction was a small pool of water that broke free of its rocky restraints and bubbled up in this place. It was the only sweet water for a couple of days' ride in any direction.

It was at this well, in the wee morning hours that the Indians watered their horses, filled their bladders, and left me behind to do my business. We said our good byes quietly, and as they rode out in one direction, I began to walk in the other until I came upon Wilpen's place, it being in the shadows at this hour. It was only a few hundred feet from the secluded pool of water and made evident by an enormous congregation of shadowy shapes and forms. Giving the benefit of doubt, I refrained from saying straightaway the entire lot was junk. I moved through the maze.

Wilpen's dwelling was constructed upon a raised ledge, some ten or twelve feet above the floor of the ravine. I suspect it was high enough to save him getting drowned by an unannounced flood. I spied a chair and a small table on Wilpen's narrow raised porch, but before I climbed the ledge to sit down, I stood in silence and studied the place that would shelter a hermit.

The man lived in a sandstone cave that I suspected he improved over the years by swinging a pick, work done no doubt to combat the sheer boredom of the place. The entrance to the cave was covered with slats of wood, making it look much like the front of a house that had been mashed flat against a wall.

There was a door with rope hinges and a rope pull cord. It had a window at its center. A roughly made shutter had been left open and exposed a piece of coarse burlap that had been fastened where a pane of glass might have been fitted. The material served to filter out something of the blowing sand and dust.

This mashed house had a very steep roof that protruded forward and downward from the wall of the cliff, its outermost edge supported on two posts. It was clearly meant to provide cover, not from the sun, but from falling splinters of rock. This was made obvious by the number of shards scattered across its top surface either embedded in the wood or too flat to slide off. A small pile of stony debris had gathered at the high side of stove pipe that jutted outward on a notable angle from within his chamber.

I was heartened to believe that the man might have possessed a sense of humor, because in cavo-relievo, he had chiseled out a row of windows across the wall that rose immediately above his porch. In spite of this artistic touch, the dwelling, the grounds, and most likely the old trader himself would share the same single-colored, rusty, weathered complexion.

Having climbed up to his ledge, I sat patiently through the remainder of dawn, watching the higher cliffs of sandstone change color. As daylight slid down their faces, it vibrated across the orange and reddish brown ribbons of an adjacent wall that abruptly disappeared around a corner. The light settled onto the floor and quietly crossed the parched riverbed as it flowed in my direction.

The glow of the eastern sky was building, working to heat the chilly air. The warming caused brief isolated gusts to spiral through the ravine. I watched the gusts twirl sand below me and pelt large, slow-moving snakes that were in search of warmth. Maybe it wasn't the fear of rising water that compelled Wilpen to build his home upon a ledge. I remained content to watch the snakes from a safe distance while wrapped in my blanket and listening to Wilpen snore in his cave as might any unhealthy bear.

In time, the rattle of his snoring was replaced by the rattle of pans, wafts of smoke from the angled pipe, and the aroma of brewing tea. It wasn't much longer before he emerged through the front door of his two-dimensional house. Without reason for caution, he stepped squarely onto the rocky outledge with a cup of tea in hand and turned in my direction. I neither moved nor spoke, but watched unfettered as he convulsed with fright upon seeing me seated in his chair.

"Eeyahhhhh!"

So unexpected was my presence, that the surprise drove him clumsily back through the cave door. His cup of tea, still snagged on a finger, was flung sideways over the ledge to rain a brown spray on his possessions below. I listened to the crashing and commotion of him stumbling over furniture or something inside—something that had many utensils to spill. Then, as if a curtain-fall at scene's end, on its own, the door slowly swung closed behind him. No applause, only the briefest silence, then... an encore.

"What 'n tarnation...! Who 'n tarnation...! Dern it! Dern it all...."

Most likely, it was the embarrassment that set him off to swearing aloud before all who might hear. There followed another brief pause and he reappeared, cautiously this time, from behind the safe end of a scatter gun. He stepped out slowly, aligning the barrel toward my head as his eyes scanned the entire ravine, wall to wall, east to west. He turned and glared at me from behind a corduroy frown that appeared to be permanent. I said nothing, allowing him time to settle down. He spoke first.

"Dern, if ya dint put the fayr a god in me lady. What in tarnation are ya…settler er injun, er jus' a freak o' nature?"

"May I have a cup of tea?" I asked.

"What!"

My request seemed to have skewered him.

"Tea. It smells good. May I have a cup, or did it all go over the edge?"

The frown affixed to his face changed ever so slightly from annoyance back to embarrassment as he peered through squinty eyes, scanning the countryside for a second time. For a second time, he turned to look at me, and then spoke.

"Lady, thur hain't nuthin' out heer save fer wind, sand n' snakes, scrub brush n' sky. Hayl, it's closer ta the moon thin the Missouri, an' heer ya be a sittin' on my porch like some kindda ghost er somethin'. Ya sceered th' bloody devil outta me. Hain't no need t' do such a thing, ya heer! No need a'tall. Tea! Tea, ya say. Humph."

Disgruntled, he ground his teeth, spit over the ledge, and went back into the cave. He returned with two large cups brimming with tea hot enough to steam the brisk air. He also produced a jar of honey. That was something I hadn't seen since last at Christopher's lodge. In these parts, it was rare indeed. He handled it as if a newborn. Again, he spit over the ledge.

"Thought ya might like it sweet," he added with an entirely new attitude.

"That's right considerate of you, sir."

He snickered, clearly delighted with himself.

"Mind if I sit wit' ya?"

"Not at all."

"Ya hain't plannin' on killin' me er nothin' are ye?"

"Not yet."

He grimaced and then went back inside the cave. He returned with another chair, which he placed across the table from me. He sat down and poured some honey into his tea. This time it was my turn.

"Mind if I ask, what would possess a man to make a home in this godforsaken crack?"

"Hain't nothin' planned, ma'am, if thet's what yer askin'."

"So…go on…tell me. Why are you here living alone in this mashed house with pretend windows?"

"Heh, heh, heh, yeh, et does sorte look thet-a-way don' it?"

He looked up and down along the length of his porch.

"Heh, heh, yeh, well…. Dit a lot o' tradin' wit' the injuns, but it were danger'us work, an' by the time I git back East-a-ways, I done spent every penny made jus gittin' there. Once er twice doin' thet an' I had enough—*enough*. No more. Problem is, I gots no other way o' makin' a livin'—gots no skill. Been a rambler my whole life—a trader. Thet's all I know. I knew 'bout this heer water, cuz o' talkin' wit' the injuns. Figered I could make ends by tradin' water an' whatnot wit' folks headin' out West-a-ways."

"And the Indians let you be? Honestly?"

"Well, now, fer one thing, they think I'm crazy-like an' thet gives 'em reason fer pause. But, I wern't no fool, no ma'am. I made my place down-a-ways from the waterin' hole so as not t' give 'em Injuns cause fer concern. 'Sides, a couple a shiny things, er sump'in metal-like, ya know, nail er needle, er an awl, sump'in

301

like thet keeps 'em happy, an' makes me worth the bother. Reckon ya might say, I pay 'em my dues."

"Does it not bother you in the least to be selling water to some stranded settler dying of thirst?"

"Now, dern if it ain't it jus' like a woman t'put it thet a-way. I hain't sellin' nothin' t'nobody dyin' o' thirst. Truth be told, I am the only blessin' they git. If they be figerin' on rain, er if I hadn't been heer t' sell em' some water, they would be dead as derned door nails, an' I'd be pilin' bodies like cordwood. I git paid cuz I'm the only person stupid 'nough t' sit out heer waitin' fer some dried out fool t'come crawlin' by. I hain't livin' rich cuz it don' happen offen.

"In fact, I might jus' add, half the time, someone swears theys gonna blow my derned head off if I don't hurry right up an' tell 'em wheer to git water fer free. Right neighborly, don' ya think?"

"You blame them?"

"Well, hayl yes, I blame 'em! Who sticks a gun in yer face an' says *gimme a glass o' water er I'm gonna blow yer damned brains out, please.* Lemme ask ya this. Wou't ya put down twenny dollers t' save the man standin' behind ya from dyin' o' thirst? Jus' tell me, now—jus' say yes er no."

"Yes, of course I would. Who wouldn't?"

"'Xactly! So'd I. So'd anybody. An' thet's what I says to 'em. Yer payin' me two dollars er a trade t' take as much water as ya can carry wit' ya, an' makin' sure I stick aroun' t' tell the next dyin' set'ler wheer t' get a drink. So, who's the bad guy?"

Wilpen traded the water for whatever he needed at the time. The settlers were either appalled or infuriated, and even after threatening him with a gun, they could do little but oblige him as they hadn't a clue where the spring was located.

Grumble as they might, Wilpen just sat indifferently until the settlers resigned themselves to accepting the hard facts...water or no water. Wilpen wasn't unfair about his trading, and he could be generous when he wished. For the most part, he simply had no competition out here in the middle of nowhere on the longest, loneliest trail along the Platte. It only helped that the surrounding water was god-awful terrible, being highly alkali and disastrous to one's vigor.

Wilpen had all the time in the world to prepare his wares for business before the next suffering traveler rode in. His prospects seldom passed through without a trade. He maintained a goodly supply of stores, odds n' ends that the subsequent settler might use. His old crusty, corroded face belied his true cunning.

"I don't offen git ta see a lady 'bout these heer parts, 'lone 'n all an'...."

In the split of a second, I leapt to my feet, drew Gracie's knife, and drove it hard, blade tip first, into the wooden table between our cups of tea. I had been waiting for the inevitable advance and put a quick end to it. Wilpen bolted backward without regard to balance. He stumbled over his heels, flipped his chair, and disappeared over the ledge. Lucky for him, he was saved from being skewered on any one of a thousand pieces of junk. So it was with a thud that he landed hard on his back. The wind had been knocked out of him. Only the shifting river of sand softened his fall.

"Uuuuuuuhhhhh. Damn. Damn."

"You lived," I confirmed.

"Uuuuuuuhhhhh. Ohhhh."

He lay still for a moment and then made swimming motions in the waterless river as he slowly worked to get back on his feet. Once up, he rolled forward and remained bent, hands on knees, staring at the lifeless earth. After catching his breath, he backed up a few paces and looked up at me with squinting eyes. He was unsure of my intent. In his haste to fall, he forgot to grab the scattergun. He now eyed it with regret.

"Dern it! Dern it all!"

"You wouldn't have been thinking lewd thoughts now, would you, sir?"

I glared down at him.

"Dern me, dern me, no ma'am, I swear it. God be my witness."

He was panting. Then he became irritated.

"Of all th' god-blessit women in th' world, I gotta meet a pure-tan. Dern it, dern it, don' it figer, don' it jus' figer."

He shook his head in disgust. He shifted his weight from one leg to the other as he stared up at me.

"In that case, I am sorry, I misunderstood your intentions. You made me nervous there for a moment. But I'm settled now. Would you join me for some more tea, then?" I asked politely.

He stood rock still, studying me from a state of consummate bewilderment. He then broke free of his mental paralysis, lowered his head like a little boy, and shuffled his way back up the ledge toward the table. He picked up the chair, placed it back on its legs, and sat down. I pried my knife out of the table.

"How comes yer dressed like thet an' carry thet dern stabber?" he grouched.

"You are rude, sir. You stink, but I don't ask why you never wash. My name is Elizabeth Dennison Claussen."

I held out my hand and he took it with the utmost caution before he introduced himself as William Pennington. I almost failed to catch his real name, for my thoughts were suddenly focused on the fact I had just used the Claussen name, as was my habit of long ago. One habit it was time to break.

Mr. Pennington continued to brood over my treatment of him, and although the tea was acceptable our conversation was strained. I troubled him for paper and quill and I penned a letter to Dorrie Anne Whipsman at Granger's Boardinghouse in Tonawanda, New York, on the canal, an agreed upon mail post.

William was correct in making a reasonably simple assumption that the letter was important to me, in view of the fact that I appeared out of the middle of nowhere to post it. He took this as a final opportunity to force me into his corner.

"This heer letter mus' be pritty dern imm-por'ant fer ya t' show up way out heer t' post it."

"That it is, Mr. Pennington. Your lucidity is noted."

"So what happins, say, it doesn't git posted th' way it oughter?"

"It would make me very unhappy. I've gone to a lot of trouble, traveled a fair distance to leave it in your trust."

"I figer'd as much."

"Like I said before, your lucidity is noted, Mr. Pennington."

Wilpen was becoming bolder in his thinking. I was waiting.

"I know thet. I heered ya th' first time. But what I'm sayin' is an intel'gent man cain plainly see thet things gotta be trade. I cain plainly see thet I offered ya tea an' honey an' hosp'tality. An' I'm also of a min' ta post this heer letter, but I hain't gettin' nuthin' in trade. Hain't fair. Dern me, I'm thinkin', jus hain't fair. Ya cain see thet plain, cain't ya?"

"What do you wish in return?"

"Y' know." He hesitated.

"No, I do not, that's why I asked."

"I don' think I gots ta say it, Eee-lizabeth. Yer real pritty an' I hain't seen a single derned flesh n' blood woman in a long time thet hain't wit' her man. An' there hain't no one in this whole god-fersaken place but me an' you. I hain't askin th' world, jus th feel ov a woman fer a night er so."

"Oh, now I understand, just for a night or so. I thought we already settled that notion."

"Yeah, but thet was b'fore ya wanted t' post this heer letter. An' theer hain't nobody out heer but me t' do it done. So unless ya like walkin' t' the moon...."

Wilpen gave me that 'I guess it's up to you' look and smirked.

"Mr. Pennington." I addressed him coolly. "You said, you are the only one out here, but I'm here too, aren't I?"

He looked at me suspiciously. He said nothing.

"You must wonder how that can be, so I'll save you the time of thinking it through."

I looked out across the plains and laid it on thick.

"I am considered a great spirit by all the Indians out there who wait for me and watch us now as we converse over tea. They do as I bid. It is I who has been hospitable by allowing you to live in peace within this wretched rocky abode. It is I who allow you to sell the fresh water of the spring, which you so carefully conceal.

"The Indians have no fear of you because I have no fear of you. I tell them, my spirit is greater, it is stronger, braver, and that is why I can protect you or destroy you. I am Vehona'e the Indian Chieftess."

At this point for effect I arose from my chair. I drew my knife and displayed it prominently before his attentive eyes.

"Should I slit your throat in the dead of night, I would only rise to higher esteem in my tribe. On the other hand, if you harm me, they will first peel your skin off in long narrow strips and then delight in your misery as they disembowel you and laugh while you watch your innards roast slowly over a fire. If they die in my behalf, while they accomplish this task, they will spend eternity in paradise, for I am a Great Spirit who will welcome them home."

I drew back my blade and took up my seat.

"You will indeed post my letter Mr. Pennington, and I will be back to take charge of a delivery. I will be watching you closely for I wish to have that for what I have written. In the meantime you will dance with the spirit of death until the parcel arrives. I have already noted your lucidity, so I need not ask whether you understand."

The man had no reason to speak. His eyes said everything. He ground his teeth and looked across the land furtively.

"Now leave me, Mr. Pennington. I wish to finish my tea in privacy as I expect my companions at any moment. I suggest you walk to the east, sir. Walk until the morning air is warm. Don't look back, and don't step out of the ravine if you value your life. If you look back before the sun stands tall, you will never have the opportunity to tell anyone we had tea. Go."

He stared at me for a moment, his mouth opening to ask a question, then, possibly thinking it better to keep quiet, he stood up and started down the ledge. I watched as he walked away with nothing more than a hat covering some hard cussing under his breath. I signaled the Indians to come for me.

While I waited, out of curiosity, I wandered into Wilpen's cave. The small door with the burlap window belied the spaciousness within. It was an amusing deception. The place overflowed with items he had forced out of the needy for a drink of water. Maybe that was unfair. Maybe he wasn't as bad a man as first thought, but I felt no remorse in helping myself to his precious booty. Having gathered what I wanted for gifts, and then some, I slung a bulging burlap feed bag over my shoulder. I stepped out of the cave and descended the ledge. I retraced my steps back along the sandy flow of the ravine and then scaled a bank that led toward the spring. I sat down, and after enjoying a cool drink, I awaited the return of the braves and contraries.

I had appeared out of nowhere and disappeared into the emptiness of the horizon, and so left Mr. Pennington in his isolation to ponder our encounter. I envisioned him weaving his thoughts, spinning his tale about 'Chieftess Vehona'e,' the knife-wielding, white-skinned, blonde-haired, blue-eyed Indian ghost' until the tale reached both coasts. Everyone would truly think he was crazy.

When we returned to camp, before a great fire, I gave account of my meeting with Wilpen, and how I put the fear of the Great Spirit into his heart. I was counting coup and my bravery was received with much applause. I then offered my sack of plunder to Ho'neheveho so he might offer gifts to the poor and thus bring honor to his name.

In spite of years gone by, I still sweated at the thought of facing anyone from my past, and so I had requested the books be sent to William Pennington's care by request of Christopher Claussen. I knew Dorrie would be astonished to receive a request from Christopher Claussen. I believed she would find it so incredulous that she would simply accept it for face value and follow his instructions. From my stories, Dorrie knew well his desire to assist others. I hardly doubted she would risk dismissing such a prestigious request after all he had done in her behalf.

As for Wilpen, he sighed with great relief upon arrival of the parcel months later. I had instructed him to tie a piece of cloth to a pole so it might flutter in the wind and signal me to fetch my parcel. I told him that the Indians would be watching him closely.

When I arrived, his place looked like a ship with flags of every color and shape flapping in the breeze.

Evidently, confident that I would return, Wilpen dug down—*way, way, down* into his past, maybe to a younger man who wasn't so brass and bitter about his lot in life. He managed to resurrect a semblance of decency and actually apologized for his behavior. It was clumsy for him and I was touched.

"Miss Dennison, I hope ya cain believe when I tell ya, thet everythin' ya might ever a heerd 'bout a man goin' plumb nuts but fer bein' alone is true. I git crazier ever' month thet gets by. Used t'be, when I see'd a settler comin', I'd git all whooped up an' hoppin' 'bout jus' waitin' fer him t' hurry up n' git here. Now, I only gits s'picious an' go fer my derned gun.

"Used t'be, I's so glad t'git some company, someone t' talk to, thet I'd 'bout give half the place away jus' t'keep 'em heer a day er two longer. D'ya heer what I'm a-sayin'? But nobody never stays. Who'd wanna stay in a place like this? No woman, thets fer sure.

"So I gits t' wheer I begin seein' folks same as rocks. Same as tumbleweed, same as a derned snake slitherin' 'neath the ledge. I don' mean nothin' to it, an' it don' mean nothin' to me. If I gits t' thinkin' diff'ernt then I gits pains from bein' lonely. When I's fixin' to have my way with ya, it was jus' my desperation actin' out. That's all. I might say as I please, cuz I got nothin' t' lose. If I ask t'be wit' a woman, the answer's most parb'ly gonna be no. But, if I don't ask, the answer most factly is *gonna* be no. I din't never used t'be thet-a-way. Well, maybe, I was. But, I hain't anymore. I'd be happy jus' t' sit an' have some tea n' talk, should ya git a hankerin' to do the same. I'd be a might grateful, iffin ya'd take my apology t' heart, an' forgive me my derned ways."

"I forgive you, William Pennington."

"Thank ya, ma'am. Does thet mean ya'll stop by now n' agin fer a cup o' tea an' talk? I'd sure like it. Now-a-days, I don' even know how t' 'magine a pretty face."

"Now n' agin? Maybe, now and then. We'll see."

In fact, I did stop by to see Mr. Pennington on a number of occasions. Having rambled and traded the whole of his younger years, the man was peculiarly interesting to engage. His stories were countless, colorful, and could entertain me for hours on end. He had been a well traveled man in his younger years.

In spite of all I stole or asked for, Wilpen seemed to have an endless supply of curios and oddities piled up in his cave. He honestly delighted in saving something special to give me when next we should tea. And except for one occasion in particular, I always took my leave in the best of moods, much like a child loaded down with candy—except for one occasion.

"Wilpen!"

"Wha?"

"What's this?" I gushed with glee.

Wilpen turned around in his chair and looked up at me. He broke into a broad acknowledging grin.

"Hain't thet a-special."

"Yes, siree. Special it is. May I have it?"

"Hayl no. Ab'slutely not."

"Why not?" I was crushed.

"'Cuz I wanna keep it, thet's why not."

"What ever do you need a map for? You never go *anywhere*." I scowled in disbelief.

"Mebbe so, but then thet there map shows me all the places I bin, shows me evry'thin' I hain't never seed, shows me ev'rything I hain't never gonna see. So now, when folks come passin' through at least I cain says *'Know it? Yes sir, knows right wheer it's at, seed it on my map many a time."*

"It isn't fair, Wilpen. I am the traveler. I travel this land north and south, spring to fall, whereas you never get out of that chair, but you figure *you* need a map. That's plain crazy. I'm willing to trade something special for it."

Wilpen stared at me with squinted eyes.

"Like what?"

I immediately realized my mistake.

"Not what you're thinking."

"Wa, hayl then, you hain't gotta single solitary thing t' catch my eye. All ya derned injuns gots is pelts an' bird feathers. I trade wit' set'lers. Thet's why I end up wit' merciful things like maps!"

"And I thought you learned your lesson. All those apologies were what—meaningless? You're lucky I don't slit your throat for what you were thinking."

"Mebbe so, but then who in tarnation's gonna post fer ya when ya be needin' more paper an' pencils, books n' stuff. An' I might like t'add thet wit'out me bein' heer, who's gonna show ya fine things like'n thet there map, huh?"

"Them fanciful things are all that's saving your hide, Wilpen."

I believe I actually hurt Wilpen's feelings. We had come to know each other over time and my rejection of his muted advance was taken personally. One thing was for sure: Wilpen was now adamant about keeping the map, most likely to get back at me. Maybe doing so was for the best. The map would be safer in the

311

confines of his cave, whereas on the trail it was bound to suffer damage and wear.

Besides, Wilpen wasn't about to give up anything that held my attention and kept me longer in his company. I could have as much tea as I could stand while staring at that spread of parchment. I slipped into a private world as I studied the grid of lines that criss-crossed the sheet. Straight and true, they intersected collections of curves and squiggles, many beneath tints of color that marked boundaries both physical and political.

The map was titled "The Western States." It was only a couple of years old, published in 1834, Boston, Massachusetts, by Harold Johnson Sons and Company for accompanying studybooks at the Bernard Mason School of Geography. It was called a picture map and was bordered by a good number of small engravings of the various bodies of government and notable events in American history.

The map focused on Ohio, Indiana, Illinois, Kentucky, Tennessee, Missouri, the Missouri and Arkansas Territories, and the Indian Lands westward to the Great Divide. It included the flow of the Missouri, Platte, and Arkansas Rivers from their headwaters, and provided a detailed depiction of the rivers and mountains.

The map seemed to tame the wildness of this vast space. What most tamed this land, and at the same time unnerved me, was the bespattering of black dots—the representation of white man's intrusion. This map was recently constructed and showed how dramatic was the westward expansion of 'civilization' from St. Louis and the banks of the Mississippi. The dots that now bordered the Missouri reached far upriver.

Looking at the map ascertained Luke would never spend his adult life running free and unencumbered across the boundless prairies, but more likely as a citizen fenced in one of those

312

newly formed dots. That realization brought uneasiness. A sense of dread welled up from deep within my soul. Sooner or later I would have to face not only that civilization, but worse—my past.

There would always be a past. Even here, even now, I couldn't escape it. I felt my throat tighten. The map was bringing back a rush of uncomfortable feelings. I felt as though it was drawing me back to Christopher, forcing me to reconnect. It returned me to his cabin. I could the feel everything about the place. I could smell Christopher's presence about his desk covered by the many maps I once studied, much as I studied this map before me. I remembered the 'Washington Map' in particular, and the large candle that illuminated it. I remembered another candle on the table next to the bed that—.

"No!"

I took a deep breath. I fought to free myself from Christopher's grip.

"No, what?" asked Wilpen.

His voice broke the spell. I looked at him long enough to regain my composure.

"No, I am not going to kill you," I mumbled.

His jaw dropped as his head tilted to one side. He huffed in disbelief.

"Yer jus' too kind, 'lizabeth. An' I s'pose fer spar'n' my life ya'd like me t' fetch ya some more derned tea."

"With honey—you can consider that your apology."

"O' course! Dern it, I shoulda thought o' thet theer myself. No wonder I cain't git a woman nohow. I got no brains."

Wilpen wandered back into his cave, shaking his head and mumbling aloud as I forced shut the door to my sickening

313

remembrances. I worked to concentrate on the map and especially the lay of rivers that crossed these plains. I did my best to burn those lifesaving waterways into my memory. I believed I might see a day when my life depended on it.

I was certain I would return many more times to chat with Wilpen, review the map, and refresh my memory. Being satisfied for now, I rolled up the document, set it aside, and enjoyed my sweetened tea. Wilpen would always hope for more than he would get, and I would always tolerate his advances in return for a connection to a world I once knew.

Although my trust and friendship with Wilpen continued to grow, I still remained protective of my Indian family and their whereabouts. I always appeared on Wilpen's porch in the same manner as I had the first time, and I always walked off into the distance at night. This was what he knew of me, and it served to entrench his stories-turned-legends, tales told of the ghostly Indian Chieftess Vehona'e.

Wilpen's trading post was on the Platte and that made it one long distant stop shy of the South Pass. Each month, more settlers traveled the Platte River Trail, and it was they who carried his story of the blonde ghost back and forth across the frontier with them. The stories were recounted in a hundred different versions. Sometimes, I was the savior of a lonesome traveler, other times a she-demon brandishing a blood covered knife. Needless to say, most of the time I appeared nude, rarely in more practical Indian leathers, or more modest dress, apron and bonnet. It was to be retold over and over again at inns amongst lonely men over pints of whiskey. Through it all, the only thing consistent was the part of the blonde ghost.

Wilpen laughed about my legendary status, and relayed all of these accounts to me. He roared with delight, conveying how he would tell a westbound traveler a tale about me, and then hear the tale retold to him weeks later by an eastbound traveler, only difference being everything he said.

Wilpen glowed at the thought of his stories traveling so far. In fact, he had a few travelers who came for the sole purpose of seeing *him* and the place where this ghost visited. He was now going out of his way to embellish his stories, for his plan was to make me the greatest legend in the West. He was selling bits of cloth from clothing that he claimed he stole after I stripped down to bathe.

Then there came one meeting in particular, one story in particular, which stayed with me. Wilpen made mention of a party of riders that had come out of the South Pass region and claimed to have gone to great trouble in their effort to locate him.

"How many were there?"

"Five. They're askin' all manner o' questions."

"Such as?"

"Ya know, wheer ya'd be stayin' n' all. Wheer'd ya come from, wheer'd ya git t' goin'. Ask't 'bout yer blont hair. Same as er'body else."

"What did you tell them."

"Same thing, I al'ays say. She 'pears in the dark o' night, an' she fades in t' the warmth o' mornin's glow."

"My word, Wilpen, you do lay it on thick."

"Heh, heh, heh, hain't it so. I gotta do ya proper. Yer a legent. Funny thing is, they 'eren't talkin' at me like I's crazy."

"No doubt the biggest surprise of all."

"Ha! Very funny, I git what yer sayin'. I git what yer sayin."

Wilpen laughed. I laughed. If only he knew of what scheming transpired beyond his awareness. Aside from Christopher's obvious attempt to locate me, there was another scheme unbeknownst to Wilpen, this one fashioned by my hand.

Unlike all my previous visits, this time I came through the ravine on horseback. Wilpen took immediate notice and sat straight up in his chair upon the ledge. He looked down at me, and I could see he was confused by this and something more.

"'Lizabeth?"

"Hello, Wilpen. How are you?"

"Well's cain be 'spected 'spose."

"You mean crazier than ever?"

"Heh, heh, yeah, thet too, I reckin."

"Good to know you're alive and well."

"I woun't be thinkin' on seein' ya so soon n' all. Not thet I'd be complainin' er nothin'. What brings ya out this-a-ways?"

"I wanted you to meet someone. C'mon down."

Wilpen stood up from his chair and climbed down off the ledge. He stood before us stock still. He was studying my companion.

"This is Eehe'e. She is a fine, strong woman, Wilpen. I wish to know whether or not you find her attractive?"

Wilpen looked at me with an expression of disbelief.

"Yer askin' if I think she's 'tractive?" Wilpen could hardly take his eyes off of her. "'Lizabeth, I been 'lone so long, I think rocks r' 'tractive. I think snakes r' 'tractive. Why in tarnation woult ya be askin' me such a thing 'bout a woman? Are ya goin' t' kill me iffin I say yes? Are ya goin' t' kill me fer havin' lewd thoughts?"

I couldn't help but to laugh.

"No, at least not just this minute. I brought Eehe'e to meet you. Her man was killed hunting bison. She is widowed and wishes not to be a burden on his family. I believe she would make you happy, and I also believe you would make her a fine mate. I know you have a good heart albeit too expressive at times. I have on many occasions seen it surface. I know to what extent you can be a gentleman when you so choose. I went to great lengths selecting someone for you, someone I thought compatible. What do you think of her?"

"She is a right handsome woman."

Wilpen spoke softly as if afraid he might frighten her away.

"I am delighted you should think so. In that case, you must listen to what I say with the utmost attention. The women of my tribe are held in the highest regard and treated with great respect. Eehe'e knows nothing less. She would expect nothing less from you. Should you determine to keep her at your side, I must be certain you will never fail to honor her. Don't ever forget what it means to be lonely. As her chief, I have given her my blessing and my permission to slit your throat while you sleep if she feels mistreated. Do you understand?"

"Yes."

"Do you believe?"

"Yes, ma'am."

As badly as Wilpen wished for someone with whom he might converse, he was lost for words. As badly as he wished for someone with whom he might sleep, he was suddenly sheepishly shy. Seemingly without thought, he removed his hat from his head.

"Might I offer you ladies some tea?"

We sat together and I eased the couple into a friendship that appeared to start amicably. I had spent a good deal of time looking for a woman whom I sensed would be good for Wilpen. Eehe'e would pour life into his empty heart. In return, Wilpen's collection of "wares" would make her wealthy amongst her people. Between his Indian wife and his connection to the white man's world, I expected Wilpen to emerge from craziness to become a powerful spirit for the tribe.

After admonishing Wilpen for his continuous spitting and his need to bathe more often, I took my leave. I bade them farewell and looked back only once, long enough to see him placing a blanket respectfully across Eehe'e's shoulders. They were sitting close together, illuminated by the flickering light of a fire burning atop the ledge. As he put his arm around her, the fire's orange glow lengthened their shadows to sway back and forth across the grooved borders of chiseled pretend windows.

I returned to camp with the braves. I left knowing Wilpen had entered a world of complete bliss. I never paid him a visit again. On those occasions when I thought of him, I always thought of Christopher. Recalling Wilpen's story of the riders left me to wonder to what extent Claus had suffered his own regrets. I thought of the riders who had taken me to him ages ago. It brought a sad and melancholy smile to my face, and the realization that, at last, I had overcome my past and the insufferable memories that distorted it. I was content. I had Gracie, I had Talk-a-Lot and Ho'neheveho; I had family. Most of all, I had my son...Christopher's son.

THIRTY-NINE

Summer was waning. Judging by the heat of day, a European would have said it was mid-September, but in truth, it was more likely to be mid-August at the latest. A Tsistsista would have said it was 'the moon when chokeberries ripen' or the time when geese lose their feathers. The refreshing greenery that covered the boundless spaces through spring and early summer had burned itself out, dissipating into the varied shades of blowing sand and scrub brush. Sand burrs and seed stuck to everything. The days had a hint of darkness, the evenings a hint of chill.

The night skies were as always, inky black and glistening. I had never been able to piece together Sagittarius, Capricornus, or any of the other constellations that put order to the stars. I was a poor student of the night sky, unable to judge time of year by the changing heavens. However, more important, I did know precisely where was the north star, the pole star, Polaris—easily found a distance five times the depth of the Big Dipper's dipper straight up and at the end of the Little Dipper's handle—Ursa Major and Ursa Minor. This I learned as a child from the old salts aboard the REBECCA.

I had no need for stars or calendar to mark the passing of time. Nature's signs, by season or by year, were ever present and most clear. To stare at the calendar was to miss the first lilies and primroses of spring opening like jewels in the sun. It was to miss the migration of geese and duck, of crane and heron on wing by the millions as they passed overhead making way for northern nests. One might not see the many visitors now arriving to summer on the plains, the Killdeer, the plovers and doves, the Red-headed Woodpeckers and the meadowlarks.

I welcomed spring at first sight of the unmistakable Red-winged Blackbirds as they flooded in to soar over our heads in flocks of thousands. For a month, their numbers flowed across the sky, thick as dark molasses, offering currents of churning aerial patterns and whirlwinds of motion all signaling summer was soon to be here. And of course, it was. And blackbirds abandoned their social flirtations to settle in pairs, quiet and unnoticed, taking up residence amidst the prairie grasses. They were our neighbors, raising their young until October and November, when they bid us farewell for warmer climates. They gave up their homes to the hawks and sturdy birds of the north now coming down to announce the approach of winter.

If not by the final thunderstorms of summer, or the occasional glimpse of gold amidst a flutter of aspen leaves, if not by the height and girth of saplings, then surely the passing of seasons could be found in the faces of those I loved. Luke, no longer a babe, hoped to be a brave. And Gracie, with the exception of her blonde hair and those astonishing eyes, possessed no trace of the flat-chested waif that rode into camp while clinging so desperately to my heart.

Never, in my most outlandish daydreams, might I have imagined a decade would pass me by while watching the coming and going of birds, or the rise and fall of flowers as I chased bison to and fro across the expanses. I spent ten years wandering foothills to pick firewood and roots. I spent ten years traversing high plain deserts that sloped gently downward from the walls of the Great Mountain divide to a sky where there perpetually rose a morning sun. With Luke and Gracie in tow, I traveled south at summer's end and north each spring thereafter in orchestration with the seasons. I had come to fully embrace the nomadic rigors of those who protected me.

To live life as a nomad was to learn how difficult could be life. It was an existence rooted in simple brutal extremes, all components of a grueling struggle to survive. I had endured the worst that nature and man might put upon me. I lived through the scorching sun, the freezing snow, the dread of sickness, injury, and battle. But what came to prevail uppermost in my mind was the haunt of hunger.

I had never before been subjected to circumstance, whereby, the search for sustenance was so clearly defined as the price of my being. From the moment we arose, to the hour we retired, every day, every week, every season of the year, our primary activity was the search and preparation of food. The ceremonies, the offerings, the songs and dances, the talk about the campfire, all centered about this one quest pivotal to our existence.

Be it the blistering heat of summer or freezing sleet under the Hard Moon, old and young alike were equally employed to confront the adversities. There were few exceptions. Men might shiver silently under cover of snow, or huddle with a spear in the dark of a pit concealed by a camouflage of branch and bush. Hunters rode hard under a sweltering sun or through the smoke of a plain set ablaze. Adversities were not only endured, but expected whenever and wherever bringing down bison or beast. The quest went on so the tribe might be fed, women and children clothed, and the old and invalid cared after.

I recalled how the gentry of Boston clamored for the thrill of the hunt. I remembered the ado over sporting the latest in fashion, the joyful squeal of young women given their first choice of the many well-groomed horses being paraded for show. Honor was defended by wagers and the men barked them out boastfully in every direction just prior to loosing dogs pedigreed and especially impatient to track their quarry be it fox, bear, or bird.

Panting horses would return the hunters late of an afternoon. The men held high their catch in hand with smiles broad and flashing across faces made rosy in complexion but for the buffeting of fresh breezes. Their watering eyes reflected the gaiety and rambunctious soaring spirits harboring within souls without worry. Their dismount signaled servants to prepare the table for a feast of food, drink, and merriment.

The Indians feasted as well. It was then that they offered thanks. They ate, they sang and danced, they bragged as did the gentry of Boston. But never once in my ten summers with the Tsistsistas did I ever understand hunting to be sport. I knew it to be dangerous; leaving many men to be led back home injured or

321

dead across the back of a horse, and often to no avail, the hunt proving unsuccessful. If it was sport, it made slaves of us all.

In my younger years, I remembered thoughtless quips often made back home about sending Indians to their 'happy hunting grounds,' and later, not so long ago, a single comment by Ho'neheveho that had been expressed in such poignant contrast.

It had been a bad day. Homa'êhesta, a chief from a neighboring tribe, had been killed. He was a familiar face, a man we all knew and respected. While at full gallop, his horse stepped into a burrow, snapped its leg, and went down. Homa'êhesta was thrown into the path of a bull enraged by the onslaught of warrior's arrows and spears. Homa'êhesta was gored mercilessly.

For Ho'neheveho, it was a terrible loss. The warrior had been a life-long friend, a respected chief, and a good and generous man who placed his people before all else. Ho'neheveho had learned much from his friend, and so looked at me with eyes reflecting his heavy heart. He was burdened with despair.

"I tired, Vehona'e. I tired. I pray to Great Spirit. When I die, I ask I never hunt again. Never. Too hard. Too hard, Vehona'e."

I cried as he lowered his head and walked away. Through my tears, I watched him escape into a field of gently swaying grass, where he chose to be alone. I wanted, so very much, to follow him and tend to his injured spirit, but I knew this was improper. He wished solitude, and this was a need that was respected by all Indians. When a man walked alone, it was known he was troubled and sought guidance. Now, it was up to spirits in the wind to wash away his wounds and lift his heart. Ho'neheveho went to find his God and pray.

Amongst all the Indians I had come to know during my years with the Tsistsistas, I never heard one express joy in the desperate and dangerous daily burden of bringing home game big enough to feed the hungry. If nothing else, I learned there was no such thing as *'happy'* hunting grounds.

FORTY

Whereas the tragedy and passing seasons served only to push Ho'neheveho and me further into the aches, the pains, and the general weariness of middle age, it brought Gracie to maturity and Luke to adolescence. Gracie was now twenty or twenty-one best I could tell, and a blossom of womanhood. She had gained all the confidence a woman could desire. I had often wondered if she might take a man from the tribe, but she remained distant and wary of any amorous attention paid her way.

Back home she would have suffered my same fate. She would have been considered a spinster at her age. But here, she was free, a bird to fly in a blue unblemished sky as limitless as her spirit. Year after year, she held tightly onto her dream to go to St. Louis. It was all of a spiritual goal nurtured from the day her dying father gave his final instructions. Of course, my unending stories and descriptions of life back east only served to put all the more ardency into her ambition to someday move on.

Luke passed his tenth spring, and grew more stubbornly independent with each fleeting year. The Indian side of these children grew up fast, strong willed, and often too unruly for me. A part of me would always be a European-bred-and-raised mother acclimated to an entirely different set of family standards. Still, the boy was beautiful with clear blue eyes and braids of blonde hair hanging well past his shoulders. He was my son and could do very little wrong before my biased eyes. I was blinded by love and pride.

In order to bring balance to their rowdy tribal upbringing, I made a concerted effort to instill within Luke and Gracie another perspective on life. I was haunted by the splattering of dark dots on Wilpen's map. The memory of that black rash and the encroachment of white man's settlements that it represented was for me most unsettling.

As a child immigrant, I knew all too well the difficulties of learning a new language in a new world. I knew the importance of speaking fluently, and how quickly one was dismissed as worthless by the utterance of a single mispronounced word. Luke began learning proper English from day one as a baby. He simply built upon that knowledge one word at a time, by the hour, day, and year throughout his childhood. For him, English came effortlessly.

By contrast, Gracie had to begin by unlearning a childhood of archaic vocabulary and impossible enunciation. It took many years to fully correct that which was firmly embedded, *"yut"* being a prime example. She was driven to succeed both by her desire to mimic me and to converse with Talk-a-Lot, who required clearly spoken words if Gracie hoped to be understood. Gracie's love of teaching English to the Indians alongside Talk-a-Lot continued to be the structure that forged her proper articulation.

I attempted to pass on to Luke and Gracie not only fluent speech, but also all of what I had been taught as a child by my European tutors in the arts and sciences. I was adamant that they regularly curb their wild spirits in order to learn proper etiquette and decorum, especially table manners. When came that day whereby I removed them to that white man's world, I expected them to understand what behavior was expected, for interaction on the wide open plains was entirely different from that of overcrowded towns and cities.

I did my best to cultivate questioning minds, curious minds. I fed that curiosity by answering every question asked of me to the best of my ability, save for one. Whenever either of them wished to know anything about Luke's father, I lied. At times the prodding and questioning from Luke was determined and unrelenting, but I never wavered. If in fact, I didn't lie, I misled them to such an extent that it might as well have been a lie.

Luke forced my relationship with Christopher to become dichotomous. My love for Claus was in perfect opposition to my fear of him. This wasn't about my fear of humiliation I would assuredly face should the truth surrounding Luke's conception be revealed. This wasn't about my fear of the wrath I would face should Luke and Christopher come to know of each other. This was something entirely new. It was a very real fear of the power that Christopher possessed to whisk Luke away from me in the blink of an eye. What hurt most was the knowing it would not be by force; Luke would go willingly and with much enthusiasm.

Aside from these fears new and old, these ghosts of my past, it must be said all other things that gave me trepidation were the very same things to be applauded by my Indian friends. Luke was strong, fiercely independent, brave beyond question, and respectful. And, of course, he was generous, as would be expected of any hopeful chief-to-be. His Indian mentors found no fault in Luke's actions whatsoever. They only laughed at my motherly concern for his safety.

FORTY-ONE

Today, Luke was restless and visibly annoyed at having to accompany me to the tree line bordering the upper perimeter of the valley. A small group of us were off to search for whatever

325

might remain of overlooked firewood and roots. Like any boy of his age, he preferred to spend his time playing sticks, fighting mock battles, or acting out pretend hunts.

"I don't want to gather roots, Momma."

"Then don't. But you are still going with me, Luke, and you will stay by my side. Do you understand?"

"But, Momma, gathering roots is woman's work. I am not a woman."

"True enough, and…you are not a mother. Keeping an eye on you is mother's work."

"Mother—."

"Luke. No more! Listen to me. Aenôheso, Heškovetseso, and Hevovetaso have all gone south for the winter. There is nobody in the camp. Practice your letters if you need something to do."

"I don't want to practice my letters. That will only make me fall asleep."

"Then fall asleep. It's better to sleep smart than live stupid. The choice is yours, but you are not going back to camp. Now, stop arguing with me. Why don't you be a good son and talk to Eškôseesehe? Ask him to tell you stories of the hunt. That will keep you occupied. Go! Now!"

"Mom—."

"I said, *go!*"

Luke let loose a defiant kick to the ground. He sauntered off mumbling his discontent, as he headed toward the brave sitting quietly on his horse. He was in denial. All of his close friends, and those who were not, were now gone, having left him behind, alone and bored. There was little I could offer to ease his frustration. Lessons in reading and writing were not about to pacify his young, energetic spirit. His entertainment was based on social relationships and social activities.

"Luke is restless as always," said Gracie .

"As always," I repeated. "He will mope until we catch up to the rest. I go through it with him every spring, every fall."

"Yut, no friends, no games."

"I know...I know."

For years, I watched the ranks of the young collect to run ragged day after day across the open fields, along the riverbanks, and in and out of the maze of surrounding lodges. I watched them make countless trips to river's edge from sunup to sunset, solely to scoop up handfuls of clay and strip the banks of reeds. They would return to the fields with these gobs of muck and fashion them into balls pressed tightly around the ends of the reeds or long grasses. Stacked in piles, or laid out in orderly rows, these collections commenced to cure hard as stone in the dry summer air.

The boys would gather up their weapon stores and face off at opposite ends of a field or our camp. They would then whip these hardened clay balls at one another with a vengeance that only boys can understand. For years, I watched them dance about, stepping side to side or forward and back in charge and retreat. These missiles represented arrows, with their willowy streamers, crisscrossing through the air in large arcs and number.

I imagined it smarted something fierce when one was struck up close, but the mock battles made for unsurpassed rushes that emanated in boisterous taunts and pitiful howls. I found myself occasionally getting caught up in the rowdiness, laughing until I hurt, witnessing some young devil in retreat run past me for all he was worth in order to avoid a good pelting by a mob screaming certain death. Occasionally older boys might even enter the charge on horseback.

These activities were always pure mayhem and perfect pleasure for a child. Year after year of this vigorous physical activity turned baby boys into strong, healthy lads. They in turn, became lean, sinewy, young men, who had developed the tenacity and endurance to withstand the harshest of rigors.

Luke was right in there, raising dust with the rest. He was a big boy for his age and could instill fear when he charged with a handful of clay projectiles. He took after his father in all ways. Even if I didn't see that particular resemblance every day of my life, Luke would still be a picture of perfection. If my pride and joy weren't enough, he stood so far apart in appearance from his black-haired brothers, he brought to me added respect and spiritual reverence.

"Wot are you thinking about ?" Gracie asked, interrupting my thoughts.

"Nothing. Thinking about Luke horsing around with the boys. Standing here watching the sun drop behind those peaks, and thinking it's the end of another day, the end of another year. It goes fast. He's growing up fast. He won't be living this life much longer. It disheartens me to know soon enough, I will be faced with some difficult decisions. I hope he handles the changes to come."

"I am certain he'll do fine. He's not that little piggy-widden anymore. Do you know when we pack?"

"No. You should ask Talk-a-Lot. She might know. Ho'neheveho has only said soon—maybe tomorrow, maybe a day or two. Are you finished collecting roots?"

"Roots? What roots? There are no roots. Everything was picked clean and eaten weeks ago. Ark a' me, it's a good thing we are leaving otherwise we'll be living off tree bark."

Talk-a-Lot emerged from the woods and into the clearing with her leather bag slightly bulging.

"Talk-a-Lot! Are you ready to go back? Are Ameohne'e, Eseohtseva'e, and the others finished gathering roots?"

"Almost."

"Good. I'm tired. I'm ready to head back down."

The tribes had camped here at the northern reach of our migration for the last three moons. The ground beneath the trees had been well picked over by this time, and it was becoming a chore to find firewood or food. We were forced to travel so much farther from the camp in order to find anything of worth that the brave, Eškôseesehe, had been sent to stand guard over us.

Even with his protection, we preferred to stay close and often settled for less than desirable pickings. As of late, we would make up for the dismal bounty by sharing our finds. Doing so allowed us to finish our work faster, being done with it before the dead of night.

"Wot did you find, anything worth eating ?" asked Gracie.

"Mostly turnips. A couple of small carrots."

"I found about twelve carrots and let's see…three…four, five, six…six turnips."

"Hmm. Not bad, considering…. Yes, you did good." I responded.

"So did I," piped Talk-a-Lot. "Look. Ma'emo'kôhtá'éne."

She held open her leather bag, which contained a couple dozen beets.

"I dig all I could find. There is no more. They are small. Take what you want."

Talk-a-Lot, Gracie, Hotoomee'e, and I passed the turnips, carrots, and beets back and forth. We shared all that we found, splitting up roots evenly for the sake of time. We then gathered up our bundles of wood, and commenced to stroll back down into the valley.

The camp looked feeble now because nearly all the lodges had been struck. The tribes had begun their migration to the south for the winter months. I knew that Ho'neheveho would soon strike his lodge, as would I, and we would be the last to head out along the ages-old trail.

Departing always filled me with butterflies of anticipation, especially when I saw so much of our camp already empty. Only patterns of round patches remained upon the earth, fading footprints of the tipis that had passed through during summer. The only people still to be found in camp were family members of the Dog Soldiers. These warriors were obligated to remain behind until the last in order to protect the stragglers.

Before the watchful eye of the brave, I was the oldest. I also tired the quickest and so I was first to signal him as I started back toward camp. Talk-a-Lot and Gracie followed a short distance behind and stepped to join me. For all purpose, sun had set, day was done. We were more than ready to return; impatient to set aside our loads, sit down, eat, and relax. The others, having no desire to be left behind, picked up their pace and scurried in our direction to close ranks. Luke would have preferred to run ahead and leave us all in his wake, but even at his young age, with end of day at hand, and in the presence of a brave; his upbringing dictated he would display courage and stay to protect us. He remained behind to walk alongside the brave and his horse at our backs.

Gracie, Talk-a-Lot, and I were taking our time, waiting up now and then, so the rest could catch up while we conversed lightly about what needed to be done before striking our tipis in the next day or so. Even a conversation about chores that still needed to be done felt tiresome, and so our discussions fell short as we willingly slipped farther into our own thoughts.

I turned around, a habit born from years of mothering, to be sure that Luke was not lingering or getting himself into trouble, and yet under the brave's watchful eye. It was precisely at the second I looked back toward my son that I glimpsed a sliver of movement streak across the narrow glen from which we were now departing.

Instantly came the knowing hiss of an arrow let loose. The sickening thud of its stone tip reached my ears as it broke through the back of Eškôseesehe. He was sitting on his horse, talking to Luke. The brave fell forward off the animal having uttered not a single word of warning. Only Luke and I had seen his murder, for the others had been facing us as they moved in our direction intent on catching up.

Luke let out a howl of warning that was at once drowned out by my own shriek.

"Luke! Luke!"

I screamed out of sheer panic. Between the almost simultaneous sounds of the hissing arrow, the disturbances in the brush, and the screeches, the others spun around in dreadful anticipation. Indians, who were unknown to us, exploded out of the wood from every direction to immediately surround us. They were covered in strange markings, and moved quickly but silently to subdue our number. Bowstrings pulled back, they stared down the shafts of their arrows with eyes that conveyed their intent to kill us without hesitation.

I froze where I stood, for the first thing done by the invaders was to restrain Luke by pressing a knife firmly to his neck. I knew well that the difference between killing Luke as a brave and kidnapping him as a child was a very thin line at his age and size. I was so afraid for his safety that I could only stand trembling and hope nothing, not the chirp of a bird, not the dart of a moth, not the sound of a prayer would provoke the strangers to slit his throat.

Ameohne'e, on the other hand, was overcome with fear and broke into a wild run. She distracted the warrior holding a knife to Luke's throat by her hysterical screaming as she fled down toward the camp. In a trice, I watched a brave sight her in and let loose his arrow. She was slaughtered within ten steps. She went down and disappeared in the grass before the sound of her scream ever reached open air.

At once, I looked at Gracie, knowing she went nowhere without her knives. I was as much worried about her next move as anything our captors might do. I watched her hand move deftly across the blades of steel.

"Keep still, Gracie," I hissed through my teeth. She ignored me.

"You hear, me, Gracie. Keep still."

Gracie snapped her head quickly as if too dismiss me. This one time, I wished she was that eleven-year-old girl, clinging to my dress, and scared beyond all reason. Instead, Gracie grew up to have absolutely no fear of the Indians she now understood, and I could see her mind scrambling for a way out.

"You'll have Luke's blood on your hands," I hissed.

She was beyond my pleas. As she assessed her options, I could only see Luke's life hanging in the balance. I had no doubt that Gracie could take down three captors before they knew what happened, but there were many more than three. And for that reason, should she take action of any kind, I would move against her. I took a step closer in her direction.

Neither plan nor intervention took place. There were too many abductors, and before Gracie could hope to throw a knife, they eyed her weapons and carefully stripped them from her side. She was then restrained along with the rest of us, we being quickly gagged and bound at the wrists. The knives disappeared from sight, they being considered a great prize.

It was certain that we were being abducted by one of the neighboring tribes or a rogue gang, probably Crow or Pawnee. We all knew it was paramount they disappear into darkness in order to lose any followers. The attack had to be well planned, late enough in the day to use the cover of night, but early enough so we wouldn't be missed from collecting our firewood for an hour or so before an alarm was sounded—by which time, it would be nearly impossible to rescue us.

Most likely, our captors had watched the camp dwindle in size for days before making their move. Most likely, they studied our habits carefully and knew precisely when to strike for best advantage. Most likely, their escape route was well planned for speed. In time, our failure to return home would be noted with alarm, and a search would be quickly underway, but any thought of a rescue party riding out in our behalf with any measure of success was probably pointless. The reason being that the last of camp was soon to be struck and all would be departed as soon as the morrow or day following. Only survival now mattered.

At once, we were forced to run. There was no thought of lagging behind. We were driven harshly for a fair piece, a good three miles back into the thick of the woods. If we slowed or stumbled, we were slapped forward or whipped with saplings. In the chaos, we had let loose our gatherings of roots, but these were picked up by the captors and eaten or forced back upon us to ferry.

I was either blessed or cursed to be seen as an elder and relieved of carrying anything that might slow our party.

Yet, I still stumbled about, falling over my own two feet from exhaustion. My lungs burned as I struggled to suck air past the gag. Worse, I fought the overwhelming urge to retch, fearing the muzzle would make me drown in my own vomit. I could not close my mouth, and so the desert air dried it out to the point of feeling like shrunken leather. The saplings never ceased to swish through the air, clipping our buttocks or legs as our captors pushed and barked out whispered orders in words we didn't understand, but in demands we did.

Our panicked run halted abruptly as we came upon a ridge that prevented us from going anywhere but along its edge or else back from where we came. The Indians ahead of us ran back and forth along that edge searching for a specific place to descend. I noticed many of our captors had disappeared during our run to the cliff. I was determined to make the best of the delay. I dropped to my hands and knees as I struggled to catch my breath. Nearly faint, I stared out into space from atop this cliff that fell away downward every bit of a hundred feet—a near perfect vertical wall.

The face of the wall was cloaked in the shadows of closing night, but I knew it would be a reddish, rusty-colored clay and sandstone feature seemingly built by rows upon rows of stacked squarish blocks. I had seen the small cliffs and ridges of this region many times over the past years when traveling north to the summer camp. They were numerous and formed a small eastern border to a more mountainous and forested high ground to the west. These discontinuous walls acted as a dividing line between the forests of the upper level and the grasses of the lower.

Once the path of descent was located, we were given scant opportunity to consider our fear of heights. Our hands were unbound, and we were at once pushed over the edge. Our sole focus being that of finding handholds in quick fashion or die by failure. Vegetation was pressed hard into much of the rock's crevices like oakum pressed between planks of a hull. I prayed Luke and Gracie's fingers would not slip off this vegetation that became greasier with each pass of grasping fingers.

I was utterly spent and working hard once again to breathe past the now loosened gag that still seemed determined to suffocate me. I was already badly weakened by the miles of running, and so finding the strength to hold my weight as I eased down the unforgiving rock, inch by inch, was fast draining what was left of me both physically and mentally.

Breasts pressed hard to rock, knuckles nicked and bleeding, I slid downward amidst a cascade of loosened sand. The commotion and falling debris startled tiny gray dippers from their cliff-side nests. "Peee-peee-pijur-pijur, peee-peee-pijur-pijur," they would cry out at me in a complaint of high trills.

On the grassy floor below me, I observed a small gang of disturbed buffalo take to running for an open field. The Indians that had disappeared now came back into view from behind the thickets and cover of trees. They appeared with extra horses in tow. As soon as we touched down, we were lifted onto the horses, and led eastward down the slopes into thickening shadows without delay. We rode for many an hour.

Save for the killing of Eškôseesehe and Ameohne'e, our captors managed a clean, silent, and speedy retreat. Unable to speak aloud but for gags and whippings, Gracie and I were only able to exchange glances. Even this was eventually masked by the fall of night, leaving us only our thoughts and luck to still be alive. In silence, I agonized for Luke's safety, for he was too young to know when best not to fight—when best to keep his mouth shut. I prayed he would stay settled.

It was true Ameohne'e had been killed with the arrow, but I was certain her death was caused by a need to maintain secrecy

335

and nothing more. Kidnapping was plenty sufficient to fulfill a vow of revenge, or to gain honor for most Indians. There was little point, if any, in killing us. We were valuable as slaves or as wives for increasing the numbers of their tribe. Torturing us might be entertaining for a while, but killing us made no sense at all, except for sacrifice, and I had no wish to think on that.

Our kidnappers came to a stop for the first time during the night. Hotoomee'e was pulled off of her horse and forced to sit upon the ground. We were about to be dragged off of our horses, but for an interruption when another party of their kind broke into our midst. This party rode up with many extra horses in tow. When their lot took view of Luke, Gracie, and I, they were visibly astonished. They stood motionless at first, saying nothing, and then delved deeply into a serious discussion with our captors.

Judging by the disturbed look in the eyes of the newcomers, it was clear they were taken aback. They hardly appeared happy. Just as with all our encounters, these men most likely never heard, let alone seen the likes of us, and to observe our blonde hair glowing in the light of the moon rocked them to their spiritual core. I considered how these Indians may have expected to abduct ordinary Indian women, and instead got much more than they bargained. We three may have unintentionally changed all their original plans.

It occurred to me that stories of a woman—a sun-haired woman possessing great medicine, may have indeed reached other tribes. Thanks to Wilpen and his prolific storytelling, if I had managed to become a legend amongst white travelers, then why not Indians? He traded with them all the time. These newcomers may have known of us as ghosts. The question being begged was whether or not our abduction would be considered a stroke of wonderfully good or dreadfully bad luck to this superstitious lot. In the meantime, we sat on our halted horses beneath a brilliant moon, staring in silence at captors and strangers alike—our hair aglow.

I looked over at Luke and then Gracie, and was suddenly struck by a remembrance of her as a child draped in those ghastly swinging heads. Had she still possessed them, we surely would be on our way back to camp by now. My mind worked these contemplations, contemplations of a desperate soul and nothing more.

While we waited, the discussion amongst the Indians apparently elevated into an argument that abruptly ceased when one of the Indians grabbed Hotoomee'e by the hair. He yanked her forcefully off the ground and threw her up onto a fresh horse amidst howls of pain. As if by silent command, a couple of lessers moved to assist the agitated brave. The men ferried the rest of us toward fresh horses, but in a less brutal manner. The remaining Indians stayed behind, fixed where they stood, studying us as we were again led out at a hurried pace. I suspect that it was for the sake of speed each of us was assigned a horse.

FORTY-TWO

It had been days since our capture, and the leather laces used to bind my wrists had long since rubbed through my skin leaving it raw, blistered, bleeding, and infected. The gag tied around my head soaked up the flow of my saliva and smeared it across my face causing my cheeks and lips to chap and split open painfully in the dry air. Many times, I thought of Rachel and the story she had told me years ago about how she and Caleb had been abducted. How they had been chained to the bed of the wagon, unable to get off their backs for hundreds of miles. Thoughts of their misery and perseverance served to bring me strength.

For seven days we rode eastward across the sandygrass desert. We stopped nightly when finding one of the small clean waterholes that frequently popped up unexpectedly. We drank deeply, ate when food was made available, and slept in the hollows huddled against the cooling night winds.

We were still bound at the wrists, but after four days, the gags were removed from our mouths. It was made clear that if we uttered but a sound we would be gagged for good. We needed little persuasion because there was not much left to say or add. Up to this point no one had been harmed, and we knew firsthand how painful the gags could be. Talking wasn't worth the misery, at least not until our mouths and cheeks healed.

As the days began to come and go, and time no longer held value, our pace seemed to slow to a stumble. The scenery was one of dulled brownish-gold grasses covering gentle swells of sand. The view never changed unless broken by shards of earth that shot up for no apparent reason other than to wreak havoc on the monotony of the scene.

The sweltering heat and wind of summer was being calmed by these autumn days, cooler, uncomfortably cool at times, but offering the freedom to travel during day as opposed to night. Of course, day brought the fear of being seen, for all strangers were deemed dangerous. The sandy mounds would conceal an intruder until time when he was so close that we had no chance to hide or escape.

It may have been for that reason we were led down into a ravine, a place safe from spying eyes, or maybe our captors simply knew of an unseen trail and were following it to a destination unknown. It didn't really matter, but we strode down the winding watershed for possibly ten miles, and only just saw a hint of flowing water, before the walls gave way and suddenly opened to an expansive, brush-filled bottomland that cradled a mostly waterless river bed. It snaked quickly and quietly out of the west and disappeared just as quickly and quietly into the east. The opposite shore edged a sizeable plain.

This river bed was large, and I knew by viewing the surroundings that during the spring thaws this was a dangerous and anything but quiet river that traversed this ground. Now, late in the year, a smattering of puddles connected by ribbons of pure sparkling water that threaded themselves delicately around numerous piles of white-washed sand was all that remained.

In this place, it was decided to call it a day. We were pulled off our horses, given water, and forced to lie down upon the ground in a group. Left momentarily undisturbed to determine my condition, I soon focused on how painfully my wrists burned, aching from fingertips to elbows. At least calluses were beginning to form. The inners of my legs were rubbed raw and my spine felt as though it had been compressed flatter than a buffalo chip. I let out an agonized moan as I looked at the others, but this was no place to air complaints for no other fared better. Twenty minutes later, two more Indians rode into our camp. I guessed they had been following behind us, on guard for warriors that might be in pursuit.

A herd of buffalo was visible out on the plain of the opposite shore. The sight of them made my mouth water. The Indians studied the herd intently for some time. I knew they were searching for a wounded or weakened animal, or one that was younger and easier to bring down with a small hunting party. In time, the men spotted what they were looking for and mounted up. They signed for us to build a fire, then proceeded to cross the riverbed. Cautiously, they rode toward the herd from downwind. They left us to do their bidding, but still bound at the wrists.

The hunt proved successful and the men returned to the riverbank with large cuts of bloodied meat strapped across their horses. We watched as they worked their way carefully across this riverbed they called Niobrara. I didn't know that name, but

I believed it was probably a river the Tsistsistas called Hisse Yovi Yoe, which meant Surprise River. I knew it as a more turbulent, faster-flowing river that we often relished for its abundance of cold, clean water that was most welcome after our long trek to the northern reach of our migration each spring. In the autumn of the year when we packed up camp for the return trip south, sometimes the water was there, but oftentimes it was not, hence the surprise.

The spirit of the Indians was much improved by their catch, and now foremost was their impatience that we women build a fire, prepare the beast, and scrape the hide. Even in captivity, we had our duties and to ease that impatience, we were finally freed of our wrist restraints, hopefully for good.

We were by now so far removed from Ho'neheveho and the tribe that it would have been pointless, even a death wish, to entertain any idea of escape. For us, there was no choice now but to follow our captors. Finding our way home would be far less likely than finding our death in all manner of ways in this desolate, uninhabited place.

Yet, there was certain advantage to reaching this abandoned ground in that we were given free rein to roam. We wasted no time in making use of that freedom, and so wandered off to bathe in the river pools, which was always a most welcome pleasure. Back on shore, the Indians were still quick to strike us for talking, but ever more frequently we took liberties. Whereas around the campfire, we kept our voices low, everything spoken at a whisper, now whilst bathing in the river we laughed aloud and carried on as we pleased.

"Thank the Lord, I still have a tongue. How are you, son? Are you alright? Let me hear your voice. Need I worry about you or what?"

"I'm alright."

"Bless you, boy. And you, Gracie?"

"Yut, I guess. If you mean besides being all plimmed up with blisters, an' rash, an' being too stiff to move. I reckon I'll live long enough to see 'em dead. Where do you figure they're taking us?"

I looked at her and shrugged.

"I worry more about you every day, child."

"I'm just saying that the Indian who stole my knives is still standing there alive. So where do you reckon they're taking us—to one of their camps?"

"Is there any part of you that's still girl?"

"Girl? My word, Elizabeth, when was I ever a girl?"

"True, true enough, but I did once hold you in my arms. In fact, you were a beautiful, headstrong girl who stole my heart. I fear headstrong matured into pig-headed."

Gracie laughed freely, and again, I shook my head with mild concern before looking about the surrounding country. I remained kneeling in the warm barely perceptible current as I studied the distant landscape. The river split the earth in two, separating a horizon of hills, ridges, and ravines to our north from endless sandygrass plains to our south. The watershed was dry and the plains grasses drier. The dryness was another of the signs of winter in the waiting.

"Honestly, I have no idea where they are taking us. We're obviously heading south. Everybody knows that. If this is indeed the same water as the Hisse Yovi Yoe, then going south takes us deeper into the sandygrass. We are still with the buffalo, but I don't recognize any part of this place. I think we must be well east of our usual hunting grounds. It would make good sense to stay well east of the Tsistsistas unless these braves have a death wish. We'll just have to wait it out, to watch and see. At least thus far nobody else has been killed."

I possessed one advantage over the rest of our group. I had actually tramped all sides of the sandy grasslands. Years before, I had entered the far west from the northern reach of the Missouri River. I had lived with Claus in the Stony Mountains beyond its western boundary. With the tribe, I had traveled south of it to our winter camp many times over the years. And finally, I knew something about the look and lay of the land east of the Mississippi. I didn't know exactly where I was, but I definitely knew the places where I was not.

"Wot do ya think they're going to do with us?"

"Again, I have no idea, Gracie. Why, are you afraid?"

"No."

I laughed. Her response was so quick and certain.

"Wot's so funny?" she asked.

"*You.* Imagine you having no fear. I wish you could appreciate how far removed you are from that little knock-kneed darling of a spit I chanced to meet years ago. The one who was scared to death of *'enjuns'.*"

"You mean the one who *saved your dried out carcass all plimmed up in the middle of the desert?* That little girl?"

"Yeah, what did they call her....*Greasy!*"

We both turned away from our captors and broke into uncontrollable laughter. The harder we tried to restrain ourselves, trying not be noticed, the harder we convulsed. We splashed water on each other to mask the noise of our blubbers and squeaks. Eventually, I had to turn away from Gracie, and splashed water onto Talk-a-Lot in order to save my ribs from breaking. I rubbed the tears out of my eyes and caught my breath.

"Get away from me, Gracie, before we get in trouble," I whispered sternly with as straight a face as I could muster.

"You are the only one here going to be gettin' in trouble," she whispered back.

Gracie nodded affirmatively. Still trying to keep composed, I turned toward Talk-a-Lot. If one thing could stop my laughter cold, it was shame. I felt it creep over me as I looked at Talk-a-Lot. Whereas Luke, Gracie, and I were unlikely to have harm come our way, this was not the case for her.

"Are you feeling well, Talk-a-Lot?"

"I am good, thank you."

"I worry for you."

"I am good."

"Are you afraid?"

She smiled, but nothing further need be said. Talk-a-Lot understood our situation. More important, she understood her situation and certainly knew her fate could be far worse. I assumed that she, like many of her tribe, believed I was so filled with good medicine that I was unlikely to encounter ill fate.

"Remember this, Talk-a-Lot. The others may have much to fear, but you are filled with good medicine. You know the white man's tongue. Wherever you go, they will see this. You will be respected. I promise you this. *I promise* you this."

I could see how my insistence calmed her. Yes, I did worry for her, and rightfully so, but I worried most for Luke, which was wasted worry, for he was probably the strongest of us all. He was as healthy as a horse. Much to my peace of mind, our captors didn't consider him yet to be a brave. If they had, he would surely have been killed. Time and time again, I thanked the Lord for that good fortune.

The bounty of buffalo meat bloated our bellies, and left us laying about satiated and lazy for an entire day. It was nothing short of a glorious rest. But it never could be a perfect rest because we all knew that we were bound for a destination unknown, and laying about was not part of the plan.

We struck camp at dawn's first light, but to my surprise, we did not head south across the sandygrass desert as anticipated. Instead, for the next five days, we followed our captors east with the flow of the river, crossing back and forth depending on the lay of the land.

The first two days we passed by land that was yet dominated by the sandygrasses, but after that the northern banks grew higher and steeper, more rugged, and strewn with cliffs and ridges, whereas the southern bank remained flatter, easier traveled, but prone to quicksand and swampiness.

By the fifth day, the river had assumed a new image. The amount of water taken on by its tributaries had increased its bluster markedly. It was now, not only wet, but often respectfully broad in width, at times appearing a quarter mile bank to bank.

In spite of the great distance across, the river remained woefully shallow and somewhat sedate. Yet, we were far less likely to cross the shallows for fear of quicksand, which seemed to be its curse. In other stretches, the river was hemmed in by rock and squeezed so tightly that the water sped through frothed as it climbed over rocks and splashed off walls in an attempt to be released from confinement.

We spent ever more time riding the southern bank, but leaving it altogether when the ground became too swampy and mosquito infested. The banks had become increasingly attractive to trees and the farther east we traveled the denser the wood along the shore. I wasn't blind to the change from forests of pines, aspen, and birch that covered the high ground where we were abducted, to the more diverse forests of oaks, elms, walnut, and ash that now fenced in the river. The sandygrasses were overtaken by thicker, richer foliage from which erupted shrubs of sumac, snowberry, and gooseberry. There were wild plum and grape vines that could be seen webbing across the stands.

Here we arrived at a sharp bend in the river that drove it almost straight north. As our captors halted our forward march in order to determine if this change of direction toward north was temporary or permanent, a very large Indian scouting party erupted into view on the distant ground ahead. We were immediately ordered off the trail and sought cover within the density of the wood. The surprise party of Indians left our captors most nervous, and we were quick to leave the area and river at this point. We headed south for a second time.

FORTY-THREE

Our route south paralleled a tributary with well-traveled trails along its banks. We followed it for most of the day until leaving the basin to track one of the trails that still worked its way south, but now across the most incredibly flat plain one could imagine. This was not a sandygrass desert with it thousands of mounds, but a fertile, thickly grassed land that mimicked the ocean in more ways than not.

The drawback here was our being in a place so flat free of obstruction that we could be spotted ten miles distant. This wasn't an assumption, for we saw many Indians crossing the horizon or coming and going along various unseen paths. The sightings were frequent enough for our captors to decide we would no longer travel by light of day.

Now, we would travel in the lesser light of evening until well past sundown at which point we rested a spell. We then continued on until just after the break of day. At that time, we would leave the trail and bed down in the grass. The horses could not be hidden and so we lashed them a short distance from where we slept, should we be found out. This was now our routine, simple in nature and successful. We traveled in this manner for five nights during which time we saw a number of campfires, and it was clear we were traveling in increasingly populated areas.

On the sixth morning, there was no need to hide, for dawn's light was replaced by a thick, smothering fog that soaked us to the bone. The air was quite chilly this morning and it appeared we would keep moving for warmth and the advantage of freedom that the fog offered. Aside from going unseen, the fog was effective in stifling the sounds of our horses and conversations. There seemed little sense in gathering up wet grass for bedding when given a few hours it would likely dry off and be far more inviting.

Soon, the reason for this abundance of fog surfaced. We came upon our second large river flowing from west to east. This was thought to be a very large river indeed, but the fog prevented us from seeing across to the other bank. We gained hints and peeks at those times when the slightest of breezes might lift the cottony blanket a few feet off the water, giving a moment's view to the opposite bank. About mid-morning, feeling worn and overtaken by exhaustion, our captors decided to take advantage of a secluded spot and the fog so we might rest in safety.

We were awakened by the Indians around mid-day or early afternoon as best I could tell. The fog had lifted in that peculiar way whereby it remains impenetrable twenty feet off the ground, but below those twenty feet you could see for a mile. Now, we could clearly discern the opposite side of the river, and it was every bit as broad as imagined. The four of us women wasted no time for permission and went down to wash.

I looked about and found myself reliving my recent past almost scene for scene. There we were once again standing huddled upon the bottom of a broad, flat, sandy, half-empty river bed washing ourselves. This land was so limitless that it made time seem to slow and actions dragged on forever. To wash on a Tuesday and again on a Friday might make one feel she had been

346

washing for a week without break. In fact, most likely there was no other event to occur on the days between the washings that might interrupt such action.

"You sure have been quiet this morning," said Gracie.

"I'm thinking about these rivers. I'm trying to sort out our whereabouts."

"Wot are you reckonin'?"

"I'm trying to recall the lay of Wilpen's maps. The trouble is, I second guessed myself so many times I no longer know what I saw and what I imagined...I'm sure it was the Niobrara to the north, then the Platte, then the Kansas.... I can't remember what river lies below the Kansas, but it wouldn't matter. We have no reason to cross the Kansas, if indeed that was the lower river. No, we might have to cross the Kansas. No...I don't think so. I give up. I can't remember."

I struggled to see those maps in my head.

"If we killed that buffalo on the banks of the Niobrara, and we worked our way south, then the only water courses I recall of this size going east and west were the Platte and the Kansas. I recall the Kansas as flowing somewhat north by east, not that that's important, but what matters is I recall no place where we might make the Kansas River without first crossing the Platte. At this time of year, I would expect the Platte to look just like this— empty. Early in the year it would be the treacherous and unforgiving flow you would expect in order to make a bed of that measure."

I pointed to the distant bank of this wide sandy floor now lying exposed to the vagaries of wind and wildlife.

"Are you saying if you figured right then you'd know where we're at?"

I didn't respond because one of the Indians was staring at us. In fact, I was bothered by a sudden realization that they had been studying us most of the day.

"Shhhh. They're watching us. I think something is on their minds."

"Are we leaving?"

"I wouldn't think so. It makes little sense to ride at night. The days are cooler now so where lay the advantage. No, I doubt we'll leave tonight."

The Indians motioned us to return to shore and begin preparing their kill for the fire. As soon as I stepped out of the river, I addressed Luke.

"Luke! Find your mother another place to sleep tonight. Pick ground better sheltered from the wind and cold. I froze last night."

"Yes, Mother."

For the remainder of the evening, Luke was kept busy running here and there for the braves, searching out grasses and buffalo dung to stoke their fire. Talk-a-Lot, Hotoomee'e, and the other two women, Mokee'eso and Pâhavooma'e, sat alongside Gracie and I as we carved up meat to skewer on spits and wrapped fish in grasses to bake in the coals.

One of the Indians gave Gracie back one of her knives. She was to use it for a short time in order to slice up the meat and fish. Obviously, the Indian had no idea that these knives were meant to be thrown or that Gracie was as dangerous as the strike of a viper if he stood within her range. I was plenty nervous knowing what could happen at the slightest provocation.

"I trust you'll keep that knife in hand."

Gracie turned to look at me. She gave me a bone-chilling smile.

"Yut."

Hardly reassuring, but when the Indians had their fill, we were called over to the fire and allowed to take whatever was left to eat. To my relief, the Indian demanded Gracie return the knife. Fortunately, between her hunger and the abundance of game and fish to distract her, we ate until stuffed, grew sleepy, and retired safe and still alive.

The night winds had grown in intensity and now blew briskly out of the west. The gusts kept driving the coals out of the campfire to streak across the sand like swarms of glowing red fireflies. I was chilled to the bone and now focused on lying down and covering myself for warmth. I summoned Gracie and Luke to join me.

"C'mon. Snuggle up tight so we stay warm."

I drew them in close. Luke, always restless, never cold, jumped up and gathered fresh armfuls of dried grasses, which he spread thickly over us for a blanket. He then brought extra armfuls of grass over to Talk-a-Lot and the women and covered them with care. It was the Tsistsista upbringing that directed him to offer what service he could for the comfort of others. It was the way to earn honor. It was the way of a chief.

At last, Luke returned to burrow under his pile of grass cover. If not for the superior windbreak of our new sleeping hollow, the winds would have blown every last blade of our grass blanket to the farthest reaches of this unending plain. Even now we had to keep our eyes and mouths shut but for the rain of sand and grit that pained the eye and made one shudder as it ground between the teeth. We adjusted the grasses over our heads, and immediately I could feel the heat of our breath and bodies warm the stilled air. The anticipation of warmth made me shake head to toe.

"Oh, my blessed lord, it feels good under here. We didn't get much sleep yesterday; tonight I plan on sleeping hard."

"Now...finish what you were telling me earlier. Where do you reckon we are?" Gracie interrupted me in a whisper. In the darkness of our cover, I could sense the two of them focused on my every word.

"I thought we were going to sleep?"

"Yut, yut, we will, but you started telling me earlier and never finished. I want to know where we are before I go to sleep. Are we close to St. Louis?"

"Oh, Gracie!" I let out an air of exasperation. "St. Louis? Not even close."

"Then where are we?"

"Well...I've been thinking. First off, we rode a good two hundred miles due east before turning south a spell and coming upon the Niobrara. We followed that flow for a good hundred and fifty miles or more as well, until we again turned south. We have been going south for six days thus far, and all of it across easy land. I figure that to be another two hundred miles bringing us presently upon this river, which I believe is the Platte.

"The Platte definitely runs into the Missouri. I remember being told by a riverboat captain that the upper Missouri begins at the Platte. I remember that river was wide, shallow, and overrun with Indians. That was then. I don't know about now.

"When I studied Wilpen's maps, I used to figure a thousand miles need be crossed if I were ever to get back to St. Louis. I suspect by now we have already put half, that's to say five hundred miles behind us. If we're not in white man's country, we are close. The problem is that these braves are doing their best not to be seen and therefore other than that large scouting party we saw at the Niobrara, I have no idea if we would now meet Indians or whites."

At that point, in spite of a plague of additional questions, I had enough. I was spent and sleep was my only intention. I offered up my final comment.

"Good night and sleep tight."

FORTY-FOUR

I arose the next morning feeling better than I had in nearly a month. The past night I had eaten well, enjoyed the benefits of a full belly, the comfort of a warm dry bed, and the blessing of an uninterrupted sleep. The night winds had calmed, and I awoke nice and warm of my own accord, no doubt because our captors enjoyed the same good fortunes, and were too lazy to get on with their day. There was plenty of leftover food cooked from the night before wrapped in grass and buried in warm earth from the campfire. This morning, the braves were more about conversing than riding, and of that they seemed to be doing a lot.

We were now allowed to talk to one another in lower tones without punishment. Our conversations soon turned from the pleasures of a good night's sleep and warm breakfast to concerns about what the braves were debating. We noticed the men were engaged in a discussion of some merit, and continually looking in the direction of Gracie, Luke, and I. Their attention wasn't doing anything for my heart's ease.

It was both unnerving and unexpected when the braves came walking toward us and suddenly ordered Hotoomee'e, Talk-a-Lot, and the other two women to their feet. My attention was riveted to the goings-on and I quickly realized that to my disbelief they

351

were being taken away. The idea of being separated was emotionally overwhelming and so without thought I jumped to my feet and ran toward Talk-a-Lot, unsure if I was about to defend her, assist her, or save myself from losing my dear friend.

"Talk-a-Lot! No!"

I reached out for her in despair, but before I had clasped her hand, I was struck such a severe blow to the side of my head that it knocked the senses right out of me. I found myself sprawled upon the ground, following a world spinning dizzily in circles. There was a ringing in my head that drowned out all other sound, and I was only just able to make sense of Talk-a-Lot through blurred vision as she was being led away on horseback. I imagined there to be tears in her eyes as there were in mine, for I sensed in truth, I would never see her again. The Indian dragged me back across the ground to where Gracie and Luke were seated and left us.

"Heaven's mercy! Are you alright? Are you alright, Elizabeth?"

Gracie's words and face mixed into an emotion of concern, I was not yet able to address. I was suspended in thoughts of Talk-a-Lot's departure before coming back to reality and my senses. With the return of my wits came the pain.

"I'll live. It doesn't feel that way right now, but I promise, I will live."

I did comprehend the look on Luke's face. He was badly shaken.

"Are you alright, Luke?" I asked.

Gracie turned to look at Luke.

"You better talk to him," she interrupted, "or we're going to have a ten-year-old killer on our hands."

"I am fine, Luke. This is no different than when you boys get to roughing about with each other and take a clay ball to the head. It smarts, but I am not harmed."

"I'm going to kill them," Luke threatened behind wet eyes and clenched teeth.

"That may be, but please, not today. Promise me you won't kill anybody today. Your mother isn't up to it. Now, promise me."

Luke glared at the Indians.

"Luke, promise me. Come on now, promise me nobody gets killed today."

"Hmmmph!"

His grunt would have to do. I worked to settle him, assuring him I was fine, but my mind was focused elsewhere as I suffered through the memory of Talk-a-Lot and Hotoomee'e disappearing into the distance. I felt as though my soul had been emptied. For Luke's sake, and maybe my own, I kept my despair hidden.

Talk-a-Lot and the others were led east along the bank of the river by two of the braves. Our party was now reduced to four braves, and the three of us—the three blondes. Within ten minutes, we were all mounted, picking our way cautiously around the beds of quicksand, and wading through the currents in order to cross over to the opposite side of the Platte. We too headed east, but along a trail that followed the river's southern bank.

The river took a large, smooth, circular bend that changed its direction from an eastern to a southern flow. We stayed on or near the trails that hugged the river's curve for a full day until the river made a hard bend to the left and again headed east. At this bend the trail formed a fork. We stayed to the right, left the river, and continued on southward. It was certain that this trail was not only well used, but well used by white men, for we passed what thus far had never been seen—*busted wagon wheels.*

353

Even I hadn't been prepared for that. Along with the wagon wheels, there was also the scattered litter of burned wooden planks. I am sure that there had been much more to these remnants, but those items were probably scavenged by the Indians. The burned planks were of little worth to either settlers or Indians and so they remained.

We camped at night under the 'the dying grass moon.' That put us more than four weeks' ride from the Tsistsistas; who by now would have understood us to be abducted, who by now would have given up their search and headed south with heavy hearts. A journey this long made it obvious we were being taken someplace for reasons I suspected had little to do with slavery, sacrifice, or fresh wives. It was about ransom. I had often heard of this while a child living on the East Coast. Of course, I also believed us to be well into the hunting grounds of other unfriendly Indians, and all this could be made moot in a heartbeat.

At the end of this day's traveling, Gracie, Luke, and I seated ourselves against a ledge of rock. We were never allowed to sit at the fire with the braves, but we were free of our bonds; and at our distance, we were able to talk without reprisal. This was due purely to our captors having no ambition to rise from the comfort of their fire for purpose of walking our way to scream, or worse, beat us. We rested, and we now talked freely within the shadows.

The days were continuing to grow colder. Unable to enjoy the warmth of fire or the benefit of blanket, we were forced all the more to huddle close together sandwiched between grasses we gathered for bedding. At least the grass was substantially taller, an average of five feet, so it provided its own windbreak. We prepared our bed much like deer tamping small cushioned areas for their beds, but we also carefully worked loose some of the grass to use as a cover. Careless yanking on the blades would slice your hands open like a fine-stoned knife.

We were working the grasses about us to form a blanket. I was wedged tightly between Gracie and Luke, talking mostly to myself, when I realized Gracie was completely ignoring me. She had grown quiet and seemed totally preoccupied with her own thoughts.

"You're awfully quiet." I whispered. "What are you thinking about?"

"I can kill 'em."

"What!" I exclaimed in shock. I sat up at once. Gracie leaned back on her elbows and looked up at me.

"I said, I can kill 'em. I know it. They think I'm weak."

"I can help you!"

Luke was quick to rush in.

"Luke Dennison! You so much as move a muscle and I swear I will break every last bone in your body. You understand me?"

I was at once furious.

"But I can help. I will kill one with my bare hands."

"You will kill nothing! Do you hear me, young man? You so much as blink, and I am going to peel the skin off your hide and tan it in front of your crying eyes. Don't you even be thinking such a thing!"

I wasn't about to deal with any ill-fated pigheaded ambitions. I turned back to Gracie, with whom I was also upset.

"You see what you have started? I can't believe what I am hearing you say, Gracie!"

"Wot's not to believe? We're prisoners, and may be good as dead for all I know. I, for one, have no intention of waiting to see wot becomes of me. Ark a' me, for I say there are only four now, and they are too confident. I get a hold of those knives, and I promise you, I'll even up the odds quickly," Gracie sneered.

"Now, just one moment. My word! Just one blessed moment, before you go off making a mess of things—."

"A mess of—."

"Hush! Hush!"

Gracie and Luke respected my command, and for a long second we sat in silence. I spoke when I felt the air was settled.

"Now just listen to me for a moment, Gracie. Keep in mind, there may be a couple of things you haven't fully considered."

"Such as wot?"

"Such as, what do you plan to do after you've murdered them?"

"Whatever I want. And, I wouldn't exactly call it murder."

"I was afraid of that, and yes, it is murder. May I explain something to you before you set out on a bloodletting rampage while I'm sound asleep?"

"Yut. Wot?"

"Maybe you have failed to notice the fact that we have been riding at a pretty good pace for the past four or five weeks, and all of it has been east and south."

"Yut, so wot?"

"So, do you remember when I first met you? You were headed to St. Louis. Remember I told you there was nothing between you and St Louis except for a thousand miles of plains and Indians?"

"Wot are you saying, Elizabeth?"

"What I am saying is that before you go off killing anybody, you might consider that to date our abductors have been escorting us across the plains; a trip that I hadn't planned in such fashion, but nevertheless a trip that could have easily killed us had we done it on our own.

"You may wish to consider that at present we are being fed and we are being guarded. We haven't had to lift a finger in order to end up somewhere near the place you have always dreamed to be—St. Louis.

"There may very well come a time to take matters into our own hands, but this is not that time. I say let us make the best of it and see how much advantage comes our way—before we start slitting throats."

"Fine. Fine!"

"Oh, thank you, Lord!" My voice strained in a whisper. "A head for reason."

Gracie could have, and would have, slit their throats. Of this I had no doubt. I had seen her deftly handle a knife a thousand times during our years together. Fortunately for me, Gracie was no fool, and she immediately understood the soundness of my reasoning.

"Do you really believe we are close to St. Louis?"

"Let me just say this for certain. We are much closer to St. Louis now than we were when you were a child. We are much closer to St. Louis now than we were a month ago. Providing you do nothing foolish, you just may live to see it, girl." Gracie studied my face and said nothing. I continued, "Now let's just go to sleep, and come morning, we'll consider our options as they arise. As for you, Luke, you keep your nose clean and your mouth shut, or you'll wind up getting us all killed. Do you hear me, son?"

"Yes, Mother."

"You're a brave boy, Luke. I can see that, and I am proud of you. Your time will come, but for now, for me—go to sleep."

"Are we never going back to camp?" he asked.

"I don't believe so."

"Never?"

"Never is a long time, Luke. Let me just say, I never knew how long I would be with Talk-a-Lot and the Tsistsistas, and likewise, I don't know how long I will be without them. But for right now, it's time for all of us to go to sleep. Now close your eyes. Good night."

"Good night, Momma."

"Good night, Gracie."

"Good night."

I was still in the habit of kissing them both good night. We pulled the grasses up over our heads and shut out the cold night air.

FORTY-FIVE

We continued to ride south and I hoped to enjoy warmer temperatures. The lay of the land hinted that the Missouri might be off to our left, but I hadn't seen anything of its banks. We had been taken from the foothills of forested slopes, led across the sandygrasses, steppes barren or covered in thick stubbly growth and short grasses, merged into mixed grasses, and now we rode through prairie grass tall enough to cast shadows on my horse's head.

For weeks, before entering this tall grass expanse, there had been little if anything of a tree to be seen at any distance from a river. Now, another change in the landscape was underway. Solitary trees were occasionally seen sprouting skyward from the thick mesh of tired grass. They presented themselves as loners, starkly obvious as they jutted vertically from the perfectly flat line of the horizon.

Ever more frequently these singular trees appeared; a tree here, a tree there, and then two, three, and finally the first grove of oaks. Of far more interest to me was the now visible line of cottonwoods far to our left, always where I assumed the river to be.

As we continued, the look of the land changed markedly. It was more fertile, and it conjured up memories of my passage years ago. I felt it safe to say, the great desert was finally behind us. I was amused by watching Luke and Gracie attempt to comprehend the vastness of the land beyond the shadows of the mountains. They understood the distance passed, but could only question and try to comprehend what distance remained.

Gracie was not about to be bothered by distance, nor was she overly troubled by being held captive, for her spirits were lifted by my assurance that every passing day brought her closer to the world that had been a construction of cloudy childhood dreams and adolescent desires—*St. Louis.*

Even I felt reasonably comfortable as of late because the Indians were obviously knowledgeable of the country. To my eye, they made this voyage appear routine. They were very relaxed in their manner, joking and laughing a good deal as of late. Only an Indian who was confident about his whereabouts would clown around in a manner such as these men. I would have deduced they were Pawnee after all, but for the fact they preferred to remain hidden and keep to the concealment of the tall grasses instead of the trail or riverbank.

In the beginning, while under strict guard, we rode in single file. Four or more braves led our troupe. They were followed first by Gracie, then Luke, then me. In line behind me rode Talk-a-Lot and the others, and finally two or more braves who kept watch over our every move and any signs of strangers that might be cause for concern. It continued this way for the first few weeks until a time in which we were too far removed from our camp to effect an escape or expect any reasonable attempt at a rescue.

After those first unpredictable weeks were behind us, after Talk-a-Lot and the others had been separated from our party, the concerns of the Indians diminished as did their number and guard. They abandoned their trailing guard, choosing instead to ride together ahead of us in a group of four so they could converse and cavort.

The three of us followed their lead, at first because we had no choice, but afterwards because we still had no choice. To be left in the wilderness with no weapons for defense or hunting spelled doom by attack or starvation followed by injury or weakness, and most assuredly death. We had to follow our captors for there was no other option.

I preferred that Gracie and Luke ride together side by side behind the Indians, but ahead of me, so I could keep an eye on them and afford some barrier of safety from behind, feeble as that may have been. This arrangement kept Luke protected on three sides.

Our days had become routine, starting the same, ending the same. So much so, we were now very quick to pick up on anything out of the ordinary. And this morning was out of the ordinary. The four Indians sat around the fire, ate, and conversed in a more serious tone than usual. Even from a distance we could perceive a change in demeanor.

"Ark a' me. Something is going on," said Gracie.

We studied the Indians, watching their every gesture and expression.

"Wot are they talking about?" asked Gracie.

"I don't know, but I agree, something is up. That much is for certain."

Having reached some sort of agreement, the four Indians stood up from before the fire. Then to our surprise, two of the men rode off.

"Where are they going?" asked Gracie under her breath.

"I don't know, but they are heading east. Maybe they are off to announce our arrival—maybe to make arrangements for a ransom. Or maybe they are just looking for fresh horses. Whatever they're up to, it proves to me that they know where we are."

"Wot luck. Now, there are only two braves and the three of—."

"Never you mind, Gracie."

"Wot do you mean, never mind. The one who that stays is the one who has my knives. Surely, that's an omen."

"Gracie!" I whispered with force. "Nev-er mind. Can we not just keep our eyes and ears open? Can we not just stay alert—just pay attention, and nothing more?"

"They're going for their horses, Momma."

"Good. Go on, then. Hurry up. Get on your horse, Luke. Come on, Gracie, mount up and let's get out of here."

"Ohhhhhhhhhhhhhh! Wot-ever you say."

Gracie let out a frustrated sigh, but she mounted up as I asked, and we rode out.

Hypocrite. That was the word for me. All the while, I was busy scolding Gracie, I was attempting to shun murderous thoughts of my own. But the truth was I had no desire to kill these men. Maybe it was because I was getting too old. Maybe it was because I no longer hated Indians. More likely, it was because I had once murdered, and it was just too sickening to acknowledge what deplorable deeds I was capable of committing.

In any event, one could not help but to entertain fresh thoughts of escape, especially at times like this when our horses headed out again to walk away the hours of our journey. I glanced over at Gracie. She concerned me, and I was becoming ever more compelled to keep a close eye on her. She was actually making me nervous with her ongoing talk of killing. I could only pray a rash judgment wouldn't cause her to carry that burden for life.

"Yut. The two of them certainly seem to be in a jolly state of mind," said Gracie.

"So, I have noticed. I would say that considering their high spirits, considering their comfort at being just two, and finally, looking at the lay of this land, I believe we are nearing our destination."

"For certain?" asked Gracie, barely concealing her excitement.

"Well...I can't know for certain, but it would make sense if they were planning to trade us or release us for ransom. Otherwise, what's the point of bringing us so far east? And we are very 'east' indeed. If they are looking for ransom, they need to bring us close to the settlements."

"You mean like St. Louis?" asked Gracie.

"Well, the St. Louis that I used to know would have been the perfect place. In those days, Indians moved in and out of the city without as much as a raised eyebrow. Of course, I can only imagine how much has changed since. In fact, according to what I remember of Wilpen's maps, there are now a slew of settlements upriver of St. Louis. We would see whites long before we entered the city of St. Louis. "

"Does that mean we are close to the great rivers?" asked Luke.

362

"Ahhh, the great rivers…yes, I believe we are, Luke. It just feels as if we are. I have been watching that line of cottonwoods that keeps appearing to the north of us and I'd bet a saddle it tracks a river."

I had spent the last ten years living in a place generally void of trees, or surrounded by aspen and firs that reached up from rocky slopes. We had left that place, crossed plains and prairie, and now entered a land of bark I recognized from my past. I remembered these trees, the cedar, the hickory, the oaks and Box Elder, and the cottonwood, especially the cottonwood. I spoke a thought aloud.

"Where cottonwood grows, the river flows. We're near water an—."

"GRRRRAARRRGGHHHHH!"

"Ahhhh!"

"Ahhhhhhhhhhhhhhh!"

"GRRRRAARRRGGHHHHH!"

The first cries were of surprise, but the second were of blood curdling death.

"Get back! Get back! Get away, Luke!" I shrieked.

"GRRRRAARRRGGHHHHH!"

"Mom!"

"Get back! Get back, Gracie! Run! Run!" I screamed.

"GRRRRAARRRGGHHHHH!"

Luke's and Gracie's horses reared up and staggered backward into mine, jarring me hard and nearly felling the three of us. My horse regained his footing as I hung on precariously, my arms gripped tightly around its neck.

363

As quickly as the Indian's arrow plunged through the chest of Eškôseesehe, so too did the grizzly plunge into the Indians before us. The beast was enormous. It was unstoppable, a flurry of growls, slashing claws, and gnashing teeth. It attacked directly from the right side, and their horses collapsed under the weight of its charge. I went white with fear and only kept my head, but for a mother's instinct to protect her young. My sanity was hardly necessary, for Luke was born to ride and Gracie was as quick as a fox.

The two of them had been ahead of me, closer to the bear, but they were already in retreat due to their horses' natural instincts— in retreat before any command was voiced. My horse was boxed in by both of their horses and a whirl of confusion. In my fight to stay with the horse, I caught glimpses of sky and earth, an image of Luke and Gracie leaving me at full speed, and finally an unobstructed view of the carnage that lay at arm's length. There was nothing now but blood and bellowing between the bear and me.

"GRRRRAARRRGGHHHHH!"

My horse reacted to the roar and the screaming that seemed to be coming from every direction. The poor creature was riddled with fear, as was I. I drove my fingers deep into its mane and clung tightly for the sake of my life. Luke and Gracie bolted past in a blur. My horse reared upward a second time as if caught by their wake, and stumbled backwards, now nearly falling over due to the mat of thick grass tangled about its rear legs.

The bear made a reckless lunge for us. Its massive front paw sliced through the air, intent on splitting open my horse's exposed underbelly. I wasn't sure if it missed the mark or not, but one of its claws clipped the bone of my ankle as my leg flailed in the air. In my state of mind, I hardly noticed the wound and felt no pain whatsoever. I was entirely focused on hanging on, determined not to find myself left alone lying upon the ground to be this marauder's next meal.

All this happened in seconds, time in which my horse's front hooves were mostly high in the air, yet to land. And it was from that stance that the horse spun its torso before falling back to earth. The very instant its front hooves touched ground, its rear hooves lashed out with a vengeance. The kick was out of pure terror, and served only to stir an already unsettled air, but it occurred just as one of the brave's horses rose back on its feet to charge off wildly in the opposite direction. This unexpected ruckus caused the bear a momentary distraction, which was all my horse needed to gain the few feet necessary to escape the animal's reach. With that advantage, we lit out faster than a rattlesnake strike and never looked back.

It wasn't as though I was riding a prize stallion or the coveted animal of a chief, but it took some serious coaxing to get this half-wild plains horse to slow down or even take note of the reins. It only happened after some persuasive maneuvering by Gracie, who saw me struggling with the runaway, and had the foresight to set off at a gallop and intercept my horse with hers. Reaching out to grab its mane, she broke its stride with her horse, forcing it to ease up.

Nervous and panting hard, the animal was brought to a halt, but not before traveling a fair distance back along the path. It may have been better had it gone farther. Gracie and I looked at each other, and I went sick to my stomach when I heard the agonizing screams of a brave being mauled to death by a beast as big as any bison I had ever seen stampeding the plains.

As the gut-wrenching screams faded into silence, they were replaced by the pounding of earth as the remaining horse came into view, galloping toward us at a frenzied pace. It sped past us, raked with deep gashes from which flowed torrents of bright red blood, now mixing in the air with a froth of sweat and spit. No one bothered to stop it. It was good as dead, yet not a word was spoken to say as much. We were too numb.

Luke rode up to meet us. We remained mounted on our horses, badly shaken, silent, and ready to flee at the slightest hint of movement in the surrounding grass. We were congregated in a perfect state of dread, hardly daring to breathe. We listened with intent, visibly shrinking like a salted slug at the slightest rustle within the undergrowth. We waited, knowing the chances were as certain as not, that the beast would break upon us in the moment. We looked to the left and to the right; we looked ahead and over our shoulders.

Rife with affright, we strained to find warning within the stalks of grass that were nearly as high as the three of us seated upon our horses. We could just see across the top of the billowing grasses. We prayed not to notice any disruption in the natural sway of the stalks and seed pods that teetered back and forth in the passing breezes. It was unquestionably one of the most terrifying episodes of my life.

As I sat still but for my trembling, I recalled a time passed when Ho'neheveho made me a chief. He told his people I had braved the bear. I remembered asking Talk-a-Lot what he meant when he said that, but she never answered me. In my years at camp, I came to learn the extent to which Indians feared an encounter with a grizzly. It was an animal that was agile, could easily outrun a man, climb a tree, swim, take down a horse, break you in half, and didn't die without taking a lot of life with it.

The warriors desired its fearsome spirit and its symbol was carved and painted onto many shields and objects of war. It was an animal especially dreaded in the blinding tall grass of the prairie or thicket where it lurked hidden from view. As God was my witness, I now understood fully their fear and their respect.

After what seemed like hours of frozen immobility, Gracie turned to face me. She dared to whisper.

"Well, now wot? I'm shaking so bad I can hardly stay on my horse."

I fought to choke out a few words of my own.

"Luke. Are you alright?"

"Yes. Did you see the size of that bear? He was huge! Those Indians are dead!"

"Quiet! Shhh, not so loud," I scolded. "Have you lost your mind? That bear will be right upon us if it hears you yelling."

A flurry of horrible images returned and brought us back to a state of nervous silence. Again, it was Gracie who broke the silence. She whispered.

"I would feel a lot better if we had some weapons."

"I can't fathom the thought of going back there." I responded. "Whatever remains to be found won't be pretty. Bears aren't fussy about where they throw their leftovers."

"Listen, I'll ride up ahead, Elizabeth."

"What!"

"Why don't you stay back here with Luke?"

"What? What are you say—?"

"Just remember, those bears are fast. If you see me high tailing it back down this path, don't be waiting to ask me why, because I'll be riding right over the top of you."

"Are you insane?" I whispered aloud. "Have you lost your mind? You will not go back there. I won't hear of such stupidity."

"I am not ins—."

"No, Gracie. No, no, no—."

"I am going back, Elizabeth."

367

She glared at me. I hadn't felt the ice of her eyes in years. Not since she was a child full of distrust. I bit my tongue.

"As you wish."

Gracie calmed down at once.

"I am sorry. I didn't mean to snap, but I'm not insane. I am however, the fastest on a horse. And it may be true that I was only a child when I lived in the mountains, but I still have more experience with bears than either of you."

"I'm afraid for you, Gracie. I don't want you going back there for any reason."

"Yut, I know, but we need the bows. We need the food in those bags. And you will simply have to accept that I am not going anywhere without my knives."

"Gracie—."

"I am going back, Elizabeth. I know to be careful. Don't worry, I will take my time. You just wait here with Luke and stay quiet. Remember, some of these bears can outrun horses."

"Oh, lord, Gracie, please—."

"Ark a' me, Elizabeth. I'll be fine. Just stay quiet and wait for me."

"You know I will never agree to this, Gracie. But if you insist, please, I beg be careful, girl. If that bear is still around, you are as dead as those braves and I will cry myself to my grave."

"Don't worry. We had bears in the mountains. My dadduh used to kill them all the time. I know to keep my eyes and ears open. I don't doubt he's still close by, and he won't have any trouble smelling any of us. But, dadduh used to say they were most dangerous when they were feeding. We must have stumbled upon him when he found some food. I should be all right as long as I keep my distance."

I nodded my head in disapproval, but said nothing in return. Luke was unusually quiet. Gracie started back up the path, while Luke and I did the only thing we could—we waited...and waited... and waited. We sat there on our horses, saying nothing, for what seemed an eternity. I was beside myself with worry. The wind was blowing gently from the southwest, which was not good, for it blew our scent all over the area that the bear was roaming. For nearly half an hour we waited.

Then came the dreaded sound of a horrific growl. Even at my distance it was enough to unsettle my horse. Instantly, I was filled with dread for Gracie. Filled with anxiety, I felt myself begin to tremble. I looked at Luke.

"You stay here, Luke. You stay put, you hear me. Stay here and stay quiet."

"Momma, don't go."

"Quiet, Luke. Stay put."

I kicked my horse hard with my heels, goading it to hurry up the path until I rounded the last bend and saw the bear hovering over the dead bodies. I halted my horse at once. The bear looked at me and growled. It then sniffed the bodies of the Indians, and looked in another direction. I followed the direction of its gaze and my blood turned cold. The beast was looking directly at Gracie who was standing perfectly still some thirty feet away, but with no horse in sight. She had retrieved the bows. Unfortunately, they were as useless as pin pricks against such a formidable animal. Gracie was as good as dead, unless I could figure out something, anything to assist.

"Whoooooooooooooo! Whoooooooooooo! Eeeeeeeeeeyaaaaaaaaaahhh!"

369

I let out a yelp, and another, and another. The bear turned at once and faced me.

"Eeeeeeeeeeeeeeyaaaaaaaaaaaaaaahhh!"

I let out another scream. The bear remained focused on me, but did not move to where Gracie might manage an escape. I had to draw the animal away. I remembered what Gracie had about bears outrunning horses. It was a fear all Indians shared. I looked back along the path to assure myself there was nothing between me and retreat. I turned back to face animal. I knew Gracie only had seconds at the most. I charged the bear, but my horse was in no mood to advance, and so resisted my commands. It was fighting my will, and caused me to yell with greater urgency. The horse refused to comply, but my outbursts caused the bear to rear up on its hind legs and growl out a warning. It sniffed the air and growled a second time. It viewed me as a threat to its food. I had its full attention.

I could only envision the beast overrunning my horse. I thought of the dead Indians and the horrible screams that marked their dying breath. I was terrified. Then I thought of Gracie, who was as much a child to me as was Luke. I drove my heels back into my horse.

"Hyaaaaaa! Hyaaaaaaa!"

I screamed at the bear.

"Come on, you miserable bastard, chase me!"

I needn't have asked. As if to grant my wish before I even made it, the animal leapt in my direction and plowed through the grass like a maddened bull. My horse was already half turned in retreat when I bolted for safety, only to see Luke sitting on his horse in plain sight. My heart stopped.

"Run! Run! Run, Luke, Run!"

Luke turned his horse and started out as I bore down on him at full speed. I turned to look behind me and to my horror, realized the bear was fast gaining on us. I was on Luke's heels and the sum of this situation was enough to cause me such stress, my eyes began to tear.

"Run, Luke, run!" I screamed with all my might. Luke was now only forty or fifty feet ahead of me, but to my heavenly relief, he was edging away. It wasn't about his ability to ride; he could outride me any day. It was about the speed of his horse. It appeared faster than mine; with every grateful breath, I gave thanks to God through my clenched teeth.

Again, I looked behind. This time the bear had dropped back. He was still running toward me, but now seemed less inclined to pursue. I had him where I wanted him—away from Gracie. I looked back, this time to see that the bear had stopped charging. I halted my horse and turned to face the animal. It stood back up on its hind legs and growled. It was standing its ground, and that was fine with me.

The longer it chose to confront me, the more time Gracie had to flee. The bear then disappeared. Instead of going back up the path toward the dead Indians, it moved directly into the grass, which came as a monumental disappointment. It left me precisely where I had been earlier, wondering if and when it would explode from within the tall grasses to deal out our doom.

I decided to leave for lack of any immediate ideas on what else might be done. Distance equaled safety in my mind, whether true or not. I was nervous. I felt the bear's presence up and down the back of my neck. I urged my horse to get on with it and soon found myself looking upon Luke. He was sitting on his horse and waiting. Seeing him safe was everything to me and at once I broke into tears.

371

"Luke Dennison, I am so angry with you that I should leave you out here to be eaten alive by that monster. If there was something here bigger than a blade of grass, I swear, I would beat you to within an inch of your life." I was flushed with joy, anger, and stress.

"I'm sorry, Momma."

"Sorry, doesn't cut it, son. It doesn't cut it. I specifically told you to remain here out of harm's way, and you disobeyed me. You could have easily gotten both of us killed. Why didn't you mind me?"

"I don't know."

"What do you mean, you don't know? What is there not to know? I said, stay here! How much clearer could I have been?"

"I'm sorry."

"Tell me, why didn't you mind me? I want to know now, this minute, why you disobeyed me when I was adamant. I was adamant!"

There was a moment of hesitation in Luke's manner. His head was lowered. Then with much guilt he answered.

"I was afraid."

His answer caught me off guard. Cowardice was unacceptable amongst the Tsistsistas. But if fear was to be instilled within a warrior, a grizzly was the only creature alive that could do it. I had never seen weakness or fear in Luke. His bravery as a child had brought me much praise from the others in camp. Somehow, I lost sight of the fact that he was only ten, still a very young boy. I was ashamed to think I might have overlooked my responsibility as a mother, the only individual who offered him sanctuary from his fears. The remembrance was enough to change my tone at once. I moved to console him.

"The bear spirit is the strongest spirit of all, Luke. I know of no man who is unafraid of the bear spirit. You needn't lower your head. Instead, raise your head with confidence and say, *I fear the bear spirit, for it is the strongest spirit of all.* That will show the world that you are honest, that you humble, and that you are very smart. Those are the virtues that make a boy a chief."

Luke looked up at me. He understood, but he was wrought by guilt. He received what I said as wise, as knowledge from an elder, but it remained difficult for him to admit fear without admitting failure. He had spent his entire life raised in the traditions of the tribes. Above all else, to be a Tsistsista was to be brave unto death. This may have been his first real test of bravery, and he felt he had failed. I understood the seriousness of this situation, and I also realized that this matter would not pass easily from Luke's memory.

"We will have plenty of time to discuss this matter in the days ahead. You will see the wisdom of the spirit that fills you. Until then, I say we do our best to find Gracie and get on with our journey. Shall we search out Gracie?"

"Yes."

With that, we turned to head back up the path for a third time. We moved slowly making as little noise as possible. Luke was certainly in no mood to talk, which made listening that much easier. I clung to a hope that Gracie was safe. I had not heard her scream, or a bear growling additional threats, both were sounds that would have carried easily to my ear. Unfortunately, there was nothing of her to be seen.

"What do we do now, Momma?"

I looked up from the path and studied Luke.

"That's a good question, Luke. I am not sure. I didn't hear Gracie scream, so I am going to assume she is alright. I don't know if we should stay here or if we should head out. Our options are poor. If we stay here, we are sitting ducks waiting for the bear to return, but Gracie will most likely find us. If we leave, we still chance an encounter with the bear, but Gracie will have no idea where we are. What would you do?"

Luke thought about it for a spell.

"I don't think it's a good idea to stay here. I think we should leave, but I think we should tie some tall grasses together and hold them up as we ride away. We can yell now and then, and if Gracie looks our way, she will see the grass bundles above our heads in the field."

Luke had proffered a sensible plan that also gave me an opportunity to give him back some of his self-esteem. I also had no stomach to remain here on the path so near dead Indians and an angry bear.

"That is an excellent idea, Luke. Let's do it."

We dismounted only long enough to uproot the tallest of grasses we could find, tie them in bundles, and get back on our horses. Once seated upon the horses' backs, the bundles reached upward three or four feet into the air over our heads. We then set out on a different path. I went north of the original path to keep our scent farthest downwind of the carnage. Every few minutes we would call out to Gracie, but there was never an answer.

"GRAAAACIEEEEEEE!"

We stopped to listen.

"GRAAAACIEEEEEEE!" Luke yelled at the top of his lungs. I was fully expecting the bear to appear at any moment.

"Keep moving, Luke. Yell again."

"GRAAAAACIEEEEEEEEEE!"

"I'm coming."

It was a distant reply but it was the sweetest sound I might hear.

"Can you see our grasses!"

"Yut. Be quiet."

Nothing else need be said. I understood her warning at once.

"Keep riding, Luke. We need to get out of here. Gracie can see the stalks. Just hold them up."

We kept up our pace, moving the horses in a northeasterly direction. At last, much to my relief, I heard her voice.

"I'm here."

Gracie appeared in the grasses to my right, riding toward us. We waited up momentarily for her to meet us. When she emerged, she had two bows in hand, two quivers full of arrows slung over her shoulders, two or three bags of food, and, judging by the glint of light that danced off her side, *her knives.*

"Oh, Gracie," I whispered aloud.

I was filled with exasperation.

"Don't say it. I know. I was wrong. I should have stayed with you. I should have listened."

"I have nothing to say, no blame. You did what you thought you must. I was so upset when you didn't come back—I am only happy to see you alive."

"Well, if you hadn't come along just when you did, I may not have been."

"What happened? I waited forever, and you never returned. I was beside myself with worry. I finally had to go see what became of you. I hardly dared consider what I might find. What in the Lord's name took you so long?"

"Well, when I arrived, the bear was still angry. It was mauling them, watching them, looking for life or movement. So, I had to wait on the path and wait, and watch." She shook her body in a spasm of disgust. "Nothing I ever want to see again. All I could do was keep still until it finished ripping them apart. I wasn't about to get pushy. Besides, I had everything I could do to keep from throwing up.

"Finally, for wot-ever reason, it turned about and disappeared into the grass. I waited another ten minutes before moving in. Believe me, I was quiet, I was quick, and I was careful. I got off the horse and grabbed whatever I could get my hands on."

She showed me the parfleches that still contained food and some flints.

"I couldn't get the blankets. Anyway, I had already grabbed all I could carry when I heard something large in the grass moving toward me. I knew. But if I had any doubts, they were dismissed the minute my horse bolted. It yanked the rope right out of my grip. The animal must have still been frightened. Anyway, I figured I was good as dead. But, I'm not, and honestly I would rather not think any more about it. I'm here now, and I have my knives."

Gracie then held up her precious knives and looked at me with a face-splitting grin. She went on to say.

"At least, I didn't have to do any murdering. That should make you happy."

I felt numb.

"They were both dead?"

"Dead? Are you serious!"

She lowered the knives and looked at me incredulously.

"I mean, I *know* they are dead—."

"They are a long, long, ways past dead, Elizabeth, and we'll be just as dead if we don't get a move on"

"Alright, alright, I get the point. I was just trying to think."

"Better think hard or in short time we will be as dead as those Indians. Ark a' me, we need to get out of here—*now*."

I was embarrassed, and attempted to move past my idiocy.

"I agree. Let's go. C'mon Luke, let's go."

"Where are we going, Momma?"

"East, same as always. There isn't much choice. No matter how much we dislike riding blind through this grass, we need to keep going east. We'll just have to pray we don't run into another bear. Let's keep our mouths shut, our eyes and ears open, and hope for the best."

"We won't have to worry about running into another bear for a while. One thing I learned from my dadduh, when they are that big, there is no other bear around unless it's a dead bear dinner. This ground belongs to this spirit, and only this spirit. As long as we don't run into him, we won't run into another for a good ways. At least for now, we should be downwind of him."

"Well, I hope you are right for all our sakes."

Gracie led the way through the thicket. Luke followed second, and I watched our behinds until my neck pained from stiffness. My stomach fluttered all the while I studied the crush of path that trailed.

"Momma, do you have any idea where we are?"

"No".

"You are one for keeping spirits up," quipped Gracie.

"You just want me to say it again."

"True. It always sounds so magical the way you tell it. Besides, it will give Luke something less grizzly to think about."

Gracie needn't say another word. I slipped into the same story, word for word.

"Fine. From the beginning. This land is split in two, east from west, by a great waterway called the Mississippi. I doubt that has changed since the last hundred times I said it. The Mississippi has its roots far up in the north country. It flows south where it is joined by another great river called the Missouri. The Missouri spills into the Mississippi and together they course southward, all the way across the land, all the way down to the Gulf of Mexico. The waters of the Mississippi reach from far left to far right of the rising sun for a distance I cannot describe, a distance you cannot imagine.

"If we ride into the rising sun, be assured we will come upon the Mississippi. That is for certain. However, if we are farther north, we could come upon the Missouri first, but that is less certain. I also believe by the number of trees in the area, especially the cottonwoods, we can't be too far away from one of these rivers, if not both.

"The desert changes to short grass prairie, which it did. And the short grass changes to medium grass—."

"Which it did!" exclaimed Luke.

"Yes, it did. And the medium grass—."

"Changes to tall grass—," said Luke.

"Which it did," said everyone in unison.

"And lastly, the prairie gives way to forest. Obviously, we are now starting to see more trees.

"The Missouri, which should be north of us, flows mostly through desert and prairie whereas the Mississippi flows mostly through tall grasses and wooded country, that is, if my memory stands correct. For that reason, we must keep ourselves headed east into the rising sun."

"And...." Gracie paused for effect, "...you've always told me that the city of St. Louis is on the Mississippi where the two rivers meet."

"That is true. It is almost exactly where the two rivers meet."

"Yut, hard to believe. I have waited my whole life for this. Naheto! Let's go!"

"Naheto!" Luke hollered out in a sudden rush of high spirits.

"Luke!" I hissed through my teeth. "There's a bear out there. Did you forget?"

Luke's eyes grew wide. He was still a child, and he was as prone to let out an Indian yelp as have a private thought. We looked around and listened for a disturbance. There was none. All I noticed from that point on was how Gracie's face was aglow but for a head full of dreams.

We set out cautiously at first, still more frightened than anything, until we felt the relief that distance offered. Thereafter, we pressed on in haste as we followed a well-used game trail. Winter was fast on our heels, and we had no winter dress nor time or means to fashion it.

FORTY-SIX

The next couple of days forced all I could muster in keeping up with Gracie and Luke. They were on the fly. In contrast, I am not sure whether it was due to their anticipation, their hopes and dreams or what, but something triggered within me a deep sense of discouragement, a cloud of apprehension that descended ever lower to stifle my spirit. I dragged. I felt as though an anchor was holding me back. I might have preferred it to be some distorted sense of relief after having endured so much and then suddenly being free—a too good to be true syndrome. Unfortunately, the more likely was my having to face that portal to my past, a door that suddenly felt wide open.

It didn't help that Gracie and Luke were hounding me to discuss St. Louis and all points beyond, those places of my yesteryears, that other world, that other dimension of my existence. I felt floodgates opening to swamp me with fears that I would be judged harshly for the person I had become. I felt a sense of insecurity that was remarkably similar to the feelings I experienced in my youth. I remembered those insecurities. In later years, the same fears, the same feelings of insecurity drove me out of South Pass and into oblivion.

I was being driven to confront the dreaded thoughts of facing Mary after all these years. I was already searching for excuses. I wasn't sure how I would explain my disappearance and any lack of effort to console her. I was haunted to know that *after all these years*, Mary could be dead as a doornail and there would be no need for explaining. That thought was amplified by an extreme crush of guilt.

I was at once pained by fury for allowing myself to again cower after so many, many years. I shook my head in disgust and decided at that moment, I would be damned before I would live in regret of my life. I had made my choices. Some were good, some were bad, but combined they resulted in experiences that no one I should meet from this day forth would likely surpass let alone be qualified to judge. My latter years had not been lived as a sheltered life. I had not lived as a pampered socialite. I had set my own course to face whatever should come my way. Because of it, I now had a son who was my pride and joy, and if for no reason other than his honor, I swore never to lower my head for any reason.

"Elizabeth?"

"Yes, Gracie."

"I was just thinking. Here I am crossing lands and distances I would have never imagined, and I am doing it in your company. I have never met anybody as smart as you. I always believed my dadduh was the smartest man alive, and for the whole of my life, you have been the smartest woman alive. I often ask myself how I came to be so lucky as to know you. Do you remember when we first met? I didn't think you were so smart back then. I thought you were completely crazy. Honest, I did. Do you remember?"

"Yes." I laughed. "You were one very frightened little girl. You were also as independent a child as any I ever met, and if I may return the compliment, quite possibly the smartest little girl I have ever known. I learned a lot from you."

"Wot could you have possibly learned from me?"

"Probably the most important thing of all."

"Wot?"

"Gracie...."

I shook my head and broke out in a broad grin.

"Wot...wot's so funny."

"My word, child, you were so independent when we met, so very independent. You were also utterly wore out and headed for a hard fall that mule—what was her name...."

"Kelly?"

"Kelly, yes, that was it. I finally talked you off that animal and onto the wagon to sit alongside me. You were so tired, in spite of all that independent nature, you lifted up my arm and placed it around you. I was completely taken aback."

"Wot? I don't remember doing anything of the sort."

"I am sure you don't. But believe me, you pressed yourself hard to my chest and fell into a deep sleep. I was so profoundly moved by your innocence and your vulnerability at that moment, I believe to this day that you prepared me spiritually for the coming of Luke. You awakened my heart unlike any child I ever encountered. You gave my heart a chance to prove it possessed the devotion required of a mother. I knew at that moment, I would have given up my last breath of life for you."

"You were a very good mother; you are a very good mother, and a great teacher."

"Thank you."

"There is something I do remember."

"What is that?"

"I remember you promising me that someday you would tell me the story of how somebody so smart could end up alone and half dead in the desert."

"Oh, my word! Timing is everything."

"Wot?"

Gracie gave me a puzzled look.

No sooner had I made my oath of *'no regrets,'* and the test was at hand. It was true we had spent hours discussing St. Louis and my travels, and I should have assumed this decade-old inquiry would be resurrected, but it felt exactly like she was reading my mind. I may not have yet crossed the Mississippi, but indeed, I had just crossed back into my old life.

"Just a private thought. I reckon you're now old enough to understand."

"Nothing like a good story to pass time."

"That too, I suppose. Tell me, Gracie, have you ever or do you ever dream about finding a man to be all yours, to love and hold forever—your own warrior, your own chief, someone to stand by you, someone to protect you?"

"I don't know. Yut. Sometimes, I suppose."

"Well, in a way, I guess you could say I fell in love with a man who was all of that and more in my eyes. He was my chief; he was my warrior. He swayed my heart for as far back as I can remember. I never knew what it was about him. I could never fully explain it. I still can't. But the man possessed the power to move me. He probably still does to this day. I just don't know it.

"Anyway, he was a generous man, Gracie. He was a kind man. It seems as of late nary a week goes by that I don't think of him in one way or another. I wish I could say it was entirely my fault that I made a god of him in my mind, but honestly I can't. I yet feel there remains something about him, a force of nature if you will, a way about him that I have never and maybe never will be able to explain. He is the most mysterious person I have ever known."

"How so?"

"Oh, Gracie! If I knew the answer to that, my life would have been completely different, I am sure."

"Do you not like your life?"

I had to think about her question.

"My life is nothing of what I foresaw when a dreamy-eyed child. Fate has changed the course of my life many times, always without warning, always without any apparent logic. Just when I believe I have gained my bearing, fate flings me along another tangent—at times a hard right-angle, and I mean *hard*. When I take time to look back, I find myself hoping a higher power has directed my decisions, because if not, I am the only one to blame for some mighty shameful deeds. I would rather there be a plan, a purpose, even if known to all but me."

"Elizabeth?"

"Yes."

"Is this mysterious man that Christopher Claussen?"

"Yes."

"Did you marry him? Was he your husband?"

"No."

"He wasn't?"

"No. Why do you ask such a question?"

"I just wondered. You said you loved him. You screamed at him something fierce when you were in labor. Afterward, you talked to him for hours while you slept. It was a long time ago, but I still remember because it frightened me. I thought some great spirit had come to care for you. I thought he was in the tipi with us."

"Oh."

I might have been unnerved by Gracie's spiritual suspicions, except I was far more mortified to think of what else I might have said, what else Gracie might have remembered.

"Is he Luke's father?"

The question slammed into me. I shuddered to think she might see the answer upon my face. I glanced at Luke. His young blue eyes were boring into me. I wasn't about to take any chances. I was pathetic. I cowered. I lied.

"No."

FORTY-SEVEN

The grasses were changed. Not only because of our position farther to the east, but also because of the cooler temperatures of autumn. The once head-high stalks that swayed in the breeze like evening waves on a sea now appeared stiff and bent over with age. The once flowering buds appeared bald. The stalks sounded hollow and scratchy and appeared to abrade and irritate each other. The youthful resilience of springtime was gone, replaced by grayish-white streaks, strands worn thin and splitting. The greens and bright ambers dulled into shades of browns and skeletal grays that smeared us with clusters of clinging seeds and burrs.

At last, the endless lay of prairie with its hidden monsters was at our backs. It was losing its dominance along the eastern horizon, overshadowed by sporadic, but ever-increasing clusters of taller wooded growth. These timbered islands quickly magnified and commenced to fold into one another, soon stunting the prairie grass that struggled to survive in their shadows. The grasses were being forcibly fenced in by the tightening pattern of impenetrable hardwoods now making claim to the once open spaces. We could breathe a sigh of relief, not only because a bear wasn't likely to jump out at us before being seen, but also because we felt as though the infamous American desert had been defeated.

In time, I found my eyes drawn to a nearly imperceptible ridge of mountains that formed to border the southern sky at great distance. I was confident that we were well within the watershed of the Missouri or Mississippi, or both, and very near to the edge of a world I left many years ago. On three occasions we observed strangers on the move. We first observed two Indians, later two white men, all on horseback, and most recently a mule-drawn wagon headed west with horses in tow. It was the latter two sightings that captured the attention of the Luke and Gracie, especially Luke, who had never been exposed to other white men.

I needn't whisper a sound to silence Luke or Gracie in the presence of strangers. We lived and learned to be as wary of strangers as we were of bull and bear, maybe even more so. Beasts might kill you, but they didn't rob, rape, abduct, or devise plans for your demise. We now deliberately coursed within short measure of safety and cover provided by the treed thickets that occupied as much countryside as did the short grasses.

We were comforted by the wooded thickets, for not only did they hide us, but with autumn days and after-dark temperatures that grew most disagreeable, the fields of shorter grass lacked sufficient height to break the buffeting night winds. In the woods, we may not have enjoyed the dense, soft, beddings of grass, or the warm blankets it fashioned, but an armful of flexible leafy twigs had far fewer spiders and ticks, and offered better protection from damp ground. Coupled with a wood-fed fire, we were able to enjoy warmth that hovered overhead like a cloudy blanket clinging to trees in the stillness of the air nearest the forest floor.

This night, while Gracie and Luke were out hunting game, I worked some dry grass and leaves to smolder, eventually bringing forth a flame. In no time, I had a roaring blaze of branches underway. I piled on larger branches until the fire was too hot to stand near. I left it to build a bed of embers, while I wandered along the tree-line grasses and into the woods looking for whatever could be eaten. I had no pot, and sought out leaves sufficient to wrap and steam.

Being this late in the year, I knew that the tubers and roots would be large and bountiful, ready to endure the winter. I wasn't disappointed. I easily located a number of potatoes and cucumbers, artichoke tubers and primrose, turnips, groundnuts, and even some late rhubarb. I also located a small spring. These thickets often flourished around such springs, and ours was no different. After a healthy drink, I washed my gatherings and laid them out by the fire. Gracie and Luke had not yet returned so I next went about collecting armfuls of dried brush, which we would later spread out and sleep upon.

All this time spent looking at the ground proved advantageous in another way. I spotted a stone that had split into a number of razor sharp wafers from the freezes over the years. Any Indian worth her salt would understand the value of such a find and it set my mind to all that I could cut. Of course, I always had use of Gracie's knives, but it was nice to have my own tools.

My initial thought was of cutting grasses for bedding and saving my hands from being sliced by the razor edges. But at first sight of a nearby sapling, my mind went immediately to thoughts of fashioning a staff or maybe two. Like Gracie with her knives, and Luke with his bows and arrows, I found my feeling of security with a staff. And so with cutters in hand I looked about for perfectly straight saplings, which I found in short order. I began at once to rake the rock edge back and forth across the smooth bark, and dropped three saplings by the time Gracie and Luke returned with dinner.

Gracie and Luke returned with a couple of turkeys, which Gracie skinned, carved, skewered, and roasted. In between the pieces of meat, we placed slices of the roots and potatoes. The rest we either wrapped in leaves and buried or piled up on flat rocks atop a thick glowing bed of coals. The rhubarb and ground nuts sizzled and exuded sweet sticky syrups that made my stomach growl. I was starved. My mouth waited impatiently and watered in preparation for this fare that produced currents of wonderful aroma.

We ate greedily. We no longer had to wait for cold or overcooked scraps left over by the braves. We ate food fresh off the coals, enjoying the surge of energy that first follows a belly filling with food. It was a luxury to have so much food left over after having had our fill.

Our spirits were high. We jabbered away, joking with one another, feeling relaxed and playful for the first time in ages. We sat around the fire lazily basking in the heat. Luke and Gracie repaired the arrows they used in the hunt, while I whittled away at my staff. A usable staff need only be made from wood that wouldn't easily fracture, one that was the right thickness and weight. Most important, it had to be the correct length for the bearer. After a couple of hours of working the saplings, I stood up and drew the staffs through the air, listening to the crisp swoosh of their speed. I had pretty much finished two staffs while we conversed.

Once Gracie had finished helping Luke repair his arrows, she went off in search of her own sapling from which she intended to fashion some throwing clubs. She was as picky as could be, intent on producing the perfect form. Her clubs had to be precise and preferably taken from the same sapling so when accustomed to one, accustomed to all. She judiciously scraped the shanks for weight, feel, and grip, then burned and smoothed the ends to a near polish. I could only imagine what pain would be had from a clobbering by one of those clubs.

Gracie's desire to have clubs was not only for clobbering, but for saving her from one unshakeable fear. She had only her knives when she came into my life as a child. Those knives belonged to her father, and not only was she wickedly murderous with the things, but she was attached to them in a mystical way. It was as if her father was there fourfold to protect her.

The problem with this attachment was that whenever a knife ricocheted off into the brush, all activity stopped at once. Nothing mattered except finding the lost knife. If it took two hours or two days, Gracie never left the area until the knife was sheathed back in its place at her side. This made any use of the weapons during the twilight hours or thereafter impossible. Those hours of murky light were the best times to hunt. The clubs came to rescue her.

One day, while horsing around with the other children in camp, she was throwing sticks as pretend knives. Needless to say, she was nearly as accurate with the sticks as she was with the knives. She could whip those sticks, one after another, faster than a skunked dog could run. It was a matter of great hilarity amongst the chiefs and braves, who noted how she could keep a determined troupe of frustrated boys at bay providing she didn't run out of sticks.

Over time, Gracie learned whereas her knives were good at killing, they were not particularly effective at doing anything less such as slowing or stopping. A stout club, on the other hand, could bust a bunch of ribs, cave in a head, knock a man off his horse, or just plain knock him out cold. If it were lost in the battle, it wasn't nearly the heartbreak of losing one of her father's knives. And in times like the present, she was always able to fashion a fresh batch of flying hell.

While Gracie worked to finish off the clubs, Luke and I packed what remained of the food for the morrow's journey. Between chores, feasting, and conversation both hands and mouths were busy the whole of the night. I answered all form of questions about what the future might hold, about the nature of life in the towns and cities we would eventually see, and about the white man's world in general.

The chatter went on until Gracie was finished, and the food worked deep enough into our guts to act like a sleep-inducing drug that made us slumberous. As we grew drowsy, we set about spreading and stacking the collected grasses and twigs for our bedding. Luke was the first to doze off. Once Gracie felt everything was secure, her eyes grew heavy and she followed Luke into a deep sleep.

I wished to sleep, but found myself slow to succumb as I wallowed in troubled thoughts that seemed intent upon surfacing. My apparent good fortunes were causing me to suffer feelings of guilt. My mind was forced by conscience to think back on Talk-a-Lot and Hotoomee'e'. I wondered how they had fared. I was worried, saddened, sickened by their predicament. They had been stolen from their families to become slaves or wives of strangers. I thought of Ho'neheveho, who most likely lost forever his wife and sister.

I needed to assure myself that I had never deceived Talk-a-Lot, Hotoomee'e', Ho'neheveho, his tribe, or any of the others about my feelings or intentions. I could say in all honesty, I thought of them as family. I was close to them in heart, and over the years I came to love them as my own. I laughed and danced with them in the good times; I cried with them in the bad times. They treated Luke and Gracie as children of their tribe, and provided all of us with sustenance and support in our times of need.

The issue of returning home had pressed on my consciousness more with each passing season, and so I never hid from them the fact that my time to leave was drawing near. They watched dispirited as I unfolded the fingers on my hand, showing them the number of years I expected to remain.

In the early days, I always presented two or three fingers when asked. And although I had never imagined being abducted, I had never raised more than one finger during these last few years while watching Luke fast approach the age of ten. The swiftness of his passing childhood made me restless. In my heart, I sensed my days with the Indians were at an end.

I thought about how many of Luke's playmates and other Indians I had taught to speak the white man's tongue, and how many could now converse or even read and write some basic English. Their taboo of having contact with the white man was dissipating into memories of the past. The allure of steel, guns, knives, and whiskey was overwhelming, and these coveted items became much sought after. There were now more and more of those who disregarded the stern warnings issued by their ancestors before the time of changes.

My students were venturing out and using to best advantage their newfound knowledge of white man's ways whenever such men should be encountered. It was a dangerous business that was apt to cost many of them their lives or worse, for I knew far better than they that there would be little choice offered them in these meetings. The influence of the native Indian upon this land was in decline, maybe not to be noticed today, maybe not tomorrow, but it was inevitable.

It was because I understood white man's ways and the meaning of those settlements unfolding on Wilpen's map that on the ninth anniversary of the falling stars, when Luke was soon to be ten, I determined time had come to tame his wild Indian manner. Seeing that he was schooled with a full understanding of European protocol and decorum was now paramount in my mind.

Sadly, I had no desire to leave the Tsistsistas for any reason in regard to my own well-being. Over the years, I grew genuinely comfortable with these people. My life was a part of theirs, as theirs was a part of mine in every respect. My life had been lived, and this was the place where I had come to settle. I was being pressured to leave the tribe out of concern for Luke's future. I didn't believe the European world of my past was going to be a better world for Luke—far from it. I believed it was the only world that would remain.

Lying here in a haze, half-asleep, listening to the crackling of the fire and the peaceful slumbering of the children, my quasi-dreams disrupted by the occasional creak of a tree or screech of an owl, I thought of my friends who slept with an unknowing innocence in their tipis upon plains so vast only God could fathom, plains so vast it was impossible to imagine a clash of cultures. In the worst way, I wished I slept with them this night.

In those last thoughts of consciousness when dreams become reality, that place where Indians believe one finds truth, Christopher entered my awareness. He was watching over me, smiling as I puzzled over the twists of fate in which I could find no logic. He understood my frustration and anxieties, and he encouraged me to dismiss them. I sensed the embrace of his love and affections, and his desire for me to move forward and fulfill my destiny. I sensed his guidance, his encouragement as though I were still a child he might shape. He filled me with confidence, but most of all, he filled me with peace. I felt as though I had been fussed over, tucked into bed, and smothered with kisses. I was glowing in the radiance of his attention.

"Go to sleep, Elizabeth."

"Yes, Father."

FORTY-EIGHT

The hour was still early, the air beyond chilly, it being down-right cold. A glance through the trees revealed a prairie glistening with frost. A thick mist poured out from a nearby island of trees betraying the secret of a warm, moist swamp hidden within.

392

During that first hour of gray morning light we remained huddled closely over the fire, stomping our feet and rubbing sleep out of our swollen eyes. We suffered to work the shivers out of our stiffened limbs.

"Oh, l-l-lord, it's c-cold," I protested.

Luke exhaled. "Look. You can see my breath."

Gracie followed suit, exhaling, in order to confirm the discomforting temperature. I was shaking uncontrollably. It certainly had something to do with my age, but more to do with having no blankets or warm clothes. Gracie seemed less cold, and Luke seemed almost oblivious after taking a moment to wake up. I, on the other hand, became one with the fire, choosing first to scorch my hands and face, and then my butt, hands, and face, butt, hands, and face, butt....

"Luke, f-fetch your mother some more w-wood, p-please? I'm so cold, I hurt."

"Yes, Momma."

Luke wandered off leaving a trail of cloudy puffs in his wake.

"Believe me, Gracie; I won't be able to take t-too much more of this."

Gracie grew pensive and responded with a hint of guilt.

"I should have grabbed the blankets when I went for the bows and arrows," "No, you certainly s-should have not! You grabbed plenty, and as I recall, you were staring that beast s-straight in the eye. As I recall, he was sizing you up for dinner. Grabbing blankets was not an option."

"Yut, that was frightening—."

"Yes-ss-ss...." I corrected her.

393

"*Yes*, that was not to think about. Oh, well...the blankets would have been nice—it is getting cold. How much longer must we travel? "

"I don't know, Gracie. Honestly...I don't know. By now, I shouldn't have to t-t-tell you how illimitable is this land."

I shook my head in dismay as I shivered.

"What I would give for a map. But even that would be useless unless I knew from where we s-started. I do remember something of Wilpen's maps, and a general lay of the land. I don't think it can be that much farther.

"The land slopes downward to the east. The creeks flow that direction—with us as we ride—but rarely toward the s-s-setting sun. We must surely be in the basin of the great rivers. I can't imagine different. I can only guess, Gracie, but I am certain it can't be more than a couple of weeks at best. G-God, I'm c-c-cold."

"We could have an early snow any day now."

"Don't remind me. I feel like it snowed on me all night. I'm not as young as the two of you. I swear either of you could sleep your way through a torrent of sleet. I don't know how you do it. I was so cold last night, I didn't sleep a wink."

"It *was* cold, and contrary to what you might think, I didn't sleep all that well myself."

"I slept fine," said Luke.

"I kept inching closer to the fire until my front side was so hot it burned. But my backside was so cold it felt like it was frozen to the bone. My feet froze no matter where I put them. I am not going to be able to do this much longer without blankets."

"None of us will," said Gracie. "It's time to hunt down some deer and skin them for the hides. Wrap up those leftover pieces of meat. I'll put them into the parfleche."

We stoked the fire and crowded it until our blood coursed good and warm. We finished a breakfast of turkey bits and conversations left over from the night before. The most important one being concluded in unanimous agreement whereby it was determined we would not be able to further endure these temperatures.

"Are you ready to ride, Luke? If we ride hard for a bit, that should keep me warm for a while, maybe until the sun is high."

"Sure. I love to ride hard."

We mounted, and I found myself caught up in a study of Luke and Gracie seated upon their horses. They would soon be shedding their garments of leather and feather—Luke soon to be trimming his long braids of hair. They sat tall on their unsaddled horses completely at ease. Not just horses, but *plains* horses, Indian horses that stood out because of their dappled coloring and speed. They were some of the fastest animals on hoof and these kids could ride them like the wind.

"Let's go. The sooner we ride the sooner we turn heads."

"Wot does that mean, turn heads?" asked Gracie after a moment of thought.

"It means that we don't carry ourselves like whites. Depending on where we are, we will or will not be wanted. Either way, we will be watched closely."

"Why would anybody want to watch us?" asked Luke.

"There are white men who don't take kindly to anything associated with Indians."

"Why?"

"Too hard to explain, honey."

It would be a sad and difficult lesson for Luke. He would not understand. He was already plenty leery of white man ways, and this approaching realization would only serve to reinforce his mistrust.

"I should be watching *them*," he protested. "I have heard of the things the white man does. He is a butcher. He wastes everything in his path. I have heard many stories from those who come the way of the rising sun."

"For those riding from the east."

"You know what I meant." Luke protested my relentless training.

"There are plenty of stories on both sides, Luke. Remember what I have always said, there is good and bad everywhere. Always search out the good, and stay vigilant for the bad."

I had tried with great care to temper his judgments and broaden his outlook. I hoped he would come to balance the cultures in his mind, never choosing to regret one in light of the other. I hoped he might see the best attributes of both worlds, for there were many good-hearted white folk who regretted the greed and insolence often exhibited by their neighbors and kin. It was a battle of conscience, much like the one over slavery. Against a barrage of ridicule and political wind, they remained level-headed and sympathetic to the sufferings of other men.

We were a couple of hours into our morning ride, alternately traversing open fields and passing through the now larger stands of trees. We always remained on our horses while crossing the fields in order to stay above the seed pods and wet, dew-covered grasses. Merely brushing past the grasses would soak one to the bone. When in the woods, if the forest floor was free of under-growth, we would dismount as a rule in order to rest the horses and stretch our limbs. Walking worked to warm the feet. Our ritual this morning was no different.

The early morning sun trickled brightly through the tall trunks, and backlit the webbing of branches overhead. The colorless entanglement, now lifted from the burden of its summer canopy, reached up in stark contrast to support the autumn sky. We walked to the sound of that fallen canopy being trampled underfoot and crunching in dried-out complaint beneath our moccasins.

I was finally somewhat limbered and so mounted up again ride for a spell. Gracie and Luke did likewise. I suspect when one is walking the forest floor deep in thought, one tends to stare at the ground and little else, the aim being not to trip while daydreaming. Only when one mounts her horse, does she look ahead to gauge the obstacles in the distance, burrows and like that break a horse's leg. And so it was, just after positioning herself upon her horse, Gracie looked outward from that higher advantage and was at once attracted to a flash of light.

"Wot's that?" she asked.

"What?" My attention was immediate and focused. We shared little stomach for unwanted surprises.

"Something over there." She pointed ahead. "A flash of light. Did you see it?"

"I didn't see any—."

"There!"

She pointed again.

I strained to see something and then, sure enough, a flash shot through the thick of the trees.

"Water."

We voiced the word in unison.

"Where? Where? Do you think it may be the river?" Luke asked aloud what was immediately on our minds.

"I have no idea. It could be a lake. A lake or river would explain the heavy dew upon the fields this morning."

"Let's go see!" said Luke.

He bolted forward. Gracie was a close second. We urged the horses to move ahead at an ever faster pace. We rode as fast as sensibility would allow while dodging trees in our haste. We were impatient to break free of the wood and sight across a clearing. In short time that view came to reveal a steeper grade stretching out before us where, at the bottom, the rising sun was skipping rays off a somewhat north-easterly-south-westerly stretch of a sizeable river.

"Is that the Missouri?" asked Luke. He could hardly contain his excitement.

"That would be good, right?" asked Gracie. "Is that it?"

She looked directly at me.

I just sat on my horse and stared. I hardly dared make an assumption of any kind.

"That would be much more than good. That would be great. It would tell me where I am."

"Well, is that it or not?"

Gracie had all she could do to stop squirming and contain her excitement.

"Let's not get ahead of ourselves. I traveled that river many years ago. If it is the Missouri, then somewhere up ahead it joins the Mississippi—and there lies St. Louis."

"St. Louis."

Gracie repeated with dreamy anticipation.

"St. Louis. The town of your destiny, girl."

"So, how far now? I don't know how much longer I can wait."

I strained to make something of the distance. It was impossible to tell.

"I don't see any sign of a city or the Mississippi, but that doesn't matter at this point. If we ride down to the river and follow it eastward, we will arrive in St. Louis, that I promise. But, hear me out. Keep your eyes open and your mouths shut. There will be many settlements along that course. You are no longer in open wilderness, but in the white man's camp. We are two women and a boy, and have little need for trouble."

I could only hope that Gracie and Luke took something of my warning to heart. They were far too giddy with delight. And yet, they could not appreciate the significance of the view. If not now, we would soon be well into the land I had left years ago. We may have merely been off the beaten track, for we were about as close to St. Louis as I would have imagined possible. Our captors knew precisely where they were heading, this I could no longer doubt.

For us to now travel along trails or cross open ground would most likely expose us to harm. Yet, this morning we shouldered that risk in open fields, for the sun was rising and offering something of the heat we so craved. It pressed warmth into our chests and the tops of our thighs. We also chose to suffer the wetter grasses in lieu of the thickets that prevented us from gauging our progress toward the river.

Within the hour, we stood three abreast staring into the current as our horses replenished themselves. It wasn't a moment without discontent.

"Why is this not good?" asked Luke.

"The water is flowing the wrong way. I didn't want to accept it, but there it is."

399

"So, we are not where you hoped, but how bad is this?" asked Gracie.

"Well, this water is flowing due north for all purpose, and that is the wrong direction. It's just wrong. It is a large flow to be sure, but too small to be the Missouri and most definitely too small to be the Mississippi."

"Wot else could it be?" asked Gracie.

"I am not sure. I do recall, while steaming westward upriver, our passing a couple of large flows that emptied into the Missouri from the south. One was the Osage. I remember the Osage in particular because it changed the color of the Missouri—turned it yellow. I remember seeing it drawn on Wilpen's map. But there were others of good size like the Kansas. There was the Platte, but I always thought of that as coming in from the west. Besides, I was certain we had already crossed the Platte. In fact, I am sure we have already crossed the Platte. That would leave me with little choice but to figure this as being the Kansas."

"So, which way do we go now?" asked Gracie.

"Well…that answer remains the same, always east or east by south. Now, I know this looks like a sad excuse for an easting, but I say we follow it, even if it does flow north. It feels wrong, it looks wrong, but it must empty into one of the two rivers. Honestly, I am not all that disheartened. I'm betting we come upon the Missouri in short measure. My senses tell me we are close and this flow will lead us to it in short time."

In spite of Luke's and Gracie's shaken spirits, they tracked a path on the west bank of the river without complaint, at times returning to the water, but generally removed to higher ground and above the heaviest mists. And there was always the morning sun. In spite of the risk, riding out from under the shadows, it was with great relish that we soaked up its warmth. We urged our horses along the bank in silent vigilance. Our moods couldn't stay dampened for long. We took the minor setback in stride.

By mid-morning we found ourselves confronting a new ponderance. We dismounted for a moment in order to stretch our legs.

"Well, now wot? The trail ends here...left or right?"

"Given a choice between east and west, we go east...to the right. I bet we will be directly upon the river's crossing. You watch, you'll see."

Luke mounted up and urged his horse to the right. He was followed by Gracie and me. It wasn't but ten minutes of passing through brush and cottonwood that we found ourselves standing on the western bank of the river bed. The dry season of late autumn had separated the watercourse into numerous strands of flat, shallow, erratic flows that were no longer able to cover the wide sand and gravel bed.

"Like I said...the crossing. And by the looks of it, folks don't proceed any farther north from here, so...I assume this is our last chance to cross over to the east bank, no doubt, the last safe crossing before the confluence. This trail looks to be a well-traveled, and speaks of the bed being solid in this area. Should we rest a while or keep at it?"

"No."

"Keep at it," piped Luke.

Their answers were swift and unshakeable.

"That's fine. We'll cross. Mount up and pay mind to quicksand."

Cautiously, we allowed our horses to pick their way across the riverbed. What often appeared as stable sand or sandbar was often anything but. One had to be judicious. Fortunately for us, this time the bed was as solid as hoped for, and we found ourselves soon safe on the eastern bank.

This new east-west trail was our only choice, but it continued to appear well traveled. It also showed the first signs of a two-track and hinted at the occasional passing wagon. The trail conveyed us eastward, and within a couple of hours the Missouri in all her low-water glory came into view.

"*That* is the Missouri! That's the Missouri!" I literally screamed with delight.

I was elated. I was ecstatic for my knowing the river at once, at first sight and without question. This time there was no doubt, no guessing. My exuberance was contagious, and all three of us laughed with great heart.

"How can you be so sure?"

"I just know it, Gracie. I just know. I'm telling you, that is the Missouri."

This new one-track-two-track trail occasioned the river's edge along the south bank, but as often as not, it disappeared, having been washed away every other mile. It never failed to return, but proved difficult to pursue.

"There has been some terrible flooding in these parts ."

My comment came matter-of-factly after seeing how badly fragmented was the trail, not to mention the amount of debris upon the upper banks.

"Only very high and fast-moving currents could push whole trees up the banks in that fashion. The high-water mark looks to be all of a rod if not more."

On every occasion, I pointed out the clumps of dead rotting trees piled up dozens deep that lined the upper bank. There was a certain stench of rotted wood in the air that I suspected must have been unbearable in the heat of the summer. Gracie considered each occurrence with curiosity, but Luke seemed oblivious. He was far more interested in the two perfectly spaced parallel paths instead of the single file path made by all travelers he had known. I smiled inwardly as I considered what impression would be made the first time he saw a paved city street.

Not unexpectedly, we reached a place where the trail had been so washed out that we were finally forced up out of the bottom and onto higher ground for good. At times the rises were high enough that when we looked down we understood how much damage had occurred in this area in the recent past.

Complete stands of cottonwood were uprooted and lying in random stacks at water's edge as far up and downriver as one could see. Great collapses of the banks exposed the earth's innards for stretches at a time. Huge misplaced mounds of sand were evident amidst swaths of vegetation bearing the scars of an enraged current that carved up the marshes and bottomland below the confluence. Especially disconcerting was the record of damage that stretched far across the basin at great distance from the present flow of the river. It must have been a flood of biblical proportion.

We rode the high ground time enough to traverse two additional watercourses of note. The second one in particular held much promise because it served to direct a trail of substantial merit toward the Missouri. The river and trail paralleled as they crossed the plains from the southwest to the northeast. In fact, *trail* was hardly the appropriate term, for it appeared very nearly a road with the earth trod down completely edge to edge. One could see it was used extensively as it cut cleanly through the grasses and over time having all stones and obstacles tossed off to the side.

As we stood admiring this marvel of a trail, looking southward as far as the eye could see, we were oblivious to a party of strangers breaking over the northern rise behind us.

"Someone's coming," said Luke.

Those words never failed to impale one with angst. Gracie and I spun around and spied the party warily. We were unsure of what to do. The party stopped unexpectedly in the middle of the trail. That was odd. We could make out six riders, three Indians and three whites.

"Wot are they doing?" asked Gracie. "Are they watching us?"

"I have no idea, but mount up. Let's head back up the trail toward that last large stand of oaks we passed."

No sooner had we started to trot back up the slope when the strangers broke into a full gallop in our direction. They didn't stay with the trail but cut diagonally across the open field in order to intercept us. I needed nothing further.

"Ride! Hya! Hya! Ride, Luke! Ride!"

"Hya! Hya!"

I could hear Gracie driving her horse as I dug my heels hard into mine. The three of us stampeded off the trail and made a straight line across a field for the woods.

"Are they chasing us?" Gracie blurted out.

"It looks that way to me."

"Why?" she cried.

"I have no idea, and I'm not about to wait around and ask. Hya! Hya!"

We plowed full speed into the woods at which point I brought my horse to an abrupt halt. I jumped off. I reached for my staffs.

"Gracie, grab your bow and stay with me. Luke, you have your bow and arrows. Run the horses back into the shadows and tie them off. You stay hid back there. And this time, you do as I say. Do you understand? I don't want to be tripping over you in haste."

"Yes, Mother."

"Go! Hya!"

I slapped the horses hard on their flanks and watched until they were safely out of view. It wasn't but seconds before the riders came up to the wood's edge.

"They're here," Gracie whispered.

The men stopped at the edge of the wood and passed words.

"Looks like they're splitting up. They're going to circle around behind us," I whispered back.

Following a brief conversation, two of the three white men split from the group. One rider galloped off to the east, the other to the west, both seemingly intent on circling the perimeter of the wooded stand. The third white man and three remaining Indians stood fast and strained to see a sign of us within the shadows from where they sat mounted on horses in the sunlit field.

"C'mon, Gracie. Let's move farther back." I whispered.

I motioned for her to follow me farther into the wood. We slipped quietly back into deeper shadows until I reached what felt to be center and safest.

"Wot are we doing?"

"I don't know. I don't dare go back too much farther. I can see bits of light back there and Luke is somewhere between us and the back edge of the wood. Those riders galloped back around to watch for whoever gets flushed out.

"Here, give me your bow and take a staff. You already have your knives and clubs."

"Wot would you have me do?" Gracie whispered.

"I don't know. I don't know, Gracie. We are trapped in here. You do whatever you must to protect yourself. This isn't about being bashful, afraid, or asking for permission. Don't worry about me, worry about you and promise you will watch out for Luke. Use those knives anyway you must. Those men aren't here for our benefit."

Gracie and I said little else as we sneaked over toward a denser growth of brush. Once in the thickest underbrush we could find, we halted and turned about to face our pursuers. Dropping low to the ground, we disappeared from view.

I strained to see or hear anything of the men coming toward us. I knew they were coming, slowly, quietly, advancing with caution, on guard. We watched and sat waiting in silence as our minds worked to assess a bad situation. Gracie broke my concentration. She looked over at me and spoke.

"Wot do you think they want with us?"

Only now, while lying in wait did I have a moment to question motives. I was at first puzzled by the gang's dogged determination to catch us, but it wasn't long before a plausible answer came to mind. I passed my thoughts to Gracie in a flurry of whispers.

"I was just asking myself that same question. The answer that makes most sense comes only after one assumes a connection between these Indians and our abductors—."

"Ahhh. You think it's them?"

Gracie's eyes opened wide upon digesting this revelation.

"It would make sense."

"No wonder they're chasing us."

"Indeed. Imagine what would be your state of mind had you abducted us for purpose of ransom, spent weeks dragging us across country and feeding us, only to have it all go up in smoke because we escaped. Even worse, your friends are dead, and we managed to do so this within days of your destination, within days of your payoff."

I pinched my fingers together to illustrate how close we were to wherever.

"They must have been furious," she hissed.

"Exactly. After all that, it would be well worth what little additional cost one incurred to recapture us."

My reasoning aired, we grew still as our attention returned to the woods before us. With no time to work out a plan of escape, I could do little more than take account of our surroundings. There was no place to go. I looked back over my shoulder in Luke's direction but saw no sign of him.

"Gracie."

"Wot?"

"Be careful." I whispered a stern warning.

My attention was riveted to her the second she moved to leave me and engage the approaching strangers. She was a fearless sort, seeking to position herself to best advantage, she crept forward. I could do little more than watch her back.

Before us, at our left, I glimpsed the first sign of an Indian closing in. I next saw the third white man straight ahead moving directly toward Gracie. The second Indian was a little to the right of him. Gracie turned to signal that she had seen the two men directly before her. I signaled to convey an Indian was somewhere in the brush to her left. She nodded her understanding and then slowly rose up behind a tree to better gauge the white man and Indian heading her way. I searched the wood for the third Indian but saw no sign of him.

Gracie withdrew two knives from her sheath. While growing up in the camp, on many occasions I had seen her let three knives fly to the mark in the same time some of the fasted archers could set and release a single arrow. Over the years, she obliged the elders by putting on shows of her talent before the chiefs and their guests. In light of her blonde hair, her legendary entrance as the child draped in shrunken heads, and her wicked delivery of steel blades, Gracie had always been revered as a significant protective spirit within the tribes.

I was attracted to more movement on my left and turned just in time to see that Indian signal to the white and others . The Indian had spotted Gracie. He signed the others to move farther across to our right which would have forced Gracie around the tree to the left and into his view. He raised his bow intent on being ready the second she stepped around. Without a second's thought, I set my arrow, stood up, and drew on him.

I let my arrow fly. Time slowed to a crawl as I took in the explosion of confusion that erupted across the woods. My arrow veered midair and slammed into the tree only inches above the Indian's head. The surprise of such a close miss caused him to let loose his arrow prematurely.

The hiss of my arrow drew Gracie's attention just in time for her to see the Indian's arrow streak toward her and slam into the tree. Instinct drove her around the right side of the trunk, opposite the approaching arrow, and into full view of the white man who spied the same tree now marked by a protruding arrow.

To my terror, I watched him take quick aim with a pistol and fire off a round directly at Gracie. The noise shattered the peace and scared me half to death. I hadn't heard the report of a pistol in years. A veil of gun powder smoke drifted through the woods and enveloped us. Gracie disappeared beneath it. Was she hit? My guts twisted into a violent knot.

"Ho-ho! You *are* a tow head!" the man howled.

Clearly, the white believed he hit Gracie. Through the dissipating cloud of pungent fog, I could barely make out his form as he dwelled a moment to observe the brush where she had fallen. That was a mistake. Gracie sprang upward into the haze and only appeared to point in his direction, but her outstretched fingers marked a path of light that flickered through the trees . I saw only a faint glimmer, but I heard the hollow thud reverberate within the man's chest. It wasn't good for the white stranger.

I never once saw Gracie miss with a knife. I hardly cared about the ending. I was overcome with relief knowing she was still alive. It seemed the white man moaned mostly from shock before tumbling forward into the brush. It was now he who disappeared from view, as did the Indian at his side.

"What in tarnation 's goin' on in there, Sol? Hey! Ya hear me? What's taken' ya so long? Hey, ya deaf or what? Don' be makin' me come in there after yas, ya hear? Hey! Ya hear me, Sol?"

Returning, as if an echo from the pistol report, came the sharp bellowing of a white man yet waiting beyond the wood at our back. The man was suddenly impatient to know if everything was in order. His edginess increased as did the force of his questioning, but no answer was forthcoming from his white cohort, Sol. The three Indians seemed even less likely to respond and give away their positions. I was growing increasingly nervous about the third Indian whose whereabouts remained a mystery to me. Knowing a third Indian was skulking around the woods made me fear all the more for Luke. I saw no sign of Gracie, and so backed away, moving closer to the vicinity where I was most likely to catch sight of my son.

Since the day of his birth, my every thought might well have centered on Luke. My every conscious moment might well have taken him into consideration. Thoughts of him fed me the courage to face down unholy nightmares and unfavorable odds such as those now at hand.

I strained to see any sign of him behind me, but the effort was pointless. I could hardly raise my head above the brush without inviting an arrow between the eyes so I hunkered down momentarily and closed them. There was no wind, the woods were still, and I prayed he was well hidden and safe. I strained to hear the slightest rustle of leaves, the faintest snap of a twig. I could just make out the dried leaves of autumn being crushed underfoot on both sides of me.

"I shoudda shot ya, ya blonde wench."

In my concerted effort to hear the most secretive betrayals, the white man's voice was as jarring as a riverboat belch at daybreak. Startled, my eyes snapped open, first from surprise, but then far more significant, from sudden realization.

"There is no excuse for stupidity!" I blurted out in return.

Obviously, Sol wasn't dead, but he also wasn't standing up to make an appearance. His comment drove home a thought heretofore unregistered. If we were to be recaptured for ransom, what possible sense would there be in bringing us harm? As Gracie used to say, *we had worth.*

"What if Sol fired his pistol only to frighten Gracie into submission?" I whispered to myself.

What if the Indian deliberately shot his arrow into the tree for the same purpose? I pondered. What if the Indian never saw Gracie throw a knife? If capture was their intent then—.

Suddenly, the brush to my right came alive and the skulking Indian exploded into view. I was completely caught by surprise and raised my staff to ward off his lunge. Out of sheer fright, I turned my face away from the attacker as I jumped up from the brush in a terrified scramble for my life. I stampeded off in a panic instinctively searching for sufficient space to swing my staff.

I risked a glance behind me and discovered there was nobody there. A second glance confirmed it. I looked again, now in shocked disbelief that was quickly followed by the dread of the unknown. I slowed my run and stopped in the first reasonable clearing. My staff was in position to attack anything that moved my way. I twirled around in quick circles searching for any sign of movement. I looked back along my tracks, but saw nothing. I remained unsure, but lowered my staff and bent over as I trembled and panted like a run-away horse. I kept a wary eye open expecting another surprise attack, my eyes darting in every direction. Only after a moment of intense spying back along my path did I see the Indian's body lying face down in a thicket.

Unfortunately, I was now standing up like a stage queen in full view of the other two Indians. I looked at them as they looked back at me with equal surprise and suspicion. I gained some solace in knowing I was now a good measure away from Gracie, and that would be to her benefit. To keep Gracie as safe as possible, I chose to make a scene. I chose to draw their full attention, and so I raised my staff high over my head in a show of belligerence, challenging the braves as if I were a dimwitted mother about to discipline them with a stick.

I had little doubt that the Indians would confront me at once, they being attracted to my bravery and the humorous futility of my challenge as a woman. I would become a plaything to taunt and rape, or take as a slave. If they determined to kill me then my last breath presented them the opportunity to absorb my spiritual power and bravery. Slitting the throat of an opponent, and savoring the power of taking life was far more rewarding that shooting one with an arrow, especially a seemingly harmless and frightened woman off in the distance.

Recapturing us had been the only thing that made sense to me, and it seemed implausible they might reduce the worth of their ticket to prosperity. Did something go wrong? Did everything change when Gracie threw her knife? I honestly believed no harm would have come to us, but now I was fully unnerved. A man was dead and there would be a reckoning.

I had to control my fear. The lives of Gracie and Luke depended very much on what I next might do. For that reason, all sense of fear was erased as their survival became my sole consideration. I studied the two Indians before me. They were moving slowly toward me.

Guns and arrows were frightening, but drawing opponents in close on my terms was entirely different. It emboldened me. At close range, I felt confident. In fact, I felt powerful for I had proved to myself many times that I could knock the largest of men senseless with a staff. At the very least, I could better these odds. I learned long ago from Dorrie how overwhelming was the element of surprise presented by a woman with a killing stick.

The two braves were spellbound by my sudden show of bravery. I knew they were summing up my spiritual power. I also knew they falsely believed I was harmless. I wasn't sure what they thought happened to Gracie or the other Indian. I couldn't believe they thought she was killed by the gunshot. Was it possible neither of them saw her throw the knife? I doubted it. What made more sense, was the Indians determining that I was the easiest problem to resolve at the moment. Afterward, they would deal with Gracie if she was still alive.

All I knew for certain was that I held their undivided attention, and that was what I wanted. They stepped toward me cautiously at first, but when the whites behind us began to holler, demanding to know what was going on, the braves' boldness was bolstered and they came straight for me.

The braves attempted to stand on opposite sides of me. They wrongly deemed my plight to be hopeless and pathetic. I could see it in their eyes. The idea of my challenging them with a stick was too enticing to resist. I poked at them like a mindless dolt knowing full well I would draw them in closer and lower their guard with my antics. They began laughing hysterically. They were insulting me.

Their first mistake came when they allowed me to step around them in our playful dance. That placed their backs to Gracie, who suddenly stood up in plain view for my benefit. Looking past their shoulders, I knew at once these men might be as good as dead. I only needed to toy with them until Gracie was also ready.

I continued to step away. They continued to follow and began to delight in taunting me with pokes and stabs from the end of their bows. Their backs remained toward Gracie. She wasted no time moving into range and then nodded it was time. I gauged my distance from the men. With a minor change in my position, I backed into the center of a clearing large enough to make the nearly invisible sweep that pulverized the knees of the Indian standing nearest to me. As he toppled forward, for all purpose and intent, my second sweep sheered his head backward off his shoulders .

The second Indian appeared so utterly astonished by what he may or may have not seen that he simply stood motionless, expressionless, as he tried to make sense of what happened in the split of a second. In the end, there was only one understanding, his friend was lying between us on the ground unmoving and most likely dead. Even worse, he had been felled by the hand of a woman, an unspeakable insult to be certain.

413

The Indian's eyes lifted upward from the bloodied body and his gaze moved over my way. The blank look of confusion was very quickly replaced by warrior hate. He glared at me. I stared directly into his eyes, and I did so with the utmost confidence. At that moment, when our eyes locked, we understood. This was no longer about capture.

The Indian had no doubts. He also had no distance or time to consider using a bow and arrow. He was boiling over with anger, and that would only work to my advantage. To approach me with a knife was certain suicide. He went for his tomahawk. It was his smartest move. Unfortunately, Gracie was standing fully upright with her hand-carved-to-perfection club in hand.

I stood still, ready to swing. The Indian never took his eyes off me. He barely moved as he reached back to launch the tomahawk. A non-moving target was too simple for Gracie. The club flipped end over end and made its mark dead center in the man's back. He was driven forward and off balance by its stunning force and I folded in the side of his head with one swing .

It was now Gracie and I who locked eyes. It was an unspoken affirmation that all was well.

"Are you alright?" I asked, only to confirm what I already knew.

"I'm fine."

"Are you certain?"

"Yut, yut, I'm fine."

"Oh, my god, Gracie. When I saw you go down in that cloud of gun smoke…. Lord, I was worried sick for you. I thought you had been shot. I prayed different, but…. And then, you suddenly pop up and save me from near certain death, not once but twice. You are a blessed child. Thank you, thank you, thank you."

I took Gracie into a firm embrace. I was beside myself with what little time I was allowed for joy.

"I di—."

"Hey, Sol! What the hayl's goin' on. You alive or dead or what?"

Our heads snapped about, looking toward the back of the wood. Gracie yelled out.

"Sol ain't gonna waste another breath of air. An either are those other two fools. And if you're tired o' breathing just set foot or go sticking your nose in here some!"

I looked at Gracie wide-eyed and lost for words to say. Lord, she was a spit.

"Ha, ha, ha. I don' think so. The only one's gonna stop breathin' air is this here kid lessn' you get yer asses out in plain view in somethin' like two flips of o' quarter. Git my meanin'."

The breath went right out of me. I felt my knees go weak. I reached over and grabbed Gracie for support.

"Oh, lord. They have Luke," she said.

"We're coming! You hear! We're coming out!" I screamed in a panic.

"Good lord, Elizabeth, wot are you planning to do? Wot do you want me to do? Should I try and sneak around and knife 'em? Do you—"

"No!" I snapped.

I glared at Gracie. She retreated as if stung. She said nothing. I felt nothing. I felt no fear. I felt only one emotion—total willingness to sacrifice everything for Luke without hesitation. I was overwhelmed by a mother's instinct to defend her young.

415

"You will drop your knives and clubs on the ground and leave them."

"Wha—."

"I said you will leave them, Gracie."

"We will walk over there appearing totally defenseless, nothing but our walking sticks. All you will do in the meantime is remember every hour we spent trying to crack each other's heads open. When we arrive, you will wait until I make the first move and then we explode their bloody skulls into oblivion. I will paint the trees with their brains. Do you understand me, Gracie?"

"Yes, ma'am. Clear as a bell."

"Good."

"What in tarnation 's taken' you women so long? I said two flips ova quarter. Ya know what the hell that means or d'ya want me t' break the kids arm t' enlighten ya?"

"We're coming! We're coming! The brush is thick in here; we're coming. Don't hurt the boy. He's done nothing."

Not a word passed between Gracie and me as we worked our way toward Luke and the two whi te men. We finally broke through the underbrush and presented ourselves as two helpless women. At first sight of Luke, with his hands tied behind his back and leashed by a rope held in the rider's grip, it took all I could muster to remain calm and not give away our deception. Luke's eyes were glued to my every move. He fully understood the meaning of our appearing with staffs in hand.

"Good lord, ahl-mah-tee! Will ya look at them two blondes. Ain't they as blonde as them braves made 'em out t' be? Damn. We're gonna get a good bit a gold outta these two. An' look at 'em, James , they know all about gettin' by in the desert."

"Hey, Bart?"

"What?"

"D'ya mind tellin' me how two half-starved, half-injun sorts can kill off Sol an ' three braves?"

"Do we know fer a fact, they're dead?"

"You sayin', they ain't answering for the fun of it?"

"Huh? Hmmm. Good point there."

Bart turned to look down at us along the length of the leash from atop his horse. He continued.

"That is a curious thing, ain't it, ladies? D'ya mind tellin' James jus' how ya managed to kill off all three o' them boys? No...tell James an' me both. This is somethin' even I gotta hear."

The men stared at us with full attention, and I didn't want Gracie to utter a word so I was quick to speak up.

"We didn't kill anybody."

"What? What? Ha! Yer tellin' me they went off an' killed themselves?"

"That's what I'm saying."

"Why would James wanna believe sump'un' as stupid as that?"

"We don't have anything to kill anybody with."

Bart studied me for a moment. He looked over at James. Then he looked at Luke.

"Yer kid here had a bow n' arrow."

"Of course. What do you expect? He's a boy. Boys always have bows and arrows. But he was with *you*."

"*White* boys have *guns* lady. Injun brats have bows n' arrows. I'm still tryin' to figure out what all o' yuz are." He sneered.

417

He rubbed his face as if to wring the confusion out of it.

"Okay, I'll give ya that the boy was with us. That still doesn't explain how Sol an' them braves died."

I jumped right in with a bold lie to hold the men's attention. I wanted full control of the situation until I could figure a way out of our predicament.

"Well, the way I saw it, there was a brave taking the lead. Sol, as you call him, was following somewhat behind at his right. The other Indian was back about where Sol stood, but over to his left. When they discovered us, I figure Sol planned on giving us a scare and so fired off his pistol in our direction. Best I can figure, the round must have hit a tree and ricocheted into the first Indian and seriously injured him or even killed him. All I know is that in a heartbeat, the second Indian turned and shot Sol with an arrow, I guess for shooting his friend or family, or at least that is what it looked like. Then the Indian walked over to where Sol was laying on the ground. It looked like he might have been going through his pockets or about to steal his pistol, but Sol pulled a knife and slit the Indian open. When we walked over to where they lay, it appeared all three were dead."

"What about the third Indian?"

"We never saw a third Indian."

Bart raised his eyebrows. He looked over to James.

"Now there's a story."

"You believe that?"

Bart raised his eyebrows again and studied James.

"Them injuns always been stupid and reckless as ever. Maybe ya wanna take another look at these two. Are ya thinkin' that two blonde-headed puffs took down Sol an' them braves? Is

418

that what yer thinkin', James? Ya think mebbe they sweet-talked 'em to death?'"

"Ahhhhh. I don' know what I'm thinkin'. Ten minutes ago there's six of us, now there's two of us. I don' know what I'm thinkin', Bart. Let's jus' get 'em outta here."

"Hey, James, sounds like more money for you an' me."

Bart turned toward me.

"Okay, now listen up, lady. The two of yous are goin' in there an' gettin' those horses of yers an' bringin' 'em out. Pull sump'un funny an' I'll slit this boy's neck ear t'ear. Understand?"

"Yes."

"Good. Git! An' be quick about it."

Gracie and I started back into the wood to get the horses.

"Wot are we gonna do?"

"Shut up, Gracie! I told you to keep your mouth shut and watch my every move. You watch my hands for the setup. You stay close to James and when I move you kill the bastard."

Gracie spoke nary a word. We reached for the horses and brought them back. When we returned to the field, I was relieved to see the men had dismounted to stretch. That greatly improved our chances.

"Okay, ladies, keep right on walkin' those horses out here into the field an' jus' remember who's got the boy."

We did as we were told. Within a couple of minutes, we were all standing together out in the open. I was constantly gauging clearance for the arc of my swing, but more important, I was watching every position that brought Gracie to advantage in her attack. She was firing glances at me as she vied for striking distance. I walked over to Luke as if concerned for his well-being.

He was standing with his hands tied behind his back. Bart was standing directly behind him, holding on to his braids. I placed my hand on his face as if to comfort him and told him in our Indian tongue to duck as soon as I swung.

"Lady, I want ya ta quit coddlin' the kid an' get on that horse. Ya best be quick about it, lessn' I lose my patience."

I turned my back toward Luke and Bart and looked across at Gracie. She was still in good position. I leaned my staff over and took its upper end into my left hand, which signaled the setup. I then coiled my body around to the left and registered the position of Bart's head. I spoke to him.

"Which horse?"

"That one."

"Which one?"

The instant Bart looked over to point at the horse I unsprung my twisted body and pulled the staff through the air with blistering speed. Luke dropped his head, his braids pulling hard on Bart's hands. Bart's attention went immediately from horse to Luke. He never looked up at me. He never knew what hit him. His brains painted the trees as promised and the only scream to reach my ears came from behind. As I spun full circle, I saw James going down on knees that were folded in reverse. He fell face down and was still supported by his arms when a second later his neck was snapped by the blow of the staff coming across it from behind. In one second it was over, both men dead . I turned to Luke.

"Are you alright, Luke? Are you alright?"

I crushed his head into my bosom. I kissed him and kissed him.

"Yes, Mother, let go, I can't breathe. Untie my hands."

I turned him around and unbound the laces wrapped around his wrists. As I did so, I looked up and across to Gracie. I knew at once something was wrong. She had not looked this way once.

"You alright, Gracie?"

"I'm fine."

Gracie still did not look my way. I turned to Luke.

"Luke, run back and find Gracie's knives. They are lying with her clubs and a bow. Go through pockets and see what else you can find, but be sure to get the knives. And grab that Sol's pistol and whatever else he has of value."

"Yes, Mother."

Luke disappeared into the wood. I stood a moment studying Gracie who attempted to look occupied, yet only looking away. She was poking James with her staff for no good reason other than to busy herself. I walked over to her.

"Is everything alright, Gracie?"

She nodded her head. I stepped around to her side and drew her shoulder back to look at her. She resisted.

"What is it, Gracie?"

She refused to face me but a sudden spasm betrayed her wish to conceal quiet sobs. I was stunned. I had never seen anything of the like in all the years of raising her from childhood. I had never seen a fearful bone or weak moment in all of her life. I was so taken aback that I didn't know how to react. She stepped away from me in an attempt to regain her composure. Gracie had never been one to show weakness. I moved toward her respectfully.

"Gracie. What is it, child? Is this about the killing? If it is, I understand. You must believe me. I do understand. Killing any living thing is hard, but to take the life of another, no matter how

421

despicable an individual can be unbearable. It goes against nature. It troubles the strongest of men, and you are but a young woman. You must not allow your conscience to destroy you. You are a fine person, Gracie. You will always be a fine person."

I tried to move around and look at her, but she wouldn't allow it. I coaxed the staff out of her hands, and took her into my embrace. I found myself tearing up. Gracie's pain would always be my pain.

"Terrible things have taken place today. It's true, but you must believe that you are above these things. You will always be above these things. We were forced into what we have done. It wasn't by choice. I know you. I know your heart, and I ask you to take comfort in knowing the reason behind our deeds. Luke is safe, Gracie. We are all safe and that is only because we did what had to be done. Not what we wanted, but what we had to do."

Gracie started crying harder. Murder was tough. She was siphoning off stress. I could do little more than hold her—this girl with a will and pith of steel.

"Talk to me, Gracie. It will make you feel better."

Gracie finally took a deep breath and sighed. She looked around. I could not remember ever seeing tears in her eyes. They gave the green of her eyes a spectacular luster. I had seen pools of pristine water in the mountains during spring thaws, ice yet floating in the current. At just the right angle, the surface picked up the green of the surrounding trees, and the combination of clarity and color could only approach the splendor of Gracie's eyes. To see them glistening with emotion simply took one's breath away. She looked up to meet my gaze and then spoke.

"Ohhhh, Elizabeth." She worked to catch her breath. "Those beasts are evil and I would kill them ten times over and not be bothered."

"Oh."

Clearly, I had missed the mark. After all my spewing, I felt a little foolish.

"Honestly, I am not altogether sure how to describe wot came over me. I don't know if it's even possible for me to explain wot I am feeling. Lord knows, you know me like no other, and I am certain you understand that there have been those times when I have felt like I live my life on the ragged edge of loneliness. I know that I keep my feelings to myself because after my folks died, I determined as a child is was easier not to get attached than to again suffer the loss of a loved one. When my momma and dadduh died, I remembered being so lost that I was completely numb to pain. I couldn't even cry. I just moved on."

She started to cry again. Clearly, this day had opened an old wound. I pulled her in and held her as tightly as I could. I smothered her with kisses.

"Shhhhhhh. Shhhhhh. It's fine, Gracie. You're fine, sweetheart. Go on, tell me what bothers you. Get it off your chest."

She straightened up and backed away. I could see her strength returning.

"Well, it's like I said. I don't know if you can understand. Let me just say that you have been e-e-every.... Everything gentle and good in my life. Even though I am older now and even though I never act like I need that comfort and.... And...well... today I watched you, and I listened to the way you spoke, and I didn't know who you were. I mean, I understand your actions were all about Luke. And I know you would do the same for me. It just.... I don't know.... It just caught me by surprise. Let's face it, Elizabeth, nobody thinks about their mother *killing* somebody."

I was stunned.

"Are you telling me that *my* killing somebody has gotten you this upset?"

She looked at me and laughed.

"Yut."

"Well, if that doesn't beat all. No.... No. I refuse to believe that. Gracie, there has to be something more to it."

I could only assume that being so close to death had triggered something deep inside of Gracie. Not unlike her hard crying as a child when awakening in the wagon after the death of her parents. She was now a woman, and I didn't buy this unexpected behavior was about me. It was about nerves. It was about walking out of a cave of fear and death, and not being able to look back into that black hole.

"No, there isn't. That was it. It was about you. In the space of ten minutes, you turned my entire understanding of you inside out, upside down. I have never known any part of you that wasn't gentle and caring. In one fell swoop, I felt as if I had been stripped of all the good in my life. I don't expect you to understand. I told you it was hard to explain."

"Well, all I can say is that I hold you to no less a standard. A more loyal and loving child I have never known, and I assure you no mother ever imagines her daughter killing somebody. If I dwell on someone so precious to me killing as many as I, well, huh...."

"Not true, you killed four. I only killed two ."

"Hardly. I clobbered Bart and laid out the two Indians. In fact, you might have killed one of those Indians with that club you threw before I ever touched him. I heard his back break. So for me, that's two kills and one questionable. On the other hand, you... knifed Sol, clobbered James, half-killed one Indian with that club you threw, and killed the third Indian with your bow."

424

"I beg to differ. I knifed Sol, the white and clobbered James with the staff. I highly doubt I killed anyone by throwing a club. You killed that Indian with a blow to his head. I saw it. That makes two."

"Wait, wait, wait…what about shooting the Indian that almost landed on top of me?"

"I didn't shoot any Indian that almost landed on top of you. You took my bow, remember?"

That was a fact that knocked me back with a jolt. We studied each other. Suddenly, we both filled with unsettling disbelief. We looked over at Luke who was returning with our horses and an armful of possessions.

"Luke!"

"Yes, Mother."

"Come over here, son."

Luke walked over and looked at me. He held up Gracie's knives.

"Thank you."

I took the knives and handed them to Gracie. I looked directly at my son.

"Tell me, Luke, did you shoot one of those braves?"

Luke stood most still and thoughtful as his eyes met mine. He turned to look at Gracie and then back at me.

"Do you remember that brave?" he asked.

"What?"

I was confused by his question.

"…That brave. He was the one that hit you before taking Talk-a-Lot away."

My blood ran cold. This time it was I who looked at Gracie. I then looked past her and into the distance feeling as if my insides had been scraped out with a dull knife. I returned my attention to Luke and studied his face.

"Is that right?"

"Yes."

He answered with an ice cold look in his young blue eyes. I nodded, but wished to acknowledge nothing.

"Gather up your things. It's time to leave."

I had no idea what to say or how to approach the issue. So, I said nothing. Luke turned to walk away and I turned to look at Gracie who was just as taken aback as I. My eyes welled up with tears. My voice cracked with emotion.

"You see, Gracie. I suffer your same feelings. I always needed my son for his innocence. He was the only part of me yet pure," I whispered.

We followed Luke to the horses. Gracie put her arm around my waist.

"Did you go through Bart's pockets?" she asked.

"Yes. Did you go through Jame's pockets?"

"Yut."

"*Yes.*"

"Yes."

"Anything worthwhile?"

"Some coins. You?"

"Same. Not much. They must have been way down on their luck. Well, at least this time a bear didn't eat the horses. We'll barter them off for cash, a couple of rooms, a bath and meals for starters. Nine horses…. Hey, Luke! How come there are only eight horses?" My concerns were voiced at once.

"That's all there were."

Gracie and I looked at each other, both feeling that twinge of nervousness.

"What do you mean, that's all there were? There should be nine horses, six for them, three for us."

"One of the riders is gone."

"What?" A rush of panic shot through me. I was at once on guard. "A rider is gone?"

"The white man."

"Are you certain?"

"Yes, Mother. There are three dead Indians and nothing more."

I turned to Gracie and let out a sigh.

"Gracie, I'm telling you, I did not need to hear this. I thought you hit him with that knife."

"I did hit him. There was no way I could miss him. I just didn't kill him."

"So it seems. Hmmph. Apparently, while we were busy killing his comrades, Bart and James, ol' Sol' was sneaking away with his life."

"I told you I didn't kill as many as you."

"Aha. Yes, yes…you did. I'll give you that."

"So, wot now? Should we go back and look for him?"

"Not on your life. I see no advantage in looking for someone who would just as soon shoot us. We should have spent a little less time killing Bart and James and a little more time killing Sol.

"Let's get out of here. Luke! Help me get those horses together. You two keep a sharp lookout. I doubt little but ol' Sol remains skulking about this wood waiting us out."

FORTY-NINE

We followed the outer perimeter of the woods, preferring to risk the open spaces versus revisiting dead bodies lying about within—or a live one lying in wait. We again made an easting down the slopes following the same trail we had traveled twice but an hour before. Now, we were intent on putting as much distance as possible between us and a second batch of dead abductors. We crossed the wagon trail without slowing a step. We had little desire to lull about further studying the oddity of two tracks. We were solely compelled to gain ground.

Little was said between us as we rode into the early afternoon sun. What was said came voiced unintentionally soft, near whispers under our breath as we worked to shed our mental pall of fear and anxiety. We shared memories we wished to put behind us, and our dispositions remained poor. The deaths draped over me like a cold rain-soaked overcoat until my depressive recounts were overshadowed by a sudden realization, a memory that quickly brought forth something known to me years before.

"The Santé Fe Trail! I exclaimed.

"Wot?"

"That wagon trail we crossed back there...." I stopped to reconsider. "I bet that's the Santé Fe Trail."

I turned my horse around and set off at a trot to return to the same intersection where earlier events turned for the worse.

428

"Where are you going?" Luke yelled.

"C'mon, Elizabeth, let's get out of here. For wot reason would you want to go back along that way?" pleaded Gracie.

I was routinely trying to resurrect long buried memories of my trip up the Missouri on the WAVERLY. I now recalled a conversation with the riverboat pilot in those days whereby he told me that Independence was the final stop on Missouri's upriver leg for most all riverboats. It was the point where folks left the Missouri to set out on foot or in wagons and follow a trail to Mexico that Indians and traders had used for centuries. The Santé Fe Trail was highlighted on Wilpen's map. It had been detailed on the maps upon Christopher's study at the cabin.

It was with reluctance and growing complaint that Gracie with Luke, and horses in tow, followed me back the mile or so needed for returning me to the intersection of ill fortune. There, I halted. I studied the trail in earnest for as far as I could see in both directions as if I hadn't seen it shortly before. It was no wonder that up close the course lost all semblance of a trail, and instead appeared to be something akin to a country road. As if to reinforce my belief, this time it wasn't a gang of no-gooders, but a train of wagons that crested over the high ground to the north and made directly for us.

Sighting the wagons did not put fear into me, but I still preferred we remain unseen.

"Let's get off the trail."

Luke and Gracie had barely slowed before I urged them to lead the horses into the woodland split by the path. I had no desire to attract attention from anyone, friend or foe. Once blended into the shadows of the wood, we stopped to give the horses a moment to catch their breaths and forage.

"Wagons and a trail good enough to be a county road...has to be Independence. Has to be the Santé Fe."

"Look at that!"

Luke was beside himself with wonder. He had never seen a wagon or team let alone a train. Gracie was just as taken by the sight, but only stared with focused curiosity. It was a convoy of large wagons. Larger than anything I had seen on wheels in my years. There were fourteen wagons in all by our count.

"Look at that, Momma."

Luke was spellbound.

"I know, sweetheart. I don't believe I have ever seen wagons so large. Look. That one has four oxen for a team."

"They're huge."

"That they are."

"Have you seen them before?" Luke asked.

"Many times, but never so large. When we arrive in St. Louis, you will see more than you can count."

"I can't wait," piped Gracie.

We peered out from the underbrush and watched quietly as the red painted spokes rotated in a slow, deliberate fashion. Wives and children could be seen sitting on the wagon benches sunning themselves and laughing or talking while most men and older boys walked alongside their teams.

"Wot all do you reckon is inside wagons so large?" asked Gracie.

"Families. Families, and whatever belongings they might ferry to make themselves a new home out west. I suspect most everything you used to strap to your pack of mules as a child when we first met can be found in those wagons, and then some."

"Wot else?"

"Things close to the heart, keepsakes, heirlooms, furniture, whatever possessions for which they feel they cannot part. It isn't any different than when we pack up camp for the season. We take what means the most to us."

"It makes me think of that wagon you used to own."

"Yes, well, that little wagon would have fit inside one of these."

We three sat in place a good twenty minutes watching the procession approach, pass by, and finally disappear in the distance over a southern rise much as it appeared over a rise from the north. When no hint of the last wagon remained to be seen, Gracie turned to me.

"Well, now wot?"

"Now we do just what we have been doing, we ride east. The difference is this time I know even better where I am."

"For certain?"

Gracie's eyes lit up.

"For certain. I'm saying this here is the Santé Fe Trail. I can't imagine any other trail so well traveled in these parts and heading so directly southwest. If I am correct, then that would mean the town of Independence, Missouri ,lies just up the way a piece, probably just below that rise, down at the river bottom. I'd stake my boots on it."

"Boots? What does that mean?" asked Luke.

I looked over at him, feeling somewhat bemused.

"I can't remember that last time I said that. It was a saying from my past. It meant that a person would bet his most sacred possession."

"Oh."

"Does that mean you know how far before we reach St. Louis?" interrupted Gracie.

"Mmmm." I had to think on that. "I am going to say mmm… ten days give or take. I wouldn't dare say less than ten days to St. Louis—but I wouldn't say more for that matter. It won't be that far now."

"Can we see Independence?"

"No, no, nooooo. I am uncomfortable enough riding into St. Louis after all these years, but some of these small towns are rough enough places for men, let alone an old lady with an attractive girl and young boy in tow. Don't forget those horses have worth. An unsavory sort will see them as easy picking. I don't believe going into Independence to be a good idea any way you cut it."

"Well, why can't we sneak up close and at least get a look at a town so we know wot to expect?"

"Not a good idea. Besides, I thought we were all about getting out of here."

"Oh, have a heart, Elizabeth. We can stay off the trail. I just want to see what a town looks like."

"Me too, Momma. What can it hurt to just have a look n' see?"

Their pleas were tugging at my heart. I took a moment to consider the risk. The dead bodies would most likely remain in the woods undiscovered for days if not weeks. There was no reason for anyone to go in there.

"Alright, the day is still young, and I guess it won't take all that much. We did see those three Indians ride out, so Indians must do business there. That's a good sign. Make sure the horses are lashed proper. We don't want to be losing them."

Gracie and Luke dismounted at once to secure the extra horses.

432

"That should do it," said Gracie.

"We're ready, Momma."

"Very well, you two ride ahead. I will follow, but be quick to take to the woods if you see hide or hair of anything that moves."

"Yes, ma'am."

It was about twenty minutes' ride on and off the trail before we crossed over the once distant crest of the road and confirmed my belief that below would be the river basin. It was at that time that we left the trail entirely so we might make our approach by way of the woods. That view would offer us the most security. We crept cautiously right up to the town's edge, but were not prepared for what we saw. The river port of Independence was far larger than anything I remembered, and also, at least in my memory, *substantially less thriving.*

So…this is a town," said Gracie

"I can't believe it. Look at this mess."

"Wot mess?" asked Gracie.

"The whole place is a mess."

"I wouldn't know. Why is it a mess?"

"Flooding. Remember what I said when we were riding a ways back and the trail along the river was repeatedly washed out? Remember as we went to higher ground, I said there had been a terrible flood?"

"I remember," said Luke. "You were pointing out all the dead trees up high on the bank."

"I was. The flood must have come through here like a tidal wave and destroyed everything. It looks as if the entire expanse of river front business has been sheered away."

"So this isn't wot a regular town looks like?" asked Gracie.

"Yes and no. It is a town, but one thinks of it as a port. A port is a town on a river where boats pay call on a regular basis. I remember this port as a place of uplifted faces, a place where the air was filled with laughter and talk of dreams. This was a place of life. If you knew this place as I knew this place, you would understand that something is now badly amiss."

"Wot?"

"Most notably, a lack of townsfolk. Aside from the obvious disarray and flotsam, there are very few people to be seen. That is odd, indeed."

"Where are all the people?" asked Luke.

"I was just asking myself that very question. I'm wondering if they might have thought about rebuilding the town, but then for some other reason—. Oh!"

"Wot!"

"Nothing."

"Nothing?"

"Sorry, I didn't mean to startle you. It was a passing thought—one best kept to myself."

"Wot was it?"

"Nothing."

"Elizabeth—."

Gracie frowned. She glared at me with annoyance for keeping a secret.

"Oh, Gracie. I had a vision of Cholera."

"Cholera!"

Gracie went white.

"See, girl, you shouldn't have pressed me. It was just a passing thought, a moment's concern due to the sight of all the standing water and wreckage. Yet, there are no bodies to be seen anywhere. I don't see anything to indicate there was an outbreak of any kind. No, I believe this is about a flood and nothing more. Folks have left or are leaving town."

"Do you suppose those wagons we saw earlier were families that were leaving?" she asked.

"A very good thought—quite possible, yes."

Little more was spoken between us. I knew better than to enter Independence even though for the most part it appeared abandoned. Instead, we just took in all that we saw without passing judgment on man or nature until I broke the silence.

"Ha! I know what's going on here," I said after considerable observation. "Imagine this—the irony in having half your town washed out by high water, and then having the river change its course to leave the remainder behind high and dry."

I pointed out across the town below us.

"You see over there, at the end of that street? That should be water's edge. Instead, it's a sandbar, an exceptionally broad sandbar to say the least. The flood changed the river's course and turned this town from a river port into a prairie post. I'll bet everybody's clearing out because they know that sandbar marks the end of profits from the river traffic. I fear the concerns of this town have been greatly diminished."

We three lay on our bellies and witnessed what little going's on took place for a good spell before I expressed my concern about losing daylight too fast in this late season. Various postings and signage proved my belief that we had reached Independence or at least what was left of it. Also, a number of signs referenced the Big Blue River, the watercourse that undoubtedly led us to town.

435

Our curiosity satisfied, there was no argument about leaving. If nothing else, observing Independence in such a state of distress was enough to distract us from the other unpleasant memories of the day. And so, we retraced our steps south along the Santé Fe until arriving back at the intersection where we resumed our easting and never looked back.

We continued with the sun at our backs until I determined the Missouri was leaving us at a bend to flow north for a considerable distance. I thought hard on whether to abandon the path or the river. We couldn't follow both. I struggled to remember Wilpen's maps and anything of my passage up the Missouri, but to no avail. I could do little more than succumb to a gut feeling that there might be a horseshoe in the river just east of Independence. That would explain why the path would leave the river to continue due east. I decided we should do the same.

We rode into the onset of night in spite of our horses' visible exhaustion. It was unkind to drive animals in such selfish manner, but Luke and Gracie were both too fired up and excited to stop any sooner. With persistence, they argued there was no need to dismount early for purpose of hunting dinner because we still packed plenty of cooked meat from our kill the night before. Even an abandoned, washed-out river town was more than enough to invigorate their imaginations about the sights to come.

My sensibilities eventually took precedence over thoughtless impatience, sensibilities fully supported by the appearance of a watercourse running south to north. The night winds were blowing stiff on the high ground and I was more than ready to investigate calm air in the bottoms. We started our descent.

Once into the ravine, the trail skirted water's edge between banks that long since evaded the sun's warmth. The sun was down and so too was the temperature within the current of mists that mimicked the river's flow. I was damp, well chilled, and expected to be wholly miserable by the time we managed a fire.

Feeling expended, the moment we descended into this steep-banked, broad-bottomed ravine freshly cleared by recent flooding of a now sleepy stream, I was insistent we set up camp for the night. Traveling in the dark was dangerous, and I had no desire to lose a horse to an unseen burrow.

Gracie and Luke weren't stupid. They understood that despite their energy, we needed to call it a day. That call was made the moment we arrived at a wide sandy flat of high ground that entered the bottoms from our left. It receded up and away from the bank to ground that was above us and free of the heavy mists. I sent Luke up onto the flat to work up a fire while Gracie and I remained to water the horses.

We soon arrived on the flat to find Luke bent over a rubbing stick. He had grass and twigs smoldering. Gracie picketed the horses, allowing one at a time to forage while I walked about gathering additional wood for the fire. In short time, Luke's smoldering kindle erupted into a flame that quickly lit up the surrounding trees and set our shadows to dancing. Gracie and I scoured the ground in search of soft grasses for bedding, which we collected into a pile next to Luke, who now had a roaring blaze underway. We broke into our stores like half-starved wolves until satiated at which point we all fell back to lie drowsily about the shimmering embers. The heat was both searing and sublime and worked with our full bellies to force us into slumber.

FIFTY

In contrast to an embarrassing number of soap-fearing, foul-smelling settlers, the Tsistsistas were commendable for their habits of cleanliness. These practices were instilled from birth, and as a rule whenever possible, the Indians would bathe on a daily basis. Even in the dead of winter, even when having to break away ice upon the river or pond, the bath was taken. It was acknowledged that frigid water invigorated both body and spirit, and that it was a great deal less uncomfortable than the rashes one attracted by not bathing.

When traveling on the open plains, a bath was but a dream on most days. We had little choice but to live with our stink until we might happen upon a creek, or better, a pond of sweet water. It was water that dictated when we camped. It trumped the rising or setting of a sun. And where food might be found, water might not.

Had we been with the tribe, we would have bathed first thing on the morrow. We would have stepped out of chilly morning waters made opaque by a reflection of gray chilly morning skies, and stepped into the warmth of waiting robes and cozy lodges until dry. Those comforts were now but remembrances in this place where we struggled solely to survive the evermore brutal discomforts of autumn's encroachment. Robes and blankets were but wishful wants during increasingly frequent predawn hours when fingers instinctively curled stiff and numb, and the rattle of teeth stole away our dreams.

Yet, so ingrained was the call for cleanliness that ,just like me, Gracie felt no less compelled to wash away her filth than to eat away her hunger. She moaned and began to stir from her nap.

"Ohhh. I can't move. I don't want to move. Why can't I just go to sleep? I swear being a woman truly is a curse."

Gracie complained aloud, but nobody responded. Having filled our bellies, I was just as lethargic, and Luke paid little mind to woman talk but had a sense that menstruation brought very bad luck.

"Elizabeth. Let's not wait until morning to wash. I don't want to. It will be too cold. I'd rather do it now, tonight. Let's wash now and then curl up here by the fire with time to dry and sleep without bother. You should go with me."

"Really."

"Please. I don't want to go down to the river alone."

"Alright, if you wish." I took a deep breath. "I reckon my belly is full, and this is about as warm as I am going to get."

"Come morning, you will thank me. I bet by sun-up it will be bitter cold. Mark my words."

"Bathe now, and we can ride out all the sooner," said Luke.

"Yut, that too. Come on, Elizabeth."

Gracie stood up and stretched.

"Alright. Let's hope the water feels warmer than the air."

I rose to my feet. I felt the currents of chilly air brush by immediately upon my retreat from the fire. I rubbed my arms briskly and looked about.

"First, let's gather more wood and build up the fire. The only reason that water might feel warmer than the air is because the air already feels like snow. We're going to appreciate a good blaze when we return dripping wet and whining."

My years with the tribe taught me that nudity was natural and acceptable, not something of which to be ashamed, avoided, or embarrassed about. However, the tribe also had strict customs regarding modesty, and I could prance around as naked as a newborn providing I did so in private or the company of other women. Out of modesty and custom, I addressed Luke.

"Luke, Gracie and I intend to bathe. Why don't you grab your bow and hunt for a spell. Bring us back something for breakfast if you are able, or go downriver and bathe yourself. In fact, bathe yourself regardless. You may not soon get another chance."

"Yes, Momma."

No explanation was needed. Luke knew well what was expected of him. We waited a moment for him to grab his bow and scale a large tree-covered bank.

I began wrestling with a large fallen branch.

"Gracie, grab the other end of this and drag it closer to the fire. I am going to strip down here so my clothes are good and warm when we get back."

"Good idea. I wish we had a blanket to take with us. I can't believe there wasn't a blanket amongst that lot in the stand."

"There was. Remember, Luke said they smelled foul so he left them. Who wants to wrap in that stink after bathing?"

Gracie looked up in the direction of Luke's departure.

"He's gone."

With that assurance, we stripped off our clothes.

"Brrrr." Gracie shivered. "Winter is somewhere out there, and I don't reckon it's too distant."

"True enough, but given a smidgen of good fortune, we should be in town before it catches us."

After draping our leathers over the branch close enough to bake without burning, I grabbed my staff for protection and followed Gracie and her knives into the shadows. We streaked toward the river on toes, crossing the upper flat at a brisk trot. Coming down off the raised flat, I followed her into the cotton-woods where we descended a slope, dodged the root-bridled trunks, and exited upon washed flats of sand at river's edge. The pale sand was highlighted by the moon's glow. With a lack of due caution, we traversed the hard-packed surface toward the water beneath a cool cloudless sky of stars.

"Keep a sharp eye for snakes," I warned.

"Yut."

"Watch out for quicksand."

"Yut."

"Watch out for Luke."

"Wot? Ugh, very funny."

"He's at that age. You know, curious."

"I know *dead* if I catch his wandering eyes spying on me."

I poked the earth with my staff to test the water-logged sand as we darted along. The air was too cold to allow dawdling. We scurried about a hundred feet farther alongside water's edge before coming upon a wide paper-thin wash that appeared to empty a spring fed pool. Unlike the uncertainties of the stream, which could appear murky and threatening, the transparent water of a shallow pool was always inviting. It was also always cold.

"Oh, this is perfect," said Gracie. "...Colder than the river, but cleaner. And, we won't have to worry about anything swimming around us."

I walked up to the water and stuck my toes into it. I was well aware of Gracie's immunity to ice water.

"Perfectly freezing," I quipped.

I immediately splashed myself freely with the ice cold water. I locked my jaws together and refused to exhibit the slightest sign of my bone-numbing discomfort. I watched Gracie, and I snickered to see her gasp as she doused herself. Ever since she was a child and we bathed together in the icy mountain stream that drew its waters from melting snow, we waged a secret war of wills. I usually lost. I struggled to speak in a steady voice.

"Gracie, I'm surprised at you. You're becoming soft as you age."

"Wot do you mean?"

"I was surprised to hear you gasp. I didn't think the water all that cold."

"I doubt it."

"Don't. I heard you gasp as clearly as the ring of a bell. And this water is nothing like snowmelt."

"Really? I don't see ya splashing about much yourself."

"Gracie, sweetheart, I'm not nearly as dirty as you."

"Oh, please!"

We instantly set out to drown each other amidst a chorus of screams that set our hearts to pumping furiously, but neither water nor air was of a temperature agreeable for such behavior. It was short-lived. In fact, at risk of quicksand, snakebite, or serious injury, we were hell-bent to overtake each other at breakneck speed as we raced back across the sandy beach and up the bank toward our clothes, now well-warmed and waiting for us by the fire.

We shot up the treed slope in a great shiver, dripping wet, and focused on the single light of the campfire, our sole source of comfort when suddenly to our left the sound of hooves emerged from the silence. The sound stopped us dead. Panting hard, we stood fast and stared nervously into the dark at our left.

"Wot's that?" Gracie whispered.

"Shush."

We strained to make something of the shadows that choked the bottoms to our south.

"Sounds like two horses," I whispered.

"Yut."

"Do you see Luke?"

"No."

"Did you hear that?"

"Hear wot—?"

"It's a wagon. Hear that creaking? It's a wagon."

We stood stock still, moving not a muscle except to better our view through the trees and shiver.

Soon the creaking of a wagon could be easily heard and within moments the driver and his rig came into sight tracking the river bank as he entered the reach of firelight.

"Do you reckon he heard us horsing around?"

"Are you serious? The way you were carrying on about the cold water—."

"Wot—."

"Shush."

"Cold wat—."

"Shush, I said. What's he up to?" I asked myself aloud.

I feared he did hear us. Sound could travel a fair stretch along the surface of water as it echoed between the banks. The stranger appeared as interested in the shadows of the river bank as the light of campfire spilling across the open flat.

We watched in quiet freezing misery as the stranger stopped his wagon between us and the fire. He sat upon the bench of his wagon, his head twisting back and forth, back and forth as his eyes pried into the shadows that surrounded him.

443

Inconvenient was hardly the word of the moment. Unbearable best described our situation as we now stood stranded within a thicket of cottonwood, in the damp night air, soaked, shivering without control, and baring our asses to the last of the season's hearty Missouri bottomland mosquitoes.

It seemed inevitable that matters would only worsen when we witnessed the stranger stand up in preparation to jump off his wagon, which he did. He then walked back along it and reached into the bed. He produced a gun. We had little choice but to hold on to each other, huddling for warmth, and watch him head cautiously toward our campfire.

My discomfort was soon being overshadowed by concerns for Luke. My eyes were locked onto the stranger's every move. When viewing the number of horses at our camp, the man at first hesitated, but soon moved amongst the animals to look them over. Next, he headed for the campfire, but there was little worth noting beyond the horses other than our parfleche and clothes. He stopped to study the clothes. He picked up one of the garments. I saw the man laugh as he turned about to study the shadows. He stood in a confrontational manner, swinging his gun to and fro, as he strained to see into the darkness of the wood.

"Wot's he doing?"

"Exactly what all men do. I assume he figured out those are women's clothes and suddenly he has no fear. Oh, oh—."

"Wot's he doing, Elizabeth?"

The stranger suddenly lifted the clothes from the branch and hurried back toward his wagon. He threw our belongings and his gun into the bed.

"Wot's he doing?" asked Gracie, most upset.

"Shhhhhhh."

"He's taking our maggoty clothes."

"I can see that. He's an ass."

"He's taking the horses!"

We watched helplessly as the stranger persuaded our horses to follow him to his wagon where he lashed them to the gate.

"There are no saddles." I uttered matter-of-factly to myself.

"Wot"

I went on mostly thinking aloud.

"He's looked the horses over and none of them have saddles. He thinks we are Indians. Because there is nothing but our clothes at the campfire, he believes there are only women about—*naked women*. What's to stop him?"

I don't believe this, Elizabeth. Are you just going to let him leave with our horses and clothes? Just like that?"

"What!"

Even in the blackness of night, Gracie knew I was staring at her in disbelief.

"*Am I just going to let him leave?* Are you kidding? What do you expect me to do—beat him with my breasts? I am no less naked than you, and a good many years slower. You have your youth and your knives, girl. Run out there and get it all back. Go on! Not only will I step out of your way, but know you have my blessing. Your beauty should mesmerize him, but if not, remember to duck when he fires off that gun."

"Never mind."

"I won't. Thank you very much."

I was almost annoyed.

"So much for warm clothes." Gracie pined.

"Maybe you shouldn't have complained about not having a blanket."

"Are you finished badgering me?"

It was that famously impassive response of Gracie's that started me giggling under my breath. Our predicament was too outrageous to be serious.

"Yes, yes. I am finished. I can't blame you for being frustrated, Gracie, but honestly, aside from freezing to death this isn't as bad as confronting bears. And more important, Luke is safe. It could have been much worse. Ask yourself, what if five or six men had been on the wagon?"

We watched as the thief reached for his whip. He laid into the team, driving the wagon onward along the trail with our clothes lying in the bed and our horses lashed to it. Now somewhat oblivious to the cold, we stepped out from the trees that concealed us, in order to watch the wagon depart along the bank.

"Now wot? I'm so cold I can't stand it, and we have nothing to wear but goose bumps. I don't believe it. Now wot? Ha!"

Gracie shook her head. This time it was she who chuckled in disbelief. I took a deep breath. I was totally lost for a plan.

"I don't know. I'm fresh out of ideas."

"You thought you were cold at the river? You think you're cold now? Wait until tonight. The night air will be the death of us. And besides that, wot are we going to do about Luke? That may be a bit awkward. Wot are we going to do tomorrow if we don't die of cold tonight?"

"A bit awkward? Being his mother, I am not sure I understand."

"Well, wot are we going to do, *Mother*?" Gracie was clearly exasperated.

"I...don't...know. I don't know! I suppose, I could ask Luke for his loin cloth and leggings, and you could ask him for his vest. I suppose we could do that. Maybe he's not as modest as us."

We were both seething with cynicism, and Gracie finally had the wit to shut up and spare me the grief. The two of us stood side by side in a wicked state of spasms, too cold to feel anything but possibly our loathing, when a horrific war cry shattered our paralyzed thought. We both knew the voice at once.

My jaw dropped as I witnessed a screaming blur of motion drop through the darkness from a high bank and crash onto the bed of the wagon. The driver leapt up off the bench even as the wagon continued to roll forward.

"Luke!"

We both blurted out our astonishment.

Caught between the urge to run naked to his rescue and the urge to remain hidden precisely because of our nakedness, Gracie and I took off in two different directions. It was an impulsive reaction, which we abandoned by the third step. However, it left us where we started, standing side by side, yet freezing, yet naked, but unlike a moment before, now utterly lost for words cynical or otherwise.

We could do little more than stare at Luke, who now had his bowstring pulled back, his arrow sighted at the stranger's chest. I was horrified by the thought of Luke wallowing in the glory of his second murder. We could clearly hear the raised pitch of nervous voices as Luke and the stranger addressed each other in the still night air. The driver was unnerved and confused.

"What the—."

"Stop!"

"Wha—"

447

"Stop or I will kill you!" Luke screamed.

At this point, nudity or not, I was only concerned for Luke's life. I began to dart through the spaces between the cottonwood, moving speedily in his direction but remaining hidden from view. My hand gripped my staff like a vise.

"Yer jussa a blonde-headed kid. You an Indian or what?"

"Don't move, or I will kill you!"

"You ain't killin' no—"

The man lunged for Luke. I went into a dead run with Gracie on my heels. I was torn between staying hidden and using the element of surprise, or jumping into view and drawing the stranger's attention away from Luke. Before I could make a determination for the best, Luke let loose the arrow. It passed more than half way through the stranger's shoulder. Before the man could blink, Luke had another arrow drawn and ready for release.

"Stop, or I will kill you!"

For a moment, the stranger must have been in shock, as was I. I stopped running but for the shock of what I had just seen. I could feel Gracie's breath washing hot across the back of my neck. We watched as the man fingered the arrow where it entered his shoulder and then reaching around to feel the arrow sticking far out his back. He quickly regained some of his senses.

"You miserable little heathen, you shot me with that arrow!"

"Quiet!"

"Take what ya want, ya little bastard. Take what ya want an' be damned sure I don't see yer face again, because next time around, I'll be doin' the killin'. Ya hear? Take what ya want an' leave me be."

"I only take what is mine. I only take what you stole."

448

"Take what ya want, ya Indian varmint. Take it an' git outta here."

Luke reached down cautiously and threw our clothes out of the wagon. He stood back up and reached for the man's gun.

"Hey, where ya goin' with that?"

"Quiet!"

The stranger ceased his protest.

"What's he doing?" asked Gracie.

I didn't answer, but seeing my head move slowly side to side, she understood my confusion. We watched as he dragged the gun to the end of the wagon nearest the rear gate. At that place, he dropped the weapon and untied the horses. I watched him walk back toward the stranger. Immediately, my stomach twisted itself into a fresh set of knots.

"Sit!" Luke commanded.

"Wot's he doing?" asked Gracie.

"I have no idea, but he bet—."

"Oh, my, word!" Gracie exclaimed.

"What?" I panicked. "What. What is it?"

"He's *taking coup.*" Gracie's mouth hung open.

"What!"

I was stunned. That idiot child of mine was proving his bravery by taking coup. He was actually stepping forward to touch the stranger. In his mind, he must have been looking to make up for his cowardice before the bear. I was dumbstruck.

"Oh, my god. Oh, my god, Luke. Have you lost your mind?" I felt as if I was about to vomit. "Surely, if he lives through this, he will die at my hand. I swear he is going to die. He is going to die."

449

We could do nothing but stand there and work to make sense of the drama within the dark as Luke eased his way forward with arrow strung and on the ready. We heard him tell the driver to face forward, which the man did at once. Luke then released the tension on his bow and reached out with his left hand. A second later he laid his hand on the man's head. The man must have believed he was about to be scalped.

After making coup, Luke backed away and jumped off the wagon. We heard him tell the driver to ride off and keep away from the gun in the back of the bed. Luke stood at the ready, watching the wagon roll away as the injured driver snapped the reins with one hand, while favoring the shoulder with the arrow sticking out its back.

Luke walked toward the campfire. He placed our clothes on the branch to again warm and turned to look in our direction. I wanted to cry.

"I don't believe it."

"That's some ten-year-old you've raised, Elizabeth. He's a full-blown bloodlettin' brave."

"That'll be enough of that!" I snapped. "Luke! Luke!"

"Yes, Momma."

"Would you turn around so Gracie and I can come back and get dressed?"

"Yes, Momma."

With that, Gracie and I ran for the fire and slipped into our heated clothes. I stared at Luke's backside, but said nothing at first. It probably would have been pointless, and I already had enough excitement for one day. I lacked the ambition to go another round with anybody. My son included. Instead, I sat down before the fire and slipped into a stupor as I tried to cook myself.

"You're awful quiet," said Gracie.

"She is angry with me."

"I am not angry with you, Luke."

"Then why don't you talk to me?"

"I just want to relax and take some time to think. It has been a day. In fact, it's been a week. What am I saying; it has been a month of trial and tribulation, one after another...after another."

"Wot were you thinking about just then?" asked Gracie.

"Just then, I was thinking how...how I never expected we would run up with face-splitting smiles, and drop on our knees to kiss the hands and feet of the first white man we encountered...and then go on to thank God Almighty in teary prayer for our safe return to the civilized world. Honestly...I never saw anything of the sort.

"And yet, that scenario would have been far easier for me to imagine than one where I am standing naked in the woods, watching my ten-year-old son shoot an arrow clean through a white man and take coup...not to mention anything about suspicions of earlier murdering, or the two of us clubbing a gang to kingdom come. I am sure you can both understand I had no idea we would attempt to butcher the first dozen white men to be met."

There was a long pause before Gracie started to laugh. Apparently, she needed to replay the scene a time or two to get the full effect. She laughed harder. Luke was grinning and then he too began to laugh. I could only look at the two of them and shake my head. There could be no denying we were savages. Well-mannered savages, but savages through and through.

"All I can say, Elizabeth, is that we have no idea what to expect. It's all new. So wot difference does it make? I doubt we'll be disappointed no matter wot happens. Here."

Gracie handed me a piece of grilled rabbit. I stuck the meat into my mouth and mumbled something incomprehensible.

"Wot?"

"I said thank you for the piece of meat, Gracie. And thank you, Luke, for your bravery in getting back our clothes. It would have been a truly miserable night if you hadn't."

"You are welcome, Momma."

"And thank you for getting us this far in spite of all we have faced, and all the worry we know you suffer to keep us safe. For whatever years I am given, I will never forget. That I promise. We love you, Elizabeth."

"Well, don't think for a moment that you are home safe and sound—."

"I don't."

"...But you are welcome."

I had nothing more to contribute. I listened to Luke and Gracie as they plunged back into their months-old conversation of yet to be worn out wishes and dreams of wondrous things they hoped to see and experience.

As they chatted away, my thoughts drifted in another direction. In a way, I felt as though I had betrayed them. They had waited so long to see the world I had planted in those dreams, and I understood that world hadn't fully arrived, but their first taste of it was one of uneasiness and reservation instead of marvelous wonder. Looking back over my years of stories, I might better have held back more on the wonders, and less on the worries. Fate was not mine to direct.

I gathered up the twigs and leaves about me, now dried by the heat of the fire, and lay down. I considered how a good night's sleep seemed nothing more than a memory I wished to relive.

This night would be unbearably cold. The stars appeared bold and distinct in the black cloudless sky, the sounds of the wood with its creaks and groans landed upon my ear undiminished. We three would have no choice but to press upon each other as tightly as possible in order to conserve a couple of degrees of warmth.

We had hoped to escape the worst of the cold open field air by sleeping within the wooded ravines of the bottomlands, but whatever bedding found was unusable, being thoroughly dampened by the mists and matted into inseparable cakes. We would have to endure the river mist without protection. Between the damp and the cold, we were no less miserable within the ravine. We spent as much time stumbling drearily around the camp looking for wood to burn as we did attempting to sleep.

There came a late hour after which we had spent so much time staggering about, complaining, collecting firewood, and trying to stay warm that we fueled the fire into a roaring blaze atop a sizeable bed of coals. I stood staring into the glow, half asleep, swaying back and forth on my feet, frying my frontside, freezing my backside, until I toppled over to be awakened with a jolt. I must have experienced that unpleasant jolt ten times before being struck with a thought.

"I have an idea."

My voice sounded broken, and neither Gracie nor Luke answered. They never opened their eyes to acknowledge me while they swayed likewise in the breeze of dreams.

"Hey!"

I hollered out, prompting their eyes to form near imperceptible slits.

"Let's bury this bed of embers under sand. If we use enough of it, we can sleep on it without getting burned. The sand will get

453

good and warm, maybe hot, maybe too hot. But I choose that over this misery."

In spite of their exhaustion, the thought of warmth was more than ample persuasion to stop them from their sway. As it was, nobody was resting well. And so, Gracie and I took turns holding our skirts out to be filled with the dryer sand of the upper flat. While one of us walked back to dump our skirt load on the fire, Luke scraped off the dew-covered surface and scooped up dry handfuls to fill the other. After about half an hour we succeeded in our effort. By continually testing the temperature of the sand we stopped when it gave off a gentle, even heat.

"Let's drag these branches around us to still the air."

"Good idea," said Gracie, "Hey, all these leaves around the fire have been dried out. Let's cover the mound and blanket ourselves with them. That should help hold the heat about us."

We completed the mound, bordered it with branches, covered it in leaves as Gracie suggested, and then lay down together. The utter bliss of something as simple as heat can only be appreciated by a soul so desperately miserable, words fail to describe. Allow me to say that after hours of just such misery, in a matter of minutes, we were soundly asleep. If we had been kittens, we would have been heard purring for miles.

The success of our effort could have been measured by the number of hours we slept before awaking late the following morn to a fully risen sun. Unlike my usual hour of restless stirring before awakening, this morning I simply opened my eyes as if my body had vomited me out of an unrealized dream. I sat up feeling ten years younger. I sat up feeling warm. Without thought, I sifted the comforting sand through my fingers. Yes, yes, yes, we could have done worse.

FIFTY-ONE

This morning, as if to fulfill Luke's prophecy, we chose not to breakfast. Before building our bed of heated sand, we had spent the night nibbling heavily on grilled rabbit while stumbling about asleep on our feet in search of firewood to stave off the disagreeable cold. All that nibbling left us to awaken with stomachs yet content. And having enjoyed the remainder of our night sleeping soundly atop the mound of warmed sand, and doing so until late in the morn, our countenances and demeanors were nothing if not wholly furbished.

With spirits so high, it was easy to forego breakfasting, and instead round up horses, belongings, and ready ourselves to ride. After those fears forced upon us by the white man in a wagon had dissipated, there remained a certain residual anticipation. For in spite of the man's black heart, he was so different in manner from an Indian that he brought with him a sense of proximity to our long-sought St. Louis.

Therefore, it was with an air of giddiness that we struck out along the same trail and in the same direction that our unwelcomed visitor had departed. From the outset, our eyes were fixed onto the track of the man's wagon wheels. The matched grooves were hypnotic and oftentimes snared me deep into my thoughts, one being a question of how well fared the injured stranger today. Visions of the man's chest skewered by Luke's arrow played over and over in my mind. The vision wasn't brought on by concern for the man, but rather concern for my son.

It was a good long time before our giddiness was fully eroded. We traveled the whole of the day, finishing it out while yet following the trail and glimpses of additional wagon tracks as they meandered through the thickets of cottonwoods, snags, and swamps. Now, dusk was close at hand and pressing us to seek out shelter, pressing us to call it quits before nightfall. The trail had led us away from water's edge as it made for higher elevations where it escaped the settling mists and pervasive damp. We were searching out sheltered ground in earnest when we rounded a bend, and from this higher terrain, spied in the near distance—*a town.*

We were all three unnerved and halted our horses at first sight in order to study what lay before us. The indistinct shape of trees gave way to the crisp edges and diagonal lines of collected structures crowded together and buzzing with activity. I knew this would happen. I knew it was only a matter of time, and I had waited the longest time imaginable. Yet, in spite of years spent thinking this moment out in my head, years spent preparing, I was fully taken aback.

Luke and Gracie sat respectively silent upon their horses allowing me time to gather my thoughts. I needed a moment to consider what was in store for us. This was not the same as seeing what remained of Independence by *'sneaking up in the woods and having a look-n-see.'* This was a full-fledged *'in the middle of the road'* town filled with citizens and activity. This town was in our way, blocking our passage. After so much freedom and wide open space, this town appeared overbearing. It felt treacherous; it felt like an affront.

Wasn't it peculiar that I should be so wary and anxious? There in the waning light of day's end was precisely the type of place I had envisioned us entering when time came to introduce Gracie and Luke to the white man's world. And halted before it, I found myself swirling within the heady realization of another fact. I actually crossed the great western desert twice to return to the world I knew years ago—*and lived to tell of it.*

To my surprise, Gracie and Luke were most restrained. During the good many thoughts and emotions that blazed through my head, the two of them continued to sit silently upon their horses staring ahead. Maybe it was more about wonder than awaiting my next word. Maybe that was a good thing because I was torn between my instincts of caution and distrust, and my memories of hot meals, warm blankets, dry beds, and a roof over my head.

I was not one to charge into anything unfamiliar, be it a river, a swamp, a camp, or an unfamiliar town. Years of living in the wild brought me to hold precious little trust in anything or anyone strange or unknown. Gracie was wicked with a knife, and Luke at his young age had scant fear of anything other than possibly a grizzly. Still, we were two women and a boy entering a man's place. As a woman, I would never be free of that ever-present understanding.

For the first time, I found myself uncomfortable about our appearance. I regretted us not being dressed in western apparel. It never occurred to me that we would be wearing Indian attire when I reached that first town. I had always imagined the three of us walking about in the simple conservative clothes of common folk as I gently exposed Luke and Gracie to the city dweller's way of life. One thing for sure, my dreams were never about abduction or ending up half-naked on the high plains without anything of value to trade or sell, exception being our recent acquisition of dead men's horses.

Gracie and Luke knew nothing of European dress and so gave no thought to the matter whatsoever. They were wholly accustomed to the thick and often stiff feel of aging skins that presently covered them. Washing buckskin often ruined it, and the sweat and body oil that kept it pliable came at a price. One generally replaced leathers only when completely wore out or putrefied, at which point the skins were far beyond stink. In any event, though not presently apparent, Luke and Gracie were generally so giddy with excitement that they well might have entered their first settlement wearing poison ivy and been happy.

In years past, no mind would have been paid to a trapper or trader riding though town in Indian dress. In fact, I dare say half the Indian garments in St. Louis had a Spaniard or Frenchman walking around inside them. It was considered a routine necessity, a matter of survival in the wilderness. When clothes wore out, they had to be replaced and the Indians were most adept at using what nature had to offer in order to accomplish this task efficiently.

I hoped some vestige of that understanding from days gone by remained to be found in this place now because clothes were expensive. Clothes required the purchase of cloth and the hiring of a seamstress, neither of which we were able to do at this time. Whatever I might gain from the sale of the horses would be necessarily put toward the food and lodging required to sustain us until journey's end. Until I could find my way back to St. Louis, to Rachel and Caleb, or a financier; we would have to save our money and wear what was on our backs.

FIFTY-TWO

Soaked in a perfect mix of anxiety and anticipation, we moved onward and observed each and every detail as the trail transitioned fully into Main Street. There was no Second Street; there was no bypass street. There was only one way in and one way out. Gracie and I entered town riding proud and abreast in plain sight with Luke in the middle. Our confiscated horses were in tow.

Our shadows, once reaching out ahead of us on the road, were now gone. The sun that warmed our backs all afternoon had since disappeared beneath the western horizon. Luke and Gracie were nothing, if not all eyes and ears. In the final minutes of waning light, their heads snapped back and forth, left to right, attempting to absorb every last detail of their strange new surroundings.

Unlike the two of them, my curiosity was tempered, for as soon as we arrived I sensed a frosty reception from those we

458

encountered in the street. I felt as though, had we been males, we might have been stopped from entering the town altogether. Memories returned of New York, Shadow Hunter, and his family of outcasts. Not to be noticed, or to be viewed as a curiosity was one thing, but I felt certain the only thing staving off immediate eviction for us was the fact we were all three blonde-headed.

Unlike the Indians of our tribe who flooded out from their tipis to greet whatever stranger arrived, these folks stopped, pointed, and stood affixed to stare. Women gasped, children were reined in, and men sneered aloud or leaned over to pass comments through the corner of their mouths. If I had any doubts about misreading the expressions of these folks, they were put to rest by Gracie.

"Are we doing something wrong, Elizabeth?"

"Why do you ask?"

"Why do I ask?" she repeated. "Look at the way they're staring at us. Don't whites smile? They look like they want to eat us. Don't whites come forward and greet visitors?"

"Not exactly a warm welcome, I agree."

"These people make me nervous."

Gracie began to take note of where stood every man about us as we rode down the street.

"Stay calm, Gracie, stay calm. Nothing has happened. There is nothing to say something will, so don't be the one who starts it. Most likely, folks are staring, not knowing what to make of us being blonde and all. The way we look, the way we carry ourselves probably makes them curious at best, and apparently suspicious or nervous at worst."

"What's wrong with the way we look?" asked Luke.

"Nothing, if you are living with the Tsistsistas or alone out in the desert. But we're not doing either of those things now. Now, we're in the white man's world, and they do things differently, Luke. Our mannerisms make us stand out."

Having been a blonde, living amidst a tribe of black haired Indians, I knew firsthand what it meant to stand out. But I also knew this wasn't only about being blonde. It wasn't just our dress. It was peculiarities, such as the way we entered town riding bareback or 'Indian saddle' as it was termed. Any white man worth his salt rode a horse seated in a western saddle if for no reason other than to visibly prove his position on Indian affairs.

Our horses with their dappled coloring spoke of Indian heritage. It was the braids in our hair; it was our manners; it was that wild look in the eyes of Luke and Gracie. It was our bows, our arrows. It was everything about us that could possibly be. We were blonde by blood, but we were Indian to the core in manner and spirit.

Most Americans would say Gracie and I had been ruined by the red man, any disposition toward honesty and trust long since fouled or abandoned. There would be no benefit of the doubt, and so I didn't expect these people to hide their disdain. The power of their opinion and poisoned hearts was fed by the strength of their numbers. Such was their ignorance and fear.

The expressions of contempt appeared all about us, looks that I learned long ago were bred out of misinformation, misunderstanding, and plain stupidity. The farther east we would go, the worse it would become. I had seen the same faces many times when traveling up the Potomac and along the Erie, and even the Missouri. I had seen the look in Albany when I asked about the fate of the little Indian girl run down by the coach. It was that same look of abhorrence and detestation.

Most disheartening was my own familiarity, my knowing how I had delivered the same disdainful sneers while in my youth, when my heart was filled and brimming with ignorance and misguided prejudices. It was Christopher who taught me to question and gauge whatever I first read or heard. It was he who stressed the dangers of being judge and jury, and the need to seek out opposing views. It was Christopher who brought me to maturity in my way of assessing the world that surrounded me.

This place was different, the time was different, but the communal sentiment appeared much the same, or possibly even more poisonous. Under my feet lie the latest frontiers to be overrun by immigrants from the eastern states or directly from Europe. People who had never lived in these parts, people who knew little if anything about living in harmony with themselves, let alone the natives. Anything or anyone standing in the way of their road to profit was despised, demonized, and ultimately disposed. It was the American way—dog eat dog, greed, manifest destiny.

When I first passed through a decade ago, the western border towns were most amiable and tolerant toward the many tribes of Indians and foreigners. Everybody was welcome providing they remained reasonably sober and acted half civilized. This time around, things didn't feel so friendly. I wondered if we had traveled farther east into the settlements than I imagined, but I corrected myself at once knowing I had not crossed the Mississippi. More likely, during my ten years of absence, eastern prejudices had traveled farther west into the settlements.

FIFTY-THREE

We three pressed forward, slowly, cautiously. The farther into town we rode, the more uncivil seemed the place. After a quick survey, I was dismayed to see nothing of Indians doing business here. The reason was as obvious as the incivility was blatant. The townsfolk were most unfriendly and easily put me on edge.

461

I repositioned my staff for confidence and a quick draw. I asked myself if I was falling prey to an overactive imagination, if I needed to calm my concerns. I worked to settle myself because I had no wish for trouble—quite the opposite in fact. I reminded myself of the need to remain level-headed long enough to allow Luke and Gracie time to ease into their surroundings.

"So this is a street, Momma?"

Luke snagged me from my worries. I hoped to mask any signs of concern.

"This is a street, Luke. This town has only one, so it usually ends up being called Main Street."

"Look at the wagons. Do all horses have saddles?" he asked.

"Oh! Elizabeth, look at the clothes those women are wearing. Are those the dresses you always tell me about?"

"And these are all stores?" asked Luke as he studied both sides of the street.

"Yes, most all horses have saddles. Yes, Gracie, those are the dresses. No, not all stores, but they are all businesses. That place over there lets rooms for sleeping, and that one over there is for eating meals. Those three establishments sell or trade goods such as hardware, tools, or dry goods."

It pleased me to see the wide-eyed expressions of wonder on their faces as we ambled along between the two rows of buildings—all this amazement from a town of such insignificance, unless of course, you happened to have never seen a town in the whole of your life.

"These folk sure look unfriendly."

There is was again, and it hurt me to hear her say as much. Gracie was growing ever more torn between her fascination for the surroundings and her wariness of the people filling those surroundings.

"Pay no mind to the stares and smirks, Gracie. We're the strangers here. They'll get used to us in time. As long as we mind our own business, we should be fine."

I wasn't sure who I was trying to convince. We did our best to avoid eye contact, and mind our own business as I suggested.

Our horses stepped along slowly, passing in and out of the glow cast by recently lit window lamps. Their light emanated from behind the frames of glazing and highlighted the varied and colorful assortments of wares. Many of the shops were closing for the night, but the townsfolk seemed to linger on the street. They seemed keenly aware of us, and I was certain their numbers were increasing. Any thoughts of this being my overactive imagination were put to rest when I clearly spied a couple of older boys slip in and out of sight as if flanking us. I noticed others moving in and out of alleys, or appearing and disappearing around corners, too many staying within the cloak of deepening shadows to be mere chance.

I could no longer disregard these actions, or deny that something was amiss. The unwanted attention was both unsettling and perplexing. My attention was at last removed from the town's amenities, and instead focused fully on the abnormal reaction to our presence. It was baffling, and I couldn't make sense of it. I was at a loss to explain such bizarre behavior when suddenly I was struck by a thought.

"It's the wagon driver—."

"Wot!" Grace's head instantly snapped about. "Where!"

"The wagon driver." I repeated. "This is all about him. I bet my life on it. When Luke shot that driver, my only concern was for Luke's safety, whereas my feelings about the driver never amounted to more than good riddance to rubbish.

"I never gave thought to seeing a town so soon, or seeing one at all, and it's more than reasonable to imagine that the wagon driver lives here or maybe even owns one of these shops. If folks saw him return with an arrow sticking out of his back, or heard him a-hooping and a-hollerin' about Indians on the outskirts of town, well…. Suddenly, we're all snakes, *and that* would explain all of this."

"My word, Elizabeth, what if he told everyone that a child shot him—one look at Luke, and there will be no mistaking us for those Indians."

Any mention of Luke effected an immediate and instinctive reaction that obliterated all other thought and activity. Those first seconds bound me fast and singly focused on his well-being. I stared directly at Gracie with undivided attention, and then weighed up her comment and the consequences.

"I doubt he did that."

"Why?"

"If you were a prideful man who managed to live after being gored by an arrow, would you lessen your story by saying a ten-year-old boy single-handedly hijacked and shot you? I doubt it. Remember, he never saw us. He never saw anybody. He would be more likely to say it was a band of Indians lurking on the outskirts and up to no good. That story would turn him into a hero, but it also would put this place on edge…and that would explain much of what we see here."

"And to them, we look like Indians?"

"And to them we just plain look strange, and yes, a lot closer to Indian than not. Honey, they don't see you in one of those fancy dresses, and I don't see a belt full of knives hanging off any woman around here who is wearing one of those fancy dresses."

Gracie studied me a moment and then leaned over to whisper.

"Well, if that's how you're figurin' it, then wot if the white man I put down with the knife lives here? I doubt he would be tellin' folks that his entire party of six got hijacked and killed off by two women."

The implication of what Gracie said went right to the bone.

"Oh, lord.... Don't even think it. If that lot is from here as well, we may never get out alive. I pegged those men for riding out of Independence. That would be their kind of place, being a near ghost town and all. But if they called this place home, or worse, if that Sol fellow rode back here to get mending for that knife wound...either way—add his bloated stories to those of the wagon driver and...."

"I'm not so sure his stories were all that bloated."

"I'm not so sure we're getting out of this town in one piece."

I looked up and down the street suddenly very uncomfortable. I looked back at Gracie and forwarded her a warning.

"You know, Gracie, it would just be our luck that those scoundrels have ties to this place. I suggest you pay close attention. Too many times in the past, pretty young things like you have paid a steep price, but for a false accusation or minor offense let alone anything the likes of murdering the neighbors even if they were scum. You be sure and keep your eyes open, child. Watch your back."

Gracie nodded her full understanding. Meanwhile, the lamps were still burning in the town's trading post and the light flowed out onto the street through a large multi-glazed window and a door that was wedged wide open.

"Can we go in there?" asked Luke.

I looked carefully up and down the street a second time. The scene only appeared to worsen. There seemed to be more people than ever, and it was with great difficulty that I tried to believe they were not all watching us. Getting out of the citizens' view seemed like a great idea.

"Yes. Yes, let's go in. Might be better to get off the street for bit, you know, out of sight, out of mind. If we disappear long enough to warm up, maybe the locals will lose interest."

We brought our horses to a halt and dismounted in that same light that spread a faint glow across the packed dirt of Main. As I worked to lash all the horses to a hitching post, Luke leapt up onto the porch and rushed to look inside. Unable to contain her curiosity, Gracie wasn't but a few steps behind. I was surprised the two of them stopped short of entering. As soon as I grabbed the pistol, a bow, and quiver full of arrows to trade for coats, I walked up behind them.

I knew that to Luke this was a lodge unlike anything he had ever seen. I could see that he was thunderstruck by all of the wares that filled the building one step forward from where he stood. To his young eyes, each and every item was utterly new and incomprehensible. The mysteries were as alluring as the pieces.

Gracie better expected what was before her, she being much older, and having spent years listening to both her parents' stories and to me going on about western ways and the things to be found in St. Louis. And yet she appeared no less astonished. She stood looking over Luke's shoulders, her eyes surveying every inch of the walls and tabletops beyond the door.

Luke turned to me and asked under his breath.

"Do I walk to the right?"

His was a question of respect. To do so, would have been polite in a lodge and hearing it made me proud.

"No, son, that's not necessary. Go ahead. You may walk in and wander where you wish, but try your best not to touch. If you break something, we will be hard pressed to pay."

"Why don't these women invite us in and offer us something?" he asked.

"It's not the custom in places of business. They might do that at their home. Their home would be more like the lodge."

"But they have many things, Momma."

Luke didn't understand why women, who possessed so much, didn't come forward to greet him and offer something to relieve his weariness. In only his first moments, he was already sensing the extent to which things would be different. Everything down to the smallest detail was strange and unfamiliar. There was much to be learned. I thought of how baffled I had been when asked if I was menstruating before being invited into the lodge of Ho'neheveho. I remember standing in the opening to his tipi unsure of what to do, standing completely at the mercy of Talk-a-Lot and her direction. I understood something of my son's bewilderment.

For now, we set aside concerns about the unfriendly faces in the street, and I encouraged Luke and Gracie to enter and enjoy looking around the store. I followed them inside, but whereas they were drawn at once to three large candy jars on a counter, I set my sights on a well-stoked woodstove that I spotted against the back wall. I left Luke and Gracie to their business as I stepped around three women also standing at the counter a few feet down from the jars of hard candy. The three had been conversing with a fourth woman, who stood alone behind the counter, possibly the shop keeper's wife. I was quick to notice how they recoiled at the sight of us.

Gracie and Luke knew from my stories that candy came in various colors, shapes, and sizes, and was often found displayed in large china or clear glass apothecary jars atop counters. They instantly recognized the containers for what they were and rushed over to peer deep into the colorful contents. Gracie lifted one lid and the next, and they took turns inhaling the sweet fragrances. It would have been better had they not touched the jars, which were undoubtedly expensive, but no harm was done. After all, Gracie wasn't a ten-year-old.

While the two of them remained fixed on the candy-filled jars, all four women remained fixed upon them with blatantly unconcealed expressions of disdain. The looks hardly escaped me. Their faces grated me to the core, not only because I sensed their distaste for my children, but also because I hated arrogance. I hated rudeness. I hated bigotry. I hated the way people could be so effortlessly hurtful. Regardless of how fanciful their dresses, how snobbish their attitude, these women were comparable to the poorest of the poor next to the wealth of Christopher Claussen, a man who possessed everything and remained the essence of humility.

I stood at the woodstove watching the four women sneer. I sensed my good nature faltering. I clenched my teeth and started slowly descending into the wrong state of mind, which when left unchecked during my younger years would have spelled explosive trouble. I so wanted Luke and Gracie to first meet the good hearted, not the abductors, not the robbers, and not now those who raised noses in an attempt to reach upper airs.

I was nothing like these women now belittling my son and Gracie while stuffed in their impractical costumes. They appeared fresh off the vine and sadly bound to the dictates of eastern society, virgins yet to be raped by the cruelties of a hard land. Unlike these prissy dolts before me, I had been taught how to swing a staff by Dorrie, shoot a gun by Luke the elder, throw a knife by Gracie, and loose an arrow by Talk-a-Lot. Most important, I had learned how much fear I could face down given the experiences of my life.

The sight of these four women prompted a rash of distasteful memories. Recollections of *'the way it was'* back home—pressures of being politely coaxed into a proper place in society—having to embrace one's status as a woman and the goodly nature of service and submission to man in the eyes of God; it all came back. I could be as offensive as any woman alive, especially in the eyes of supposedly genteel women such as these, who wouldn't understand why I would never take a tongue-lashing from any man unless it suited me. And it seldom suited me.

To have the wealth and power of the Claussen name behind one, and yet experience the patronization, the constant reminders of the mindless and feeble tendencies that supposedly suffered my gender, the inability to endure the pressures of life, the incapability to comprehend higher learning or anything aside from needlework, cooking, cleaning or washing—well…let us say in spite of my knowledge of geography, mathematics, and literature, in a man's world, I would always be best at lying on my back and having babies.

Unfortunately for society, it had been impossible for me to conform to a mold of such design. I was too spirited. I may not have been born with teeth to tear, and it was true that I grew up in comfort, but I was not spared all of life's brutality. There were hard lessons, lessons that stiffened my spine, but only once was my spirit ever broken, that being the death of Lady Rebecca. Only Christopher could understand the depth of that pain, a suffering he shared. He put that tragedy aside, and in all other things he applauded my grit and encouraged me in every way to stand my ground. Something I was well primed to do right now.

These four would eventually be broken or transformed, finding dirt under their nails and sand between their teeth as they learned the earth of the west where common women worked hard but were appreciated, considered equal and competent. Out here they worked the ground alongside their men, and they earned the respect deserved from their labors and their neighbors.

I left the heat of the woodstove, and walked toward the counter where I entered into the midst of these women who seemed more annoyed than fearful of our presence. The three women regarded me with an air of revulsion. I could accept an air of revulsion because I knew in their eyes I looked like an Indian and probably reeked of horses, sweat, and old leathers. But more important, if they had overheard any rumors of murder or mayhem, they would have displayed an air of fear at the sight of me. The women averted their eyes at once, only to pass furtive glances in my direction or that of Luke and Gracie.

"Begging your pardon, ladies. I wish a word with the proprietor if you'll allow me to pass."

I was unmoved by the frailties of the three customers, visitors, or whatever they might be, and looked at them unswervingly until they gained enough sense to step back out of my way. They offered no protest, but were too nosey to take their leave. I went on to address the young woman behind the counter.

"Good evening, madam. I was hoping you might do me the service of accepting this finely crafted bow and quiver filled with arrows, along with this sturdy pistol, in trade for something warm for us to wear. I would also require a few pieces of candy, a single sheet of parchment, and enough postage to get a post off to St. Louis. That would be considered an exceptionally profitable trade by anyone. Do you not agree?"

The woman appeared jolted by the fact I spoke better English than most. She took charge of the pistol, flipping it over repeatedly to assess its wear and worth. She set the weapon down upon the counter and took up the bow to study its workmanship as well as

470

that of the quiver and arrows. She began to nod her approval, judging the items to have value much to her advantage.

"May I ask your name?"

"Miss Dennison."

"Well, Miss Dennison, the pistol appears in good condition and the bow, the quiver, and the arrows are indeed well-fashioned as you have said. Take however many drops you wish. I will fetch a sheet of parchment. There are shawls, wraps, and blankets over there against the wall." After pointing across the store, she turned back toward a desk and produced a piece of stationery along with a quill and well. She placed all three upon the countertop with an air of expectation.

"Do you wish me to pen something in your behalf?"

"I thank you for your kindness. If I may...."

I reached for the quill, dipped it in the well, and began writing a letter in brisk clear penmanship. I could feel the silent stares and disbelief in all four women. I knew with certainty it would be rare indeed if any one of the other three knew how to read or write. I finished my missive and folded it.

"If I may use your wax, madam."

I flipped the letter over and addressed it. I then sealed it with wax.

"If you would see that this is ferried on the next available run to St. Louis, I would be most grateful."

The young woman behind the desk was flushed with amazement or embarrassment. I could see it in her cheeks and eyes.

"Yes, ma'am. The next pick-up."

"Thank you."

I turned away.

"Excuse me," the counter lady called out.

"Yes."

"May I ask from what parts west have you come?"

"The Stony Mountains—the Rockies. Been out ten years."

Her eyes opened wide. I heard a gasp from behind. No doubt, there would be much to gossip about tonight.

"Gracie."

"Yut?"

"Come with me, sweetheart."

Gracie said nothing. She was so taken by the displays in every direction that she simply followed my lead.

"Mmm, that candy smells good. I take it you like anise," I said.

"I love it. Honestly, it is splendid." Her eyes went dreamy. "Wot's this smell?"

"Lemon."

"This?"

"Orange."

"This?"

"Ginger."

Gracie was rotating through her pieces of candy, holding up one after another for me to test.

"That is sassafras. I drank a lot of sassafras tea when a child. You don't often see it here like back east."

"This is mint. I know that smell. It's all over the woods," she said.

"Come look at this dress, Gracie."

I drew her toward the rear of the room so she might see a couple of fine dresses that were hung on display.

"Beautiful aren't they?"

"Very."

Gracie looked up at the garment on display.

"It is unusual to see such a dress, especially here in a small town. You will see plenty of them in St. Louis, but as a rule, out here one only finds bolts of cloth, like those over there leaning in the corner."

I pointed to a nearby assortment of cloth. Gracie spied the material but returned her gaze to the dress.

"This is so fine." She reached up to rub the material gently between her fingers. "Who could make such a dress?"

"A seamstress. Usually, if a dress is already made up such as this, it is the work of a widow or spinster, who earns her keep by sewing. A talented seamstress is often given space by a store owner, who will gladly display her work for a modest fee or sometimes he'll do it for free just to draw in customers."

"Who would wear this?"

"Anybody, but especially a beautiful young woman like you."

"I would wear something like this?" Gracie remarked with surprise.

"Of course."

"I don't think so." She turned to me. "You would wear something like this?"

"I have many times."

"Mmmmm. I...don.... There's no place for knives...."

473

"Gracie, Gracie, Gracie...." I gave her a look full of sympathy. "You are correct. I admit there is no place for knives; I give you that. However, the dress is pretty. Is it not?"

Gracie reached carefully for the wonderfully embroidered garment, sliding her fingers lightly over the ruffles of white fabric and lace. I could see reality replacing the imaginings that occupied so many places in her mind. I brought the dress down off the hanger and laid it across the counter.

"Look. Here. Look at the quality." I ran my finger along a seam. "Look at the skill of this seamstress. Look at these backstitches. Oh, my. Look at how nice is all of this hemstitching—beautiful, absolutely beautiful. Here, see how nice she did this button-stitching. This woman is particular about her work; it took a lot of time and patience. This dressmaker is very good.

"Gracie, I understand this seems strange to you, and you cannot see yourself wearing such a fine garment, but you will be expected to do so in St. Louis. We both will."

"I can see you in this dress, but not me."

"I can see you in—."

I was about to conclude my lesson of sorts, when distracted by a ruckus outside on the street. At the first sound of commotion, I looked over toward Luke. He was safe and presently studying a wooden toy horse and an iron-headed hatchet.

From the darkness beyond the door that was still wedged open, came a disturbance, a spattering of voices in excited tones. A clamorous group had formed in the street for what reason, I was unsure, but my instincts warned me to be on guard. I looked at the four women, still standing at the counter. Their gossip was stilled as all four were now only staring out the door at something in the street. My eyes shifted from them to the window, and through it, I could see at once there was a gathering of lanterns in the darkness—many lanterns.

I knew it mattered none whether one was white or Indian, hysteria was truly an insidious self-feeding storm. It could be fed by fear, love, hatred, suspicion, or greed; it mattered little. It could engulf the hearts of young and old, weak and strong alike as it spread from soul to soul faster than wind-whipped wildfires. And beware, for those fires would burn the innocent unlucky enough to be in the way. Suddenly, a boy of twelve or thirteen ran in through the front door and yelled.

"Lucinda! It's bein' sayid that injuns with bows n' arrows n' knives are skulkin' 'roun' town. It's bein' sayid, they got some women an' children taken hostage agin' thay'r will! They're sayin' it's the same vermin that shot Mr. Roderman an' stuck that feller from Independence!"

I felt my blood surge. The women instinctively turned to look our way prompting the boy's own eyes to follow suit. His eyes found the three of us standing on guard and studying him, which did little for his brief show of bravery. In fact, it did so little that the boy sprang back into the darkness like a jackrabbit, only his mouth to be heard outrunning his feet.

"There's Indians in the post! There's Indians in the post!"

I listened to the young boy's proclamations fade into the din of the crowd. I feared it represented the beginning rather than the end of our troubles. Lucinda, the counter girl, said nothing. She stood nervously in place glancing back and forth at the three women and us.

I could only imagine what variety of frantic hearsay was escalating in the street. A sizeable gathering must have collected beforehand in order to feed the lad enough courage for him to stumble inside and warn Lucinda of Indians. Added to that were the blackness of night, the strangeness of the frontier, the overall ignorance and hatred that runs rampant. I fully appreciated the potential storm that appeared to be headed our way.

Luke set down the wooden horse and hatchet, and became focused on the commotion beyond the door.

"Luke," I called out to him.

He made a move in that direction.

"Luke!"

I called out to stop him, but he was incurably inquisitive. Pretending not to hear me, or else just plain ignoring me, he walked over to the door to investigate. He was rolling a piece of candy in his mouth while looking out into the shadows of the street, shadows now fragmented by the rising number of torches.

"Get away from the door, Luke, I won't say it twice!"

Having no desire to upset me, Luke turned obediently to walk back my way at which point a man stampeded through the door in his direction. He grabbed a startled Luke firmly around the neck with one arm, holding him hostage, while pointing his gun every which-way about the store ready to shoot the first thing that moved.

"Run, get out now! Martha, get out now!"

Apparently, the man was connected to one of the three women. He may have been her husband or fiancé, maybe a brother, maybe a man whose heart wished madly to impress the lady. Whatever the relationship, he succeeded in only one thing.

He scared the living daylights out of all of us by the manner in which he burst through the door, and commenced to hollering and swinging a gun every which-way. He frightened the four women so badly that they collapsed to the floor, going down in a fit of hysterical screams while scrambling on all four to remove themselves from harm's way. Their combined screaming only added to the already heightened impression that mayhem and murder was underway inside the trading post.

All sense of order quickly disintegrated, and I focused on only one thing: my son. Above the screams in the store and the shouts in the streets, I yelled out to Luke in the language of the Tsistsistas, the tongue he knew best.

"O'óhtá! Bite! Bite!"

I implored him to bite the man and run. This he did. The man shrieked with pain, his howl of agony surpassing the rest, his grip loosening just enough for Luke to slide down to the floor. Luke bolted at once along the length of the counter attempting his escape.

Cursing without conscience, and wishing to keep Luke at all cost as a shield or a bargaining chip, the man dove forward with an outstretched hand and came crashing down belly first onto the floor with one hand yet ahold of the gun, and the other locked firmly onto Luke's ankle. Luke fought to get free. At the same time, I broke into a run to assist him. I was now as panicked as the rest.

Unencumbered by concerns of consequence, Gracie acted in a perfectly predictable manner. A glistening sliver of light sped past my shoulder as Gracie's knife slipped from her hand and blistered down the aisle. It was invisible except for the dance of light on its keen edge, a reflection of an oil lamp. It slammed into the wooden counter base with a sound like the slamming of a door to Hell. It split the wood as it embedded itself only inches from the man's forehead. This was no longer the weak throw of a spindly ten-year-old.

She forced a gasp of stunned surprise from the stranger's throat. The closeness of the call must have shaken him badly. His eyes were suddenly fixed upon the blade of death nearly touching the end of his nose. Before I could intervene, the man turned his head just in time to see a second blade streaking toward him. He

477

recoiled as the second blade embedded itself in the wooden counter, six inches closer, and precisely where had been his head. Gracie would have killed him on the spot.

The stranger had involuntarily let loose of Luke's ankle when pulling back to dodge death by a split skull. Sensing the moment and seeing the distracted look of surprise upon his attacker's face, Luke took aim and kicked out hard with the heel of his foot, splaying the man's nose wide open. The blood gushed from his face in a torrent of red.

The stranger wailed in agony a second time, scrambling in retreat as he brought his hands to his face. The pain flooded his eyes with tears, which blinded him. He was wholly incapable of defending himself from attack, and fearing the worse was about to happen, he swung his pistol about and fired blindly to put off any advance on our part. Behind the rolling cloud of gun smoke, women screaming, and the sounds of shot ricocheting about the room, he fell back through the doorway and disappeared into the darkness, a frantic bloody mess.

The lantern had been snuffed. I failed to believe any man so high strung could have mastered swinging a pistol that wildly and yet take out the only lighted lamp in the store by intention, but that is how it went. Darkness clamped down upon us once. Added to that was the hovering cloud of gun smoke, and I was now unable to see anything in the front half of the store. Still, no amount of shadow and smoke could dampen the sounds of men outside hollering for the women to run. I barely made out their movement in the torchlight that entered from outside, but I heard their screams of terror fade as they ran from the store in a fit of panic.

The mob went wild. The crowd burst into a fresh rage. Their anger peaked at once and they began to chant a chilling cry.

"Kill, kill, kill, if that's God's will.

Burn, burn, burn s'how heathens learn!"

Over and over they chanted working themselves into frenzy. Next came a rain of hard knocks and thuds as stones soared through the doorway to bounce around the room.

"Momma."

"Over here, Luke. Over here."

Luke scurried back along the aisle, away from the doorway and the front counter, back to where Gracie and I knelt behind any available cover.

"Kill, kill, kill, if that's God's will!

Burn, burn, burn s'how heathens learn!"

Then came the first fearfully expected blast of a shotgun. Its discharge produced a flash of light that briefly illuminated the entire room. A crush of destruction followed as the load of shrapnel shattered the storefront window and demolished an entire wall of dishes, pottery, and jarred goods that fell to the floor in a storm-like cacophony of clinking hail.

Fragments of debris flew in every direction, peppering us as we dropped to the floor badly frightened, but free of injury. When the value of property no longer held sway in the decision of the crowd, it was time to die. The mob was now without conscience. Whether for the wagon driver's revenge or simple misunderstanding, emotion overruled logic and blood was all that mattered.

"Kill, kill, kill, if that's God's will!

Burn, burn, burn s'how heathens learn!"

The chanting continued—the tempo building. A second explosion again thrashed the store goods and pumped more smoke into the room.

"Wot are we going to do, Elizabeth?"

The sound of Gracie's voice moved past me like a wave of peace. I couldn't see her, and in spite of the fact she was choking on the smoke, the calmness of her voice belied the nervousness of heart. It went a long way to relieving my own stress, much of which was brought on by my fear for Luke's life. It seemed if she was managing, so too would Luke. For a moment, I felt collected.

"I don't know, Gracie. We have to find a way out of here."

Gracie moved into view. I shook my head with doubt.

"The mob is out for our blood. But for all the noise and bluster, we couldn't talk sense into them if we wanted. Besides, they care little to know what we have to say." I turned to my son. "Try and keep your head down, Luke."

"Kill, kill, kill, if that's God's will!

Burn, burn, burns s'how heathens learn!"

A third shot ricocheted through the store, but this one had a consequence. We cowered, covering our heads for protection, closing our eyes tight, but after the flying debris subsided and we looked up we noticed a faint glow at the back wall. The three of us studied the soft glow, and at first sign of flickering, my heart stopped.

"Fire," I whispered with utmost dread.

"Oh, no, fire," repeated Gracie.

The words floated out of her mouth as soft as a breath. Fire was my Achilles' heel. Fire instilled within me a fear so profound that my muscles failed to respond. My lungs refused to fill. I was struggling from inside to free myself. My mind was racing in cross-currents of confusion, each thought opposed by another to leave me paralyzed. I was unable to play out what options were before us in the final moments before the inevitable inferno.

The memory of Lady Rebecca's death hijacked my senses. I felt as though I passed through the veil of time, and was standing at the back of the Boston Community Church. I saw the bright white glare of an inferno streaming out through a partially open door and nearly blinding me. I saw a clear vision of Lady Rebecca's hand reaching out from behind the blocked door, reaching for the cool air of life. I was choking, frozen, unable to move. I could only watch from a distance.

"Elizabeth! Elizabeth!"

"Wha—."

"Quick! We have to put out that fire!"

The intensity of the memory and its emotion slapped me back to reality and the call of Gracie's voice. She shoved me hard away from the flaming lamp oil, and in doing so snapped me out of my paralysis. I got on my feet and rushed toward the back wall. Frantic, I searched for anything that might quickly snuff the blaze. I remembered the bolts of cloth, one of which I grabbed and quickly unspooled.

I attempted to smother the air from the fire, but the cloth wicked up the oil too fast, and only served to encourage the flame further. I wrestled with the pile of burning cloth now heaped over the fallen lamp, when suddenly out of the corner of my eye I saw a flame streak across the floor and scale the wooden planks of the back wall. The pistol shot had splattered lamp oil all across it.

The fire's path upward was blocked only briefly by the shelves of broken pottery. Between the dried out floorboards and wall planks, the flames grew incredibly fast with heat to match. Instinctively, I shielded my hair and jumped sideways directly into Gracie, who was hovering close. We both fell over.

The fresh blaze lit up the room and invigorated the crowd, which now clearly had little concern for the owner's impending loss or our lives. Howls and cheers rose into the black night sky. The only good thing about the raging flames was the way it held Gracie and I momentarily spellbound. We were still lying toppled on the floor next to one another looking up at the flames, and out of harm's way, when the next shotgun load of nails and barbs burst through the doorway to spread across the room above our heads.

Burn, burn, burn s'how heathens learn!"

"What do we do, Momma?"

"Let me think; let me think."

There seemed no choice but to face a crowd that wanted our blood. I was concerned for myself, sick for Luke, and this time, possibly more worried for Gracie. She was a beautiful girl, and for her to be left to the whims of a maddened horde was a thought I couldn't bear to consider.

At least the fire lit up the store and I was able to search for something, anything that might aid us in an escape. I spotted a stand of pry bars, which prompted a plan, and I immediately scurried across the floor on my knees to reach them. I grabbed three and threw them back across the floor, one at a time, to Gracie and Luke. Nervously, they watched my every move.

"The floor! The floor!"

"The floor?"

Gracie only questioned my words for a split second before understanding exactly what I meant. I returned to them, and we began scrambling on all four in search for a place to pry up a floorboard. We had ample light from the fire now moving overhead, but the smoke was making it harder to see the cracks. The acrid smoke burned our eyes, causing them to spill tears in a torrent. We found the best plank ends, the biggest gaps, at the rear right side of the building, farthest from the door where we entered.

We drove the pry bars into the joints with force, wedging and stabbing, trying to get a bite on a plank sufficient enough to pry it up off its nails. In quick order we realized we had another problem to overcome. The floorboards were too long to simply pry up. Counters, bins, and tables stacked high with wares rested upon the planks either entirely or sufficiently enough to prevent us from raising them. Meanwhile, the fire was now racing across the ceiling at full speed.

"Gracie, go find me a saw."

"Wot's a saw?"

"What?"

"What's a saw?" she asked, now visibly frightened.

"Forget it. Luke, grab that axe, over there!"

Burn, burn, burn s'how heathens learn!"

The roar of crowd was now our blessing because it masked the considerable noise we were making inside with our bashing and pounding.

"Clear this stuff away. Now!"

The three of us worked at once pushing and pulling anything we were able in order to clear some open space to where we could bend a board upward from its end without interference. At the same time, we repositioned one of the counters to block some of the growing heat.

"Start prying up those ends. Hurry! Cough, cough."

Burn, burn, burn s'how heathens learn!"

My eyes and lungs felt like they were burning as hot as the room. We were all three choking as much as breathing, and slicing pieces off the cloth bolt to cover our faces and filter the smoke. Using the pry bars and Gracie's knives, we hastened to work loose one of the ends. As soon as possible, we wedged the bars between plank and floor and dropped onto them with all our weight, forcing the squealing nails to give up their grip. Slowly the wood lifted off its joists. We pried up the first plank to a point whereby I brought the axe down with all my might, but instead of snapping the board, it bounced the axe straight back up, hardly denting the wood. Fear bore right through me. We had no time for even a minor setback. The axe was useless.

"Luke, when Gracie and I lift this plank you slide this axe handle underneath it as far back as you can."

Gracie and I wedged with the pry bars, forcing the board up farther until Luke was able to slip the axe handle under as instructed. We continued to rock the pry bars with all our weight as Luke inched the axe handle farther across the floor. Across the top of the axe handle, the plank was bending dramatically upward against the grip of the nails. We still needed to raise another plank in order to make an opening big enough for us to escape.

Burning cinders had now set fire to the wares in the bins atop the counters, and those flames were now licking at the already burning ceiling. The heat was intolerable and I almost failed to retrieve more axes. My eyes were so irritated, so full of tears, I could barely make out the floor or anything else for that matter.

The only relief was found in the rush of cold fresh air being drawn up from the ground through the plank we had raised. It was breathable and served to cool our skin, but it also fueled the fire overhead. I studied the next plank, but instead of looking for an end, I looked for a knot or crack. I found just what I needed and brought the axe down with every ounce of terrified mother's strength I could muster.

The honed steel edge made contact true to the mark, and the dry floorboard shattered into splinters across its weakest point. We were now forced to breathe over the opening, for the rest of the room was so filled with smoke that the fire was no more than a bright orange glow like morning sunrise through a dense fog.

"Pry it up! Pry it up!" I screamed.

We struggled to free the second board from its nails, and we succeeded. One by one they popped until we had it high enough that we could lie down and slide underneath both raised planks. Gracie was the smallest, so Luke and I eased her first down between the joists, and into the dark void beneath the opening.

"Go, Gracie, hurry. Go! Go!"

"Go, Luke. Go! Go!"

One after the other I fed them through the meager opening and to a second chance at life. I then dropped down and started to wiggle my way underneath the angled planks when I felt myself being held back.

"I'm stuck, I'm stuck!"

"What?"

The admission came out as part scream, part panicked cry. A moment of terror took hold of me and choked off my breath. My head and arms were in the cool air of the outside as they hung from the hole in the floor, but my torso and legs were beginning to cook in the heat above. Luke and Gracie were pawing all over me, trying to pull me through. I wiggled and twisted in a state of fright until at last I realized my leather garment was snagged on one of the nails embedded in the joist.

"I'm hooked on one of the nails! The leather is gathered up and won't tear. You have to pull me through. I have nothing I can grab or reach for leverage. I'm stuck. You're goin—."

Something large came crashing down or came apart inside the store and a ball of red hot cinders blew through the room. The crowd outside began to howl. The hot cinders rolled across the floor and down through the opening branding me wherever skin was exposed. My legs still above the floor were resting in a spread of tiny hot embers that were falling from the ceiling. I quickly latched onto a piece of fabric and covered part of my legs.

"Gunpo!"

"Pull! Pull! Pull me through now! Pull. Pull hard!"

I was beside myself, overwhelmed by both the burns and fear. Gracie and Luke pulled with all their might, I let them twist and turn me and when the garment finally gave way, the nail sunk deep into my thigh and ripped its way through my flesh. I cried out sharply in pain. Then I just cried between my moans of agony. But at least I was crying with cool night air. I was bleeding badly, but I was bleeding on cool damp ground. The garment came through with my legs and I used it to sop up blood.

"Gun—der!"

"Are you alright, Elizabeth?"

486

"Yes, yes. I…I—."

"Are you badly hurt? Are you burned?"

"Gracie!"

I turned to look at her in the red glow seeping through the floor.

"Yut?"

"I'm alive. What else is there?"

We were now trapped beneath a burning building, still very short on time in which to determine how we might escape the inferno overhead. The heat was radiating through the floor and making us glisten with sweat in spite of the cool air. Much worse were the small burning embers that streamed through those cracks in the floorboards to land in our hair with that horrible smell, or on our skin causing much discomfort, and forcing us to continuously shift our position. We dared not look up for fear of catching an ember in the eye, so remained focused on what ground lie in the flickering shadows beyond the store. We were in need of a route to run.

The crowd, which had grown solemn, no doubt due to reflecting upon its murderous actions, began growing rowdy again. The increased level of commotion was most notable even from where we were trapped. There was a considerable amount of yelling and we watched as feet turned to move away from the burning structure. Was it over? If the crowd was quick to back away, we might escape without further ado. And that they were.

It took a minute to sort out what was being said amidst the confusion, and when I realized what was being said I went numb. Two or three men were yelling out across the din. It was a warning for everybody to get back, to stand clear because of a keg or two of gunpowder at the back of the store that was certain to blow any minute. *My god*, I thought to myself, what else could fate possibly throw at us?

No sane person would ever set fire to a business or, worse, intentionally kill innocent people inside. It may have been naive on my part to believe this, but I did. What I feared in life were those thoughtless or demented hooligans who were mean by nature and enjoyed carrying a prank as far as it would go.

Unfortunately, unexpected surprises, such as a couple of kegs of black powder, brought about unexpected results. Everybody would proclaim their shameful involvement as bystanders, and express their sorrowful guilt by association, but someone would still be dead—someone being us.

All I had now was prayer, and I was pleading all over heaven. I prayed to my Christian God. I prayed to my Indian Great Spirit. I prayed to Lady Rebecca. But then most earnestly, I prayed to Christopher Claussen. I didn't question why I would pray to Christopher over all my gods. It was as if I became that child long ago who never doubted Christopher could calm the seas. I pictured him in my mind and at once I was filled with peace. I prayed that fate had not spared me a horrible death as a child in a church fire long ago only to see an inferno devour me and my child at a later date. Only Christopher could understand the intensity of that fear.

"Your child." I cried.

It was time to run. Our chances, once seen by the townsfolk were next to none, but our chances beneath this burning building and kegs of gunpowder were *none* by any measure. We had to run and we had to run now.

FIFTY-FOUR

Above the din of the onlookers, above the roar and crackle of the burning framework over our heads, came the sound of something new. It came from all directions at once. It was a sound so familiar to my ears that at first I didn't hear it at all. It was the only sound fitting to be heard at a fire of this size. It was the sound of war drums.

Boom, boom.

Boom, boom.

Boom, boom.

The rhythm reverberated through the valley, through the half bare trees and to the farthest reaches of the river. It echoed along the streets, bounced between the walls of the buildings, and worked its way underneath them into the foundations where we lay trapped. Finally, it pounded fear deep in the chests and consciousness of the crowd.

Boom, boom.

Boom, boom.

Boom, boom.

As if doused by a fire bucket of cold water, the townsfolk went dead silent with shock. All the bold, free-flowing talk of justice and payback for the skulking Indians burning up in the trading post came to an abrupt halt. In a flash, the acclamations and backslapping turned into a rampage of terrified shrieks, wailing cries, warnings of torture, scalping, and slaughter.

A state of pure dread swept through the crowd, leaving them anything but interested in the yet spectacular blaze raging over our heads. Even the impending explosion of gunpowder kegs seemed to fall short when compared to the perceived Indian barbarity about to befall them.

I could see the crowd turn their backs to us as they spun about, fearfully looking over their shoulders into the black of night where firelight cast shadows carved into hard sharp edges. The colorless images quivered in a maddened frenzy as if also driven into panic by the resounding beat of drums.

Cries of attacks were heard. Sightings were claimed. Arrows were produced. Indians were said to be lurking about the woods just beyond the buildings, just beyond the light of lamps. The mob scattered, thinning dramatically. I witnessed groups of women and children crying aloud as they fled the fire for the security of the inn. The call was out to fort up. The men peeled away in waves as they barked out orders and scrambled for weapons.

A frightening crash occurred overhead as part of the structure or something large collapsed upon the floor. By this time the floorboards were opening up, their edges being eaten away by flames. The heat was stifling. It was forcing us out. The crash caused showers of burning embers to fall like streams of glowing sand. We were jumping around as if we'd upset a wasp's nest.

We had to run. We might live or we might die, but I witnessed one horrible death by fire, and I was not about to fall to that fate. I would fall only to the fire of a gun. It was time to run. Mayhem was calling out to us. The street was full of it, and it could only play to our advantage.

"We have to run! We have to run! This is our only chance! Go! Go!"

"Come! Elizabet, come!"

A deep voice resonated from behind. Badly startled, we all turned over to look, and to my utter disbelief I saw in this red glow of hell, lying upon the ground just beyond arm's length, the most unexpected and fulfilling answer a pleading prayer might bring—*Shadow Hunter.*

"Taa?" Taa?

I was too stunned to express anything more than his name. My eyes flooded with tears. I would never know how Christopher did it, but I knew in my heart that he answered my prayers just as he calmed the seas. I knew it.

"Come, come." He waved us toward him.

"Go! Go, quickly! Go! Go! Go!" I screamed.

I shoved Luke and Gracie, pushing them in his direction even as my mind worked to accept what was taking place. We slithered faster than a shot-up snake. Taa pointed to an area of darkness beyond two shacks that were brilliantly lit by the blaze.

"Go!"

He dragged Gracie and Luke out hard-handed and sent them off stumbling into a run. From bellies, to knees, to flying feet, in less time than it took for a second breath, we struck out across the open ground. Out of the corner of my eye I spotted a man with a gun and his shadow, a perfect twin holding fast upon the wall. I turned to see them hunker down and bring their weapons to bear. But before I could fear for Luke and Gracie, I heard the hiss of arrows streak invisibly through the night air behind us. The man never fired.

Thud. Thud. Thud.

The Indians didn't kill him, but their arrows struck the wall with solid hits, impaling his shadow only inches from where he stood. The warning served to petrify him sufficiently enough. He dropped his aim and nearly dropped his gun as he retreated in haste, fleeing toward the street where he sought out safety in numbers. He disappeared beyond the fire, but I could hear him hollering out additional cries of an Indian attack.

We lost ourselves in the dark of night beyond the shacks, and were met by two more Indians. They turned and ran ahead of us, escorting us safely into the pitch black depths of the wood. Shadow Hunter followed fast on our footsteps. Within the safe haven of hardwoods, we came upon a party of seven or eight additional Indians who approached Taa and conversed briefly in excited whispers. He then stepped away from the Indians and came to my side.

As soon as I caught my breath, I threw my arms around this friend from another time and place. I squeezed him so hard I literally squealed with joy. I don't remember ever being this happy to see anybody, maybe not even Claus. Taa allowed me to express my gratitude in this physical manner, which was unlike him. It wasn't any action on his part that ended my show of emotion, or Luke's and Gracie's silent stares of inquisition, but rather a monumental explosion.

The earth suddenly flared skyward in an eruption of blinding whitish-blue light that penetrated every crook and cranny of existence. It was immediately followed by a thunderous concussion that plowed into all of us. I let loose of Taa, and in unison with the rest of our company, I instinctively turned toward town. I stood numbed, my senses momentarily stalled, as I witnessed a massive orange plume of rolling fire ascend high into the night sky.

Then, a notable lapse, and as if infuriated by the burn from below, the heavens cast down a plague of debris that pummeled the town and any living thing within earshot of the event. We could hear all manner of clatter, bits and pieces of the former trading post and neighboring structures returning to what rooftops remained. Even where we stood there was danger, for remnants of the town were dropping through the treetops all about us.

The reality of our situation only a moment before was too horrible to contemplate. Now, we were but insignificant souls unworthy of bother in light of an inferno consuming the establishments and the commotion of a panicked crowd caught fearfully between losing everything to fire or imminent massacre by an ill-perceived attack.

Having regained something of my composure, I turned to question Luke and Gracie on their condition. Satisfied of their well-being, I next bent over to address my injured leg. It was bleeding sufficiently for concern. I was still holding on to what I assumed was a garment of small significance. Only upon closer observation in the light of the moon, did I discover that in the choking, smoke-filled store, I had unknowingly grabbed the splendid work of the seamstress we had so admired.

I was dismayed to think of the dress, now soiled and bloody, and the financial loss one luckless widow or worse would bear. I would ask Taa to seek out the owner if possible, and make reparation in my behalf. I also realized that I was out a pistol, bow and quiver full of arrows, not to mention the post I penned, and half a dozen horses.

The wailing from afar continued to permeate the woods. I stood up straight to again look toward the burning fires in town. The town appeared fully engulfed by flame, its light pushing back the dark that surrounded us, and illuminating Luke and Gracie. I was heartened to see them now much settled, appearing safe and secure.

In spite of what seemed a litany of luckless disasters, in the end, we always pulled through. We always resurfaced, always found ourselves able to look back, even if in utter amazement. I reckon if we were anything, we were lucky through and through. If I didn't believe that, then I was left with only one troubling explanation. Christopher Claussen.

I shuddered at that thought. I turned my head quickly to look away from a powerfully vivid mental image of Claus and found myself the focus of Taa who yet stood close at my side and was looking directly at me. I hoped he didn't hear me mumbling to myself or worse. Thankfully, he was quick to speak.

"We go."

FIFTY-FIVE

Shadow Hunter sounded older, but in one respect, he remained true to memory. He was yet a man of few words.

"Come, Elizabet. We go now."

Taa escorted me to a fresh horse. Gracie and Luke were already mounted and ready to head out. The larger party of Indians gave each of us a handful of pemmican to ease our hunger. They gave us blankets to ward off the cold of night. They bid us farewell in silence, and slipped quietly back into the shadows.

Taa and his two fellow guides set out at once, taking the lead to test the path that Gracie, Luke and I were to follow. For a good two hours, we pressed the horses as hard as we dared in the moonlight of night before easing up. The extent of commotion and mayhem back in town was certain to keep the townsfolk entirely occupied, with little time left over for chasing our party.

However, realizing how determined would be some to seek vengeance, and knowing nothing fulfilled that obsession like a dead Indian or black man, was enough reality to spur us on in haste. The cold did us little good, but served the horses well by easing their weariness. In time, we slowed from a trot to a walk. In a single file, we kept close on each other's heels; yet, scant conversation ensued, but for an air of apprehension and urgency that stifled our excitement at finally being safe.

During this slower pace, while I no longer rode in fear of my horse stumbling in the dark, my mind became obsessed with the impossibility of being saved by Shadow Hunter. Mentally, it was inconceivable. I thought back to when our abductors split up, and one party left us to ride out ahead. I remembered telling Gracie that they were probably setting up the trade, scouting for someone who might have guns or something else of worth. Logic dictated it had to be during that time our presence became known to others.

I suppose one needn't question the whys. All that mattered was our now being in good company, our feeling safe and warm with fresh blankets and food in our bellies. It was in that content frame of mind that we rode for another two hours until the moon grew feeble behind a dense wedge of clouds. At that point the path was lost to absolute darkness, and it was agreed that to press our luck further would be unwise. Taa made the call to stop and bed down. I doubted anyone was more grateful to rest. Now that the horrors and anxieties of the night seemed behind us, I found myself drained of emotion and physically spent. It had been a long brutal day. I felt we were all relieved to dismount.

Taa joined his companions, who immediately busied themselves building a fire. I called out to Gracie and Luke, and together, the three of us set out to relieve ourselves. Upon our return, we three sat down for the first time thankfully wrapped in the warmth of blankets that warded off the night's frost. The fire provided warmth to the bone and comforted me while I took time to inspect, clean, and dress the wound on my leg. To be sure, it was every bit a nasty and painful wound, badly swollen about the gash, but it wasn't a snake bite.

Taa and the others soon sat down beside us, and again passed out some dried meat and fruit. It was too dark and late to hunt fresh kill, but what food was on hand was sufficient to calm even the growl of Luke's young stomach. We were all three surely beyond content, possibly blissful.

In this less traumatic atmosphere, I again introduced Gracie and Luke, who were now fully taken with curiosity about these strangers who mysteriously appeared from my past. They were all ears, whereas I was all questions. I was yet unable to grasp the impossibility of the rescue. I wasted no time in seeking my own answers to the mystery.

"How in the name of god did you manage to find us, to save us? I can't believe it, Taa. You saved our lives. I mean, you *saved* our lives. We were good as dead. Honestly, I was on my last prayer. Those fools wanted our blood in the worst way, and just when they are about to get it, you show up out of nowhere. How is that possible? I have driven myself daft over the last three hours trying to imagine how that could possibly happen. It obviously wasn't coincidence."

At first, Taa said nothing. For the longest moment, he just studied me as Luke and Gracie studied him. I imagined he was struggling to find something he might recognize beneath the years that had aged me. A smile broke across his face, and his deep voice went on to speak of another time, a place long lost to memory.

"You remember schoolboat, Elizabet?"

The question was nothing like I expected under the circumstances. I felt my foundation shake. I was instantly catapulted into a place that was in the realm of bedtime stories for Luke and

Gracie. Their eyes went wide at hearing a familiar name as they sat intent on capturing the essence of every word Taa put forth.

"Yes, of course. How could I ever forget the schoolboat—Dorrie, Rachel, Buzzy, and Carter? Those were hard times, Taa, but they were special times. Yes, I remember it, but why would you ask me that of all things?"

"One night you say we pray. Everybody pray to God. Everybody pray thanks for food, thanks for friends—."

"Thanksgiving!"

"Yah." Taa nodded his head.

"Yes, I remember it fondly. It was a wonderful night. We all prayed. We prayed together. We thanked the Lord for our food and shelter and the meal. Remember the meal? Who was it... Gunninks...Schuellers and Gunninks! Aggie and Opal, what a pair...they brought us dinner to be sure we didn't go without. My word, I haven't thought of them in ages. I suspect they have probably passed on by now. Remember all those street urchins, poor things. We bathed the lot, bathed and fed all of them." I paused a moment while the feeling of the memory lingered. "Yes, we thanked the Lord for a lot of things that night. I thanked Him for our friendship, Taa. Oh...but that was a blessed night."

My face felt all aglow as other memories of that time rose to warm my heart, each offering something of joy and peace to balance out a night so tilted toward terror and mayhem. However, my need for answers was hardly diminished.

"What does the schoolboat have to do with this?"

"I remember we raise our drinks. All people say '*to Elizabet, the chosen one. Elizabet is chosen one. Elizabet is chosen one.*' I always remember. I dream many times. Every season, every moon, in my dream I ask Great Spirit where is Elizabet *the chosen one*? Great Spirit say, you will see, you will know. He say soon you find her."

I thought it peculiar, even unsettling, that in spite of the fact I hadn't heard those words in many, many years, I was profoundly affected nonetheless. I didn't feel joy, nor did I feel sorrow. What I felt was a sense of duty, a wave of commitment or responsibility that arrived on my shore from some distant, far away sea, from somewhere over the horizon of my awareness. For a fleeting moment, the words made me intensely uncomfortable, enough so that I worked to dismiss them and instead focus on what else Taa might have to say.

"A long time I ask, I think maybe you dead, but I remember you strong spirit. I think of blue brush. I remember strong medicine. Many years ago, I hear Indians, I hear scouts speak of woman Great Sun Head Spirit. She live in desert. She live with Tsistsistas, the Cheyenne. Always, I ask; always, I listen.

"Five days ago, I hear talk of whites for trade. Indians want guns for white women. They say hair like sun...eyes like sky. I listen. I ask. I hear say two women and boy. I think...*boy*.... And I know. Boy is reason you *chosen one*. I hear name Elizabet, I know. I know. I know. In my dream, you, Elizabet, have great son."

I was fascinated by Taa's dream story. It was romantic, and Taa spoke of it as though he was an oracle, but I was more interested in actual facts that could explain away the seemingly impossible rescue.

"How did you know where to begin looking for us?"

"I know many Indians. Many here, many everywhere—everywhere. They come; they go. We come; we go. I travel up and down the river. I have friends in Independence. When I go there, they tell me you on trail. Indians use old trails always. All

Indians know trails. I know what trails to watch, where trails go and come."

"And you have been following us for how long?"

"We not follow you. We raft down river from Independence. We come to do business. We hear say from Indians, whites with sun on head on trail to town—come from west. We hear say big trouble in town. We not stay in town, not safe. We think maybe you have big trouble. We ride up to hills and watch trail from high. We wait.

"When sun go down we not see you come. We not see you go by. We ride down for closer look, but too late. We see you go into town and think maybe you white, maybe you safe. But, we see big trouble. In town, we see mob, angry folk, too many people. We cannot meet you.

"When you go into trading post, we stay back; we see mob grow. We think very bad for you. We think mob too big. We go for help. We ask tribe to beat drums, to call spirits. We say ask spirits to make whites go. We say ask spirits to guide us to you. You lucky, Elizabet."

Taa concluded his story, which prompted Gracie without hesitation to follow with her own question. She looked directly at me.

"Wot did he mean by *chosen one*?"

"Oh, lord, Gracie, it was nothing more than a quip made by an old lady when I was a child. But I have to admit, after tonight; even I am starting to wonder. Honest to goodness-god, I am starting to wonder."

I looked back at Taa.

"And, Taa…just so you know, I do have a *great* son."

I turned to look at Luke with all the admiration a mother could muster. I rubbed my hand across the top of his thick braided blonde hair. Suddenly, I felt a drop of water on the back of my hand, then another, and another. I looked up into a dark starless sky above our fire, and a fine spray of rain commenced to fall upon my face.

If there was one thing that could make misery more miserable it was cold rain on a cold night. I released Luke to Gracie, watching them both scurry off in search of bedding on higher ground that would not be swamped and leave them to awaken in a pool water. Racing the raindrops, they sat down side-by-side and hurriedly spread blankets across their legs. They grabbed the edge of the oil cloth and yanked it up over their heads as they fell onto their backs and disappeared from view leaving only the sound of quiet laughter and whispers.

The rest of us were also on our feet, moving to keep from going to bed soaked. I asked Taa if I might sleep next to him for warmth, and he obliged me, if for no other reason than to save us both a soaking while we discussed other sleeping arrangements. After months on the road watching out for others, having someone I fully trusted watch over me as I slept was bound to assure a good night's rest—probably as good as I might have had sleeping in my old bed at Mary's.

In fact, stealing a warm dry bed from one's memory was routine when trying to fall asleep out in the wilds. Sleeping in a tent could be every bit as comfortable, and often, considerably cleaner than sleeping in most of the bug-infested boarding houses. But, sleeping on the open ground was something else. That was a place where snakes slithered, and that thought did little for slumber.

A perfect case in point was my present situation beneath an oil cloth that spared me a soaking, but was bent on suffocating me, and useless against the pelting of rain drops on my forehead. I was as I said—*on open ground*. To be sure, an oil cloth on the open ground was better than no oil cloth, but far from the joy of a tent. In any event, I was not one to fail considering that only the night before we would have killed for a wet blanket. I cared not to think how miserable we three would have been this night had we been caught in the weather. I shuddered as a chill coursed through me head to toe.

The sound of the rain's even patter relaxed me, but it also made me aware that in all of our travels to date, we rarely experienced rain. Was this more of Christopher's work? Did he command rain to dampen the spirits of anyone with a hankering to track us down? Was I playing games in my mind as I dozed off, or was I going to believe such nonsense and accept my lunacy?

Truth be told, most of our travel was in the desert of the high country, a place unknown for much in the way of rain other than the occasional unexpected cloudburst. It was only of late after we entered the tall grass prairie that we might expect a good sustained soaker. For us rain was long overdue. It rained because we were well into November, the latter part of the year when cooler temperatures and the change of seasons brought turbulence, wetter skies, and heavy dew. Obviously, I was not a lunatic, and this had nothing to do with Claus.

For me, the wet of autumn was worse than the snow of winter because one could usually manage to stay warm if dry, but staying dry was always difficult—and damp went right to the bone. How fortunate for us that Taa and his scouts traveled fully prepared for any weather. Their life was lived on the trail as guides or escorts and blankets and oil cloths were nothing more than standard fare.

The heat of the fire that had been felt beneath the blankets was slowly being doused by a deliberate shower. Yet, I felt comfortable, cozy in fact. I pulled the blanket up across my ear and shivered for no good reason. I snuggled up as close to Taa as possible. It was nice to have him near. His presence further opened the door to years gone by. An unsatisfied curiosity put off much of my drowsiness. I propped up the oil cloth forming a tunnel to fresh oxygen. It was cool upon my face. I inhaled a deep breath of the rain-scented air and addressed Taa in a low voice as I expelled it.

"You must tell me about Little Deer and Snow on Ground. How are they? Please tell me they are safe and happy."

"Yah, ha, ha." I imagined a broad smile crossed his face. "They good. Little Deer not so little. A woman. Very nice. Very smart. She live with a man now. Snow on Ground is good. She live with Little Deer. She is happy."

"Oh, thank you, Great Spirit. I am most happy to hear that news. It does my heart good. And where do they live?"

"Near Missouri River, twelve days up."

I wanted very much to ask Shadow Hunter if he knew anything about what had become of the blue brush and mirror, but after some thought I decided to let it pass. If the brushes were one and the same, I suspected Taa would have liked it returned to Little Deer. But, the brush and mirror set was the last gift that Gracie's father had given her, and she would have been distraught to give them up. Along with my ship's blanket, it was amongst our dearest possessions. Sadly, all of it and more was left behind in the care of the Tsistsistas, or so we hoped.

Instead of discussing the blue brush, in brief fashion, Shadow Hunter and I exchanged other stories about our lives and what we did over the last decade. He could barely believe that I had lived with Indians for the last ten years. I could not believe how successful he had become in the community as a guide for white settlers. We shared one or two tales of joy and sorrow until I could no longer keep my eyes open. I drifted off with the soothing resonance of his voice in my ear.

I dreamt of Christopher. I hadn't dreamt of Christopher in... well...I couldn't remember when last. Thankfully, I was spared my usual assortment of troubled and nightmarish memories recounting my last days in his company. The stress and embarrassment fell way to the deeper emotional attachment that I had known and cherished in my youth. My dreams escorted me into the sanctuary of Christopher's comforting and protective embrace. The dreams may have been due to my sleeping alongside a man I trusted. They may have been due to the realization I was close to home. They may have been due to Christopher....

And it may have been the combination of all three, or other reasons that escaped memory upon awakening, but I awoke in a supreme state of mind. It was as if I had been caressed by a lover the whole of a sunny afternoon. It helped that Taa let us sleep late to awake at our own will, which I did, and so awoke as invigorated as I was elated. Once arisen, we set out upon the trail, bypassing breakfast because the wood and surroundings were soaked from the night of rain and a morning of heavy fog.

"Two weeks, if we ride sun-up-to-set."

"Two weeks! Are you certain?"

Gracie's eyes were wide open with anticipation.

"Two weeks. I ride this trail many, many times, many years. Two weeks to St. Louis."

"The city of your dreams, Gracie. Only, no more dreams, honey. It's as real and as close as the end of your nose."

"My dadduh always wanted me to see St. Louis. I remember that about him."

"Well, Gracie, I can promise you this. The St. Louis that your father knew, as splendid as it was, will not compare to what you will see now. Have no doubt, as fast as those towns were growing, well...I wouldn't dare venture to imagine."

"Ha, ha, ha." Taa laughed.

"What's so funny?" I asked.

"You have been gone ten years. It will be *you* who does not know St. Louis."

END OF PART ONE VOLUME THREE

www.ingramcontent.com/pod-product-compliance
Lightning Source LLC
Chambersburg PA
CBHW031050260626
47172CB00001B/12

* 9 7 8 0 9 8 2 2 2 1 3 8 9 *